GOD IS THE LORD BY WHOM WE ESCAPE DEATH

PSALM · LXVIII

LLEWELLYN.

THE DEAN'S WATCH

A rich and beautiful story set in a Cathedral
city in the 1870s. There the formidable Dean
struck up a friendship with a genius of a
clockmaker, Isaac Peabody; there Job, who
promised to be an even finer craftsman than
Isaac, courted Polly, Miss Peabody's irrepres-
sibly happy little maid-of-all-work; and there
many other events, some as delightful as they
were unexpected, befell those living in the
shadow of the great Cathedral.

THE DEAN'S WATCH

by

ELIZABETH GOUDGE

Drawings by A. R. Whitear

HODDER AND STOUGHTON

Printed in Great Britain
for Hodder and Stoughton Ltd.,
by Richard Clay and Company, Ltd.,
Bungay, Suffolk

*Here lies in a horizontal position the outside
case of*

George Routledge, Watchmaker

*Integrity was the mainspring and prudence
the regulator of all the actions of his life;
humane, generous and liberal,
His hand never stopped till he had relieved
distress.*

*So nicely regulated were his movements that
he never went wrong, except when set going
by people who did not know his key.
Even then he was easily set right again.
He had the art of disposing of his time so well,
till his hours glided away, his pulse
stopped beating.*

*He ran down November 14, 1801, aged 57,
In hopes of being taken in hand by his Maker,
Thoroughly cleaned, repaired, wound up, and
set going in the world to come, when
time shall be no more.*

Contents

CHAPTER I   *Isaac*

I

THE candle flame burned behind the glass globe of water, its
light flooding over Isaac Peabody's hands as he sat at work
on a high stool before his littered work-table. Now and then he
glanced up at it over his crooked steel-rimmed spectacles and
thought how beautiful it was. The heart of the flame was iris-
coloured with a veining of deep blue spread like a peacock's tail
against the crocus and gold that gave the light. He had oil lamps
in the shop and workshop but lamplight was not as beautiful as
his candle flame behind the globe of water, and for work re-
quiring great precision its light was not actually quite so good.
And he liked to feel that through the centuries men of his trade,
clockmakers, watchmakers, goldsmiths and silversmiths, had
worked just as he was working now, in their workshops after the
day's business was over, alone and quiet, the same diffused light
bathing their hands and the delicate and fragile thing they
worked upon. It banished loneliness to think of those others,
and he was not so afraid of the shapeless darkness that lay
beyond the circle of light. He did not like shapelessness. One of
his worst nightmares was the one when he himself became
shapeless and ran like liquid mud into the dark.

For any painter it would have been a joy to sit in the corner

11

of Isaac's workshop, unseen by Isaac, and paint him in his pool of light, but only Rembrandt could have painted the shadows that were beyond the light. They seemed to hang from a vast height, as in Rembrandt's Adoration of the Shepherds, and if here they were looped back to show not the holy family but one grotesque old man, yet adoring wonder was not absent, for Isaac had never grown up and things still amazed him. He was amazed now as he looked worshipfully at the beautiful thing he held. This child's gift of wonder could banish his many fears but the balance was precariously held.

He looked safe enough tonight in his halo of warm light. He was a round-shouldered little man with large feet and a great domed and wrinkled forehead, the forehead of a profound thinker. Yet actually he thought very little about anything except clocks and watches, and about them he not so much thought as burned. But he could feel upon a variety of subjects, and perhaps it was the intensity of his feeling that had furrowed his forehead, lined his brown parchment face and whitened the straggling beard that hid his receding chin. His eyes were very blue beneath their shaggy eyebrows and chronic indigestion had crimsoned the tip of his button nose. His hands were red, shiny and knobbly, but steady and deft. He dressed in the style of twenty years ago, the style of the eighteen-fifties, because the clothes he had had then were not yet what he called worn out. His peg-topped trousers were intensively repaired across the seat but that did not show beneath his full-skirted bottle-green coat. The coat was faded now, and so was the old soft crimson bow tie he wore, but the dim colours were eminently paintable against the great draped shadows, and richly illumined by the moony light. His soft childish mouth was sucked in with concentration except when now and then he pouted his lips and there emerged from them a thin piping whistle.

He was happy tonight for one of his good times was on the way. Everything he did today, anything he saw or handled, had shape as though the sun was rising behind it. Presently it would happen to him, the warmth and glow of self-forget-

fulness, and after that for a few moments or a few days he would
be safe.

He had finished. The Dean's watch was now once more
repaired and he knew he could not have made a better job of
it. He held it open in the palm of his hand and gazed at it with
veneration, his jeweller's eyepiece in his eye. It was inscribed
"George Graham fecit, 1712". At that date Graham had been
at the height of his powers. The inscription took Isaac back
to the old bow-windowed shop in Fleet Street, next door to the
Duke of Marlborough's Head tavern, which had been a place
of pilgrimage for him when as a lad he had served his apprenticeship in Clerkenwell. Graham had worked in that shop, and
lived and died in the humble rooms above it. Charles II's
horologist Thomas Tompion, whom men called the father of
English clockmaking, had been Graham's uncle. Both men had
been masters of the Clockmakers' Company and they had been
buried in the same tomb in Westminster Abbey. Whenever he
held the Dean's watch in his hands Isaac remembered that
George Graham's hands had also held it, and that perhaps
Tompion in old age had looked upon his nephew's handiwork
and commended it.

For it was not only a beautiful watch but an uncommon one.
It had a jewelled watchcock of unusual design, showing a man
carrying a burden on his shoulders. Isaac had seen hundreds
of watchcocks during his professional life, and many of them
had had impish faces peeping through the flowers and leaves,
but never so far as he could remember one showing a human
figure. The pillars were of plain cylindrical form, as in most
of Graham's watches. He had never favoured elaborate pillars
for like all great craftsmen he had always made ornament
subsidiary to usefulness. Isaac closed the thin gold shell that
protected the delicate mechanism and turned the watch over.
It had a fine enamelled dial with a wreath of flowers within the
hour ring. The outer case was of plain gold with the monogram
A.A. engraved upon one side, and upon the other a Latin
motto encircling the crest of a mailed hand holding a sword.

Isaac laid the Dean's watch down on his work-bench,
amongst the others he had finished repairing today, and opening a drawer took out an envelope full of watch papers neatly
inscribed in his fine copperplate handwriting. The majority of
horologists no longer used these but Isaac was attached to the
old customs and liked to preserve them. In the previous century
nearly every watch had had its watch pad or paper inserted in
the outer case, either a circular piece of velvet or muslin
delicately embroidered with the initials of the owner, or else the
portrait of the giver, or a piece of paper inscribed with a motto
or rhyme. Isaac had collected and written out many of these
rhymes, and he would always slip a watch paper into the outer
cases of the watches of the humbler folk, for their amusement
and delight. He did not dare to do so with his aristocratic
customers for he feared they would think him presumptuous.
He shook out the papers and picked out one here, one there.
This would do for Tobias Smalley, landlord of the Swan and
Duck, who was a rare old grumbler.

> "Content thy selfe withe thyne estate,
> And send no poore wight from thy gate;
> For why, this councell I thee give,
> To learn to dye, and dye to live."

And this, he thought, for Tom Hochicorn, one of the Cathedral
bedesmen, a very good old man who believed in God.

> "I labour here with all my might,
> To tell the time by day or night;
> In thy devotion copy me,
> And serve thy God as I serve thee."

He slipped the watch papers into their various cases and then
wrapped the Dean's watch in wadding and laid it away in a
stout little box. Tears were in his eyes for he would not see it
again until the Dean once more overwound it or dropped it.
His fear of the terrible Dean was always slightly tempered by
anger, because he took insufficient care of his watch, and then
again by gratitude because but for the Dean's carelessness he
would never have the lovely thing in his hands at all, for its

n and women of the city because he loved the city. It
ty. He had been born within its walls and had never
ept for those seven years in London.

ck that Isaac was making now he did not visualize in
vindow because it was so much a part of him that he
re as easily visualized his eyes or brain or hands in the
s this clock. He did not think about its future because
future. He did not consciously tell himself that it was
ty but he had a confused idea that the dark would not
et him while the pulse beat on in this clock.

ng before the solid oak table which was sacred to his
ne his heart beat high with joy at what he saw. No
vould have seen anything except a confused jumble of
m, but Isaac saw his clock as it would be. He saw the
shed thing and knew that he would make it, and that
be his masterpiece. Like all creators he knew well that
eeling of movement within the spirit, comparable only
st movement of the child within the womb, which
e victim to say perhaps with excitement, perhaps with
ion or exhaustion, "There is a new poem, a new
a new symphony coming, heaven help me." The
t had been unusually strong when he first knew about

to be a lantern clock in the style of the late seventeenth
the kind of timepiece Tompion himself had so de-
create, the clock face surmounted by a fret that hid
of the bell above. Isaac nearly always used the
al eastern counties fret, a simple design that he liked,
his clock he was designing his own, inspired by the
iothic fret which Tompion had been so fond of, only
f the two dolphins and the flowers and fruit he saw
s and the beautiful arrow-head reeds that grew upon
bank outside the city wall. Isaac could paint on ivory
skill of a miniaturist, and his clock face was to be a
ie heavens. The twelve hours were to be the twelve
ie zodiac, painted small and delicate in the clearest and

mechanism was faultless. Because of this anger and gratitude
he possibly had a warmer feeling for the Dean than most people
in his Cathedral city.

Isaac took his own watch from his pocket and looked at it.
It was a severely plain silver timepiece with tortoiseshell pair
cases. He had made it for himself years ago. It said three
minutes to eight and Isaac was dismayed, for it was later than
he had realized and if he did not hurry he would be late for
supper and incur his sister's displeasure. Yet the dismay quickly
passed for today nothing had power to disturb him for long.
He waited, his watch in his hand, for in a moment or two the
city clocks would strike the hour and he liked to correct their
timekeeping by his own faultless watch. It was quiet in the
workshop, no sound but the rustle of a mouse behind the wains-
cot. It was a frosty October night of moon and stars and there
was no wind. The city was still. There was no rattle of cab-
wheels over the cobbles, no footsteps ringing on the pavement,
for everyone was at home having supper. Isaac was aware of
all the lamplit rooms in the crooked houses, little and big, that
climbed upon each other's shoulders up the hill to the plateau
at the top where the Cathedral towered, looking out over the
frozen plain to the eastern sea. Another night he would have
shivered, remembering the plain and the sea, but tonight he
remembered only the warm rooms and the faces of men and
women bent over their bowls of steaming soup, and the children
already asleep in their beds. He felt for them all a profound
love, and he glowed. The moment of his loving was in the world
of time merely sixty seconds ticked out by his watch, but in
another dimension it was an arc of light encircling the city and
leaving not one heart within it untouched by blessedness. Then
the clocks began to strike, and the light of the ugly little man's
moment of self-forgetfulness was drawn back again into the
deep warmth within him. And he understood nothing of what
had happened to him, only that now, for a little while, for a
few moments or a few days, he would be happy and feel safe.

The Cathedral clock, Michael, started to strike first, in no

hurry to precede the others yet arrogantly determined upon
pre-eminence. Its great bell boomed among the stars, and the
reverberations of its thunder passed over the city towards the
plain and the sea. Not until the last echo had died away was
the city aware that little Saint Nicholas at the North Gate had
been striking for some time. Only two of his light sweet notes
were heard, but little Saint Nicholas was dead on time. Saint
Peter in the market place waited for Nicholas to finish and then
coughed apologetically, because he knew that his deep-toned
bell was slightly cracked and he himself half a minute late.
Saint Matthew at the South Gate struck a quick merry chime
and did not care if he was late or not. Last of all Isaac's clocks
in the shop all struck the hour, ending with the cuckoo clock.
He kept them all a little slow so that he could enjoy their voices
after the clocks of the city had fallen silent. Having refereed
them all in past the tape he put away his own timepiece and
rose slowly to his feet to set about the ritual of the Friday night
shutting up of the shop.

In an old leather bag that had a lock and key he reverently
placed the mended watches of those gentlemen and gentle-
women of the city who were too incapacitated by rank, age or
wealth to do their own fetching and carrying. These he would
deliver tomorrow, for on Saturday the shop remained closed
and he spent the day delivering watches and winding clocks.
Every clock of importance in the aristocratic quarter of the city,
the Close and Worship Street, was in his care, intimately known
to him and loved and cherished during half a lifetime. There
was a smile of great tenderness on his face as he remembered
that tomorrow he would see them all again. The watches of
the great locked away in the leather bag, the watches of the
lesser folk were placed in a drawer to wait till called for, but
with no less reverence either for themselves or for their owners,
for Isaac's humility did not discriminate between man and man
and scarcely between man and watch. In his thought men
were much like their watches. The passage of time was marked
as clearly upon a man's face as upon that of his watch and the

marvellous mechanism of his body
by evil hazards. The outer case
carter's corduroy or bishop's bro
pulse was the same, the beating o
breaking illusion of eternity.

The watches put away, his eyes
making in his spare moments. The
at it tonight but he could spend a
adoration. He was always making
most of them after the patterns of t
loved the best, but enriched alway
that was all his own. For Isaac wa
He did not need to employ anoth
cases or do his marquetry for him.
ceived his own brain and hand a
fection without help from another.
he could have had an apprentice, r
city with watches and clocks and se
pupil. He was a born teacher ar
impart his knowledge. But it was i
training insisted upon by the Cl
years as apprentice and two as j
necessity of producing a masterpiec
the Company before the apprentice
workmaster, was daunting to poor b
if one here or there should aspire
London as Isaac himself had done.
for the unattainable, for with a good
would have had more time for the cr
seldom failed to sell when they app
so lovely were they and so cheap.
he mostly forgot to send his bills in a
the watches of poor men for nothing
the value of his clocks, but even if he
century they would be eagerly soug
of Europe he would still have sold th

to the m
was his
left it ex

The c
his shop
could ha
window
it was th
his eter
entirely

Stanc
clock al
one else
mechar
accomp
it woul
strange
to the
causes
exaspe:
picture
movem
this clc

It w
centur
lighted
the ba
traditi
but fc
famou
instea
two s
the ri
with
dial c
signs

loveliest colours he could encompass. Each picture lived already
in his mind, completely visualized down to the last scale on the
glittering silver fish at twelve o'clock and the golden points of
the little shoes the Virgin wore peeping from beneath her blue
cloak at six o'clock. Within this circle of stars Isaac had planned
the sun and moon balancing each other against a blue sky
scattered over with tiny points of light that were the humbler
stars, but whenever he stood and looked at his clock the sun
would not stay where he wanted it, as did the moon, but swam
upwards and placed itself like a golden halo behind the fish.
Again and again Isaac had replaced the sun floating just off
shore from nine o'clock, but it was no good, it always went back
to the meridian. And so now Isaac had given up and as he
looked at his clock tonight he acknowledged the rightness of
what he saw. The glittering silver fish and the golden sun
formed one symbol, though of what he did not know. His heart
beat fast and music chimed in his head. The bell of this clock
was to strike the half hour as well as the hour, for according to
tradition the spheres were singing spirits. "There's not the
smallest orb which thou beholdest but in his motion like an
angel sings." Isaac did not believe it but he had the kind of
mind that delights to collect the pretty coloured fragments of
old legends that lie about the floor of the world for the children
to pick up. As man and craftsman he knew that he would touch
the height of his being with the making of this clock. He
covered the lovely thing with a cloth and turned away. It was
hard to leave it even though there was nothing under the cloth
except a medley of bits of metal and some oily rags.

He put on his caped greatcoat, that once had been black but
was now so stained by age and wind and rain that it was as
miraculously full of colour as the plumage of a black cock,
picked up his battered hat and the locked bag that contained
the watches of the great, blew out his candle and felt his way to
the door that led into the shop, lifted the latch and went in.
He had not yet put up the shutters and the shop was faintly lit
by one of the new gas street lamps that the city had recently

installed. It was so small, and its bow-window so crowded with clocks, all of them ticking, that the noise was almost deafening. It sounded like thousands of crickets chirping or bees buzzing and was to Isaac the most satisfying sound in the world. Standing behind the counter he listened to it for a moment with his eyes shut, especially to the ticking of the cuckoo clock that he had made just before he had started work on the celestial clock. It ticked louder than any of the others and the cuckoo in it was a gorgeously aggressive bird, who exploded full-throated from his little door at every hour. Since the cuckoo clock had been in the window the children of the city were continually blocking the pavement outside the shop. Isaac was quite used now to looking up and seeing their faces pressed against the glass. There was someone there now even though it was late and dark. Opening his eyes Isaac could see the pale gleam of a face, dark eyes and a thatch of untidy dark hair. A boy, he thought, and then suddenly it seemed to him that it was not a boy but a sprite beyond the window, light and eager like flame in the wind. But sprites were children's tales. He was a convinced but hardworked rationalist, always hard at it re-convincing himself of his convictions. During his bad times this was not difficult, but during his good times the bright shards on the floor of the world had a trick of turning into shining pools that reflected something, and he was distinctly startled until he saw a ragged sleeve come up and wipe the misted glass clear. Only a boy. He had been breathing on the glass like they all did and the lamplight had blurred beyond it and played a trick upon his eyes. But he did not want to frighten the boy and he crept forward inch by inch, hoping to reach the shop door unobserved and call out a reassuring word as he opened it. But it was no good. The boy saw him and vanished.

2

There was a look of sadness on Isaac's face as he came out into the street, put up the shutters and locked the shop door. He had a pied piper attraction for boys and they did not usually flee from him, but he supposed he had looked grotesque in the half-dark, shuffling across the shop. For a few moments he was so grieved that he saw nothing as he stumped up the street, the moon behind his shoulder and a grotesque shadow of his tall hat bobbing along the pavement in front of him, and then the sorrow passed because nothing could sadden him for long during his happy times. He was ashamed of this, but he could not help it, any more than he could help it that in his dark times all the beauty and glory of the world did not gladden him. And of this too he was ashamed.

He began to whistle one of his tunes, for the city about him was magical. His repertoire of tunes was small, all of them variations of a striking clock. He went through them one after the other almost without cessation when he was happy, driving his sister Emma almost crazy. In spite of the sharp incline he chimed twelve o'clock in every possible way all the way up Cockspur Street, his eyes on the crown of frosted stars above the Rollo tower of the Cathedral. Isaac did not like the Cathedral. It frightened him and he had never been inside it. Yet he always had to look at it. Everyone had to.

At the top of Cockspur Street, that was so steep that all the little bow-windowed shops had short flights of steps leading up to their front doors, Isaac turned right and was in the market place. Here too there were shops on the ground floor of the tall old houses with their higgledy-piggledy roofs, and a small tavern, the Swan and Duck, where Isaac went sometimes when he was feeling low. The town hall with its fine Georgian pillars was here too, the Grammar School that Isaac had attended as a boy, and St. Peter's that was nearly as old as the Cathedral itself, a little dark musty church, battered and apologetic. Isaac had not been inside it since his boyhood, and in those days had suffered much within it and had hated it, but now after so many years of passing it as he went backwards and forwards to his shop he had come to know that his misery within it was not its fault and to love its old scarred face, and the small dark porch with the notice board where the papers

seemed always torn and askew. The bell in the low squat
tower struck the half-hour as Isaac passed beneath it, and its
cracked old voice seemed calling to him. "Good night," said
Isaac.

Just beyond Joshua Appleby's bookshop he turned sharply to
the left and climbed a flight of steps between two high garden
walls, a short cut to Angel Lane where he and Emma lived.
It was a steep twisting cobbled lane bordered on each side by
very old houses and crossed at its upper end by Worship Street,
which curved about the great old wall which encircled the high
plateau where the Cathedral towered, with the houses of the
Close clustered about it. Those who lived within that wall were
in the thought of the city the great men, the aristocrats, individually liked or disliked according to their individual
characters but as a body venerated because they always had
been venerated, the heirs of a tradition that was still sacrosanct.
Worship Street was just one step down in the social scale, a
gracious leisured street to which the ladies of the Close moved
when their husbands or fathers died. The doctors and solicitors
of the city lived here too, with a small sprinkling of retired
generals and admirals whose fathers had once been deans or
canons of the Cathedral. The city did not commend itself as a
place of retirement to those whose roots were not in it, for the
climate was bleak, but it had a way of drawing back to itself,
sometimes almost against their will, any who had once lived
in it.

Angel Lane to the west of the Close, with Silver Street to the
east, housed those whom the city considered to be the more
worthy and respectable among the tradesmen; not butchers or
grocers or publicans, but Joshua Appleby of the bookshop,
Isaac, the chemist and the veterinary surgeon, together with
schoolmasters, lay clerks, and many poverty stricken maiden
ladies and widows who would rather have died than let anyone
know how poor they were. The houses in Silver Street and
Angel Lane were small, and their rents low, but their nearness
to the Close and Worship Street, their age and picturesque

appearance, gave them an air of great gentility. In them one could be desperately poor and highly respectable at the same time.

Isaac's little house was nearly at the top of the lane but before he turned to it he glanced eastward, and then stood spellbound by what he saw. Across Worship Street he could see the archway that led into the Close, the Porta, flanked by two small towers, cavernously black against the brilliance of the moonlit wall. Beyond and above it was a darkness of motionless trees, the great elms and lime trees of the Close that rose even higher than the wall. Beyond and above that again were the three towers of the Cathedral, the Phillippa and Jocelyn towers to the right and left and the central tower, the Rollo, soaring above them into the starlit sky with a strength and splendour that was more awful in moonlight than at any other time. Like the moon herself dragging at great waters the Rollo tower in moonlight compelled without mercy.

And the mailed figure above the clock face in the tower also compelled; above all he compelled a clockmaker for he was the finest Jaccomarchiadus in England. Like a fly crawling up a wall Isaac crawled up Angel Lane towards him, scuttled across Worship Street, cowered beneath the Porta, got himself somehow across the moonlit expanse of the Cathedral green and then slowly mounted the flight of worn stone steps that led to the west door within the dark Porch of the Angels. At the top he stopped and looked up at the Rollo tower, trembling. Then suddenly his trembling ceased for he was looking at the clock. He forgot his fear of the Cathedral, he forgot where he was, he forgot everything except the clock. He saw it from a distance every time he delivered watches in the Close but because of his fear of the Cathedral he was close to it only when as, tonight, he had been compelled. It was a Peter Lightfoot clock, less elaborate than Lightfoot's Glastonbury clock which had later been removed to Wells Cathedral, but in Isaac's opinion far more impressive. The Jaccomarchiadus stood high in an alcove in the tower, not like most Jacks an anonymous figure

but Michael the Archangel. He was life size and stood upright
with spread wings, his stern face gazing out across the fen
country to where the far straight line of the horizon met the
downward sweep of the great sky. Beneath his feet was the
slain dragon, and his right foot rested on its crushed head. One
mailed fist gripped the hilt of his sword, the other was raised
ready to strike the bell that hung beside him. His stance was
magnificent. Had he been a man it would have seemed defiant,
but the great wings changed the defiance to the supreme certainty and confidence of the angelic breed. Below him, let into
the wall, was a simple large dial with an hour hand only.
Within the Cathedral Isaac had been told there was a second
clock with above it a platform where Michael on horseback
fought with the dragon at each hour and conquered him. But
not even his longing to see this smaller Michael could drag
Isaac inside the terrible Cathedral. No one could understand
his fear. He could not entirely understand it himself. Yet
every now and then, in spite of it, Michael compelled him to
come and stand as he was standing now and look up at the
clock, and then to turn and look out over the city from the
central hub and peak of its history and glory.

I

IT was a compact city, and on a night such as this one it climbed towards the stars like one of those turreted cities seen in the margins of medieval manuscripts.

It was so compact because although the city wall had largely disappeared as such, existing now only built into the walls of houses or bordering a stableyard or vegetable garden, yet the city had not straggled beyond the old confines. Its population was not increasing, for its chief industry, the making of osier baskets in the slum district at the North Gate, where the river came in a silver loop quite near to the city wall, did not attract the younger men and they were tending to leave the city and seek work in the distant towns. Yet the city remained fairly prosperous, for it was the market town for the surrounding country. On Saturday, market day, the market place was crowded, and on every fine day there was a constant gentle flow of traffic on the narrow roads that led from the villages out in the fen to the city.

These villages were widely separated from each other for they existed only where a small hill had in old days made it possible to build above the floods, and they housed a courageous but dour and silent people. Life had been a tough and lonely

25

struggle for them in days gone by and though now that the fens had been drained, and banks built against the menace of the river and the sea, they were a fairly prosperous farming community they remained self-contained, suspicious of strangers and inclined to be morose even to each other. Great churches crowned the summit of each small hill but they were mostly empty, for the fen people were not devout, and in the cold windswept vicarages their priests frequently despaired and died. There were lonely manor houses here and there where many a squire preferred to drown his loneliness in drink rather than be bothered to ride miles through the wet to forgather with anyone else, and where his wife and daughters lived chiefly for the days when he let them have the dogcart and go and shop in the city.

There were happy days in the fen country as well as dour ones, glorious hot summer days when the harvest fields were gold as far as the blue horizon of the sea, spring days when riding parties cantered down the centuries-old grass roads between tall hedges of flowering crab apple trees, winter days when everyone went skating on the flooded fields close to the river, or sometimes in a very great frost on the river itself, while overhead the great sky flamed slowly to a sunset of almost dreadful splendour. Nowhere else in England could one see skies quite like those of the fen country. Something in the quality of the air gave them a weight of glory that seemed to crush ant-like men and their tiny dwellings to dust upon the flat ground. Only the Cathedral could stand up against them, towering in black ferocity against the flame and gold. Yet the happiness did not predominate and those who went away from the fens to live elsewhere took with them a memory of endurance rather than joy.

Within the city the atmosphere was different. The same tough breed dwelt there but greater safety and prosperity within the walls had fostered a greater gregariousness. The city had a long history and a civic pride and had always known something of the pleasures of pageantry, for the plateau at the top of the hill had from the days of the Norman Duke Rollo onward been one of those places where men feel that they must assert themselves. The strange tall hill rising into the vast sky out of the vast plain had seemed to challenge both and on top of it men had felt themselves conquerors. Here they could see their enemies coming and defy them when they came. Here they could laugh at floods and storms. Here they could play the part of a god in the sky towards the poor peasants beneath, and oppress or relieve them as they chose.

Duke Rollo, who had been the first to assert himself on the hilltop, had been an oppressor. His great castle had frowned angrily upon the poor folk who had toiled for him below, catching fish for him, tilling for him the few fields that could be salvaged from the waste of waters, fighting and dying for him when he bade them, afraid of him and hating him yet dependent on him for their life. A little town came into being below the castle, and strong walls were built about it, a town of huddled houses and twisted unsavoury streets, housing the duke's men-at-arms, armourers, grooms and scullions, with their toiling wives and savage half-clad children. These did not hate him as did the peasants for he brought excitement into their lives. His banner streamed from the castle-keep above their heads and his trumpets rang out from the walls. When he and his knights clattered up and down the narrow streets on their destriers they cheered him, for he was a mighty man, a great fighter and reveller, and they admired his courage and vitality and neither expected nor desired that he should pity them. He died suddenly, in full carousel in his banqueting hall, and the fearfulness of his death, unshriven in the midst of his sins and drunkenness, sobered the mind of his young son, Duke Jocelyn.

In Jocelyn's day mass was said daily in the castle chapel for the repose of the soul of Duke Rollo, monks as well as men-at-arms passed up and down the streets, and the people no longer died in droves in times of famine for they had only to climb up to the castle and Jocelyn would give them all they needed. He was merciful to the poor. On Maundy Thursday he washed the feet of the twelve dirtiest old men whom his people could dig out of the slums around the North Gate and hound up the hill for that purpose. He kept vigil for long hours in the castle chapel and his people called him the Good Duke. Yet he did not win from them the admiration they had given to his father. They missed the pageantry of the good old days, the excitement and danger that had glamourized Rollo's brutality. And they felt in some vague way that the old duke had embodied the spirit of the strong grim place which he had created. Jocelyn did not. He took after his mother the Lady Phillippa who had died young of Rollo's boisterousness. He was timid and anxious, delicate in body, increasingly obsessed as time went on with the thought of his father's end and the fear of hell. He was already a dying man when the thought came to him that he should destroy the castle, whose stones were stained with the spilt blood and wine of his father's murderings and feastings, and build in its place a great church, and a monastery for holy monks, in reparation for his father's crimes. He would endow the monastery with all his wealth, and the monks should pray without ceasing for his father's soul and for his own; for as his sickness increased so did his conviction of sin. He too, though men called him the Good Duke, had his secret mean little sins and they whispered about his bed at night when he tried to find rest there from his pain, and in the day they seemed to him an obscene fog that choked him when he tried to draw his breath.

His dying was long-drawn-out, taking years where men had expected months, for it seemed that he could not die until he saw his great project in a fair way to fulfilment. He had always at his right hand driving him on, pouring as it seemed his own strength into the duke's failing body and mind, his Benedictine chaplain and confessor William de la Torre, later to be spoken of with bated breath as Abbot William. Many monks ruled upon the hilltop in the course of the centuries but they were not remembered in after years. Only William de la Torre and one other were remembered, William's stature in men's minds almost equalling that of the Cathedral itself. It was said he was well over six foot and could fell a man with one blow of his great fist. He was a man of powerful intellect, iron will and keen ambition. Moreover he was a genius. Duke Jocelyn's wealth procured the services of the finest masons and craftsmen in the country, men who could work in stone and wood and stained glass almost as though they were God himself forming the crested mountains, the forests and birds and flowers with fingers that could not err. It procured too a vast mass of suffering labour. The whole fen country travailed to build the church and monastery. Men groaned and sweated dragging stones up the hill. They sawed wood till they dropped with exhaustion. They caught the ague working upon the walls in the rain and bitter wind. It was accounted as nothing for men high up on the scaffolding of the great tower in cold weather to fall suddenly, as birds fall from a tree in a great frost. They died but there were plenty more to take their place. Looking out from the plateau and seeing the trains of ox carts bringing the stone and wood along the rough tracks through the fen, and the barges coming up the river laden with precious metals, velvet for faldstools and hangings, breviaries and sacred vessels, it seemed as though the whole world was converging on the strange hill in the wilderness. And William de la Torre held it all in the hollow of his hand.

At some time during the building Duke Jocelyn died, actually at the last in fear, and unshriven as his father had been, because William de la Torre, sent for in a hurry, dallied discussing plans for the chapter house with his architect and strolled along to the duke's bedchamber too late to be of any assistance to him. Jocelyn's body was enclosed in a leaden coffin with not much ceremony and forgotten until such time as William de la Torre deemed it politic to bury it beside the high altar of his church, on the day of its consecration to Saint Michael and All Angels, preaching over it a sermon so eloquent and moving that the vast congregation wept unashamedly. William de la Torre also wept. It was part of his power that he was so fine an actor that he could convince himself as well as others. Duke Jocelyn died without issue, though he left a child widow, Blanche Fontaine, who lived out the rest of her short life in a house at the monastery gateway, later called Fountains, where centuries later Isaac Peabody called weekly to wind the clocks for old Miss Montague.

And so, in the absence of heirs, Abbot William reigned supreme; though that he would have done in any case for supremacy was his rôle, and he could be great in it as this world counts greatness. He was a great abbot. The towering church that was his creation more than any man's dominated the whole country for miles round. The monastery buildings surrounded it, chapter house and infirmary, library and dorters, kitchens and cloister, all fine buildings in themselves but dwarfed by the leap of walls and towers and battlements above them. The poor little town that struggled up the hill became almost swamped by storehouses, granaries and stables. The people lived in mean little houses crushed between the monastery buildings and the city walls, and they toiled for the Abbot as once they had toiled for Duke Rollo. But the Abbot had more thought for them. The monks cared for the sick among them, taught their children in the monastery school, fed them in times of famine and kept them safe in time of war. Works of learning as well as mercy were accomplished on the hilltop, books were written, manuscripts were illuminated and music was composed. The singing of the monks in choir could be heard on still days far across the fen, as could the pealing of the bells, and men working in the fields would stop and turn and lift up their eyes to the great church and praise God.

The monastery never wanted for wealth. Its fame was so great that men flocked to it bringing their riches with them. Among the monks were not only noblemen expiating their sins, and scholars, artists and musicians desiring peace and quiet, but men who desired to pray. It was a great house of prayer. It was great. "It is great," were the last words of Abbot William upon his deathbed. He died, aged eighty-eight, unhumbled to the last. The great bell of the Rollo tower tolled for him on a night of storm but the next morning dawned calm and still,

and a little boy who lived down by the North Gate said he saw
two swans circling over the Rollo tower. Yet men's hearts
failed for fear. The Abbot was dead. What now would happen
to them? He *was* the monastery. He was subsistence itself.
Men could not conceive of life without that hated, feared,
indomitable man to goad them through it. By his command he
was buried almost obscurely behind the high altar beneath a
slab of black stone. He had had the bodies of Rollo and
Phillippa moved from their burying place and entombed inside
the monastery church in a wonderful chantry, and Blanche
Fontaine too had her chantry, and the tomb of Duke Jocelyn
beside the high altar had his mailed figure lying upon it in a far
greater dignity and beauty than had been his in life, but
William de la Torre had known he needed no monument to his
memory. The great church was his monument and he would
not be forgotten as long as it endured. His choice of an
apparently humble tomb had been the last gesture of his pride.

2

In fearing that they faced disintegration without him men
had forgotten the momentum that men of genius leave behind
them in their works. The life of the monastery moved on in the
course he had appointed for it for several centuries, the only
major change being that a succeeding Abbot became the first
Bishop of a newly formed fen diocese, the monastery church his
Cathedral, and the Prior of the monastery became its head.
During these years the church was beautified in many ways and
the Lightfoot clock, and the statue of Michael the Archangel,
were placed high in the Rollo tower. Bishops and Priors came
and went and some were saints and some were not, and some
were beloved in their day and some were hated, but none was
remembered excepting only Prior Hugh, who was Prior at the
time of the dissolution of the monasteries.

He was a little man, quiet and peace-loving, so that men
were not surprised when they heard that he had commanded
his monks to yield humbly to the command of the King's Grace

and to offer no resistance when the commissioners came to drive them from their home. Yet when they arrived, with a formidable array of armed men as escort, and on a cold snowy day rode up the hill to the monastery to take possession of it in the King's name, it was found that the Prior had schooled his monks for a departure of dignity and grandeur. He himself in his simple monk's habit came out from the Cathedral and stood in front of the west door, at the top of the flight of stone steps that led up to it, and it seemed to the townsfolk and peasants who had come crowding and weeping up the steep streets to see the last of the monks who had looked after them for so many years, that he was a much taller man than they remembered. His voice, as he cried out to the commissioners and their men to stand aside that his sons might pass out, had an authority in its tones that none had heard before. Then the great door of the monastery, that opened upon the wide greensward that stretched from the front of the steps to the Porta, swung open and the monks came out in procession singing with splendid vigour the fighting psalm, the sixty-eighth, "Let God arise and let his enemies be scattered." Their great gold processional cross, and their banner of Michael the Archangel, were forfeit to the King, but at their head walked the youngest novice carrying a large cross made of two bits of wood nailed together. As they passed beneath the foot of the steps their Prior raised his hand and blessed them, and he kept his hand raised until the last of them had passed out through the Porta. They could be heard singing as they went down the narrow cobbled street that led to the North Gate, and across the bridge over the river to the rough road beyond that led back through the fen to the world they had renounced. Their singing died away and what happened to them no man ever knew, though for centuries afterwards it was said that on nights of wind and driving snow the chanting of the monks could be heard sounding through the storm.

When the last of his sons had disappeared the Prior dropped the hand he had raised in blessing and turned and walked back into the Cathedral. They found him later lying dead before the altar, the knife with which he had ended his earthly life lying beside him. It was not the action of a true priest, who may not himself dismiss from life the soul that is God's, but it was an act for which men nevertheless remembered him with sympathy and admiration. Even his enemies were grieved and defying the law that those who take their own life must not be buried in consecrated ground they buried him where they had found him, laying over his coffin a flat black stone such as covered the body of Abbot William. No man afterwards dared disturb his bones, and for years it was remembered that some poor half-crazed girl had vowed that on the day of his death she had seen two swans flying over the city towards the setting sun, and their wings were of pure gold. And so these two men, the first Abbot and the last Prior, lay the one behind the high altar and the other in front of it. Four centuries divided them but in the life of the great Cathedral that was no more than the exhalation of a breath.

The years went on and the city on the hill endured many and sometimes terrible vicissitudes. The monastery became the property of the King and its lands and buildings were given by him to one of his favourites, Harry Montague. Harry gave a great banquet to celebrate his arrival and as it was fine summer weather many of his cronies rode all the way from London to assist at the junketings. It was almost like the old days of Duke Rollo come back again, with men and horses clattering up and down the cobbled streets of the city, music and revelling, and succulent smells of baked meats floating on the wind. But the people of the city were sullen and miserable. They had been utterly dependent on the monastery and they did not know what was to happen to them now. And they felt disorientated. Through the years they had come to feel, if only subconsciously, that the city existed for the Cathedral and monastery and the Cathedral and monastery for God. The city had been God-centred and now they felt as though God had forsaken them. They did not like the Lord Harry.

They liked him even less when at the end of the final banquet he and his cronies, being all of them as full of wine as their skins would hold, carried the priceless books and manuscripts out of the library, flung them in a great pile on the green at the foot of the steps where Prior Hugh had stood to bless his monks, and made a bonfire of them. The leaves of the books were many of them yellowed and brittle with age, like the petals of dried flowers, and they burned brightly. Harry and his friends, most of them young men and wild as well as merry with the drink, were intoxicated by the leaping flames. Tumbling over each other in their excitement they ran into the dorters and refectory, coming back with hangings and chairs and tables which they flung yelling on the bonfire. The flames leaped so savagely that the whole sky was lit up, and could be seen right across the flat country, even as far as the sea coast, and when sparks carried by the high wind caught the thatch of the little houses down below, and the city too was on fire, it seemed to the awed watchers in the fen villages that the whole hill was being destroyed by fire from heaven. They remembered the singing of the monks upon that night of wind and snow six months ago. "Let God arise, and let his enemies be scattered; let them also that hate him flee before him. Like as the smoke vanisheth, so shalt Thou drive them away; and like as wax melteth at the fire, so let the ungodly perish at the presence of God." And then they saw the great Cathedral rising like a rock from the fire, its tall towers stark and black against the flamelit sky. It was a tremendous presence there and it seemed that it trampled on the flames. Slowly, gradually, they died. The stars and the moon entered once more into possession of the sky and the great fire was over.

It had been extinguished with great courage by the citizens themselves. Running cursing from their burning houses the men formed chains of buckets down to the river and for hours they fought the fire and at last they conquered. Throughout the fight they were aware of the presence up above them, the great strong thing that could not be destroyed. Many a man said afterwards that the Cathedral fought with them. But there had been some among them, children and old people, who had died in the fire and the city did not forget. Nothing Harry Montague could do now would ever lessen their hatred of him. When some years later he was stabbed in the fen by an unknown hand the city glowed and gloated.

His descendants lived on for a while in the fine house that Harry had made out of the central part of the monastery buildings, the kitchen, refectory and dorters, and the Prior's chamber and chapel. The rest, the library, the infirmary, the offices and outbuildings, gradually fell into disrepair. The walls and roofs remained intact, so strongly fashioned were they, but inside the bats haunted them, there was moaning in the chimneys and broken doors screamed eerily on rusted hinges in the wind. The Montagues did not stand it for long. They vowed the place was haunted. The people of the city did not grow tired of hating them and they were always afraid. They went away and lived in a great house by the sea. Only one of them, Harry's youngest son Thomas, remained behind and lived in a little house in the city. He was a gentle and kindly man and wore down the people's hatred. He married the mayor's daughter and finally became mayor himself. His descendants always lived in the city, the last of them being old Miss Montague of Fountains.

Then another hierarchy came into being at the top of the hill. The King's Grace appointed a Dean to administer the affairs of the Cathedral, and Canons, lay-clerks and choristers to preach and sing the services. During the reign of the Montagues there had been an outbreak of the plague, failure of the crops and bitter poverty that they had done nothing to relieve. The people had felt there was a curse upon the city because the monks had been driven away, but now that the men of God were back, even though they were no longer monks, hope was re-born and men went to work with a will. The Cathedral bells rang out again, sounding far across the fen as in the old days, and on summer mornings and evenings, when the west door was left open, men and women pausing in their work could hear the singing of the lay-clerks and choristers as once they had heard the chanting of the monks. There were no more empty buildings on the hilltop. Harry Montague's house became the Deanery, and the other buildings were incorporated in the new houses for the Canons, a choir school and almshouses for the poor of the city. The new men of God were good to the poor, and the city began to feel itself again. Without that life of praise and prayer and charity at its heart it had been like a wheel without a hub, as purposeless as a godless world. The men upon the hilltop might at times individually fail them, might grow loveless or indolent, but what they stood for was always the same.

3

The centuries passed again. In the great days of the first Queen Elizabeth all went well with the city and the fen villages, apart from the normal hardships of a countryside where life was never easy, but the Civil War left ugly scars behind it. The fen country was predominantly for Parliament but there were a few royalists in the city and the most determined among them was the Dean, Peter Rollard, a round rubicund little man with a red beard and a temper to match. His determination had been increased by the fate of the royalist Bishop, who was in prison. He had now to be loyal for the two of them. Commanded to discontinue the use of music and ritual in his Cathedral, and to worship God there in the full starkness of the puritan faith, he refused, and the Cathedral worship continued as before until on a cold grey day of east wind Lieutenant-General Cromwell himself, with a company of his Ironsides behind him, rode into the city. They clattered up the cobbled streets, rode under the great Porta on to the green and dismounted at the foot of the steps where Prior Hugh had stood to bless his monks. Evensong was being sung in the Cathedral at the time, and the triumphant Magnificat rolled out to greet the Lieutenant-General as he leaped up the steps and went in through the Porch of the Angels to the open west door beneath the Rollo tower. His spurred boots rang on the paving stones of the nave as he strode up it, and his harsh grating voice, raised to the full echoing apocalyptic roar of an enraged prophet, preceded him.

The lay-clerks and choristers heard the roar and the clanging before they saw the Lieutenant-General and their voices wavered, but when they saw him striding down upon them, black-cloaked, his tall black hat increasing his great height, their voices died away altogether and Dean Peter Rollard sang the last two verses alone. He was not a musical man but his vocal chords were powerful. The Lieutenant-General was not able to make himself heard, and taking an unloaded pistol from his holster he flung it at Peter Rollard. It struck the Dean's right shoulder and the pain was so intense that his right arm hung useless. A lesser man would have discontinued the altercation, but Peter Rollard, perceiving that Cromwell was sacrilegiously wearing his hat in the house of God, picked up his service book in his left hand and aimed it at the hat. His aim was entirely accurate. Cromwell's men, who had followed him at a respectful distance, closed about the Dean and he was marched off to the city prison.

The Ironsides spent the rest of that day, and the next, in destruction. Every carved angel and haloed saint within reach, inside the Cathedral and out, had its head knocked off. The chantries of Phillippa and Rollo, and of Blanche, that were full of angels, were a shambles of angelic heads. The glorious carved and painted wooden screen, with its panels depicting the life and death of the Virgin, was hacked out entirely and burnt on the green together with all the Cathedral vestments. At sight of the flames the citizens, puritans though most of them were, remembered Harry Montague's bonfire that had ushered in much suffering for the city, and they trembled.

High up in the Rollo tower Michael was beyond the reach of destruction. His haloed head safe upon his mailed shoulders he looked down in scorn upon the destroyers below, and the light of the flames seemed to glint upon his sword as though it was dipped in blood. At him too the citizens glanced anxiously, for there was something about his looks that they did not like. The Cathedral too, as the grey cold twilight of the second day drew on, had a menacing look. It seemed vaster than usual, colder, blacker, and yet terribly alive. Those whose duty compelled them to crawl about like ants beneath it had a feeling that it was towering up and up and might curve and break over them like an annihilating wave. Lieutenant-General Cromwell and his men had meant to leave at dawn the next day, after a late afternoon spent in smashing the Cathedral windows, but they found they were pressed for time and decided to go at once, sparing the windows but taking Peter Rollard with them for incarceration in a safer, deeper place than the city prison. They clattered down through the cobbled streets with the Dean riding in the midst of them, a trooper leading his horse because only his left hand was of use to him. The last that his people heard of him was his unmusical voice singing the sixteenth verse of the sixty-eighth psalm as loudly as he could. "This is God's hill, in the which it pleaseth him to dwell; yea, the Lord will abide in it for ever." His enemies feared to silence him for there was such a numinous terror upon them that evening that they were frightened of him. Dean Peter Rollard was another of those men whose vital, doughty spirit could be as daunting as the spirit of the Cathedral itself.

The years of the Commonwealth ground slowly by, and perhaps the sorrows of the citizens during that time were not really greater than is normal to human life, perhaps it was only their fancy that made them seem so, and swung their sympathies slowly over to the lost cause. They grieved over the death of their royalist Bishop in prison, shuddered at the murder of the King, and when his son returned to his own they rejoiced. But when Peter Rollard also came back to his own the whole city nearly went mad with joy. It was Christmas Eve, one of those spring-like Christmases that do occasionally visit even the bleaker parts of England. The Commonwealth had suppressed Christmas as smacking of popery, and through the grey years there had been no Christmas services and no ringing of the bells. But upon this afternoon of the Dean's return the bells rang again. It was a day of pale sunshine and in the morning the city had been permeated with the strange smell of violets that comes sometimes in a mild midwinter after shed rain, though there are no violets. All day it was very quiet except for the low hum of happy preparation. As the afternoon wore on the pale sky deepened to a fen sunset, not one of the terrifying ones but a scattering of small pink clouds all over a sky of deepening blue. The river, and the pools and streams among the reeds, reflected the sky. The swans, seeing themselves lapped in colour, floated in a mazed stillness. The great distance was very clear and the fen villages on their small hills could all be seen, their church towers rising black and clear. Very clear too were the little figures of two horsemen approaching far off upon the road from the north, that curved itself about the villages as it approached the city. It was known that the Dean's servant Tom Lumpkin, and he only, had gone to meet him at his special request, but even so the watchers on the city walls could not have been certain who these two were had they not heard bells pealing. So faint and lovely was the sound that it might have come from heaven itself, and for a moment or two the citizens looked at each other with wondering awe, before they realized that the village churches were ringing Peter Rollard home.

Then the bells of the Cathedral began to swing and soon their tremendous clamour was shaking the Rollo tower, and the citizens were streaming joyously out of the North Gate to welcome their Dean. He was not only their Dean, a courageous man who had endured much for the sake of the faith that was in him, but a figure who, whether they understood it or not, symbolized for them the spirit of this place. He was a descendant of those others, of Duke Rollo, Abbott William and Prior Hugh. Their mantle had fallen upon him. With him away the life of the city, and of the Cathedral upon the hill that was the reason for the city, had sickened, as it had in the days after the monks had gone away. Now, as the shuddering tower lifted its weight of music towards the sky, the spirit of the place leaped upward into new life.

Peter Rollard was much changed. His red beard was streaked with grey and his face was furrowed, and as he rode up through the city towards the Cathedral with his people exulting about him he actually wept. No one had ever expected to see Peter Rollard weep, and he had not himself expected that he would be so overcome and had taken no prevenient action. He was without a handkerchief and Tom Lumpkin had to supply one.

That Christmas Eve the villagers in the fens saw light shining from the Cathedral windows and heard organ music and the sound of a mighty singing. The whole city was inside the Cathedral, they judged, excepting only the sick and the babes and those who must care for them. Once more, after the dreary years when there had been no Christmas, they were welcoming Christ to his manger throne.

Peter Rollard lived for six years after his return, a much gentler man than he had been, and much beloved. A new Bishop was appointed, Josiah Farran, and he too was loved. These two died within a few weeks of each other and were buried in the south aisle of the Cathedral nave, and the sorrowing city caused beautiful effigies of them to be carved in coloured marbles and laid upon their graves. On the afternoon of the day on which Dean Rollard died an old shepherd, coming in from the fen, looked up and thought he saw two swans far up in the sky. After a moment's consideration he decided it was only his fancy, for he had never known swans to fly so high.

4

The years passed and the life of the city flowed on with no great upheavals. There were wars abroad and years of scarcity

at home that took their toll of life, but there was never a day
when the praises of God were not sung in the Cathedral, or a
Sunday that the bells did not peal. Bishops and Deans and
Canons lived and died in the old houses about the Cathedral,
and some were holy and some were strong-minded and a few
were both but none of them seemed quite to have the stature
of the great men who were gone, none of them seemed quite to
be the city. None of them, that is, until in the year eighteen-
hundred and sixty-five the terrible Adam Ayscough was
appointed Dean.

He came to the city at a time when a miasma of evil had
corrupted it. The city had endured onslaughts of evil before in
its long history, for as a fortress of God it had always been
especially obnoxious to the devil, but the attacks had been
overt ones and recognized for what they were. But this time
there had been few robberies, no violent quarrelling and
murdering, but instead a creeping nastiness of sloth and deceit,
indifference and self-indulgence, that most horribly seemed to
emanate from the Cathedral close itself. The Dean at that
time was a melancholic recluse and the Canons dined too well.
There was no active wickedness among them, they were all too
comfortable for that, but the absence of good left a vacuum that
was quickly filled. The slimy film on the surface was not in
itself alarming, merely a dirty Cathedral, gabbled services,
soiled and torn surplices and insubordinate lay-clerks and choir
boys, and the only man who fully realized the satanic nature of
what was beneath was the Bishop, an incorruptibly holy man
but too old now to be able to come to grips with any problem
except the almost overmastering one of shifting his aged body
about its duties. Yet when the melancholic Dean died he knew
what to do, for that very morning he had seen in *The Times* the
announcement of Adam Ayscough's resignation from the
presidency of a famous college. He had met him only once or
twice but he knew what manner of man he was. Adam Ayscough had already cleansed the Augean stables of a corrupt
public school and made it the finest in England, and the college

he was leaving had possessed neither virtue nor repute before
he took it in his grip. If he could not through the grace of God
cleanse the city no man could. The old Bishop wrote to him,
inaugurating a long tussle between them, for Adam Ayscough's
mind was set upon retirement and it was not his habit to
yield his will to another. Yet, surprisingly, the old Bishop
won, and within a year Adam Ayscough had been installed as
Dean.

Within three years the small ecclesiastical world upon the
plateau at the top of the hill had been scoured in every cranny.
They were years of terror for all concerned, for the Dean drove
upon them like a gale from the sea. The fabric of the Cathedral
was dangerously decayed in places, the roof was leaking, ladders
and broken chairs blocked one chantry, the droppings from
jackdaws' nests littered a second, a new organ was needed and
a new choir-screen to replace the one destroyed by Cromwell.
For a while, as the Dean attended to these things, masons,
carpenters, woodcarvers and the like descending upon the city
and dirt and debris flying in the air, it almost seemed as though
Abbot William was building the Cathedral all over again.
The human element was not neglected for concurrently with
the flying of the dust the Dean was campaigning against those
evils in it which had resulted in dirty surplices and gabbled
services. He reorganized the choir-school and the almshouses
and dismissed a sadistic headmaster and an incompetent
organist. He put the fear of God into the whole lot of them,
from the Sub-Dean down to the smallest choir-boy, and the
battle of the plateau was watched with much enjoyment by the
rest of the citizens down below.

And then, suddenly, it was their turn. It was of no use to
protest that the affairs of the city were not the business of the
Dean. Adam Ayscough was deaf. His terrible anger uncovered
the deplorable state of the workhouse, and revealed to a
horrified city the conditions under which women and girls
worked in the labour gangs in the fens. He exposed graft,
exploitation of children and the weak, hypocrisy and greed

wherever he found them, and however bitter the opposition he encountered he nearly always beat it down. During the years of battle he was only seriously defeated once. The slums about the North Gate, where most of the basket makers lived, were a breeding ground of sickness and misery, but their destruction, and the building of healthier homes on higher ground, was something that even he could not encompass. The slums, though appalling, were picturesque and contained some of the oldest houses in the city and he had all the sentimentalists and antiquarians against him. He had the people of the district themselves against him, for the basket workers had always lived by the North Gate, close to the osier beds, they were used to their dirt and squalor and were traditionalists to a man. But what finally defeated him was the fact that influential men owned property there, and the public houses that dominated every street corner were a source of income to the wealthiest man in the city, Alderman Turnbull the brewer, who lived in the market place. In his own way he was as much a colossus as the Dean and the fight they had over the slums was something the city never forgot.

But in all else the Dean triumphed, and for a period of some six or seven years it seemed that the city lay helpless in his grip, and then very slowly there came a strange stirring of new life, a springtide freshness and energy. Men and women did their work increasingly well, with growing pleasure and pride in what they did. The Cathedral became known all over England for its music, and the dignity and beauty of its services. Its bells rang out with power. Its fabric was perfectly cared for and a spirit of good craftsmanship grew up in the city. All that was great in the past seemed very much alive and men and women looked with new hope to the future. It seemed to them that the one blight upon the place was the Dean himself. For years, after the battle of the North Gate slums, his enemies had carried on a campaign of vilification against him and he was cordially disliked. Yet the city was proud of him. When he ploughed his way doggedly along the streets, his broad shoulders a little bowed beneath the weight of the ten years he had spent in the city, his craggy face set like granite and his unhappy eyes peering out beneath his shaggy grey eyebrows with no friendly recognition in them for any whom he passed, men and women felt a thrill of pride as well as dislike. He was, somehow, the city.

I

A TREMENDOUS music broke out over Isaac's head, and for a moment he was startled nearly out of his wits, for standing looking out over the city his mind had gone back to other years. Then a thrill of awe went through him. He did not look up, though he was vividly aware of the mailed fist striking the great bell and the stern face of the Archangel, but remained looking out over the past. Nine times the great bell boomed out, the sound rolling over Isaac's head and away over the city to the fens. Nine o'clock, the hour of the old curfew. Then far down below him he heard the homely church clocks striking. In all the houses of the city other little clocks were striking too though he could not hear them. Then there was silence, deep and profound, and suddenly he was terrified. It seemed to him that time was opening at his feet and that he stood looking down into an abyss of nothingness. Behind him the Cathedral soared like a towering black wave that would presently crash down on him and knock him into the abyss. Unable to move he stood there sweating with terror, as helpless and hopeless as in those nightmares that visited him during his bad times. But this was not one of his bad times, it was a good time. His mind suddenly gripped that. He remembered what had

45

happened an hour ago and the memory was like a cry for help.
Again and again he cried for help and slowly the memory of
love became love, welling up from the depths of him and
quietly enveloping himself and the city, time and the abyss, all
that was. He was set free.

He walked quietly down the steps, wiping his face with his
handkerchief and vowing that never again would he go near
the terrible Cathedral in moonlight. He went across the green
and under the Porta, crossed Worship Street and was in Angel
Lane, and presently he was so far recovered that he started
whistling the bells of St. Clement's shakily but with enjoyment.
He was still whistling when he went up the two worn stone
steps to the front door of number twelve, where he lived with
Emma, and did not begin to run down until he stood in the
dark little passage taking off his muffler and his greatcoat, and
remembered suddenly that it was long past supper-time. The
silence in the house was ominous and even though it was one
of his good times he fumbled stupidly with the handle of the
parlour door and nearly lost his footing on the wool mat on the
threshold. Emma had a little wool mat made by herself before
every door in the house. They were her pride and joy and it
must have been Isaac's fault that they always slid from beneath
him, for Emma herself never lost her footing on them.

As her brother came in she rose silently from her hard chair
and pulled the long tasselled bellrope that hung beside the fire.
The bell clanged like a fire-alarm in the kitchen next door, a
signal to their little maid Polly to bring in the overcooked
supper. Their evening meal was supposed to be at eight but
Emma always waited for Isaac however late he was. That was
one of her principles. Another of them was that she never
reproached Isaac however maddening he might be. She had
accepted him as her cross and she carried him uncomplainingly,
for she was a very virtuous woman. "Wash your hands," was
all she said now.

Isaac slunk back again into the passage, slipping this time
on the kitchen mat, for he had to pass through the kitchen to

the scullery. As he came in Polly straightened up from before
the kitchen range and she and Isaac smiled at each other, but
did not speak for fear Emma should hear them. Isaac tiptoed
through to the scullery and lit the candle there, and a moment
later Polly popped up at his elbow with a jug of water. "'Ot,"
she whispered. He looked down into her round greenish-hazel
eyes, bright with laughter in a plain freckled little face from
which the ginger hair was drawn back to be hidden beneath a
big mob cap. He was small but she was smaller, reaching only
to his shoulder. She was a brat from the city orphanage and
Emma had got her cheap. She was sixteen years old, tough
as a pit pony and a wonderful worker. She did not find
drudgery monotonous and was possibly the happiest person
in the city. She adored and protected Isaac, she adored Sooty
the cat and would have protected him had it been necessary.
She pitied Emma. She had never hated anyone, not even
those who in the past had cruelly misused her. She was
intuitive and looking up now into Isaac's face she knew it was
one of his good times. While he soaped his work-soiled hands
she darted back into the kitchen and returned with a rough
towel which she had been warming in front of the fire. "'Ot,"
she whispered again, and felt in her own body the glow of
Isaac's happiness and of his hot water and hot towel. Warmth
was acceptable in the scullery for it was cold and dreary there.
The kitchen regions of the picturesque old houses of Angel
Lane were stone-floored and damp, the happy hunting ground
of blackbeetles and mice, and the cats who had to be kept to
keep down the mice. However scrupulously clean they were
kept, and Polly scrubbed the stone floors of number twelve
every day, they retained their distinctive smell; damp, mice,
beetles and tom cat flavoured with onion.

"Thank ee, Polly," said Isaac, and pinched her cheek.
"What's for supper?"

"Shepherd's pie," said Polly. "'Ot."

Polly's pies, even when kept waiting too long in the oven,
were good, and Isaac stepped across the kitchen with alacrity,

his mouth watering. But seated at the round table in the parlour, opposite Emma, he found that he was not hungry any more. It was odd, the way he always felt hungry in the kitchen with Polly but unable to eat much in the parlour with Emma. And yet Emma was always solicitous about his meals and subsequent indigestion. It was another of her principles that a man's stomach should be a woman's first care. Emma presiding over a meal was like a high priestess offering sacrifice at the altar of a pitiless god. Grimly, as she and Isaac sat waiting for Polly to bring in the pie, she looked the table over to make sure that everything required for the coming ritual was in place. The oil lamp in the centre was trimmed to perfection, the white tablecloth, exquisitely darned and laundered, was spotless, the thin old table silver highly polished. The cruets were not quite at the right angle but she adjusted them. Isaac's post-prandial bismuth mixture was by his glass.

There seemed nothing wrong but she sighed, weighed down by the perennial sorrow of having no dining-room. Number twelve was one of the smallest and cheapest houses in Angel Lane and had only four rooms, the kitchen and parlour on the ground floor and Emma's and Isaac's bedrooms above. The two attics in the roof, Polly's and the box room, hardly counted as rooms because they were so tiny. The poor poky little house was not suited to gentlefolk, and a gentlewoman Emma had been born and a gentlewoman Emma would die, even though Isaac had demeaned himself by becoming a common tradesman. It is the status of the father that determines a woman's exact position in the social scale, she would tell Polly, who so far as the orphanage could tell her had come into the world with no father at all, and Emma's father had been a clergyman of the Church of England. She never forgot the great days of the past but there were those in the city who did. There were many now, she feared, who thought of her as Isaac Peabody the clockmaker's sister, rather than as the daughter of the Reverend Robert Peabody, rector of St. Peter's in the market place.

She sighed again and Isaac looked at her in anxious self-reproach, knowing how often he himself was the cause of her sorrow. Though she was three years older than her brother she still had the gaunt remnants of her early dark good looks. She was straight as a ramrod, big-boned, tall and thin, with a long melancholy face and profoundly sad dark eyes. Her clothes were nearly as old as Isaac's but she looked after them so well, brushing and folding them daily with such care, that there was nothing slovenly about them, and she brightened them with a gold locket and a mourning brooch containing her mother's and father's hair. The home that she had created for herself and Isaac was like herself and her clothes, scrupulously clean and neat, sad, saturated with the past. Everything in the parlour had come from what Emma called "the old home", and she had added nothing new in all the years. The fireside chairs, with seats so slippery and hard that one slid off them if one tried to relax, the prickly horsehair sofa, the faded curtains of dark green hanging at the window that Emma scarcely ever opened, the picture of the Day of Judgement hanging over the sideboard and the enlarged photo of their equally terrifying father hanging over the mantelpiece, were each of them for Isaac a reminder of his miserable boyhood. Wherever he looked it confronted him. On the sofa his adored mother had lain when she was dying. At this same table he had sat for an hour at a time, refusing to eat his congealed mutton fat and suet pudding, and under the picture of the Last Judgement his father had thrashed him. Even the fire on the hearth was the sullen fire he had always known, for they had always had to economize. The only thing his eye lighted upon with any pleasure was the clock on the mantelpiece, a black marble Benjamin Vulliamy clock with two figures of Time and Death standing one on each side of the dial. As a child it had frightened him almost as much as the picture of the Last Judgement, but now it was a comfort to him for though it was ugly it was at least a clock and it kept good time.

The door opened and Polly came in with a heavy tray laden with the pie, warm plates and a large brown steaming teapot.

D

Her face was flushed and beaming and instantly the atmosphere
of the cold stuffy room was subtly changed because she was
happy. Polly's chief joy in life was feeding people. She was of
the pelican breed and would have nourished those she loved
with her own flesh and blood had she had nothing else to give
them. "There!" she said, dumping the pie down triumphantly
in front of Emma, for Emma always served the food, Isaac
being far too lavish with it.

"You must place the dishes in silence on the table, Polly,"
said Emma wearily. "How ever many more times must I tell
you that!"

Polly, having placed the teapot on its stand in silence,
tipped Isaac the suspicion of a wink before she went to stand
beside Emma with her hands behind her back, while Emma
doled out her helping of pie on to a cracked white kitchen
plate and cut her a slice of dry bread. The parlour plates had
a pink and gold border, and it always hurt Isaac's feelings
intolerably to watch Emma seeing how little she could give
Polly. It did not hurt Polly for the pelican breed do not concern
themselves with their own feeding.

"Thank you, ma'am," said Polly briskly, and whisked out of
the door with her plate, her voluminous print skirts crackling,
her small feet tapping out their quick vigorous light tattoo
upon the stone floor of the passage. She never slipped on the
mats for she had the sure-footedness of the single-minded. The
kitchen door clicked behind her and there hung in the heavy
air the faintest suggestion of music.

"That girl isn't singing is she?" Emma asked suspiciously.

"No," said Isaac, and began to talk loudly and incoherently
about the weather and the people who had come to the shop
that day. His sister transferred her suspicions to him and her
nose began to twitch nervously. "Isaac," she whispered, "have
you been drinking again?"

That was one of the things that made Isaac such a heavy
cross for her to bear. When he was having one of his bad times
he did, occasionally, get drunk. Those nights when he came

home from the Swan and Duck singing at the top of his voice
all the way up Angel Lane caused her a humiliation that was
agony to her. Their father had been president of the Tem-
perance League and she and Isaac had both at his command
signed the pledge in infancy. After one of Isaac's lapses she did
not go out for several days for she was too ashamed.

"No, Emma," said Isaac gently, but now he could think of
nothing else to say and became silent, for he was as ashamed
of his lapses as Emma was. Luckily at this point the Time and
Death clock, and all the clocks of the city, struck ten, and the
faint music within the house was merged with the music outside.

Supper ended, and the table cleared by Polly, they sat one
on each side of the sullen fire, Emma reading her evening
chapter in the family Bible, that was kept on a small round
table with a red plush tablecloth beside her chair, and Isaac
holding a newspaper unseeingly before his nose. In their
childhood their father had held family prayers after supper,
reading the Bible aloud to them and their mother and the little
maidservants in a voice of such doom that even when he read
of the love and mercy of God it made no sort of sense to his
hearers. Only the doom came home to them, and the anguish
of his conviction of sin and doubt of salvation as he implored
the Almighty to have mercy upon them. Broken upon the rock
of his stern and joyless character and faith his delicate wife
had failed and died and Isaac had lapsed into unbelief. Only
Emma had had sufficient strength of character to take the iron
of her father's teaching into her own body and soul, to revere
and imitate him while he lived and mourn him now that he
was dead. There could no longer be family prayers with
Isaac what he was but Emma always read her Bible at the
appointed time, with a faint hope that by so doing she might
win Isaac away from his wickedness before it was too late.
Isaac was not exactly the object of her affection, for no one
had ever taught her anything about love, but to care for
his delicate body and save his lost soul was the object of
her existence. Isaac knew it and his worst moments in this

house were when Emma was reading her chapter while he sat trembling on the edge of his chair, as obstinately determined not to be saved as he had once been determined not to eat the mutton fat. There was nowadays an integrity about his obstinacy, for his refusal to accept his father's God had in it something of the courage and fire of the true faith. But he was a weak man and it cost him dear. He never read a word of the paper he held before him. He did not even see it. He only saw the face of his father, whom he had hated.

Robert Peabody had been perhaps not entirely sane, brave, utterly uncorruptible, pitiless to himself, his wife and children only because he had to be. Hell yawned for them all and he had not dared to let them forget it. Above all he had not dared to let Isaac forget it, for Isaac had always been a delicate and abnormally sensitive child, prone as the delicate are to seek a little comfort for himself here and there, and dangerously indulged by his equally delicate mother. Never for one moment had Robert Peabody allowed Isaac to forget the wrath of God, and Isaac had spent his childhood in a state of cringing fear of the deity, domiciled in his imagination within the Cathedral. The only time he had ever actively defied his father had been when Robert tried to take him inside the Cathedral. He had fought like a wild beast. Brought home and chastised he still would not go, and the attack of asthma he had had as the result of this battle had been so severe that Robert had let the matter drop for his wife's sake. For Maria Peabody was always worse when Isaac was worse, for Isaac was the only reason why she held to life. But her hold on life was not strong and when Isaac was fourteen she died.

For two more years Isaac had struggled on at the hated city grammar school, mercilessly teased by the boys there, and then he had done a base and terrible thing; he had stolen three pounds from a drawer in his father's desk and run away to London. He knew that for such a deed the wrath of God was held in store for him, but he was so miserable that he scarcely cared. And there was always the hope that there was, after all, no God. This hope was fostered by his maternal uncle, to whose house in Clerkenwell he betook himself when he reached London. This uncle, his mother's only brother, was a notary, a stout and jovial person so very much addicted to the pleasures of this life that his brother-in-law, after one visit from him, had felt himself unable to receive him in his house again lest he corrupt the children. The notary, chilled to the marrow by that one visit, had not wanted to be received again, but he had been fond of his sister and had never ceased to correspond with her, and when she died he had written a little letter of condolence to her son to whom through her letters he had taken a fancy. The warm sympathy of that letter had been something new to Isaac. He had carried it for two years in his breast pocket and then had gone to seek the writer of it.

His uncle had been good to him, had taken him into his warm untidy bachelor establishment, taught him to laugh, to swill mild ale, to eat a beefsteak with enjoyment, to disbelieve in God, to take a clock to pieces and put it together again. Then, finding that his nephew took a thrilled interest in his own hobby of horology, was expert at it and excited beyond measure to find himself in Clerkenwell, at the very hub of the clockmaking industry, he apprenticed him to a clockmaker friend of his. It was done only just in time, for a few days after the deeds were signed and sealed Robert Peabody managed at last to find his son. There was a sad and bitter scene between them but Isaac, backed up by his uncle and bound in honour to his master, stood firm, and Robert went back heartbroken to the city and never saw his son again.

Those years in London had been the happiest in Isaac's life, yet his father, and the city on the hill, were never far from his thoughts. He tried to forget them and could not, and they were linked together with the thought of the God from whom he ceaselessly fled. His father, his city, his forsaken God. A man may build as he chooses upon his foundations but he cannot change them or forget them, and if at the last the superstructure of his own building falls about his ears he tends

to rediscover them at the end as the only rock he has to cling
to. Isaac was still a young man when his father died yet
immediately he packed his bag and went back to the city, and
when on the evening of the funeral his sister Emma, whom he
had never been able to like, told him it had been their father's
dying wish that she should devote the rest of her life to him he
did not hesitate. The tiny sum of money that their father had
left her was hardly sufficient to keep her in clothes. She had
been trained for no profession and in any case ladies did not
work for their living. He must come back to the city and
support her until she married, for his foundations demanded
it of him. She had never married. The years he had spent with
her seemed to him now a long time. The years he had spent
in the city seemed timeless. The years he had spent making
clocks and watches had upon them the light of eternity.

2

Half-past ten struck and Emma closed the Bible. "Ring the
bell," she said to Isaac. Summoned by the clanging Polly re-
entered with three bedroom candlesticks, highly polished brass
for Isaac and Emma and cracked china for herself. Solemnly
Emma lit the candles, as she did every night punctually at ten-
thirty, inaugurating the ritual of bedtime. Then the parlour
fire was raked out, the window firmly latched and the lamp
extinguished. Then all three processed to the kitchen where
the same was done. Emma asked, "Is the cat put out?" and
Polly replied, "Yes, ma'am." Then they went back to the dark
passage and Isaac put the chain across the already firmly locked
front door, while Emma locked the parlour and kitchen doors
upon the outside, lest burglars break into the kitchen or parlour
in the night. Then she went slowly up the narrow steep stairs
with her candle, followed by Isaac with his candle, Polly
bringing up the rear with hers. On the landing above Emma
halted and said severely, "Good night, Polly," and stood
watching while Polly climbed up the tiny flight of uncarpeted
stairs that led to her attic. When the door of that apartment

had been heard to latch behind her Emma said, "Good night, Isaac," and bent to kiss him. Then she went into her bed-chamber over the parlour and shut the door behind her. Isaac went into his room, put his candle down on the table beside his bed and let out a sigh of relief that was almost a sob. He would not see his sister again until the morning.

Safe in his small hard bed, his tasselled night-cap on his head, he pondered miserably for a little while on the pitifulness of the affections and hates of human beings. He hoped he did not hate Emma, but when every tie of blood and duty and gratitude demanded of him that he should feel affection for her she affected him like some disease from which he shrank and cowered. His nerves quivered in her presence. What was the cure for this rasping of one personality upon another that brought one near to desperation and the breaking of the mind? What could one do? There was never any answer to this question, and there was none tonight, except the white radiance of the moon that bathed his bed and the slow rising within him of the waters of peace. Abruptly he forgot Emma in profound astonishment and thankfulness. It was still here. He was still having one of his good times. The unhappy evening with Emma had only been a momentary cloud upon it. He was still safe. He stretched his misshapen little body in the bed, he worshipped the moonlight and fell asleep.

In the large gloomy four-poster which had been her parents' bed, and which almost filled her room, Emma wept. No one had ever seen her cry, no one knew she could, but the gift of quiet weeping was one that had been vouchsafed to her of late years. She wept because she was tired right out, soaked with tiredness like a sponge with water, heavy as lead. Her exhaustion was not physical, for Polly did all the hard work of the house and Emma was a strong woman; it was the weariness of failure and betrayal. She knew now that she would never change Isaac, never turn him into a sober business-like gentlemanly good man. After all her years of prayerful struggle he remained what he had always been, a bad man.

Yes, a bad man; a man who had stolen from his father and broken his heart, a man neither sober, honest nor God-fearing. And yet, and this to Emma was the bitterest thing in all her bitter lot, this bad man was so often happy. She, who had been a woman of exemplary virtue all her life, who had let no day go by without prayer and Bible reading, who Sunday by Sunday attended divine service, who scraped and saved to put money in her missionary box and took no sugar in her tea in Lent, was vouchsafed no reward for virtue. God had betrayed her. She had done her part but he had not done his. Peace. Joy. They were only words to her. She had seen peace in the eyes of the unregenerate Isaac, and joy dancing in Polly's eyes, but neither the one nor the other so much as touched her with a wing tip in passing. In the face of such injustice it was hard to believe the Bible promise that the righteous shall be rewarded. She wept on into her pillow and sleep came at last, deep and dreamless. She did not know what a blessing it was that she could sleep so well.

Polly always let the cat out at night, as commanded, but as soon as she had gained her small hard bed in the cold attic she let him in again. It was about the best moment in all her happy day when she jumped into bed, opened the dormer window beside her and called, "Sooty! Sooty!" He did not come immediately, even though he had been sitting on the roof waiting for this moment ever since he had been put out, for he had his dignity to think of. He came when it suited him, slowly and with condescension, somewhat astonished at the last to find himself on Polly's bed. He stood for a while upon her chest, kneading her disdainfully, his enormous tail twitching, his eyes like green jewels, heartless as beautiful. Polly scarcely dare breathe lest he depart but she never closed the window until he had decided to settle down. She understood his independent pride and knew that to coerce him would be to lose not his affection, for he had none, but the partiality of his tolerance.

Tonight he sat down on her chest, his back to her, his twitching tail tickling her nose, but still she did not dare to close the window. There was a long silence in the room and then a sound so faint that it was more a vibration than a sound. It increased, sending sympathetic tremors through her body, increased slowly and steadily until sound was perceptible, a faint humming, and then a louder humming as of innumerable bees approaching at speed, and then at last Polly's whole body was shaken by the full glorious organ music of Sooty purring. Then she shut the window and lifted up the top blanket to make a warm cavern beside her body. Into this Sooty condescended to insert himself. For a while the organ music continued beneath the blanket, then it sank to the bee-like humming, then to silence. Sooty slept.

Polly remained awake for a little while looking out over the kingdom. Winter and summer alike she slept with her bed across the dormer window, that she might see it in the evening and the morning and when she woke up at night. Angel Lane sloped steeply below number twelve so that Polly's window at the back of the house commanded one of the finest views in the city. When she had entered into possession of her attic at number twelve she had for the first time in her life owned privacy and a view. Just at first she had scarcely known what to do with either of them. The silence and loneliness had frightened her, and it had made her feel dizzy to see the roofs of the city tumbling away below her southward down to the river, and then the vast plain beyond stretching to the end of the world. Then slowly deep needs of whose existence she had scarcely been aware began to be satisfied and there woke in her the question, who am I, a question that she had not asked in the crowded orphanage days. The solitude of her room made her aware of herself and the illimitable beauty it looked upon made her aware of something beyond herself, so far away that its unattainable perfection broke her heart. And yet it was near. It was far as the brown brink of the horizon before dawn, and near as the yellow rose that climbed from the walled garden below and in June propped itself upon her window sill and scented her room. The scent of a flower is a very close and intimate thing, she thought. It can seem to be a part of your body and blood.

Polly's name for her view, the kingdom, she had picked up from attending Saint Matthew's at the South Gate on Sundays with all the other orphanage children. The prayers had for the most part gone off her like water off a duck's back but that one perpetually repeated sentence, "the kingdom, the power, and the glory", had stuck in her mind like a phrase of music and now it sang itself there whenever she looked at her view. Tonight it was moonlit and sparkling. Frost glistened on the tumbled roofs and great stars burned in the sky. She could just see the church towers crowning the little hills in the fen, far away and small like toy towers, and here and there the gleam of water, but the power and glory in the vast singing sky had crushed the earth to nothingness tonight. It was not her own idea that stars sang. Isaac sometimes taught her to say bits of poetry when they were together in the scullery, and he had taught her the bit about the singing stars. All the rags and tags of verse that Isaac knew, taught him in his childhood by his mother, were gradually passing from his memory to hers. There they were in safe keeping for Polly had a remarkable memory. The orphanage had not been very successful in teaching her to read or write, for she had been there for too short a time, but anything she had heard with attention she remembered. On Saturdays, when she went marketing and Emma handed her a shopping list, she was too ashamed to say she could not read it, but luckily Emma always read it aloud before handing it to her and she never forgot anything.

Suddenly she remembered that it was market day tomorrow. She had been feeling chilly in spite of Sooty's warmth, for the blankets on her bed were poor and thin and the frost thrust its fingers through the ill-fitting little window, but now she began to glow. Tomorrow in the market she would see Job. The warmth of her joy tingled upwards from her toes to her cheeks and they were a faint rose colour in the moonlight. The stars came closer and she swung up to meet them, yet when she was among them they changed from singing spirits to flowers and she saw them as lilies growing in a field beside a stream. In her dream she and Job were together in a small dancing boat, and the quick water was carrying them out into a mystery. It was a dream full of expectancy and it often came to her.

CHAPTER 4

I

THE sudden appearance of Isaac Peabody in the shop had
sent Job running down through the streets of the city as
lightly and silently as a phantom. Though he possessed a pair
of broken boots he went barefoot when he could because it
made escape easier. He was not by temperament an escapist,
for he had extraordinary toughness and courage, but he
retained his sanity by living as much as possible within his own
private world. When he had to come out of it he did what had
to be done as well as he could, and endured stoically what had
to be endured, and escaped back to it again. He had not been
afraid of the clockmaker, he had fled only from force of habit.
He had caught glimpses of Isaac many times before tonight
and the old man and all his clocks lived with him in his world,
together with Polly and a few others. Very few were admitted.
It was a signal honour to be admitted by Job to the place
within himself.

As he descended the hill towards the river and the North
Gate he imagined he was climbing down the escarpments of a
mountain. It was always as a mountain that he thought of the
Cathedral. Shut at night within the safety of his world he
would sometimes try to imagine what it was like inside, and he

would try and choose between one and another of the amazing
landscapes that drifted cloudlike through his heaven and try
and fit it inside the mountain. But none of them was great
enough. When they touched the stone of the mountain they
dissolved into nothingness. The mountain kept its secret and
it never even occurred to him that he should climb up to it and
see if it possessed a crack in the rock that would let him in.
He was not, like Isaac, afraid of it, but people did not go
inside it whose clothes were dirty and who stank. He had
absorbed that fact with the air he breathed when he first came
to the city. He did not resent it, for he was kept from resent-
ment by a piece of knowledge which to him was as factual as
his boots; that if he could keep himself from going under there
would be a way through his present bad luck to good luck.
But he must not go under. If he did the easy thing that he
often longed to do, if he stopped washing under the pump and
cracking the fleas and let himself sink back into the slime and
obscenity of Swithins Lane, he would lose the way. Upon this
fact he had grounded himself.

He reached the flight of stone steps that led down from the
respectable part of the city to the slums below and paused and
looked back. He could see the Cathedral above him towering
against the stars and as he gazed Michael struck the half-hour.
Then with his head up he turned and ran down the dirty steps.

He might be lucky tonight, he thought, as he padded past
St. Nicholas at the North Gate into the darkness of Swithins
Lane, and get to bed without a belting. He was late but if his
master was still at the pub old Keziah would not tell on him.
He was apprenticed to Albert Lee the fishmonger, whom he
hated and who hated him, but old Keziah, Lee's mother, was
kind to him after her fashion. Job was used to being hated
and did not much mind because he knew the reason for it;
he was different, and he exulted in his difference. The hidden
exultation gave him a slight air of arrogance, though actually
he had no more pride than was necessary for the preservation
of decency, and increased his illusiveness. There were times

when Lee thought he would burst a blood vessel if he could not get a good grip on the boy and beat the superiority right out of him. Yet at the end of a belting he had somehow done neither.

The moonlight that flooded the heights of the city scarcely penetrated to Swithins Lane for the upper stories of the old houses jutted over the lower, turning the lane into a dark, filthy tunnel. Garbage squelched under Job's bare feet and he heard the rats scuttling. There was a faint glimmer of candle-light behind some of the small dirty windows, and now and then through an open door came the usual din of children screaming, and exhausted and maddened women shouting at them. A few drunken men lurched along the gutter but most were still at the pubs. The stench of the place was nauseating but Job was as used to that as he was used to the smell of fish that penetrated his appalling clothes, and already there was a part of him that was running on ahead to sanctuary. He could almost see it, a wraith that had his shape but was made of white flame, himself as he would be when he had passed through. He did not know whether he had imagined this wraith or whether it was real. It ran swiftly, leaping over the heaps of refuse and the scummy pools, and he ran after it, losing it sometimes and then glimpsing it again. He did not catch up with it until they had reached the side door of the shop, that stood ajar on its broken hinges, and then again it was gone and he was alone.

He edged in cautiously, for the half-open door meant that one or other of them was still in the kitchen behind the shop. If he could once leap up the narrow stairs at the end of the passage to the dark landing above, and then scramble up the ladder that led to his attic under the tiles, he was safe. Lee, a heavy man, could not negotiate the rotting ladder even when sober, when drunk he couldn't even find it. Job reached the end of the passage and leaped for the stairs, but even as he did so he was aware of the heavy body lurching through the kitchen door, and a vast hand grabbed his bare ankle. At the same moment he was equally aware that the other boy was back again, leaping into his body to share the torture with him. He did not struggle, for it was useless, and also he knew intuitively that his contemptuous acceptance of the inevitable maddened Lee. They were a queer couple of enemies, for the boy too had his weapons. He enjoyed the many ways in which he could use his quick slim body and agile mind in a wordless taunting of Lee's sodden stupid clumsiness. And Lee was slightly in his power, for the skill of the apprentice was the mainstay of the business. Job knew that whenever he ran up to the city after dark Lee was in a fright that he would not come back.

But he had not yet attempted to run away for he knew the consequences. He had been apprenticed to Lee for three years and only one year had passed. If the cops caught him he'd be prosecuted and imprisoned under the Master and Servant Act, and he would not be allowed to plead for himself. He had a morbid dread of prison and of all dark and shut-in places. But the beatings were bad. Some night there might be one which would be too much for him.

Lee dragged him into the kitchen and set about it by the light of a candle stump and the moonlight that flowed through the window. The light was dim and he was drunk, and some of his blows went wide, but those that cut true had the force of the man's strength and hatred full behind them. Job never sobbed or cried out because he knew Lee wanted him to, and beat him largely for that purpose. His gasps he could not control but the man's own laboured breathing covered them up. It did not last long, for Lee was in too poor shape to keep it up, but while it lasted it was indeed very bad and almost the worst was the ending of it, when he was sick and faint with pain and exhaustion and yet must get himself up and out of the room without letting Lee know that he had broken him. It was easier tonight for that boy had not left him and was a strength in his body. He moved through the moonlight to the door with his head up and vanished silently up the stairs. Lee flung his belt into the corner of the dirty kitchen and cursed, and then the sobs that he had been unable to tear out of Job clawed at his own chest. He sat hunched on the wooden chair, his great red hands dangling between his knees, and maudlin tears made streaks upon his face that were as hot and stiff as the streaks on Job's back. Of the two of them he was the more wretched. He was possibly the most miserable man in the city that night.

Job gained his attic, did what he could to help himself and lay face downwards on his wretched bed. The attic was no more than a roof-space with boards laid across the beams below to hold his bed and a broken chair. It had one small dormer window but the roof sloped so steeply that there was only one place in the little room where he could stand upright. All the same, he loved this eyrie because it was his own and no one but himself could get to it. And because here he could sleep and dream and gain his world.

He lay still for a long while upon the threshold, but he could not go in yet because the pain was too bad. He knew how to keep still, not only physically but inside himself, so that when the pain ebbed in his body the tumult in his mind quieted too. The window faced not upon the squalor of Swithins Lane but towards the river and the fen, where the frost was crisping the grasses and the tall pointed reeds. The night flowed in through the window, filling the room with the coldness of well water. He could hear the faint sound of the river flowing past and gazing down, as though he lay on the river bank itself, he could see in imagination the silver of the moonlight lying on the water, trembling where it splintered silently about the stones at the water's edge and the spears of the reeds. All his life he was to find the sight and sound of flowing water one of the greatest solacements of grief.

2

He had been lying on the riverbank like this, face downwards and looking at the water, on that day when as a small boy he had run away from his governess to fish for minnows and the gypsies had got him. He could still in nightmare feel the hand grasping at his clothes, lifting him up, and smell the huge dirty palm clamped over his mouth that he might not scream. He had lived for two months with the gypsies and they had given him his name, Job Mooring, but he did not remember much about it now except the perpetual swaying of the van, the barking of the dogs, the blows and curses. But he did remember how the rolling country of the midlands had flattened out into the fen, and that he had liked the fen, and that one day in a green grove he was sold for eight guineas to Dan Gurney, a chimney sweep of the city, to be his climbing boy. That the kidnapping of small boys to be chimney sweeps was a frequent occurrence during the shameful years of the exploitation of the children he did not know. Working for Dan he seemed alone in his wretchedness and knew nothing of the army of other children who toiled and died in the mines and factories and chimneys of England. That he too did not die was because of his extraordinary toughness and because when it got to the point where he could not bear it any more he was delivered.

The man who had saved him was the first whom he had admitted to live in his world, and was in fact the creator of it, for his great stature and compassion could not be held within the hard tight walls of a small boy's suffering. Job had to make space about him and in his mind he made it, and then as time passed the space grew and became a world of illimitable fancy where this man walked as a giant. Job only vaguely remembered his governess, and a big house with many servants where a man painted pictures and a woman played the piano and had no time for him. He believed now that they had been relatives but not his parents for he had no memories of love. He had encountered love for the first time, and then only briefly, in his short encounter with the giant.

In the quietness, with the pain growing easier, he looked down and saw the encounter as though he were looking through the wrong end of a telescope, with the moving figures small and far away. Yet it was happening within him too, it was always happening, because it was the point of his salvation. The water, then, had welled up through the broken ground to give

E

a living freshness to his whole life. The timelessness of salvation was something he did not understand yet but he was aware of the freshness whenever he remembered that day.

He wished he could remember just how he and Dan Gurney had got there. It had still been dark when Dan had dragged him out of bed and cuffed him and told him to get on with it. In one way Dan had been a better master than Lee for he had been too lazy to beat him, but in all other ways a worse one. Lee's cruelty was largely the emanation of his wretchedness but Dan had enjoyed his.

Carrying their sacks they climbed up through the steep streets of the city, and they seemed to climb interminably. The light grew as they climbed but there was a thick mist so that Job had no idea where they were. Nor in his wretchedness did he care. They went under an archway and the tread of their boots rang hollowly upon the paving stones beneath it. Then they passed under tall trees, invisible but dripping with mist. The cold drops fell on Job's face and made tracks through the grime. He was a stunted little creature in those days, thin but very agile, and invaluable as a climbing boy for he could get through very narrow flues and so far had had the wit to get himself out again. It was bad for a sweep's reputation when a boy got stuck and died.

They came through the mist to the back door of a great house and when he saw its size Job was frightened, for these big old houses of the gentry were the worst. Most of them had their old wide chimneys contracted, so that they should not smoke too much, to a space only just large enough to allow a boy to get up and down, and the flues were winding passages with sharp angles. They were hot and dark and stifling and it was easy to lose yourself. It was then that the fear got bad and it was difficult to keep steady enough to use your wits to save yourself. It was, for Job, getting increasingly difficult. During his first year with Dan his natural pluck, a healthy body and great curiosity had given him resilience, but as the months dragged on and he grew weak with semi-starvation and the foul air of the chimneys the fear grew. Today, as the butler let them in to the darkened house, it seemed to stop his breath altogether and there was a clawing sort of pain in his guts. As he followed Dan and the butler up a long passage he thought he was going to be sick. He would have been if there had been anything in his stomach.

They came to a big room shrouded in dust sheets, and now there was a housemaid in a mob cap and apron as well as the majestic butler. It was light now but the grey mist was still muffled against the windows. The great chimney gaped. To one side of it stood a basket of kindling, waiting for the relighting of the fire when the chimney should be swept.

"Up with you, boy," said Dan.

But Job stood where he was, trembling violently. It was the first time he had refused a chimney.

"Go on, you young bleeder!" said Dan low and savagely, but still Job did not move. Dan cursed and struck him, and the butler and maid coaxed gently, promising him a slice of cake when it was over, but he would not go. Except to protect his head with his arms when Dan struck him he did not move.

"The boy's shy-like," said Dan to the butler. "Ain't never been in a house as fine as this before. You leave 'im to me, sir. You too, ma'am. 'E won't be afeared alone with me."

"Don't strike the child," said the maid. "If we go, mind you treat him gentle."

Dan swore that he always treated Job gentle and the boy was as fond of him as his own father, and rather reluctantly the butler and maid left the room. Dan did not waste time. He seized Job and thrust him bodily up the chimney. His arm came after him a little way, forcing him up with blows, and mechanically Job began to climb. He went on for a little way and then stopped. He couldn't do it. His mind went blank and he clung where he was, completely still. He heard a rustling below but he did not wonder what it was until the flames leaped up. To light a fire beneath him was a very old trick for making a boy climb but it was new to Job. He gave a choking cry, clung for a moment with his head hanging back, caught between the darkness and the flames, and then the blackness and the fire seemed to rush together and he let go and fell.

He realized later that it must have been a small fire, only a few bits of kindling lit to frighten him, and someone must have quickly flung a sack over it when he cried out, for when he slithered down it was not into the flames. A strong pair of hands took hold of him before he could fall, lifted him out of the chimney and put him gently into a big armchair covered with a dust sheet. To Job in his dazed state the room seemed full of people, and a vast and terrible anger like a thunderstorm. It seemed that everyone was being washed backwards and forwards by the anger as though they were straws in a flood. Only he seemed immune, lying on some rock above the flood and safe from it. Curiosity killed the cat but it can also be very reviving. Job wriggled up in the chair and looked out over its high back as though he were looking over a garden wall. No one saw him and from this vantage point the scene of battle was spread out most splendidly before his eyes.

The room was not full of people after all, only Dan, the butler, the maid and a huge man in black clothes, old and ugly, with a hooked nose and eyeglasses perched upon the summit of the nose. It was he who was so angry, and he was an alarming sight in his anger, but he did not alarm Job. The butler, however, stood at attention like a criminal in the dock, the maid was crying and Dan was trembling. Job had not known Dan could tremble and the sight astonished him. It also astonished him to find that the old man was not making as much noise as he had thought he was while he was still so bewildered. He was just saying what he thought, and though his voice grated like a saw it was much quieter than Dan's when he was in a rage. A few of the things that he said lodged in Job's mind and he remembered them afterwards.

"It was my express command that no climbing boy should ever be employed in this house," he said. "The apparatus for sweeping chimneys without a boy now exists and should be used." His terrible beak of a nose turned towards the butler and his eyeglasses flashed. "You have flagrantly disobeyed me."

The butler flinched, as though at a whiplash, but he did not answer, and it was the maid who sobbed out something about the mistress having said to have a climbing boy, and to promise the boy a piece of cake if he wouldn't go up. Then it seemed that the old man flinched himself. A sort of spasm twisted his face. Job couldn't understand it. Then it was Dan's turn. The nose and the eyeglasses turned in his direction and he flattened himself against the wall as though they pinned him there.

"You are aware of the law, I presume. In eighteen-hundred and sixty-four it was made illegal for any boy under sixteen to help a chimney sweep. I shall have you summonsed for the breach of that law."

Dan began to stammer out that Job was sixteen last month. He was small, that's what it was, small for his age, but sixteen if a day. And that was the truth, guvnor, so help him Gawd.

"Where's the boy?" asked the terrible old man, and they all looked vaguely round. It was the old man who spotted him first, looking gravely at them over the top of the armchair. Only his grimy face was to be seen, and two filthy hands clasping the top of the chair. His dark hair was cropped short so that the soot should not get into it and he seemed all bones, but they were fine bones and his large dark eyes were remarkable. He gazed at the old man and the old man gazed at him. "What's your age, boy?" he barked. Both his bark and his scrutiny were most alarming but Job stood up to them very well.

"Dunno, sir," he said.

"Come here," said the old man.

Job scrambled out of the chair and came round to stand in front of him. He ducked his head, as one did to the gentry, and then stood squarely with his hands at his sides and looked up at the old man. Soot fell from his diminutive person on to the dust sheets on the floor.

"Eight or nine," barked the old man. Then he turned and

looked at Dan, who was still pinned against the wall. "You will be summonsed and appear before the magistrate, but later I will see to it that you are provided with the necessary equipment for sweeping a chimney without the assistance of a climbing boy. You may go. The boy remains here." He turned to the butler. "See that this child is cleaned and fed. I will make the best arrangements I can as to his disposal and inform you of them in due course."

He turned and walked out of the room, his great head thrust forward and his hands behind his back. He had an extraordinary walk, as though he were forging along against a steady head wind. He had not looked at Job again, and had spoken of him as though he were a stray kitten who would have to be drowned if no suitable accommodation could be found. But Job's feelings were not hurt.

For the rest of that day he was rather miserable. The servants of the great house meant to be kind but there were so many of them that their talk made his head ache. He was allowed to eat his fill of wonderful food but it was too rich and he was sick. It was a painful business being scrubbed clean and having the sores on his body attended to, and afterwards he had to sit on a chair with nothing to wear but a blanket, his filthy rags having been burnt. During the afternoon the second housemaid, who had young brothers, went to her home and came back with a most peculiar assortment of male garments, all too large. In these he was draped and they were almost as uncomfortable as the blanket.

The next day, suddenly, a bell pealed and he was summoned to the study. The butler took him there, opened the door and pushed him through, indicating a writing table in the far distance to which he must set his course. With his trousers in coils round his ankles, and only the tips of his fingers showing below his sleeves, he journeyed across acres of carpet towards the table. It took a lot of courage but when he got there he found the old man sitting at the table, looking at him over the top of his eyeglasses. Job ducked his head and then looked back at him, his arms held rigidly at his sides. He was not afraid of the man but he began to tremble, because he had a feeling that he had now been disposed of. The man loomed up above him like a great mountain.

"Boy," he said in his hard grating voice, and then he stopped and took off his eyeglasses and put them on again. "Boy," he said again, and now his voice was harsher than ever, "there are in this city a couple of charitable institutions known as Dobson's orphanages. Boys and girls without homes are cared for and educated there and afterwards apprenticed to suitable trades. The boys' orphanage is at the East Gate, the girls' at the West Gate of the city. I have arranged for you to be received at Dobson's at the East Gate and you will be taken there today. I trust you will be happy."

There was a silence and Job felt that something was expected of him. He ducked his head and whispered, "Thank you, sir." Then he just stood there, and he felt very cold. He did not know why he was sobbing. He did not know what he had expected, or why the word "orphanage" had made him feel afraid. He knew he ought to turn round and face the long journey back to the door, but he couldn't. The journey to the table had been to the man, but the journey back to the door would be away from him. He knew his nose was running but he hadn't got a handkerchief. The silence lengthened and the room was full of desolation. Then a large heavy hand came down upon Job's shoulder, feeling through the folds of his ridiculous coat until it could get a grip on the meagre bones beneath. Looking up at the man Job saw that he had taken his eyeglasses off and was peering down at him, and he was as miserable as Job was. Indeed far more miserable, for everything about this man was vast, his anger and his sorrow and his love. The grip upon his shoulder was Job's first experience of love. He did not recognize it, but he stopped sobbing and wiped his nose on his sleeve. He began to feel warmer, and not so wretched. The grip on his shoulder gave him a sense of his own identity.

"Boy, listen to me," barked the man suddenly.

Job listened, but for a few moments the man said nothing. It was almost as though he did not know what to say. Then he cleared his throat so loudly that Job jumped, and said, "Boy, all things pass. You are a brave child and a remarkable one. You will not be defeated and for the undefeated there is always a way through."

Then he lumbered to his great height and with his hand still on Job's shoulder walked with him to the door. Outside the butler was waiting. Job was handed over and the door was shut, with him on one side and the old man on the other. When a little later he left in a cab in the custody of the butler, bound for the orphanage, it was raining so hard and he was crying so much that he did not notice where they were going. And so he never knew that the great house in which he had lived for two days and a night was right under the stone mountain at the top of the hill.

Job was not happy at the orphanage, though he slept in a clean bed, was adequately fed and taught to read and write and cipher. He was not happy because he was different. The other boys disliked him because he learned more quickly than they did, and they punished him for it with many subtle cruelties. Mr. Fennimore, the master of Dobson's, a man whose comfortable rotundity and hearty laugh had deceived the whole city into thinking him the kindest of men, punished him too, whenever he could for whatever he could. The boy was brilliant, curious yet secretive, odd, and a challenge to Mr. Fennimore's understanding that he could not meet. Even the smallest pin-prick in his self-esteem was gall to Mr. Fennimore and he detested the boy

In spite of the cruelties Dobson's did much for Job. He recovered health and strength and he became literate. He thought he had forgotten the lessons with his governess but they came back to him now and helped him to learn. It was the literacy that gave him his great joy at Dobson's, for in the schoolroom there was a shelf containing a few tattered books, given by some kindly citizen, and the boys were allowed to read them on Saturday nights. Few made use of the privilege, for they couldn't read well enough, but Job read them all. He read among others *The Pilgrim's Progress, Gulliver's Travels, Robinson Crusoe* and *The Cloister and the Hearth*, spelling them out as best he could to begin with but soon reading fluently. All the books had pictures in them. The books were like rooms in a great house and the pictures were lamps lit in the rooms to show them to him. As he read his dreams slowly changed. The nightmares of being stuck in chimneys that suddenly started to get smaller and smaller, squeezing him until he woke up choking and screaming, gradually gave way to dreams of forests full of great trees, where fabulous beasts galloped down the cool green aisles, meadows full of flowers and celestial mountains musical with streams. He dreamed of the sea that he had never seen and of ships upon it, and of caves where the tide washed in and out. And gradually the dreams became his world and he walked through it night by night with his hand in that of the old man. Sometimes by day too he would go away inside himself and he would be there. He never spoke of the old man and of his two days in the big house, and no one bothered to ask him how he had come to Dobson's. The whole experience of those days was part of his world and his private treasure. He scarcely related it to everyday life as he knew it.

He had another joy at Dobson's, and that was Polly. The boys and girls of the orphanage, the boys living at the East Gate and the girls at the West Gate, came together only on Sundays in church. Dobson, a wealthy divine who a hundred years ago had been Rector of St. Matthew's at the South Gate, had laid it down as law that on the Lord's Day all the children must attend matins at his church and for a hundred years they had done so. Every Sunday morning saw them walking through the city, two crocodiles converging on St. Matthew's, still dressed in the garments Dobson had decreed, the girls in long grey gowns and cloaks, and black bonnets tied with black velvet strings, the boys in grey coats and breeches and grey worsted stockings. Both boys and girls wore buckled shoes and the boys carried little three-cornered black hats. The people of the city loved to see them marching two by two to church, they looked so demure and old-fashioned, and so well cared for. The great munificence of old Dobson in providing for these children was, they felt somehow, to their credit. They were a generous city. Everyone smiled at the children as they passed by.

St. Matthew's was a lovely little church that might have been designed by Wren. The children sat in the front pews, boys to the right and girls to the left, and it was on a Sunday in spring that Job first glanced across the narrow aisle and saw Polly. He was feeling desolate that morning, having been caned by Mr. Fennimore the day before and having had one of his nightmares, but the moment he met her eyes he felt a sense of warmth and safety. They could never speak but they looked at each other each Sunday for a month, and then he did not see her again, but she joined the old man in his world.

Job was at Dobson's for four years and then he was apprenticed to old Nat Cooper the undertaker. Nat was kind but stern. He was a hell-fire dissenter and scarcely let Job out of his sight lest the devil run off with him. On Sundays he took him to a tin tabernacle at the opposite end of the city from St. Matthew's, so that he never saw Polly, and he always took Job with him when a corpse had to be placed in a coffin, so that the boy should learn to think upon his latter end. Job did think upon it, and his nightmares came back. One thing, however, Nat did for him. He taught him carpentry. He learnt to distinguish between the different kinds of wood, to love them and understand their ways. Realizing that the boy had great skill with his hands Nat gave him a few tools for his own and taught him woodcarving. Job had these tools still and when he was sent out into the fen, to find the flowers for the posies Keziah sold in the market, he would bring back bits of wood and make little gifts for Polly. First the books and then the wood. Each was a milestone for him on the way through.

After two years together Nat died and Job was back again on Mr. Fennimore's hands, and Mr. Fennimore re-apprenticed him to Albert Lee. He could hardly have chosen a trade less suited to Job's temperament and talents, but he was interested in neither. If there was anyone in the world whom Job hated more than Lee it was Mr. Fennimore. Job was never resentful but he was a good fierce hater. There was a lake of fire in the hollow of the mountains in his world in which he had already deposited Dan Gurney, Mr. Fennimore, Lee and a few others. They had not died in it but lived there in the perpetual torment which the old undertaker had described to Job as the state of the damned. It was an exquisite pleasure to picture them there, but on the nights when he was travelling through his world with the old man he could never find the lake of fire.

3

He fell asleep at last, waking after a few hours to the dull misery that always gripped him when he first woke up. Another day of the fish and the stink and the blows. Two more years of it. He moved and the pain ripped across his back. He burrowed his face into the dirty old pillow again and tore at it with his teeth. It could not have been more tattered than it was but it eased him to feel that he was doing to something that belonged to Lee what Lee was doing to him. He wished he could have done it to Lee. Then suddenly he remembered something; it was market day and Polly would come to the fish stall. Instantly he was quiet and knew the dawn had come and was slowly filling his room. He could hear bird voices crying out in the fen, for the river and the fen were forever bird-haunted. Presently he edged out of bed and moved cautiously to the window, for his back was stiff and sore. The stench of the earth closets behind the houses made it impossible to smell the freshness of the morning, but he could see it. The river, though it was scummy where it flowed past Swithins

Lane, was yet brimming with light and already arrowed here and there with the swift dart of moorhens. Beyond it the fen was wreathed in low silver mist to the horizon. Willow trees and clumps of reeds rose from it frosted and sparkling. There was a village on a hill a few miles away and the cock on its tall church spire took the glint of the morning. Three swans beat across his line of vision, blindingly white, the sound of their great wings tremendous in the morning silence. They passed and the scene settled again to its repose.

Job's was a temperament that swung easily from one extreme to the other and now misery was lost in a joy that seemed lifting him off his feet. At this moment personal wretchedness seemed to him a small thing in comparison with the vast shining outer world that was always there, sustaining and holding him even when he did not remember or notice it, small even in comparison with his own world that he held within himself. The two, echoing and calling to each other, reflected some mystery that was greater than either.

There were shouts and the banging of doors, the smell of cooking. Swithins Lane had awoken to another day. He left the window and crept stiffly down the ladder and went out to the back to wash himself at the pump.

CHAPTER 5

The Watch

I

THE sun soon conquered the mist and Isaac, as he passed
under the great elms of the Close, looked up and saw pale
gold leaves trembling against the blue of the sky. Down below
there was no wind but up there a faint breeze fingered them.
The frost had weakened their hold and even such a faint touch
was too much for them. One after another they came slowly
spinning down and one or two touched Isaac's upturned face
in falling. He stood looking up, entranced, and his hat fell off.
But there was no one to see and laugh at him for at a quarter
past nine in the morning the Close was deserted, except for a
few well-fed ecclesiastical cats sunning themselves on the tops
of the old walls that enclosed the gardens of the Cathedral
dignitaries. In these sheltered gardens flowering time was not
quite over and the pungent scent of chrysanthemums drifted
from them, to mingle with the scent of the bonfire in the
Deanery garden and the smell of the wet fallen leaves. How
well Isaac knew these scents of autumn and the butterfly touch
of falling leaves upon his face, sad or happy as his mood might
be. Winter, spring and summer did not accommodate themselves to one's moods as autumn did. They lacked its gentleness.

The Cathedral was in one of its kindlier moods. Blue mist

veiled the starkness of the Rollo tower and sunshine spilled down the walls and buttresses. It looked almost ethereal, as though built of air and light, and so benign that Isaac decided to venture as far as the south door and deliver his watch to old Tom Hochicorn in person, instead of leaving it for him at the almshouses. He walked down the lime avenue and then climbed the steps to an archway that led into a narrow cloister. Here on a stone bench beside the south door Tom Hochicorn sat with his hands upon his knees, wearing the long gown of dark blue frieze and the crimson skullcap that the Cathedral bedesmen had worn for centuries past. The Cathedral had four bedesmen, one to take care of each of its doors, all old men from the almshouses. Aware of a figure approaching Tom rose and bowed. There was only one thing in the whole city more charming than his courteous bow, and that was his smile as he welcomed worshippers to his Cathedral and put out his hand to open the door and let them in. Tom loved and trusted the Cathedral as deeply as Isaac hated and feared it. As the years had passed the conviction that he owned the whole place had grown upon him. Yet no one, looking at old Tom, would have guessed at the fiery love and burning pride that inwardly possessed him. He had meek eyes, a long white beard flowing down over his chest and a gentle deprecating voice and manner. Yet if any desperate man had tried to harm the Cathedral in any way Tom would have been capable of violence, and any stranger who dared defile the cloister with a careless word or too loud a laugh heard what Tom thought of him.

"No, Tom, no!" cried Isaac on a note of panic, as Tom put out his hand to the door. "Don't open that door! It's me—Isaac."

Tom sat down again and motioned to Isaac to sit beside him on the stone seat. He knew all about Isaac's fear of the Cathedral, and humoured him as he would have humoured a nervous child. "Listen, now," he said encouragingly.

Inside the Cathedral the organist was practising, and few men could play the music of Bach as he did. Isaac could not

but be quieted and listening to the music he began to see a
picture in his mind. He saw great pillars soaring upwards like
the trees in a forest, and a vaulted roof, very high, lit with
dim glory as when the wind blows light cloud across a moonlit
sky at night. He saw wide pavements of stone splashed with
pools of colour, and small chambers like caverns hollowed out
and carved and beautified by the surging of wind and sea.
Dead men lay here upon biers of dark stone, their eyes closed,
their hands upon their breasts. He saw strange vast curtains
of shadow and shafts of light that pierced down from beyond
sight to light upon old cloudy banners, a gilded throne, a great
rood lifted high up and far away in appalling loneliness. The
organ music grew louder, swelling, mounting. It was a dark
tide of bitter salt water, the same tide that had fretted out the
caverns and turned the dead men to stone upon their biers.
Then it was a thundering of wind in the trees and all the tall
columns were swaying in it. Then it was darkness, heavy and
hot, shapeless and pitch black, and the cry that tore across it
seemed to stop his heart, to enter into his blood and bones.
Yet he could not get up and fly from it for his limbs were like
lead, heavy as the limbs of the dead men on the biers. The
music stopped.

"Pretty, eh?" said Tom Hochicorn. "Weren't that a pretty
tune?"

"I've brought your watch, Tom," said Isaac hoarsely, and
bent to unlock the leather bag. "Here it is."

"Thank ee," said Tom, opening the worn gunmetal pair
cases. "Why, there ain't no watch paper! You always give I
a new watch paper."

"There's a watch paper," said Isaac.

"No, there ain't," said Tom, disappointed.

"You've dropped it," said Isaac.

The two old men searched the pavement but could find no
watch paper. "I must have dropped it in the shop," said Isaac.
"I'll put it in an envelope and post it to you. Good-bye,
Tom."

"Now there's no call for you to be off so soon," said Tom. "'Tis close on ten o'clock matins. If you was to sit 'ere with me you'd hear 'em at matins. 'Tis just so pretty as a lot of singing birds."

"No, Tom," said Isaac. "I've all my clocks to wind." And he fled.

Outside in the lime avenue again he looked back. Tom Hochicorn was sitting as before, motionless with his hands on his knees. Isaac had the fancy that he and the stone bench he sat on, and the stone wall behind him, had become one. "He'll never get away now," thought Isaac. "It's got him." And he vowed that never again would he yield to the pull of the tides that last night and this morning had nearly got him too. Never again would he even go and look at the Jaccomarchiadus.

2

There was a seat in the lime avenue and he sat down to wait for ten o'clock to strike. After ten o'clock the Dean would be in the Cathedral and he would be in no danger of running into him while he was winding the clocks. For years he had wound the Deanery clocks and had succeeded in never seeing either the Dean or Mrs. Ayscough. Sitting quietly in the dappled sunshine he had recovered from the terror of that music but he had not forgotten the cry of loneliness. He would never forget it.

Ten o'clock struck and he made his way towards the high wall of the Deanery garden, and followed round it until he came to the cobbled stableyard. Crossing it he arrived at the back door, set hospitably wide under its high stone arch. Pigeons wheeled in the warm sunshine of the yard and in the tall elms of the garden rooks were cawing. In the harness room a boy was whistling as he polished the harness and from the stable door came the smell of hay and horses. As he knocked humbly at the open door Isaac wondered, not for the first time, what it must be like for a man and woman to live in a great house like this and have so many servants. Not very homely, he thought. But then of course the Dean and his wife would be a comfort to each other. Not like himself and Emma. A man could choose his wife. He blushed with shame, realizing suddenly that he was comparing his lot with that of the Dean. It was a presumption. They were such poles apart that they could scarcely be said even to inhabit the same earth.

From the dim, warm interior of the house a stately presence could be seen advancing slowly down a long passage. It was Mr. William Garland, the Dean's butler. There was no more impressive man in the city. He was of middle height and well-proportioned, though slightly protuberant in the region of the waistcoat. Whether in motion or at rest his carriage and stance were equally magnificent. His impeccable garments might have been made in Savile Row. His fine head, with glossy black hair and whiskers just touched with grey, was that of an elder statesman. His benign countenance and finely modulated voice would have become an Archbishop. Reaching the door he slightly inclined his head and enquired, "Mr. Peabody?"

Isaac replied, "Yes, Mr. Garland. Peabody to wind the clocks."

"Will you be so good as to step this way, Mr. Peabody?" enquired Garland.

Turning on his heel he progressed back up the passage with the same slow dignity with which he had come down it. Reaching a green baize door he opened it. "Will you be so good as to precede me, Mr. Peabody?" he enquired. "I can then shut the door behind us. To shut noiselessly, it requires the handling of one accustomed to its ways. Thank you, Mr. Peabody."

Every Saturday Garland received Isaac at the back door at exactly the same hour, with exactly the same words and ceremony. Had he appeared to know without questioning him who Isaac was Isaac would have felt utterly put out. They were men of about the same age, men of tradition, and they liked to do things in exactly the same way year after year. It gave them a sense of security.

F

Once through the green baize door they were in the spacious hall, with its shining floor, dark oil paintings of departed Deans, and jardinières of hot-house plants. It was Isaac's undeviating rule to minister first of all to the grandfather clock in the hall, a very fine Richard Vick timepiece with a Chippendale case. From there he progressed to the drawing-room to wind the Louis Sixteenth cupid clock, and from the drawing-room to the dining-room and the First Empire marble clock. The clock in the Dean's study he kept till the last. It was an eighteenth century pedestal clock by Jeremiah Hartley of Norwich, of ebonized wood with brass mounts, the dial and back plate exquisitely engraved, very simple but very perfect in all its parts. He loved it second only to the Dean's watch.

"I have the Dean's watch here," he said to Garland, putting his bag down on the hall table and unlocking it. "I finished it last night."

"Ah," said Garland. "The Dean was enquiring for it." He always said this when Isaac brought the watch back. Isaac did not suppose it was true but he admired the ceaseless quiet vigilance with which Garland kept all who ministered to the Dean's wants, tradesmen as well as servants, up to the highest possible peak of performance in their duty. Were he to mend the Dean's watch with the speed of lightning it would still be just not quite quick enough.

"I'll take it up to him at once," said Garland.

"At once?" asked Isaac, and suddenly his heart missed a beat. For the first time in years something was not as usual. "At once?" he whispered. "Is the Dean not at matins?"

"A considerable hoarseness," said Garland, tapping his own throat with solemnity. "Consequent upon a feverish cold caught at the Diocesan Conference. Doctor Jenkins advised a few days indoors."

"In bed?" asked Isaac.

"Not today," said Garland. "I expect him downstairs shortly."

"To the study?" asked Isaac.

And now Garland also realized the seriousness of what had occurred. The Dean was seldom put out of action by his indispositions, not even by his lumbago, for he had great fortitude, and had never before been absent from Saturday matins unless he was away. The Saturday routine was disturbed. The two looked at each other, Isaac clasping and unclasping his hands, which had become clammy in the palms, and Garland reflectively stroking his jaw with his forefinger. Then inspiration came to him.

"You must attend to the study clock first, Mr. Peabody," he said, and there was in his voice that note of challenging certainty that is noticeable when strong men take desperate decisions on the spur of the moment. "Such a thing is contrary to our routine but we have to consider that should the Dean be down before you leave the house we run the risk of his finding you in the study." He opened a door behind him and waved a hand towards the room beyond. "The study, Mr. Peabody. You know where to find the clock. If you will give me the Dean's watch I will take it up."

Garland departed soft-footed up the great staircase and Isaac entered the study. It was a book-lined comfortable room with windows looking on the garden, the Dean's writing table set at right angles to one of them, but Isaac never paid much attention to the room, so anxious was he to greet his old friend the Jeremiah Hartley. Generally he lingered over his examination of it, testing the mechanism, dusting it carefully with the square of soft old silk he kept in his bag for that purpose, rubbing the ebony and brass with a bit of soft chamois leather, but today he was so terrified that he merely wound it and then hurried back into the hall to the Richard Vick with the Chippendale case. He had done no more than open the glass door which covered the clock face when Garland returned hurriedly down the stairs, soft-footed as he had gone up them.

"The Dean is coming down *now*, Mr. Peabody," he said, "and unless we are to risk the danger of your being seen in the hall I think——"

"The drawing-room?" Isaac interrupted, "or the dining-room?"

For a moment or two, so upset was their routine, they could not remember which came first. Then Garland recovered himself. "The drawing-room precedes the dining-room, I think," he said. "And there is no danger of Mrs. Ayscough coming down. She has indifferent health and does not leave her boudoir until twelve o'clock."

Safe in the drawing-room, Isaac still trembled. He heard steps come down the stairs, a harsh grating voice complaining of the lateness of the post, Garland's voice in soothing reply, and then the closing of the study door. From behind it came three stentorian sneezes and then silence. Now he could relax and turn his attention to the Louis Sixteenth clock. It was not in him to dislike any clock but he was not very fond of this one. The mechanism was satisfactory but he did not like the garland of gilded languorous cupids surrounding the dial. Their too-plump hands carried wreaths of impossible flowers, violets and snowdrops blooming at the same time as lilies and roses, and just as large. The room was beautiful but Isaac thought it too luxurious and for the first time he wondered what the woman was like who lived in this room after twelve o'clock. He had heard that she was beautiful. He had also heard that she and the Dean were childless. He was glad to escape from the pink languor of her room to the rich but impersonal glow of the dining-room mahogany, and the severity of the First Empire clock, a monumental marble edifice which inspired respect rather than affection.

But the Richard Vick in the hall inspired both. It had beautifully worked gilt spandrels of winged cherub heads, austere little creatures who had nothing in common with the cupids in the drawing-room. It struck the hours with a sonorous and deep-toned bell. The Chippendale case was plain and dignified, with three gilt balls surmounting the hood. Isaac was so absorbed in his careful winding of this treasure that he actually forgot the Dean. Then a bell clanged impatiently in the regions behind the baize door, Garland reappeared and went to the study. On the other side of the door the harsh voice rapped out a question and Isaac, his work finished, clutched his bag and groped blindly for the baize door, for he was suddenly in the worst fright he had known in all his frightened life. He had half-heard the question and it had seemed to enquire, "Is Mr. Peabody still in the house?" He was just escaping when Garland gripped him by the skirts of his voluminous old coat. "The Dean wishes to speak to you, Mr. Peabody," he said.

Isaac was hardly aware that he had moved into the room until he heard the door shut behind him. "Good morning, Mr. Peabody." The Dean's voice was always harsh and ugly but when he had a cold it had a graveyard quality that chilled the blood. Yet Isaac found that he was crawling slowly forward across the carpet towards the tall black figure standing in the central window, and though all but submerged by his own terror he did think it was a lonely figure. The Dean had his back to the light and Isaac could scarcely see his face, but as he came nearer he was acutely conscious of how very clearly the Dean must be seeing his, and not only his face but his sins. He was quite sure he saw him stealing the three pounds from his father's desk and knew about his getting drunk and not believing in God. Then suddenly personal terror was lost in professional anxiety as he saw that the Dean was holding his watch in one hand and the pair cases in the other. Had he failed in his mending of the watch? Had it stopped again? He came nearer and his heart nearly stopped, for a white circle was gleaming inside the pair cases. A watch paper! By mistake he had put one of the watch papers he kept for his humbler clients inside the Dean's watch. It must be Tom Hochicorn's watch paper. And what was on it? He couldn't remember. Several of his watch papers were comic ones. Some were even vulgar. His eyes on the carpet he swallowed several times and said, "Forgive me, sir. It was an accident. Please forgive me, sir."

The Dean had been slightly deaf from childhood, when his father had boxed his ears too hard at too early an age, and being morbidly conscious of the nuisance the deaf can be he had formed the habit of not asking people to repeat themselves. To those who did not know him well, and very few did, his ignoring of their remarks, when they could manage to summon up enough courage to make any in his presence, took nothing away from his reputation for arrogance. Terrified and unforgiven, Isaac found to his horror and shame that a tear was trickling down his cheek. He fumbled for his handkerchief, could not find it and had to wipe his face with the back of his hand, and then was startled nearly out of his wits to hear the Dean say, "Thank you, Mr. Peabody. I needed the reminder." He looked up then, he was so astonished, and found that the Dean was looming over him like a predatory vulture. The craggy, beak-nosed face was so ugly, so seamed and yellow, that he would have recoiled had he not seen the man's eyes, profoundly sad and obviously very short-sighted. "He did not see my sins," thought Isaac suddenly. "He can scarcely see me."

Putting his watch down on the writing table the Dean picked up the eyeglasses that hung round his neck on a black ribbon and perched them on the summit of his nose. With their help he read out the inscription.

> " 'I labour here with all my might,
> To tell the time by day or night;
> In thy devotion copy me,
> And serve thy God as I serve thee.'

Yes, Mr. Peabody, I needed the reminder. Please God, I will give Him better service in the years that remain to me. I will learn of my watch."

Afterwards Isaac could not understand how he could have had the temerity to say what he did. He said, "It's a beautiful watch, sir, and you should take better care of it. You overwind it, sir." And then, intuitively realizing from the bewilderment in the Dean's face that he was deaf as well as short-sighted, he raised his voice and loudly repeated himself.

"You are quite right," said the Dean. "I will try to do better. Thank you, Mr. Peabody. Can you spare me a few moments? Will you sit down?"

Mr. Peabody sat down in the chair indicated, facing the Dean across his writing table. He placed his leather bag on the floor and laid his hands upon his knees. Though he was no longer afraid they still trembled a little. He had an unfortunate habit of turning his feet in when he sat down. They were turned in now, toe to toe. His bright child-like blue eyes were fixed expectantly but nervously upon the Dean's face. The Dean altered the position of the silver inkstand upon his table, and then of his gold pencil and the miniature of his adored wife, and then put them all back where they had been before and wondered what he could say. All his life he had loved children and poor people, and such child-like trusting little oddities as the extraordinary little man sitting opposite to him, all those whom Christ had called "the little ones". But he never knew what to say to them and his unfortunate appearance always frightened them . . . at least nearly always, for once there had been a small chimney sweep who had seemed not to be afraid. . . . He had become a priest that he might serve the poor but lacking what is called "the common touch", and being quite unable to preach a sermon that could be understood by intellects less brilliant than his own, he had been such a failure in his various parishes that he had been obliged to turn to school-mastering. That he had been a famous schoolmaster, and a great one in all eyes but his own, had not comforted him at all.

Peering across his desk at Isaac there came back to his mind an incident of his schoolmastering days which seemed to him to epitomize the greatness of his failure. Walking one day down the main aisle of the school library, his great head thrust forward, hands behind his back, he was suddenly aware that the place was not, as he had thought, empty. Crouching in a corner, trying not to be seen, was a terrified new boy with dirty smudges of tears upon his face. Instantly his headmaster had known how it was with him for he himself, handicapped by his deafness and ugliness, had been hideously tormented in his first year at his public school. His heart gave a lurch of pity and he bore down upon the boy with intent to comfort him. But the boy, his eyes bright and wild with terror, swerved aside and fled.

Trying to think of something to say to Mr. Peabody the Dean suddenly remembered that incident, and that his nickname among schoolboys and undergraduates had been "the Great Beast", after the alarming creature in the book of Revelations. The little man with his trembling hands reminded him of that small boy. He said to himself that it would be the same again. He could never reach the simple humble folk whom he loved the best. He could fight for the children, he could carry the sins of men, he could command their obedience and respect, but not their love. Something wrong with him. A man can change very much in his own fortune through his own efforts but the kind of man that he is he cannot change. He will hang about his own neck, like a dead fowl tied round the neck of a dog, until the end. The Dean's thoughts were always inclined towards anxiety and gloom, and never more so than when he had a cold. He sneezed violently and trumpeted into his handkerchief. Reappearing from its folds he said anxiously, and without premeditation, "Mr. Peabody, I should not have asked you to stay. I fear you will catch this cold."

Oddly enough this approach seemed the right one, for Isaac brightened up immediately. "I have just had it, sir," he said with all the complacency of a man who sees another enduring a misfortune from which for the moment he is immune. "It's about in the city. A terrible cold." For a few minutes they told each other about the great colds of their lives, and then anxiety again rearing its head the Dean asked, "Am I encroaching upon your time? At leisure myself this morning I am forgetting that other men are not."

"I am at leisure, sir," said Isaac. "It is my clock-winding day. I don't open the shop on Saturdays."

"You enjoy your work, Mr. Peabody?"

"Enjoy it, sir?" Isaac was so astonished that the question could even be asked that he could not for the moment answer it. Then he said, "Clocks and watches, sir, they're alive. They live longer than we do if they're treated right. There's nothing in this world so beautiful as a well-made timepiece. And every one different, sir. Never even a watchcock the same."

"What is a watchcock, Mr. Peabody?" asked the Dean.

This time astonishment deprived Isaac of the power of speech. That a man could carry the most beautiful watch in the world about with him in his pocket for half a lifetime and never open the inner case to look at its works was to him incredible. He supposed a rich man like the Dean, who owned so many lovely things, took them so much for granted that they meant little to him. A man of a certain type might even long to be free of them all. Isaac had great intuition. He had realized earlier the Dean's loneliness. Now he realized his weariness. Finding his voice at last he said, "Your own watch, sir, has a watchcock of unusual and beautiful design. If you will let me have it I will show you."

The Dean handed him his watch, saying with that painful contortion of the facial muscles which so few people realized was his personal version of a smile, "Be careful of my watch paper, Mr. Peabody. I treasure that watch paper."

Isaac carefully removed the pair cases and the paper and opened the watch. "There, sir," he said with triumph. "Though the mechanism of a watch is not seen it is a point of honour with watchmakers to make it as beautiful as possible. You'll never see two watchcocks the same, and you'll never see one as unusual as this one of yours." Then seeing with what difficulty the Dean was peering through his eyeglasses Isaac produced his jeweller's eyepiece. "Put this in your eye, sir. You'll see better that way. Now did you ever see anything so beautifully wrought as that little figure? The odd thing is, sir, that I've never seen a human figure on a watchcock. Faces, often, but not a figure."

The Dean was silent, gazing intently at the man bent nearly double by the burden on his back. "Who is he?" he asked.

"I don't know, sir," said Isaac. "That's what I hoped you'd be able to tell me."

"At a guess I should say it was Christian," said the Dean. "You know your *Pilgrim's Progress* I expect, Mr. Peabody. You remember how Christian carried his burden up the 'place somewhat ascending' where there was a cross, and at the foot of the cross it fell off him and rolled away. Or it might be the Son of God Himself, carrying away the sin of the world." Isaac shifted uncomfortably in his seat, embarrassed as he always was when the sore subject of religion came into the conversation. Though he had not lifted his head the Dean knew all about his embarrassment. "Did you notice the Ayscough family motto, Mr. Peabody?" he went on. "It is on the back of the watch."

The suggestion that there could be anything at all about any watch that came into his hands that he did not notice so amazed Isaac that his embarrassment vanished, as the Dean intended it should. "Yes, sir," he said, "it is beautifully engraved. But my Latin is rusty, sir. I left school too early. I am not certain of its meaning."

"It is from the twenty-eighth verse of the sixty-eighth psalm," said the Dean. " 'Thy God hath sent forth strength for thee.' Sometimes I think how odd it is, Mr. Peabody, that I should be spending my old age as Dean of this city whose history is so bound up with that particular psalm. You will remember Prior Hugh's monks singing it as they passed away from the city into the storm. And then Dean Peter Rollard— 'This is God's hill, in the which it pleaseth him to dwell.' Do you attach importance to coincidence, Mr. Peabody?"

"No, sir," said Isaac.

"Then you will laugh at me when I tell you that I believe I

do. Take this bad cold of mine—is it a fortuitious accident that it kept me from going to matins this morning? Well, Mr. Peabody, whether it is or not I shall thank God tonight for the pleasure of your acquaintance."

Isaac was not more astonished by this speech than the Dean himself. Never could he remember talking to anyone with the ease with which he was now talking to Mr. Peabody. And the little man was speaking up well and clearly and losing his nervousness. It would not last, of course. Sooner or later he would blunder in some way, and see his friend afraid of him. For a moment his own mind beat about in fear, and then he remembered that Mr. Peabody was master of a craft about which he knew nothing. There were not many subjects about which he was ignorant but by the mercy of God horology was one of them. If he could sit at Mr. Peabody's feet as his pupil, he the poor man in his total ignorance, the little man would not be afraid of him for knowledge does not fear ignorance.

"I think the maker's name is engraved inside the watch, Mr. Peabody," he said, peering through the eyepiece. "But I cannot read it. Can you enlighten me?"

"Yes, sir," said Isaac eagerly. " 'George Graham fecit, 1712'."

"A well-known horologist?"

"One of the greatest. Thomas Tompion's nephew, sir." The great name of Tompion seemed to leave the Dean where it found him and Isaac was both grieved and shocked at the depths of his ignorance. Like all good teachers he was scarcely able to bear ignorance on his own subject and he said in a breathless rush, "I could tell you about them, sir, one day, if you had the leisure—if I would not be presuming."

"I will hold you to that, Mr. Peabody," said the Dean promptly. "I shall be delighted to be your pupil. Seventeen hundred and twelve. This watch was, I believe, a gift to my great-grandfather when he came of age. It has come down from father to son and has seen much history for all my ancestors were fighting men. Our crest, as you see, is a sword. I broke with family tradition when I went into the Church and my father never forgave me." The Dean, his watch in his hand, had almost forgotten Isaac as his mind wandered back over the past, but now he looked up anxiously. "I must be boring you, Mr. Peabody. Old men are at their most tedious when garrulous."

"No, no, sir!" said Isaac, and his eyes were so bright with interest that the Dean smiled and said, "Well, Mr. Peabody, you have taught me to put a greater value on my watch. You must feel surprise that I have had so little curiosity about it, but the fact is that when my father thrashed me it was always for five minutes by this watch. Five minutes can seem a long while to a small boy." The Dean's sallow face suddenly flushed, for in excusing himself to Mr. Peabody he had been betrayed into disloyalty to his father. Self-excuse was contemptible and always led to something worse. "Do not misunderstand me, my father was a man whose son I am proud to be. Discipline is necessary for the young. As a schoolmaster I have myself thrashed hundreds of boys." He smiled at Isaac. "Mr. Peabody, if I take greater care of my watch in future I am afraid that you will miss it. We must arrange something. Shall we—"

But Isaac was not told what they were to arrange for Garland entered, throwing the door wide. "Archdeacon Fromantel," he announced, and the Archdeacon entered, impeccably gaitered, a man of fine presence. At sight of Isaac his eyebrows shot far up his expressive forehead. The Dean sneezed with great sadness, but he rose from his seat with dignity and courtesy.

"You know Mr. Peabody, Archdeacon?" he asked.

But Isaac had sidled behind Garland like a terrified crab seeking cover behind a rock and when the Dean looked for him he was gone.

With Michael striking half-past eleven Garland and Isaac paused for just a moment's whispered chat, but the disintegration of the Deanery routine caused them to do it on the wrong

side of the green baize door and their sin found them out. A
drift of perfume reached them from the direction of the stairs,
and a soft frou-frou of silk petticoats. "Mrs. Ayscough!" gasped
Garland. "Half-an-hour early!" Caught in the guilty act of
this unlawful communication he and Isaac were for a moment
rooted to the spot, their eyes unable to leave the beautiful
woman descending the stairs. Elaine Ayscough seemed to
Isaac to be a figure of legend. In appearance she might have
been Dante's Beatrice, or the Elaine of her own name. Sunshine striking through a window gleamed on her pale gold hair,
smoothly parted and drawn back into a chignon. Her white
neck rose swan-like from the plain collar of a soft grey dress.
She wore no jewels apart from her wedding ring and the little
gold shells in her ears. Her face seemed designed for the pale
gold setting of a cameo ring for even in the glory of the sun it
lacked the warmth of living flesh. Isaac was unable to understand how a woman so simply dressed, even more simply
dressed than Emma, could give such an impression of fashion
and elegance. It was true that Mrs. Ayscough was a tall
woman, but then so was Emma. If he had known how
much the simple grey dress had cost he would have understood
better.

At the foot of the stairs Mrs. Ayscough paused. She had
apparently not seen Isaac, but she seemed to see Garland and
her delicate eyebrows arched very slightly in a manner
reminiscent of Archdeacon Fromantel, except that his eyebrows had shot up in unpremeditated astonishment and the
movement of hers was intentional. "The gentleman who winds
the clocks, madam," said Garland.

"Oh?" said Mrs. Ayscough, and for a moment her grey eyes
met Isaac's as she moved across the hall towards the drawing-
room. Garland reached a fumbling hand behind his back and
pulled the baize door open and Isaac scurried down the
passage behind it and fled.

Sitting on the seat in the lime avenue again he could not
forget Mrs. Ayscough's pale cold eyes and compassion for the

man he had just left welled up in him, and after that amazement at his own compassion. He had never thought of the Olympian figures of the Close as in need of compassion and nor, he supposed, had anybody else in the city. All of them, and especially the terrible Dean, had seemed to live in a world where compassion was not necessary. He saw now that it was the very first necessity, always and everywhere, and should flow between all men, always and everywhere. Men lived with their nearest and dearest and knew little of them, and strangers passing by in the street were as impersonal as trees walking, and all the while there was this deep affinity, for all men suffered.

CHAPTER 6 *Fountains*

I

TWELVE o'clock boomed out and Isaac shot up out of his seat. Twelve o'clock! For twelve years he had progressed from the Deanery to Canon Wiseman's to wind the Dresden clock, from there to Canon Willoughby's, to the Rimbault chiming clock, and then to Miss Montague at Fountains. The Palace and Worship Street were reserved for the afternoon. For all these appointments he had never been a moment late, arriving on Miss Montague's doorstep punctually at a quarter-to-twelve to minister to the Michael Neuwers and the Lyre clock. Whatever would Miss Montague and Sarah think? They would fear some disaster had happened to him. Isaac was a comic figure as he literally ran down the elm avenue to the Porta. He stood panting on Miss Montague's doorstep at five-past-twelve. The Dresden and the Rimbault must wait, for Canon Wiseman and Canon Willoughby would not be so disturbed by his non-appearance as Miss Montague and Sarah.

Fountains, after the death of Blanche the widow of Duke Jocelyn, had become a part of the Priory. After the monks had been driven away it had been left empty but later had been restored and made into a private house again by Thomas Montague when he became mayor. It had remained in the

possession of the Montagues ever since. Fountains actually
formed part of the Porta. Miss Montague's drawing-room was
over the arch and her front door was within it. A small brass
plate above the letter box had "Fountains" inscribed on it in
letters that were nearly worn away. Beside the door was an
ancient iron bellpull but it had to be pulled out a good four
inches before anything happened, and as it was very stiff only
the strongest could get it out far enough. The elderly, by Miss
Montague's special instructions, lifted up the brass flap over
the letter box and dropped it, and went on lifting and dropping
until Sarah came. This morning Isaac lifted and dropped once
only before she opened the door, her face puckered with
anxiety beneath her snowy mob cap. She pulled him in, shut
the door and gave him a good shaking. Although she was
round about eighty years of age, and scarcely bigger than a
marmoset, her shake had surprising strength. "Do you know
the time, Isaac Peabody?" she demanded. "There's twelve
gone by Michael five minutes past, and you due in this house
at a quarter-to-twelve and not a minute later. You've had us
all of a tremble. . . . He's here, ma'am," she called up the
stairs to an unseen presence, "and none the worse, drat him!"

With swift monkey-like movements she clawed Isaac's hat
from his head and his coat from his back. He laughed. Miss
Montague and Sarah were perhaps the best friends he had in
the city and at Fountains he was at his happiest. Though he
came here every week he looked round him in delight, sniffing
the fragrant smell of Fountains, stretching his spirit in its particular atmosphere of antiquity and peace. It was so old that
to come inside it was like coming into some abode of ancient
knights hollowed out of the sheer rock. The lancet windows
looking on Worship Street were set in such thick walls that
they did not let much light into the stone-floored hall, but
there was nearly always a log fire burning there and it gleamed
on the tapestries on the walls and upon the old oak chest that
Sarah polished till it shone like glass. Miss Montague was
fond of pot-pourri and there were several bowls of it in the hall,

scenting the warm air that was already pungent with the smell
of the burning logs. Fountains had at all seasons of the year an
autumnal warmth and graciousness, and no chill of winter in
spite of the great age of the house, its mistress, of Sarah, of
Araminta the housemaid and Jemima the cook.

"There now," said Sarah, taking a clothes brush from the
chest and belabouring Isaac about the shoulders. "Don't that
Polly of yours ever brush your coat? Don't ee waste time telling
me now what you've been up to. You go on up to the mistress
and she'll tell me later."

Two staircases led up from the hall, one being a circular
stone staircase leading up to a room in the tower. Of the two
small towers that flanked the Porta, Fountains contained one
and the almshouses the other. The second staircase of dark
oak had been put in by Sir Thomas Montague in the sixteenth
century and led to the bedrooms and drawing-room. Up this
Isaac climbed, turning left at the top where firelight gleamed
behind a half-open door.

"Come in, Mr. Peabody," called Miss Montague. She had a
clear voice, with only an occasional huskiness in it, and no one
hearing it would have guessed that she was older than Sarah.

Mr. Peabody entered the room and standing at the door
made a beautiful bow. His bow was memorable, being of the
same period as his antique garments. Miss Montague acknowledged his bow with an inclination of the head that oddly
combined, as did her whole presence, the dignity of a great
lady with a saint's humility and a gamin's impish humour.
She sat erect in her chair beside the fire, her thin fine old hands
caressing the cat in her lap, her small feet in black velvet shoes
resting upon a footstool. She had left off paying any attention
to fashion forty years ago and dressed as she pleased, in a plain
old black gown, a fichu draped over her shoulders and a square
of lace flung over her plentiful white hair. Whether she had had
any beauty in her youth it was impossible to say. She was now
a dumpy old lady with a soft face of indeterminate feature, and
faded blue eyes that were both shrewd and tender. Those upon

G

whom her eyes rested immediately thought the world of themselves, for it was obvious that she saw with one glance all the
good in them to which their own families seemed so strangely
blind. She did not as a rule talk very much herself but then
she did not often get the opportunity, so eager was everyone
else to talk to her. No one ever seemed to know very much
about her. She was just old Miss Montague of Fountains, and
she had always been there, as changeless as her room.

It looked west over Worship Street and east into the elms
and lime trees of the Close, with in winter a view of the west
front of the Cathedral through their bare branches. The east
window was always open in warm weather and birdsong filled
the room, the smell of the lime blossom in its season and at all
times the music of the bells. At morning and evening there was
sunshine, and nearly always the fire on the hearth. There were
beautiful things in the room, for Miss Montague had inherited
the treasures of the past, but they were all a little dimmed with
age and they did not intrude themselves. They had kept their
stations in this room for so long that they looked rather as
though they were painted upon its warm restful shadows.

"You are well, Mr. Peabody?" asked Miss Montague. "And
your sister? And Polly?"

"Very well indeed, ma'am. And Emma too, and Polly."

A slight shadow of anxiety passed from Miss Montague's
face. She did not ask him why he was so late because she was
not an inquisitive woman. If she could be told that all was well
with her friends she did not need to be told anything further.
"Michael Neuwers is five minutes slow by Michael the Archangel, Mr. Peabody," she said.

"Five minutes slow?" ejaculated Mr. Peabody, and was
beside the Michael Neuwers in a moment. It stood in the
centre of the mantelpiece, in the post of greatest honour, and
with the exception of Michael the Archangel was the oldest
and most valuable clock in the city. It had been made in the
late sixteenth century by the same clockmaker who had made
Gilbert Earl of Shrewsbury's gilt clock, made to the Earl's

instructions. "A small fine hand like an arrow, clenly and strongly made, the dial plate to be made of French crown gold, and the figures to show the hour and the rest to be enamelled the fynelyest and daintyest that can be, but no other colour than blew, white and carnalian." Miss Montague and Isaac were quite sure that the Montague Michael Neuwers was quite as beautiful as the Earl of Shrewsbury's. The case of silver gilt was surmounted by a little gilt lion and on the dial plate the Montague lilies and roses, white and crimson, were wreathed about the hour ring. After three centuries the lovely thing still kept good time but Isaac was always a little anxious, just as he was always a little anxious about Miss Montague herself. Though it seemed that the changes and chances of this mortal life did not touch either of them yet life remained mortal and they were old.

He adjusted and wound the Michael Neuwers with infinite care and tenderness and turned to the Lyre clock. He had no anxiety about it for it was an Isaac Peabody. It was the first clock he had made after he opened his shop and Miss Montague, driving up Cockspur Street in her little pony carriage, had seen it in the window, had stopped and come in. It had been their first meeting, though of course he had known her by sight and by repute, for in those days she was often to be seen in the city. He had been proud to see her in his shop and had bowed very low behind the counter. He could see her now standing in the dusty sunshine, a little middle-aged woman in a black bonnet and shawl, her figure inclining in those days to plumpness but otherwise not so very different to what she was now, for her hair had whitened early. She had dropped him a little curtsey, though she was a great lady in the city and he was only the clockmaker, and smiled at him, and he had loved her from that moment. Then she had asked him if she might buy the Lyre clock. He saw that her hands in their black silk mittens were trembling a little and that she looked a little scared, and he wondered why. Then she told him. "I have never bought myself a present before."

"You like birds, ma'am?" he had asked, for the clock was wreathed in birds.

"Yes. You see, I live among them. The trees of the Close come right up to my windows. In spring I find young birds on my drawing-room floor. They have hopped in through the window. They never seem afraid of me."

"Ma'am, you must have the clock," he had said firmly.

"Won't you be unhappy to part with it?"

"I made it for you," he had said, and was quite sure that unknowingly he had.

So she had taken her worn purse from the capacious pocket of her black gown and counted out a few gold sovereigns, and though it was a small price for such an exquisite clock he could see in her eyes that she was uneasy at spending so much on herself. Lest she change her mind he had wrapped it up and carried it out to her pony carriage, and put the reins in her hands and clucked up the old fat white pony rather hurriedly. But she had understood the reason for the hurry and when she drove off she had been laughing.

And now the Lyre clock stood on her escritoire close to the window that looked out into the trees of the Close, and the shadows of flickering leaves on moving boughs caressed it. The Lyre was one of the loveliest of his clocks. The upper part of the pendulum was formed to represent the strings of the instrument, the lyre itself was plain and simple, its only adornment a few curved leaves at the base, and at the summit a crested lark with spread wings. But the clock face in the centre had a wreath of tiny enamelled birds about the hour ring. The clock had a happy tick, very quick and gay, and chattered to the Michael Neuwers that answered with its slow soft beat. No one could feel lonely, Miss Montague said sometimes, with these two clocks for company.

"Perfectly in time with Michael," said Isaac, putting the Lyre clock back on the escritoire. "A good clock."

"Made by a good craftsman," said Miss Montague.

"They have their own life," said Isaac. "Clocks are like

children. You can start them off right but you can't do more."

"Here's your glass of wine, Mr. Peabody," said Miss Montague, as Sarah came in with a glass of sherry wine and a thin sweet biscuit on a silver tray. "Sit down and tell me your news."

Isaac always had a glass of wine at Fountains, and he thoroughly enjoyed it, sipping it slowly and making it last as long as possible while he talked to Miss Montague of his affairs. He was not as a rule much of a talker but at Fountains he chattered as fast as the Lyre clock. There was only one thing he did not speak of with Miss Montague, his unhappiness with Emma, for that would have seemed to him disloyalty to his sister. Yet always when he left her he felt as though he had spoken of it, for the bitterness in his feelings seemed subtly withdrawn. He never asked himself why this was. Everyone took Miss Montague for granted. But today he had nothing to say about his home affairs because he had to tell Miss Montague about the Dean, watching her all the time that he might see surprise, amusement, delight, affection, lighting her face one after another as he poured it out. Talking to Miss Montague was rather like playing on some musical instrument superbly well. The response one wanted was always forthcoming. Isaac played the last chord and sat back very well pleased with himself.

"Now that is wonderful," said Miss Montague, able to speak at last. "Horology will be an ideal hobby for the Dean. Up till now I do not think he has had a hobby. He has his religion, of course, but religion is not a good hobby for religious people."

Isaac was surprised at this for he knew Miss Montague to be a religious woman and in past years he had been a little scared lest she should try and convert him. He was not scared now for he had discovered that she never spoke of her opinions unless specifically asked to do so. And so, free from fear, he found her the one person in the world with whom he could mention the sore subject of religion, just casually in passing. He asked with twinkling eyes, "Why not, Miss Montague?

I thought you considered religion to be the pre-eminent need of man."

"So I do," said Miss Montague. "Like food. But a man can't be always eating, Mr. Peabody. He must do something else between meals or he'll get indigestion and grow sad and moody."

Isaac laughed, and then said sadly, "But I shall not see the Dean again. Great men speak kindly to lesser men and then forget what they have said."

"He will not forget," said Miss Montague. "But you may have to wait some time before he can summon up enough courage to claim your friendship. It is always thought, Mr. Peabody, that men put on self-confidence with gaiters and crowns. They don't, you know. A shy man is a shy man whatever he puts on. How glad I am that the Dean is to take better care of the beautiful watch."

A clear bell-note seemed to come soaring down to them from the height of heaven and after it a silence so profound that Miss Montague and Isaac did not even hear the ticking of the clocks. Michael was like that. He had only to speak once and one did not hear another voice. The charmed moment passed and Isaac was on his feet at once, for Miss Montague had luncheon at one o'clock. It was the moment of English history when mealtimes were in a state of flux. Many people still preferred their main meal of the day at five-thirty but those who followed the fashion were now firmly attached to luncheon, afternoon tea and late dinner. Miss Montague was indifferent to fashion but Sarah insisted that she conform to the social habits of the Close. Regretfully, for she preferred him to her luncheon any day, she held out her hand to Isaac. He bowed over it and went away.

2

While Isaac was still with the Dean Polly was walking down Angel Lane on her way to the market. She still wore the out-door clothes the orphanage had given her, a grey gown and

cloak and a plain black bonnet, but with her very first earnings
she had bought some cherry coloured ribbon to replace the
black velvet strings, enough to make two rosettes and a large
defiant bow that tied beneath her chin, and the glory of that
ribbon gave her self-confidence among the other girls at the
market. She sang softly to herself as she walked along with a
big market basket on her arm, and colour came into her cheeks
with the exercise, the singing and the joy. Several tired women
peeped from behind their draped window curtains to see her
pass, envious of her lightness and gaiety. And she an orphanage
brat! They did not of course know about Job. Nor did they
know what she was singing, though they supposed that gay
words must go with such a merry tune. The words were these.
"A box of pins and a reel of black cotton. One yard of black
sarsenet. One eel, fresh. Oranges and cloves, pepper and pigs'
trotters. Grey darning wool and a scrubbing brush. A pound
of onions and an ounce of liquorice allsorts. Fishheads for Sooty.
Fishheads. Fishheads. For Thine is the kingdom, the power,
and the glory. Amen."

She took the same way to the market that Isaac followed
when he went to his shop, running lightly down the flight of
steps that he had climbed so laboriously last night. She passed
Joshua Appleby's bookshop with an awed glance for all the
books inside, and she wondered what it must be like to be able
to read. She thought it must be wonderful and it surprised her
that the gentry who were able to read could be bored. Yet they
were. What was the matter with them? She was sorry for the
gentry for there always seemed to be something the matter
with them. She passed St. Peter's church with a friendly glance,
for Emma took her there on Sundays. Just beyond the old
porch she turned on the pavement and there before her, with
the grave classical town hall for a backcloth, was all the
splendour of the city's market. She stepped off the pavement
on to the cobbles with the ecstasy of a duck taking to water or
a saint entering heaven, and in a moment was lost sight of in
the ebb and flow of noise and colour all about her. What did

she want with books, she thought suddenly. No book could open the door to anything more strange and rich than this.

If not quite so marvellous as she thought it the market was a famous one in the fen country and served a wide area. The yard of the Swan and Duck was full of the gigs and carts and carriages that had brought the farmers and gentry of the villages to the market, and the inn stable was full of nags and ponies. Since dawn the drovers had been bringing in the cattle, the pigs squealing in netted carts, the poor sweating cows driven along the fen roads and up the cobbled streets of the city amid a cacophony of shouting men and barking dogs. The only thing that Polly did not like about the market was the fear of the animals and she never went near the town hall end of the square where they were imprisoned in their pens. But the rest of the market was sheer bliss. The stalls ran in long lines across the breadth of the market place, with lanes between them packed with eager women and children in their gayest clothes, laughing and chattering. The men were mostly at the far end, intent upon the beasts, but sometimes a young farmer would elbow his way through the crowd intent upon a fairing for his sweetheart or toys for his children. The choice was wide for almost everything was sold in the market. Many of the goods on the stalls were for sale in the shops any day of the week but they were cheaper in the market and somehow much more exciting spread out like this in the sunshine. There were vegetables and fruit, flowers and fresh farm eggs and butter, ribbons and laces and rolls of coloured cloth, toys and sweets, bonnets and shawls, pots and pans and gay china cups and saucers, needles and pins and coloured glass beads, chestnuts and gingerbread, pots of honey, willow baskets and clothes pegs, eels and fish caught in the river, picture postcards, corn cures and mousetraps. Four square about the noise and gaiety and colour stood the old grave tall houses, and far above it all the Cathedral towered into the sky and Michael tolled the passing quarter hours, echoed by St. Peter's, St. Nicholas's at the North Gate and St. Matthew's at the South Gate. The busy shoppers were hardly aware of the bells and yet they were a part of market day, their music woven into the laughter and chatter like a thread of gold into homespun cloth.

Polly made her purchases with deliberation because Emma, a careful shopper herself, expected her to take her time, and all the while that she was comparing one stall with another, asking the price of this and that, and singing her gay little song of the needs to herself to refresh her memory, she never once looked at the fish stall. But at last everything except the eel and fish-heads was in her basket and she made her way towards the old mounting block close to the Swan and Duck. On the mounting block, week by week, sat old Keziah Lee with her basket full of bunches of wild flowers from the fen, marigolds and water forgetmenots and yellow irises in their season, with in autumn crab apples for jelly and in winter posies of everlasting flowers dyed in bright colours, and beside her Albert had his fish stall. Keziah was like an old witch to look at, tiny and shrivelled in her black bonnet and ragged shawl, and Albert looked like an operatic tenor gone to seed. Since Job had been with them their business had improved. Their fish was cleanly gutted, their eels fresh caught in the river and displayed both in the shop and on the market stall with a curious beauty, laid in shallow woven rush baskets among fragrant leaves of water mint. How such a disreputable couple could encompass the artistry of the little posies, and the general air of freshness that pervaded their shop and stall, was one of the unsolved mysteries of the city. Job, barely visible as a shadow moving noiselessly at the back of the shop or stall, was vaguely thought to be weak in the head, for Keziah and Albert were perpetually shrieking imprecations at him, as though maddened by his incapacity. Their curses seemed to envelop him in a murky shroud of nonentity and no one except Polly ever really saw him.

She would never forget the first time she had seen him. She had come to Dobson's from the workhouse, after the terrible row about it which had shaken the city to its foundations and resulted in the dismissal of the workhouse master and most of his staff, and the clearing out of a few surplus children to Dobson's. The row, she understood, had been caused by the terrible Dean whom everyone hated, but she did not hate him because it was he who had commanded that every year three girls and three boys, the six most promising children in the workhouse, were to be passed on to Dobson's at his expense. She was proud to be one of the first six chosen, and thankful to leave the workhouse. She never thought about it after she had left it, for she had a wonderful capacity for letting evil things slough off her, but she did not forget the Dean. She had never seen him when he was at the workhouse but she had heard him once from the other side of a closed door. She had trembled, as one did at a peal of thunder, but she had exulted too.

Both she and Job had been at Dobson's for some while before they saw each other, and they might never have done so had they not had their places in church rearranged, so that they sat just across the aisle from each other. To turn the head only very slightly towards the opposite sex was punishable if noticed by authority, but Polly and Job were both so diminutive that the larger children in front of them and behind them screened them from view, and their eyes met often. Polly was a year older than Job, and already motherly, and when she saw him first her heart seemed to stop, and not only with compassion. She did not analyse the thing that was not compassion but was aware of it as a relief, as though there was a purpose somewhere. She looked at Job and Job looked at her, that first time with shy interest, but the second time with delighted recognition. The third time his eyes were alive and bright and the fourth time they clung to her face with an entreaty that tore her to pieces and afterwards, at night, made her sob into her pillow because she was leaving Dobson's to be maid-of-all-work to Emma in Angel Lane and would not see him again.

But a long while afterwards she did see him again. Emma sent her one day to buy fishheads for Sooty at the shop beside the North Gate, and he was there in the shadows gutting fish.

He looked much the same except that he was taller and his hair had grown into an untidy black mop. She went close to him and not knowing his name she said gently, "Dear." He looked up and his black eyes suddenly blazed with light. Then Albert loomed up. One of his great fists landed in Job's left eye and the other in the small of Polly's back, sending her lurching back into the front of the shop. She paid for Sooty's fishheads and then for Job's sake fled without looking at him again.

That had been a year ago and now they met weekly at the market, exchanging a whispered word or two when they could. They met at other times too, for after the shop was shut Job sometimes climbed up the hill to Angel Lane and scratched like a mouse at the back door. It opened most conveniently into the scullery, where they could be together for a few minutes and yet if Emma came into the kitchen Job could be gone in a flash. On the rare occasions when Emma was out he would creep into the kitchen and sit warming his half-starved body by the fire. The strong aroma which haunted the kitchen, after his fish-impregnated wet clothes had been steaming in front of it for a short while, could always be ascribed later to Sooty's fishheads which had gone off.

For where Job was concerned Polly was without conscience. Followers were forbidden by Emma but when interrogated Polly would look her mistress straight in the eye and say, "No man or boy ever sets foot in my kitchen, ma'am, excepting only the sweep in the way of business," without a blink of an eyelash. She was prepared not only to lie for Job but to steal for him, and she did sometimes steal a little of Emma's flour to make the pasties he adored; but the meat and potato inside them were what she had saved from her own plate when Emma dealt her out her portion in the parlour. Out of her meagre earnings she bought cough lozenges for Job, and salves for his cuts and bruises, and he on his side did what he could to serve her. He brought her blackberries and nuts and made nosegays for her, and from bits of wood he carved robins and wrens and mice for her amusement; she had a box in the attic full of these treasures. And treasures they were, though neither of them realized that the skill of his fingers amounted to genius.

Polly chose her eel and her fishheads without a glance at Job and then took them to him behind the stall to wrap up for her. He slipped into her basket, on top of the fishheads, a posy of sprays of scarlet blackberry leaves and soft grasses from the fen, and her hand went into his pocket holding a pasty whose filling was her last night's portion of shepherd's pie. Their eyes met and their hands touched for a moment, and the sun was warm upon them and the bright air trembled with the ringing of the bells. Polly when she went away took the brightness, the music and the warmth with her, but darkness fell on Job.

CHAPTER 7   *Miss Montague*

I

A FEW days later Sarah cleared away the tea and lighted the
lamp that stood beside Miss Montague's chair. She would
have drawn the curtains but Miss Montague stopped her.
"There's sunset still in the sky," she said. "Is it not beautiful?"

"I don't let such things worry me," said Sarah. "Ring the
bell when you've had enough of it."

After she had gone Miss Montague sat apparently idle, her
hands caressing the cat in her lap. Beyond the west window, behind the steep old roofs of Worship Street, the last of a fiery sunset was burning itself out. Through the east window she could
see through the branches of the elm trees the west front and the
three great towers glowing with reflected light, so that it seemed
as though the whole Cathedral was built of rosy stone. Evensong was over and everyone was having tea. There was no
sound but the ticking of her clocks and the cawing of the rooks
in the elms. Motionless in her chair Miss Montague left her
room and went up and down the streets of the city, seeing the
remembered pattern of its roofs against the sky, the leap of the
Cathedral towers seen now from one street and now from
another, knowing as she turned each corner exactly what she
would see, for she had the city by heart. She went out of the

South Gate and down into the fen, and saw the great flaming sky reflected in the water. She told over the names of the villages on their hills as though they were a string of jewels, and came back into the city again and found that the lamplighter was going his rounds and the muffin man was ringing his bell. Lamps and candles were being lit in the houses now and she looked in through the windows and saw the children having their tea, but nobody noticed her. If anyone at this moment was thinking of her it was as a very old woman who never left her house except to go to the Cathedral in her bath-chair when she was well enough, and perhaps they pitied her. They did not know how vivid are the memories of the old and that only the young are house bound when they can't go out. Her memories ranged back over more than eighty years and covered a long span of the life of the city, and the birth and life and death of many men and women all of whom had been and were her friends. She did not forget a single one of them and now that she was so old she did not distinguish very clearly between those who were what the world calls dead and those who still lived here. No one had ever been so blessed with friends as herself. It astonished her. But then her whole life astonished her and caused her considerable amusement as she looked back upon it.

2

She had been born in this house. Her grandfather had been a famous judge and in his day Fountains had been only the holiday home of the Montague family, but her father, lacking the ambition possessed by nearly all the Montagues and gaining a rich wife, had retired early from the army and had lived for most of his married life at Fountains. His daughter Mary had come fourth in his family of six children, all of them attractive except herself. She had been from the beginning a plain little thing, and when a brother in a fit of temper pushed her down the tower stairs and she broke her leg the accident did not improve her looks. The leg, unskilfully set, mended badly and afterwards was shorter than the other. She had hurt her back also in the fall, and it caused her much suffering, but of this she never spoke after she had been told it was only growing pains. In a family of six aches and pains were not much noticed, least of all in the least noticeable of the children. And so she grew up stunted in her growth and slightly lame. She was shy and never had much to say for herself, and no one could have guessed, seeing the little girl sitting like a mouse in the corner with her kitten, that the ambition and the adventurous spirit that had made the later generations of Montagues such a power in the land was more alive in her than in any of the other children.

Through her early years she lived withdrawn from the others and their rowdy games, in which she could not join, happy in a fantasy world of her own. As soon as she could escape from lessons and the sewing of her sampler she would climb the tower stairs to the little room at the top, called Blanche's bower because it was said that it had been beloved of the duchess Blanche, and here she would sit in the window seat, wrapped in a shawl, with the cat in her arms, looking out over the roofs of the city to the fens and the sea, and dream of the great things she would do. She would be an explorer and discover unknown lands, and be adored by the natives there. She would be another Elizabeth Fry and her life would be written and she would be the friend of kings and queens and everyone would love her. She would marry an ambassador and live in fabulous Russia and have twelve beautiful children who would worship the ground she trod on. She would be a great actress like Sarah Siddons and every man who saw her would fall in love with her. There was no end to the entrancing careers that she mapped out for herself, and in all of them her starved longing for love was satisfied up to the hilt.

Her awakening in adolescence was sudden and terrible. Her eldest sister Laura was to be married. It was the first wedding in the family and was to take place in the Cathedral and be a great social occasion. It never occurred to Mary that she would not be Laura's bridesmaid with the other sisters. She was only

a little lame and she could stand for quite a time when she had
to. Yet the shock of being excluded was not so great as the
shock of finding that in all the excitement of the wedding
preparations no one, least of all her pretty careless mother,
seemed to think it necessary to explain to her why she was left
out. She realized that they had never thought that she would
expect to be a bridesmaid. Towards the end of the wedding
reception her back was hurting her so much that she could
hardly bear it. She crept away, no one seeing her, grabbed the
cat and went up to Blanche's bower and sat on the window seat
wrapped in her shawl, for although it was a warm spring day
she was cold. She heard, as from a great distance, the joyous
turmoil down below, and presently she saw them come out into
Worship Street to watch the bride and groom and the chief
bridesmaid, her second sister, drive away for the honeymoon.
They were all there, her father and mother, the two brilliant
brothers and the pretty younger sister who was already taller
than she. Then full realization came to her. These brothers and
sisters would do the kind of things of which she had dreamed,
but she herself would never do them because the Mary Montague of her dreams was not the Mary Montague of the actual
world. She was two people but until now only one had been
really known to her, and she did not want to know the other.
Characteristically she did not stay for long where she was, waiting for someone to come and find her in the gloaming and offer
her sympathy, but as soon as she was physically rested went
downstairs to forestall it, but no one had missed her.

She had humour and commonsense and she soon knew what
she must do. She must have done with her dream world, laugh
at the ridiculous Mary who had lived in it and get to know the
Mary whom she did not want to know, find out what she was
like and what her prospects were. It sounded an easy pro-
gramme but she found it a gruelling one. The fantasy world,
she discovered, has tentacles like an octopus and cannot be
escaped from without mortal combat, and when at last her
strong will had won the battle it seemed as though she was

living in a vacuum, so little had the real world to offer the shy
frustrated unattractive girl who was the Mary she must live
with until she died. But free of the tentacles she was able now to
sum up the situation with accuracy. She would not marry and
being a gentlewoman no other career was open to her. She was
not gifted in any way and she would never be strong and
probably never free from pain. She was not a favourite with
either of her parents, both of whom were vaguely ashamed of
having produced so unattractive a child, and yet she was
the one who would have to stay at home with them. And there
was nothing to do at home. The prospect was one of lifelong
boredom and seemed to her as bleak as the cold winds that
swept across the fens, even at times as terrible as the great
Cathedral in whose shadow she must live and die. For at that
time she did not love the Cathedral and in her fantasy life the
city had merely been the hub from which her radiant dreams
stretched out to the wide wheel of the world. What should she
do? Her question was not a cry of despair but a genuine and
honest wish to know.

She never knew what put it into her head that she, unloved,
should love. Religion for her parents, and therefore for their
children, was not much more than a formality and it had not
occurred to her to pray about her problem, and yet from somewhere the idea came as though in answer to her question, and
sitting in Blanche's bower with the cat she dispassionately considered it. Could mere loving be a life's work? Could it be a
career like marriage or nursing the sick or going on the stage?
Could it be adventure? Christians were commanded to love, it
was something laid upon them that they had to do whether they
liked it or not. They had to love, as a wife had to obey her husband and an actress had to speak her lines when the curtain
rose, and she was a Christian because she had been baptized
and confirmed in the Cathedral and went to matins every Sunday in her best bonnet. But what was love? Was there anything or anybody that she herself truly loved?

A rather shattering honesty was as much a part of her as her

H

strong will and her humour, and the answer to this question was
that she loved the cat and Blanche's bower. She fed the cat and
nursed him when he was sick, and she dusted the bower and
kept a beau-pot of flowers on the window sill. Her eyes were
always on them, watchful for beauty to adore, for the ripple of
the muscles under the cat's striped fur, the movement of sun and
shadow on the walls of the bower. And watchful for danger
too. She had got badly hurt once rescuing the cat from a
savage dog, and when the bower's ceiling got patched with
damp she gave her father no rest until he sent for the builder
to mend the roof. She was concerned for them both and had so
identified herself with them that they seemed part of her.
Making a start with the cat, was it possible to make of this concern and identification a deliberate activity that should pass out
in widening circles, to her parents and the servants and the
brothers and sisters and their families, to the city and its people,
the Cathedral, even at last perhaps to God himself? It came
to her in a flash that it must be wonderful to hold God and be
held by him, as she held the cat in her arms rubbing her cheek
against his soft fur, and was in turn held within the safety and
quietness of the bower. Then she was shocked by the irrever-
ence of her thought, and tried to thrust it away. But she did
not quite succeed. From that day onwards it remained warm
and glowing at the back of her mind.

So she took a vow to love. Millions before her had taken the
same simple vow but she was different from the majority because she kept her vow, kept it even after she had discovered the
cost of simplicity. Until now she had only read her Bible as a
pious exercise, but now she read it as an engineer reads a blueprint and a traveller a map, unemotionally because she was not
emotional, but with a profound concentration because her life
depended on it. Bit by bit over a period of years, that seemed
to her long, she began to get her scaffolding into place. She
saw that all her powers, even those which had seemed to miti-
gate against love, such as her shrewdness which had always
been quick to see the faults of others, her ambition and self-

will, could by a change of direction be bound over in service
to the one overmastering purpose. She saw that she must turn
from herself, and began to see something of the discipline that
that entailed, and found too as she struggled that no one and
nothing by themselves seemed to have the power to entirely hold
her when she turned to them.

It was then that the central figure of the gospels, a historical
figure whom she deeply revered and sought to imitate, began at
rare intervals to flash out at her like live lightning from their
pages, frightening her, turning the grave blueprint into a
dazzle of reflected fire. Gradually she learned to see that her
fear was not of the lightning itself but what it showed her of the
nature of love, for it dazzled behind the stark horror of Calvary.
At this point, where so many vowed lovers faint and fail, Mary
Montague went doggedly on over another period of years that
seemed if possible longer and harder than the former period.
At some point along the way, she did not know where because
the change came so slowly and gradually, she realized that he
had got her and got everything. His love held and illumined
every human being for whom she was concerned, and whom she
served with the profound compassion which was their need and
right, held the Cathedral, the city, every flower and leaf and
creature, giving it reality and beauty. She could not take her
eyes from the incredible glory of his love. As far as it was possible for a human being in this world she had turned from herself.
She could say, "I have been turned," and did not know how
very few can speak these words with truth.

Through most of her life no one noticed anything unusual
about her, though they found her increasingly useful. The use
her family made of her, however, was more or less unconscious,
because she was always there, like Fountains itself, and because
she was as unobtrusive as the old furniture whose quiet beauty
seemed painted on the dusk of the ancient house. She was just
Mary, plain, dumpy, lame, one of those people who do not
seem to alter much as the years pass because they have no
beauty to lose. The sons and daughters of the house enjoyed

their visits home because Fountains was a peaceful sort of place.
The servants were happy and contented and the work of the
house ran smoothly. The grandchildren, especially those whose
parents were in India and who were sent home to be looked
after by their aunt Mary, were more perceptive than their
elders. When in after years they looked back on Fountains as
upon a lost paradise they saw the face and figure of Aunt Mary
as inseparable from it and they knew that they loved her. A
few of them loved her as they loved no one else. Each one of
them was quite sure that she loved him as she loved no one else;
which was true, for seeing as she did the love of God perfectly
in each creature of his creation and care she could love the
creature as though it were all that existed, and she loved almost
without favouritism.

   Almost, because she was human. There was one who was
dearer than all the rest, her brother Clive who had pushed her
down the tower stairs. He, alone among her brothers and
sisters, grew to be more perceptive even than the children, because he never forgot what he had done. He intuitively knew
that she endured constant pain and slept badly, though no one
else knew; her strong will had enabled her not only never to
speak of it but also for all practical purposes to overcome it; and
he knew also, because she made him understand this, that she
set some sort of value on her pain and thanked him for it. Just
what its value was to her he could not understand, because ex-
planation of the inexplicable was never Mary's strong point. It
deepened love, she said, and sharpened prayer by making them
as piercing as itself if drawn into them. But this was beyond
him. What was not beyond him was delighted comprehension
of her impish humour, which she was too shy to reveal to many.
With him she gave it full play and they had great fun together
over the years. He alone of the family did not marry and though
they met seldom, because as a soldier he was abroad a great deal,
the bond between them grew stronger as they grew older. In
late middle age his health failed and he came home to Fountains. In his forty-eighth year he died a hard death after a long

hard illness through which Mary and Sarah nursed him, and after his death darkness enveloped Mary.

She was forty-five years old and she had not believed that such a thing could happen to her. Through the years her faith had grown so strong that she had not believed that she could lose it. The living light that had made love possible had seemed too glorious ever to go out, yet now it had gone and left her in darkness and the loneliness of life without love was to her a horror quite indescribable. It had a stifling nightmare quality. A cold darkness, she thought, would have been easier to bear, but this hot thick darkness brought one near to the breaking of the mind. It had been for nothing, she thought. It was not true. It had been for nothing. The wells of water to which she had always turned for refreshment had dried up. When she opened her Bible it was just a book like any other, and that revered historical figure, as self-deceived as herself, was as dead as Clive, killed like him by suffering so great that she could not let herself think of it, for they were not the only ones to pass into nothingness through that meaningless agony. Even the current cat could give her no joy, for it was spring and when she tried to find a little comfort in the garden she was perpetually stumbling over the young birds that he had killed. The Cathedral, huge and glowering, oppressed her with a sense of the colossal idiocy of man and she could have wept to think of all the men who had suffered and died to build it. Why pour out all that blood and treasure for the glory of a God who if he existed at all existed only as a heartless tyrant? She went on going to the Cathedral services as usual but they bored her so intolerably that she could scarcely sit through them. She went, she supposed, from force of habit. It was part of her routine.

Later she realized how much men and women owe to mere routine. She had for years led an extremely disciplined life, and now discipline held her up as irons hold the body of a paralytic. No one except Sarah and Doctor Jenkins found her at all changed. Her parents, old and ailing now, her father growing blind and her mother bedridden, propped their whole weight upon her just as usual, the old people in the workhouse and in Swithins Lane listened as eagerly as ever for the sound of her pony-carriage coming down the cobbled lane, and found her just as satisfactory a source of supply as she had ever been. But Sarah kept trying to make her put her feet up on the sofa, and Doctor Jenkins called upon her on his own initiative one day and placed a bottle of pink medicine on her escritoire.

"What's that for?" she asked a little tartly.

Doctor Jenkins was a young shy man in those days but he was not abashed by the tartness, unusual though it was, because he loved Miss Montague. When he had first come to the city as assistant to old Doctor Wharburton he had felt scared and lonely and had not liked the place, but as soon as Captain Montague's gout and Mrs. Montague's asthma had brought him to Fountains he began to feel different. He had had no idea what an intelligent and attractive fellow he was until he had met Miss Montague. Now he sat down in his favourite chair, realized afresh how likeable he was, relaxed happily and told her at length how exhausted she was by her brother's long illness, and by her father's gout and blindness and her mother's asthmatic heart and querulous temper. She must rest more and take this tonic. "It has iron in it," he finished.

"I'll take it, Tom," Miss Montague promised for love of him, though she did not believe a word of it.

Yet at the end of the first bottle of tonic she began to wonder if there was something in it. She was used to feeling exhausted and paid no attention to it, for it was her normal state, but this abysmal fatigue both of body and mind was not her normal state. She was in darkness but how much had the miasma of fatigue contributed to it? Was it possible that a bottle of tonic and putting one's feet up could affect one's faith in God? Shocked at the unaccustomed way in which her thoughts were dwelling on herself she drove down to the workhouse in her pony-carriage with six flannel petticoats and a dozen packets of tea and baccy. Coming back up Cockspur Street her eyes were caught by the window of the new little shop which had just been

opened by young Mr. Isaac Peabody. It was a very long time
since her attention had been caught by anything, but there was
a clock there shaped like a Greek lyre and Clive had taught her
to love all things Greek. Before she knew what she was doing
she had stopped the pony-carriage, climbed out, and was gazing
at the clock, fascinated by the circle of bright birds whose
bodies would never fall and die. The lark at the summit of the
lyre was so beautifully fashioned that she could see the quiver
of his spread wings and the pulsing of his throat as the song
poured from his open beak. In old days her mind had been full
of poetry she loved but in this darkness she had forgotten it all.
Now as she looked at the lark one of Shakespeare's sonnets
seemed to be struggling to make re-entrance into the darkness of
her closed mind, beating against it like a bird beating against a
shutter.

> "I all alone beweep my outcast state
> And trouble deaf heaven with my bootless cries."

How did it go on? "Precious friends hid in death's dateless
night." No, it wasn't that one. Then suddenly the shutter
crashed down and the bird flew in on a beam of light.

> "Haply I think on thee, and then my state,
> Like to the lark at break of day arising
> From sullen earth, sings hymns at heaven's gate;
> For thy sweet love remember'd such wealth brings
> That then I scorn to change my state with kings."

She leaned against the window as the children did. "Thy
sweet love remember'd." Clive. Clive. And he whom she had
thought had turned her and got her. What wealth had it been
to love them, even if now they were dead. Even if there was no
God, even if dateless night was the end of it all, how could she lose
them while she lived and remembered, and when she no longer
lived then loss, like every other pain, would be over for her.

She opened the shop door and walked in and young Mr.
Isaac Peabody came forward from the room behind the counter,
an oddly bird-like creature with arms that were too long for
him. He moved them up and down as he talked as though they

were wings and he meant to take off at any moment. It showed how much good the tonic had done her that the moment she set eyes on him she knew she had a new friend and was glad. A short while ago she had wanted no new friends. Somehow, against her conscience, she bought the Lyre clock, and when she reached Fountains the delighted Sarah carried it up the stairs for her and put it on her escritoire, and she sat down on the sofa and put her feet up and looked at it. From then onwards, whenever she had a few moments, she put her feet up and looked at it and the bright ring of birds seemed to gather all the sunshine to itself.

That was not the end of her darkness, which continued for a long while yet, but it was the first bit of comfort in it. She began to sleep better and sometimes now when she woke in the mornings it was not to that indescribable despair but to a quiet sadness, and with the name of her God upon her lips. But it was autumn before joy was restored to her again, and then it was not the same joy.

She found herself, one wet Wednesday afternoon in October, with an hour to spare, an unusual state of things in her hard-pressed life. She was to have taken the chair at a women's missionary meeting but the speaker had been taken ill and the meeting was cancelled. She had arranged for Sarah to sit with her mother, and for a friend of her father's to have tea with him and read aloud until she came back, and the wild idea came to her that she would do with this hour just what she pleased. But she must go out, for her household did not know that the meeting had been cancelled. Feeling like a truant from school she put on her bonnet and cloak, found her umbrella and let herself out of the old front door into the cool dark cavern of the Porta. Beyond it was a drizzle of fine rain and Worship Street looked grey and dismal, but in the greyness of the Close there were gleams of gold, as though sunrays were enmeshed in the rain, because the bright leaves were not yet fallen. So she went that way, limping slowly under her umbrella, and the air seemed fresh and sweet after her mother's overheated bedroom.

But where should she go? She could only go a short way, for now that the rheumatism had settled so firmly in her bad leg and her back such a thing as going for a walk was not possible for her. She could call at any of the houses in the Close and be warmly welcomed but she felt too tired for social calls. She thought she would go to the south door of the Cathedral and sit there on the stone bench and talk to the old bedesman, old Bob Hathaway whom she was very fond of, for she found poor people much more restful than the well-to-do. She walked slowly, for there was that whole hour stretching before her with its blessed emptiness, but even so she was tired when she reached the south door and found it oddly comforting to have old Bob clucking at her like a fussy hen, helping her to shake the wet out of her skirts and put her umbrella down. He was a crusty old man, without the courtesy of Tom Hochicorn who years later was to succeed him, but he was almost as fond of her as she was of him and the scolding he gave her was a pleasure.

"Abroad in all this wet!" he growled. "Why don't ee wear pattens, ma'am?"

"They don't suit my rheumatism, Bob," she explained.

"Sitting on this 'ere cold stone at your age, ma'am!" he went on wrathfully.

"You sit on it," she said, "and you're older than I am."

"Old enough to be your father, ma'am," he said, "which is why I'm giving ee a piece o' my mind."

He went on giving it for some while, and then they talked of rheumatism in general and Bob's in particular, and the terrible wind he had after fried onions, and Miss Montague was just beginning most wonderfully to enjoy Bob when she had the misfortune to sneeze and he got angry with her again. Either she must go home, he said, or she must go into the Cathedral and have a bit of a warm by the brazier. It was lit. She did not want to go home and so to please him she said she would go into the Cathedral for a few moments. He opened the door for her and she went in.

It was very dark in the Cathedral, except for the glow of the

large charcoal braziers that were lit here and there in its vastness. They did practically nothing to conquer the cold of the
great place but they were pretty as flowers. She made her way
to the nearest and held out her chilly hands to its comfort. It
burned beside the carved archway that led into the chantry
of the duchess Blanche and glowed rosily upon the stone, just
as the sunset glowed upon the stone of Blanche's bower at home
at Fountains. Miss Montague moved forward into the chantry
and sat down on the old rush-seated chair that was just inside.
It had a hole in it, for in these days, before the coming of Adam
Ayscough, the Cathedral was not well cared for, and her
spreading skirts stirred up the dust. Then the dust settled, and
with it the silence, and she realized that she had never before
been quite alone in the Cathedral. There were the old bedesmen at the doors but they seemed far away, and it was dark.
Vast curtains of shadow fell from the invisible roof and they
seemed to move like a tide of dark water. She felt very lonely
and she wished she had the cat on her lap.

In the dimness she could just see the little figure of the
duchess Blanche lying on her tomb, by herself because her husband had been buried beside the High Altar, but not lonely because there was a dog at her feet. Her hands lay on her breast
placed palm to palm in prayer. It was said that she had had her
humble part in the making of this place. She had not lived long
enough to see the great church of her husband's dream completed, for she had died young, but every day of her widowhood she had come to the Cathedral and knelt down in a particular spot to pray for the repose of her husband's soul, and for
a blessing upon the builders of his dream, and after her death
they had built her chantry about the place where she had knelt.
It was too dark to see it now but Miss Montague knew how
lovely it was, small and delicate like the little duchess herself,
with cherubs in all the nooks and crannies. Cromwell's men
had defaced these, and Blanche's praying hands, but they had
not succeeded in spoiling the chantry's beauty, only in giving
it a look of battered but enduring patience.

"You've been here so long," Miss Montague said to Blanche, "praying with those wounded hands." For though her mind told her that Blanche was either nowhere, or somewhere else, but anyhow not here, yet she could not this afternoon quite get rid of the feeling that Blanche was here. And high up in the darkness that her sight could not penetrate he was there upon the rood. Her hands folded in her lap Miss Montague shut her eyes, for she was very tired. She ceased to feel lonely. Blanche was here, and the man on the rood, sharing the same darkness with her and with a vast multitude of people whom she seemed to know and love. How much more friendly it is when you cannot see, thought Miss Montague, and how much closer we are to him. Why should we always want a light? He chose darkness for us, darkness of the womb and of the stable, darkness in the garden, darkness on the cross and in the grave. Why do I demand certainty? That is not faith. Why do I want to understand? How can I understand this great web of sin and ugliness and love and suffering and joy and life and death when I don't understand the little tangle of good and evil that is myself? I've enough to understand. I understand that he gave me light that I might turn to him, for without light I could not have seen to turn. I have seen creation in his light. He shared his light with me that I, turned, might share with him the darkness of his redemption. Why did I despair? What do I want? If it is him I want he is here, not only love in light illuming all that he has made but love in darkness dying for it . . . And she said, I will learn to pray.

It was a promise. She said, Please may I begin to learn here with Blanche, and she whose prayer until now had been the murmuring of soothing and much loved words in the tired intervals between one thing and another, or the presentation to Almighty God of inventories of the needs of the city as she drove about it in her pony-carriage, abandoned herself for the sake of those she loved to silence and the dark, understanding however dimly that to draw some tiny fraction of the sin of the world into her own being with this darkness was to do away with it.

Bob's hand fell upon her shoulder and she looked up. It was now almost entirely dark in the Cathedral and she saw his anxious puckered face only dimly by the light of the brazier. "Ma'am, ye's been here near an hour," he said crossly.

It had seemed five minutes. She got up with his help and they went back to the south door. He opened her umbrella for her, while she settled her cloak and shook the dust out of her skirts. Then she smiled at him and thanked him and went away into the rain. She seemed, he thought, "bit moidered", yet she looked younger than when she came.

She did not despair again, and though the darkness came back at times right up to the time when she was a very old woman she was always able to welcome it. Yet if these times came when her health was low she would remember that first bottle of tonic and ask Doctor Jenkins for another, for true darkness and the murkiness of ill-health could be intertwined, to one's confusion, and she would remember that other sonnet of Shakespeare's and know she must not

> ". . . permit the basest clouds to ride
> With ugly rack on his celestial face,
> And from the forlorn world his visage hide."

After her parents died the city noticed with dismay that she was what is called "breaking up". But increasing physical weakness did not distress Miss Montague, for the enforced lengthening of the tired intervals between one thing and another meant more time to learn the work of prayer, and the house where she now lived alone with the old servants became more and more a place where everybody came because she was more often in it than she had been. As the years passed she was disturbed, almost alarmed, by the growing peace and serenity of her days. Surely it was wrong to be so happy. Then, abruptly, she knew it was not wrong. This was the ending of her days on earth, the dawn of her heavenly days, and it had been given to her to feel the sun on her face.

And so she was happy in old age and vastly amused to find

herself a personage in the city, almost an institution, beloved, revered, and apparently the hostess of a salon. Shrewd as she was she could not but be aware that her chair by the fire had become a throne, and that when she went to the Cathedral in her bath-chair it was a queen's progress. When she looked back on the unloved girl she had been, on the toiling drone of her middle years, on the shabby prayerful recluse of her elderly years, it was all beyond her comprehension. But she enjoyed it and with a slightly mocking amusement dressed up for the part with velvet shoes on her feet and lace about her shoulders and over her head. She knew her own worthlessness and so did God, though he loved her none the less, and this false idea of her that the city had got into its head was a private joke between them.

3

Outside it was nearly dark, but she did not call Sarah to draw the curtains; she did not want even the footsteps of dear Sarah on the stairs to enter the silence that held her. But presently other footsteps entered it, slow and heavy, as of a man carrying a heavy weight. They came into the dark cavern of the Porta beneath her room and the flap of the letter box was lifted and dropped once. Miss Montague smiled and her happiness became deeper. It was the Dean.

It had never been her habit to examine love, or to compare one affection with another, for as love had grown so had reverence for it, but she did realize that Adam Ayscough had brought again to her life something that had been withdrawn when Clive had died. To him alone of all her friends could she speak out of the depths of herself, and from him alone did she receive as much as she gave. In the two intimacies there were differences. Clive had not always understood her but the Dean knew far better what she was talking about than she did herself. Clive had told her everything about himself that there was to tell, Adam Ayscough told her nothing. Yet mysteriously she knew much. She thought sometimes it was as though he kept all his grief in a locked box. Being the man he was he could not show it to her but he had given her the box, and possessing it gave her much power to comfort him. Their friendship had been of slow growth, so shy and self-abhoring was the man, so long did it take him to realize that their need of each other was mutual. And even now he came only seldom to see her, afraid to trespass on her hospitality and afraid to tire her. She wished he would come oftener but like all the old and infirm she had accepted with rueful humour the fact that she must be visited oftenest by those she least wished to see. It was the sensitive, the gentle and humble who feared to come too often lest they tire her. The coarse-fibred had no such inhibitions.

"The Dean, madam," said Sarah.

He bowed over her hand, for he had an archaic courtesy not unlike Isaac's. He still called every woman "ma'am". "I hope you are well, ma'am? I trust you have not suffered from the damp?"

"Thank you, Mr. Dean, I am pretty well. And I hope you have fully recovered from your cold. Will you please sit in that chair? You will not feel the draught there."

An exchange of courtesies flowed between them until Sarah had left the room, and for a short while after. There was never any intimacy in the manner, only in the matter of their conversation with each other. Not even in their thoughts did they use Christian names. The easy manners of the later generations would have shocked both of them.

"Is Mrs. Ayscough well?" asked Miss Montague, and then, with generous warmth in her voice, "I could see her from where I sat in the Cathedral last Sunday. I thought I had never seen her look more beautiful."

For a moment the Dean's face lit up almost miraculously, then settled again into its habitual sombre sadness. "She is not too well. The harshness of our climate has never suited her. She has an extreme delicacy."

Miss Montague had her own opinion of Elaine Ayscough's extreme delicacy, but it lent no asperity to her gentle words of sympathy. She did not know which of the two she was sorrier for, the man whose habit of hopeless love no indifference seemed able to break or the woman who had to bear year in, year out, the ennui of his unwanted devotion. Their predicament saddened her and she turned thankfully to a happy subject.

"Did you enjoy Mr. Peabody? He told me of your conversation together."

Again the Dean's face lit up. "I am much obliged to you for suggesting that we should talk together. It was a great privilege. I had not known quite how to approach him but the opportunity for conversation presented itself happily."

"I am delighted, Mr. Dean, that for once in your life you have condescended to allow Almighty God the happiness of giving you a little pleasure."

The Dean was frequently startled by the unexpectedness of Miss Montague's remarks, and also, once he had got over the first shock, by their insight. "You are right," he said slowly. "You are quite right. Years ago I decided that joy was not for me. Yes, I see. The decision was my own, not his, and therefore most presumptuous."

"Though most natural," said Miss Montague. "With so many burdens to bear on your shoulders it must have been difficult to look about you. But now you must, for you've not much longer to gratify heaven by taking a little joy. I have discovered, Mr. Dean, that in old age God seems to delight in giving us what our youth longed for and was denied. You know what that was in your case."

"And so do you, I expect," said the Dean, smiling at her. "Sometimes, ma'am, I think that you know everything."

"Certainly not," she said a little tartly. "But I do know that you will hurt the feelings alike of heaven and Mr. Peabody if you do not make a real study of the art of horology."

"I am certainly very ignorant of it," said the Dean humbly, "and far too unobservant. I have heard the ticking of your clock but I have never looked at it." He adjusted his eyeglasses, located the Michael Neuwers on the mantelpiece and got up and looked at it. "This is a very beautiful clock."

"I will tell you only that it is three hundred years old," said Miss Montague. "You must ask Mr. Peabody to tell you about the man who made it. My Lyre clock was made by Mr. Peabody himself. The city is very proud of Mr. Peabody's clocks. Have you ever noticed my Lyre clock? Over there on my escritoire." The Dean crossed to her escritoire and bent and peered at the little circle of enamelled birds. "The little man made this lovely thing himself?" he ejaculated.

He came back to his chair and sat with one hand behind his ear while Miss Montague told him about the day when she had bought the Lyre clock and made the acquaintance of Isaac Peabody. Only with Miss Montague was he sufficiently at ease to betray the fact that he was deaf. He knew that she did not mind speaking slowly and distinctly, for she was so perfectly leisured. "I was in trouble at the time," she said. "I believed that I had lost my faith. Then Isaac put his clock in the window and gradually I found that I had not lost my faith. I shall be delighted if you will laugh at me."

"Why should I laugh?" asked the Dean. "Genius creates from the heart and when men put love into their work there is power in it, there is a soul in the body. You have never seen my watch, ma'am. Mr. Peabody thinks it remarkable. He tells me it has a most unusual watchcock."

"Please to be so good as to hand me my magnifying glass from inside my escritoire," said Miss Montague.

Five minutes later they were sitting side by side absorbed in the watch. Then Miss Montague looked from the watch to the window, where she could just make out the great shape of the Cathedral towering like a mountain against the last of the afterglow. They were both so intricately, beautifully, wisely and lovingly fashioned that the only real difference between them was the unimportant one of size. She had been told of people who could hold some beautiful object in their hands and it would reveal the past to them. How powerful they must be then, these things that had been created from the heart. What beneficence had this watch already wrought? What blessings had it yet to give before some idiot smashed it? A deep shudder went through her.

"You are cold?" asked the Dean.

"No. I just thought of destruction. Of evil. Nothing is safe, not even the Cathedral. I felt afraid for the Cathedral. I felt afraid suddenly for the world. When evil gets a grip on men it always drives them to destroy."

"Evil has hard work to get its hands on what it really wants to destroy," said the Dean. "Which has eternal value, this watch or the love that made it? The body or the soul? How extraordinary that I should be asking this question of you, of all people!"

Miss Montague smiled but did not answer. There was a silence in which each spoke to the other though not in words. Love. The only indestructible thing. The only wealth and the only reality. The only survival. At the end of it all there was nothing else.

CHAPTER 8

I

ON the following Sunday the crisp beautiful autumn weather was still holding and there was something of an air of festivity over the city. It was a century when Sunday was still important, and a cleavage between weekday and holyday as real as noticeable. The bells seemed to ring all day and all respectable people went to church except a mere handful of unbelievers such as Isaac, and they felt so much in the minority that during the hours of divine service they incarcerated themselves in their kitchens or libraries behind the newspaper, defiant or uncomfortable according to temperament, and did not issue out until church-going was accomplished. Sunday clothes were very glorious in the city in those days, and Sunday dinners rich and succulent. A rustle of silk petticoats, a frou-frou of frills and flounces, made a soft murmuring undercurrent to the music of bells and voices during churchgoing hours, and as the morning wore on the mingled scents of roast beef and Yorkshire, onions and apple pie became ever more delectable.

In the houses in Angel Lane, which for the most part boasted only one small maid like Polly and yet where the appearance and customs of gentility must be upheld, the strain contingent upon getting into one's best clothes, getting the dinner and getting to church all in the space of a few morning hours was very great. It was especially great at number twelve because Emma felt it her duty to take Polly to church with her in the morning instead of leaving her at home to mind the joint. She feared to let Polly stay alone in the house with Isaac, lest he corrupt her with his terrible freethinking notions, and she also feared to let her go to church by herself in the evening lest she collect followers. Indeed she scarcely dared let Polly out of her sight all day on Sunday lest some sort of evil befall her. At least that was what she believed to be the motive in her ceaseless vigilance over her little maid. She was unaware of her own terrible jealousy of Polly. The sympathy, laughter and comprehension that spun like sunlight between Isaac and Polly, as once they had spun between Isaac and his mother, was something she refused to know about. Nor would she know that the orphanage child had in her that vital glow that she had never had. She lived too close to despair to have any strength left for selfknowledge. She might have been able to acknowledge herself unloved but to know herself unloving was beyond her strength.

That Sunday morning Polly was hard at it from an early hour, lighting the fires, getting and clearing breakfast, washing up, making the beds, peeling the potatoes and onions, putting the joint in the oven and making custard. The pastry she had made the day before, and she had cleaned all the shoes and starched Emma's Sunday petticoats. While she was darting here and there, trying not to dance and sing, Emma was laying the table with meticulous care and Isaac was winding the clock and trying not to get under foot. Usually he hated Sundays but this one he felt was going to be different. His spirit was as sensitive to such things as a barometer and this morning he was aware of a change in the wind, disturbing perhaps, but eventually beneficent. When Emma, who had been upstairs changing into her Sunday best, came into the parlour drawing on her black kid gloves he turned to smile at her, swallowed nervously and gulped out, "You look nice, Emma. Is that a new bonnet?"

Emma stared at him. Her big black bonnet, with a sad black

ostrich plume rearing up on top of it like a bedraggled cock
about to crow, had been new five years ago. Her voluminous
black bombasine gown was older still and she was glad to cover
it with her mother's cashmere shawl, old too but so soft that its
folds still retained their first beauty, and a whiff of the perfume
that their mother had always used. Mrs. Peabody had kept all
her maternal love for Isaac, and Emma, though nursing her
mother with apparent devotion, had retaliated with many
subtle cruelties, but she had persuaded herself now that there
had always been perfect sympathy between them and she never
failed to put orris root between the folds of the shawl.

"That is our mother's shawl," said Isaac.

Emma had been almost on the point of returning his smile
but now a dead shut look closed down over her sallow face.
Isaac was always blind and stupid in all that concerned herself,
instantly alert if anything recalled their mother. She turned
from him in silence and took the big brass-bound prayer book
from a bookshelf. Then she rustled and crackled through the
door calling, "Polly, I am waiting." Polly came stepping very
demurely down the stairs, but the demureness emphasized the
gaiety of the crimson ribbons on her bonnet and the sparkle in
her eyes, and as she came the bells began to ring. Isaac opened
the front door and light and air and music poured in, broke
against Emma like bright water against a dark rock, flowed
round her, joined behind her, and to Isaac's fancy filled the
house. "Shut the door, Isaac," said Emma sharply from the
pavement. Isaac did so and then leant against it chuckling.
"Too late, Emma," he said. "It's in."

He stayed where he was, almost too happy to move. The
bells seemed to him to be ringing almost in the walls of the little
house, and the reverberation of organ music came nearer and
nearer. Two great eyes burned in the dimness of the passage, a
majestic presence approached and the music boomed about his
legs. A solid softness was pressed against him, now here, now
there, as Sooty weaved and turned and hummed. There were
now no women in the house, nor would be for a blessed ninety

minutes. Sooty led the way to the kitchen and the two males ensconced themselves before the fire. Isaac took his coat off and sat in his shirt sleeves, his feet on the fender and his pipe in his mouth. Emma did not allow him to smoke, but he had discovered that if he left the window open fresh air and the smell of the roast counteracted the aroma of tobacco, and his sins did not find him out. He placed his spectacles upon his nose and opened the paper. He read and smoked a while. Sooty purred, then slept. From the garden the sharp sweet autumnal song of a robin pierced him and then ceased. He continued to hold his paper in front of his nose but he no longer read it. When the bells fell silent he always tried hard not to think of the city's preoccupation at this hour, but yet he always did, with anger and guilt. Yet today he remembered it without anger, even with a certain nostalgic pleasure, and one of those flashes of vision that came in his good times.

In all the old churches of the city the congregations had rustled to their knees. In St. Peter's in the market place Emma was kneeling beside the black marble tablet on the wall that commemorated their father's virtues, her sallow face hidden within her bonnet, with Polly beside her peeping bright-eyed through her interlaced fingers. In the Cathedral the Dean knelt with bowed head in his carved and canopied stall, his ugly strong hands clasped on the white page of the great book that lay open before him. Somewhere within the shadows was an old lady in a bath-chair, her mittened hands folded together on the rug that covered her knees. As quietness grew in Isaac he became aware of a multitude of men and women kneeling in churches all over the world, thousands of them, and heard the murmur of their prayer rising louder and louder like a mounting wind in forest trees; yet in the forefront of his seeing those two pairs of clasped hands, old and misshapen, held his attention with a sense of symbolic strength and beauty. The wind shook him, coming from he knew not where and going he knew not where, but a harsh grating voice in his ears was audible to him above its power, speaking for him and for the city. "O Lord, have mercy upon us, miserable offenders. Spare thou them, O God, which confess their faults. Restore thou them that are penitent." He would have tried to escape, as he had escaped from the Cathedral a few nights ago, but it was for the city, and he had opened the door to it himself. They were deceived, they prayed to a vacuum, to that dark shapelessness that terrified him, but the love with which they prayed had reality; he knew that, for he had experienced love.

He knocked his pipe out. His paper rustled to the floor and his spectacles slid down his nose. His hands, red and shiny, lay relaxed on his knees. He abandoned himself to the quietness and the warmth of sun and fire. Autumn was a strange paradoxical time of the year. It was the season when he was happiest and yet it was the season when he was most vulnerable and most aware, and that was not always a happiness. Yet he liked autumn. As he dropped asleep he heard again the sharp sweet robin's song.

He woke and saw a mouse on the floor, by the coal scuttle, not three feet from where Sooty slept. He looked at it for several minutes, admiring the delicate ears and the curve of its tail, happy with it, until it slowly dawned upon him that this close juxtaposition of himself, Sooty and a mouse, was unusual. He stirred Sooty with his foot, woke him up and indicated the mouse. Sooty yawned, looked at the mouse, glanced contemptuously in Isaac's direction and went to sleep again. Isaac leaned forward and poked the mouse with his pipe stem. It did not run away. He leaned still further forward and picked the mouse up by its tail. Then he carried it to the window and stood there holding it, excitement mounting in him. It was a wooden mouse with a tarred string tail, a common enough toy but fashioned with such love of mouse that it was almost more mouse-like than a real one. It revealed, so to speak, the essence of mouse, swift and slinking, endearing and alarming all at once. Who had made it? Not Polly. She was of the pelican breed, not the beaver kind. She was not creative. But this craftsman was such another as he was himself. He could have made this mouse and its creator could have fashioned the cuckoo that flew out of the clock in the shop window. Isaac's face was pink with pleasure, for he was not a man to begrudge another proficiency in his own craft. He had never felt jealous in his life. He wrapped the mouse carefully in his clean Sunday handkerchief and put it in his pocket, for Emma must not see it. She was perfectly capable of putting it in the dustbin. What had Polly been thinking of to leave it lying on the floor? For it must belong to Polly.

He went back to his chair, lit his pipe again and looked at the clock. Three-quarters of an hour had passed and stillness held the city. It must be sermon time. He saw Polly sitting very upright on the hard bench, her eyes fixed on the preacher's face, her own small countenance rather wickedly demure within her bonnet, for her thoughts were not where they should be. He shrunk away from the dark figure of Emma beside her, for he did not want to see Emma. Instead he tried to see the Dean sitting in his high canopied stall. But he was not sitting, he was kneeling, his face hidden in his hands. To his side came a man in a black gown, bearing a golden wand, and the Dean rose and followed him. They paced slowly beneath the huge shadowed roof from which the sunbeams fell like spears, and then the Dean was mounting up and up as though, Isaac thought, to some scaffold, or to some high place that was as fearful to him as a scaffold would have been. The pulpit, thought Isaac, the pulpit. I did not know he hated to preach. Isaac was distressed. What could he do? There was nothing he could do and he was suddenly so unhappy that he opened the paper and immersed himself in the sporting news.

2

Polly did not dislike churchgoing, indeed she loved it, though she could not read the prayer-book in which Emma so carefully found the places for her, or understand a word of the Reverend Augustus Penny's rambling sermon; in fact few people could, so ancient was Mr. Penny and so muddled in his head. She loved it because sometimes, when she and Emma came in, she saw a shabby figure at the back of the church, hidden in a dark corner by a dusty marble monument. Job. Walking in behind Emma she dared not even smile at him and when she came out again he was always gone, but even that much of Job was enough to make her day glorious.

Today, walking with quick short steps beside Emma down Angel Lane, with the bells pealing and the sun warm on her face, she felt that he would be there. Else why was she so specially happy today? She hardly knew how to contain herself. As they turned to go down the flight of steps that led to the market place she turned and looked back up Angel Lane to Worship Street, and saw a river of colour flowing under the Porta. It was the gentry going to the Cathedral, the men in curly-brimmed top hats and cut-away coats of bottle green, russet and mulberry, the women in little hats with wonderful full skirts swinging over stiffened petticoats. Polly loved to see them, they were so gay. "O look, ma'am!" she cried to Emma, but after one contemptuous glance Emma walked on down the steps with her head in the air. She, by birth, belonged to that bright galaxy of stars, but she had fallen from them because her brother had gone into trade and got drunk at the Swan and Duck. And they had let her fall. Well, let them go to the Cathedral. She was going to St. Peter's, her father's church, for that had fallen too. With Mr. Penny so old and wandering in his head it had become lonely and almost derelict, with a congregation so sparse that in bad weather it did not always go into double figures. Yet it was rich in possessing the whole of the affection and loyalty of which Emma Peabody was at present capable.

They came out of the sunlight into the dark porch, and from there into the dim mustiness of the church. Out of the corner of her eye Polly saw Job beside the broken monument, and her heart leapt. She could only give one quick glance but after it she could see him as clearly as she would ever see anything in this world. He wore a peat-brown coat that was now much too small for him, strained across his chest and buttoned tight so

that no one should see the state of his shirt, blue trousers with
patches at the knees, and broken boots. He had scrubbed his
face until it shone, but being pressed for time at the pump that
morning he had not continued the good work to ears and neck.
He sat crouching a little forward, as though he thought he
would be less noticeable that way, with his brown hands on his
knees to hide the patches, and his eyes under the tumbled dark
mass of hair on his forehead were bright with mingled pleasure
and fright. To sit behind Polly and look at the top of her bonnet appearing over the back of the pew was bliss, and he liked
old Mr. Penny, but he did not like it when the other members
of the congregation stared curiously at him. It was a measure
of his love for Polly and his affection for Mr. Penny that he
came at all.

St. Peter's did not frighten Polly because it was broken and
neglected, and she was so sorry for it that she was fast coming to
love it. The paving stones were cracked and uneven, the hangings faded and torn, the tall old pulpit looked tottering into
ruin and there were cobwebs everywhere. Every available
space was crowded with memorial tablets, surmounted with
cherubs with broken wings, funeral urns and skulls. Yet it had
beauty, for there was very old glass in the windows. It darkened
the church but when the sun shone it spilled deep and glorious
colour all over the cracked paving stones, the dusty pews, the
chipped cherubs and skulls and urns, and the congregation.
It was shining today and when they settled themselves for the
sermon Polly saw that the meagre congregation was arrayed in
all the colours of the rainbow. Her lips parted in delight, for
they were as royally dressed as the gentry had been. Seeing her
smile and afraid she was about to giggle Emma hushed her, for
Mr. Penny was smoothing out the crumpled bits of paper on
which he had written out his sermon, and looking down at
them pleadingly, his mouth trembling. Polly lifted her face,
and the smile was for him now, because his torn old surplice
was lilac, crimson and gold.

He was a tall old man, thin and hoop-shaped, with wispy

white hair and bewildered watery blue eyes. For a great many years he had been vicar of one of the loneliest villages in the fen, but after his wife had died there he had become somewhat melancholic and ten years ago the Bishop had brought him to the city. But the move had come too late to do him much good, for though he had never lost faith in his God he had lost faith in himself. Years after the great church out in the fen had remained half empty, while year after year the cold damp vicarage had mouldered to pieces about himself and Letitia, because it was one of the poorer livings. And now year after year the congregation at St. Peter's grew smaller and smaller. The vicarage was less vast here, the stipend a little more, but that did no good to Letitia. It was a pity that they had not thought to move him before Letitia died, but he bore no grudge. Only he could not help it going round and round in his head, as it was doing now, so that he could not remember his text, which he had failed to write down at the head of his sermon. He looked desperately up and down the pews and saw how the girl in the black bonnet and grey cloak, a girl whom he liked almost as much as the shabby boy who hid by the monument at the back of the church, was smiling at him. And her bonnet was golden and her cloak rose-colour and saffron. "The king's daughter is all glorious within," he said. "Her raiment is wrought gold." Then he rambled off into a sermon about something entirely different and everyone went to sleep except Polly and Job. Polly stayed awake thinking about Job and Job stayed awake thinking about Polly.

It was when the service was over that the wonderful thing began to happen. Polly, coming out into the porch with Emma, saw to her astonishment that Job was still there, his back to the people, intent upon one of the torn bits of paper that flapped from the notice board. He did not turn round and she scarcely even dared to look at the back of his head and his unwashed neck as she stood waiting for Emma to finish her conversation with old Mrs. Martin from the baker's shop. Emma, as the daughter of a former vicar, was a person of importance in the tiny St. Peter's congregation, and she loved queening it among them. "Yes, ma'am, my daughter Mary's home," said old Mrs. Martin. "The one who went out to America. You remember her, ma'am? Your dear father baptized her." And then, as Emma was graciously pleased to remember Mary, she went on, her old face flushing at the presumption of what she was about to ask, "I suppose, ma'am, you couldn't honour us by drinking a dish of tea with us today?"

"Thank you, Mrs. Martin," said Emma, "but I never leave my brother alone on a Sunday."

"Mary's leaving for London tomorrow, ma'am," said old Mrs. Martin sadly. She was very disappointed and she feared she had presumed too far. Polly could not bear her disappointment.

"Ma'am, I will give Mr. Peabody his tea," she said. "And he will have the paper and Sooty. He will not be lonely. He would like you to have the pleasure."

"It would be such an honour, ma'am," said Mrs. Martin. "I remember as though it were yesterday how your dear father—." She stopped and wiped away a tear, caused actually not by remembrance of the late Mr. Peabody but by a draught operating upon weak eyesight. But Emma was touched. She was also torn two ways by jealousy of Polly presiding over Isaac's tea and a sudden longing to be made much of. No one even in her childhood had petted her. The nearest she had ever come to a knowledge of tenderness was occasionally now in her later years, with these old women who saw her through the rainbow mist that softens all outlines of the past. She was not aware of saying yes but without her knowing quite what happened she found herself climbing the steps towards Angel Lane very flustered and out of breath, and committed to it. She stopped and looked accusingly down at the top of Polly's bonnet. "Polly, did you hustle me?" she asked sharply.

"O no, ma'am," said Polly from within her bonnet. Her face could not be seen, and her voice was small, correct and demure, but Emma had a sense of small bells chiming, of jubilation and laughter all inside the bonnet. She put out her hand against the wall to steady herself, then climbed on. At the top of the steps she stopped again and asked, "Who is that disreputable boy who was in the porch just now?"

"I don't know, ma'am," said Polly within the bonnet, adding severely, "he should wash his neck."

3

Elaine Ayscough settled back in her seat with a sense of almost unbearable malaise. Adam had just climbed up into the pulpit. It was a high pulpit with a great sounding board and when he got to the top at last, and stood there with his big head hanging a little forward, his ugly nose jutting beak-like from his sallow face, peering out and down at the congregation, with that hideous thing curved over his head, she thought he looked like the Punch of a Punch and Judy show. She thanked heaven that, as Dean, Adam did not have to preach often, and she took it as a personal injury that the Canon in residence should have sprained his ankle and forced him to preach today, for she hated hearing Adam preach. She hated it as much as he hated preaching. Marriage was a queer thing. She did not love Adam, but yet she knew things about him. She knew preaching made him miserable, though she did not know why, and when he was in the pulpit every nerve in her body seemed to be taut. With an effort of her very strong will she tried to detach and calm herself, for she did not want to have another of her headaches; they were ageing her. Adam's sermons were always very long, entirely incomprehensible, and often inaudible too because his deafness made him raise his voice too much, so that it just boomed in the sounding board like surf in a cave and nobody heard a word. She could feel in all those nerves in her body that were not yet quieted how the congregation was resigning itself; to endurance, to meditation, to the planning of menus or wardrobes, each mind running to its own habitual harbour as a ship runs to shelter in a rising wind. But none of them was turning to sleep. In other churches in the city people were possibly sleeping through a sermon, but not here.

People did not sleep when the Dean preached. Subconsciously they were too disturbed.

Elaine, having severed her connection with Adam, let herself drift into the sanctuary of her own beauty. Looking down she saw with pleasure how her wide silk skirts were faintly patterned with the far colours of the stained glass windows. Her slim gloved hands lay in a patch of purple light, as though she held violets. She was aware of the great Cathedral soaring about her and felt more kindly disposed towards it than she usually did. It was beautiful in sunlight, a fit setting for her loveliness. She was not a religious woman but she did feel a profound and at times almost a humble thankfulness that she had kept her beauty. It had been the same today as it had always been. As she had rustled up the nave to her pew of honour beneath the pulpit, tall and slender, and sunk gracefully to her knees, her face devoutly bowed into her hands, she had felt all the eyes upon her just as she had always done. She did not mind if they stared in envy or even dislike so long as they stared. It was not so much that she wanted admiration as that she wanted comfort. Years ago when there had seemed nothing else to live for she had made a *raison d'être* of her own beauty, not realizing that as life goes on a *raison d'être* becomes increasingly possessive. Sometimes, during the wakeful hours of the night, she knew that she no longer owned her beauty, but that her beauty owned her. Then she would be very afraid, wondering if when it left her she would be simply a thing dropped on the floor.

The grating voice above her obtruded itself again. The severance had not been complete; it never was in marriage. Her hands made a sudden convulsive movement of exasperation in her lap, and she had the fancy that Adam had seen it. The deanery pew was too close to the pulpit; far too close when it was your own husband who was preaching. They were too close. She folded her hands again, gently, for she must not crush the violets in her lap. She must not hurt Adam who had given them to her. Fool, she said to herself, they're not flowers, they're light. But it was too late now to tell herself that, for she was already back again in the little Chelsea drawing-room and Adam had just put the violets in her lap. A drifting mood, encouraged, is like a current at sea. You have no control over where it will take you.

They had met each other first at a dinner party, her first party after the ritual period of mourning for her young scamp of a husband was over at last. She had been gay that night. She had finished with her black clothes, with lawyers and con-dolences, with pretending to be grief stricken when she was not, with the whole boring business of widowhood, and could enjoy herself again. She had very little money and would have to do something about that shortly but meanwhile she was gay, and ready to be entrancingly kind to the grotesque middle-aged man who had taken her into dinner. He was distinguished and scholarly, she had been told, well born and well off, or she would not have bothered with him. She rather admired breeding and scholarship and was adept at concealing her own lack of both. She was a clever woman, with the chameleon's gift of taking colour from her environment. Her gaiety that night was not obtrusive but it gave an enchanting warmth to her usually rather remote and classical beauty, a warmth that seemed to the desolate man beside her a glow of heavenly kindness.

Adam just at this time was extremely desolate. He had al-ready been a schoolmaster for some years, having failed as a parish priest, but he was not enjoying it. He did not make friends easily. He knew little of women and had always been rather afraid of them. He fell in love now, at forty, for the first time and it could scarcely have gone harder with him. It was months before he could bring himself to propose to Elaine, so inhibited was he by the thought of his own unworthiness, so scared of in some way hurting her fragile purity with his clumsiness, and he could never have done it had she not been a widow. That somehow was a help. But even so his wooing was so stumbling and constrained that Elaine, involved with other men, did not recognize it for what it was, and when at last he made his humble declaration she was so taken by surprise that her usual finesse failed her. The mask slipped and though after a moment or two she answered him correctly enough he had seen the astonishment, the slightly contemptuous amusement. She saw that he had seen, saw him flinch, and she was sorry. He had touched something in her.

Like so many beautiful women Elaine had a flair for making disastrous marriages. Her French marriage was a degrading exhausting business and it was now that she began to build her life about the fact of her beauty and find sanctuary there. Her beauty was her armour. While she looked as she did she could preserve her pride. Luckily neither of her earlier husbands had learnt the trick of survival and after six years in France Elaine came back to England a widow again, as delicately beautiful as ever but also as impecunious as ever and not quite as physically tough as she had been. She was actually feeling as fragile as she looked, and there was a vague fear in her mind. What next? It was a wet November and the friend whose Chelsea home she had chosen as her refuge seemed with each day that passed less and less sensible of the honour done her. The fear grew.

The rain passed and there came a Saturday of sunshine. She was not fond of walking, but to escape from Rosamond she went to Kensington Gardens and walked there. She still wore her widow's weeds and they were shabby now, and her nose was pink at the tip from a slight cold. She was not looking her best and she knew it, and the knowledge did nothing to cheer her. The sun was warm and golden, and droves of gentle yellow leaves floated about her, but her fear obsessed her mind and she did not know it, and she did not see the tall black figure coming towards her. But he saw her, solitary and fragile, a poignant note of sorrow in the drifting golden glory. His heart seemed beating in his throat and for an instant he did not know whether to go back or go on. Had it seemed that all was well with her he would have turned back that he might not obtrude an awkward memory upon her, but to see her drifting towards him with the leaves, as though as lost as they, kept him where he was. He could perhaps be of service to her.

"Madame Blanchard," he said gently, for he had known about her marriage. She stopped, recognized him and held out her gloved hand to him. He bowed over it and offered her his arm. "Madame, shall we walk together a little way?" She accepted his arm and they strolled on together, conversing of the weather. He was as ugly as she remembered him but she was instantly aware of a new ease in him, a new dignity. Humble as ever he yet had an air of authority. His clothes had been well brushed by butler or valet, his top hat was immaculate. She read the signs and looked up at him with a smile of entrancing sweetness. He murmured a few gentle words of condolence and for a moment she wondered how she should accept this sympathy. With pathos, drooping on his arm like a bird with a broken wing, or with the truth? She decided for the truth. "You need not condole with me, sir," she said with bitterness. "I am thankful that my marriage has ended."

She had made the right decision. He was shocked, and a compassion so vast overwhelmed him that all diffidence, all sense of shame because of the past, was lost in it. He asked her if he might serve her in any way and she shook her head. He asked her if he might take her home and she accepted his offer. She took him up to Rosamond's pretty drawing-room, where the lamp had been lit and the tea table laid before the fire, and the two pretty women made much of him. He told Elaine that he was still a schoolmaster, in town for today only, but he would be spending his Christmas vacation here. Might he call upon her then? She smiled agreement as she bade him goodbye. After he had gone it transpired that Rosamond knew about him. He was now headmaster of a famous school. Her nephew had been caned by him. She seemed not to mind now if Elaine stayed with her till after Christmas.

Elaine conducted her distinguished lover through his second courtship with admirable skill, and as the days went by with real sincerity. The greatness of his love for her by turns touched, exasperated and frightened her, but she was grateful, for it was sweeping her to honour and security. And he was a good man. It was his sheer goodness, she realized now, that had touched her before, touched her innate fastidiousness. She believed herself utterly sick of carnal men. She would try to make him a good wife. She hoped that they might be happy. A week after Christmas he brought her a diamond ring and a bunch of violets, kneeling beside her to put them in her lap.

Then began that strange long sorrow that had worn them both down. Elaine did all she could. She possessed a sense of drama, of fitness and occasion, and only the most discerning guessed that she had not been born to the position she filled with such grace. She moved through her days with dignity and correctitude, a beautiful hostess and a mistress able to command the obedience if not the affection of her servants. She conducted her flirtations with such skill and decorum that again only the discerning were aware of them, and she was meticulously careful in all the outward observances of the religion that was her husband's life.

But that was all she could do. Adam's life, behind the façade of the material comforts and elegances they shared together, was something that he longed to open to her, but could not. Sometimes, stumblingly, he tried to speak of the things that were life to him, but she did not understand. Nor could he on his side understand that the luxuries that so desperately wearied him, that he endured only because his position in the world demanded it of him, were life to her. It would have been all right, she sometimes thought, if he could have stopped loving her, if they could have settled down together into that easy indifference that is the refuge of so many ill-assorted marriages, but they could not even share indifference, and his love, increasingly of the sort that she neither understood nor wanted, bored her almost to distraction. Her dislike of the love of carnal men had, she discovered, been only a passing ennui.

Yet she did not leave him. She wanted to, several times she had almost done so, especially when he had decided that instead of moving to London, chosen as the place of retirement because she loved London, they must come to the bleak city in the

K

fens. Over that they had a heartbreaking struggle. Adam, torn
between the will of his adored wife and what he finally came to
believe was the will of God, could make only the one decision.
She had not understood it, and she could not forgive him, but
he had a hold upon her that she could not break and she went
with him to the city.

But she was more unhappy now than she had ever been.
Until now her married life had been spent in places where there
were at times great social occasions and her surpassing beauty
could be arrayed and displayed worthily. In the little old city
such social occasions as existed were boring in the extreme.
Clothes were years behind the fashion and all the men who
were not parsons were over seventy. And the climate did not
suit her. She was not so well as she had been and not quite so
beautiful. She was in a panic about her beauty and so was her
husband, knowing that it was her axis. And about Elaine herself he was in anguish. He had loved her for so long, and it
seemed so unavailingly, and he had not made her happy. He
had, he thought, utterly failed her. He did not know what her
life had been before their marriage, and so was unaware of the
significance of that one fact that lay like a nugget of buried gold
at the heart of their life together. She was still with him, still a
woman who because of something in himself had remained
through all the weary years a decent woman and a faithful
wife. Those who had any affection for Adam Ayscough disliked Elaine. Even Miss Montague, who disliked no one and
would have taken Elaine to her heart had that been a place
where Elaine had the slightest wish to be, did not do her
justice. For there had been a battle and it had been, if hardly,
won.

The sermon ended at last and Elaine was aware through her
whole body of her husband's relief, his relaxation of tension.
Aware too, when he had gone to his canopied stall, of the reaction of misery that took its place. He would be impossible to
live with for the rest of the day now. He was never at any time
a cheerful man and after a sermon his depression was as im-

penetrable as a fen fog. When the last hymn had been sung, and the blessing given, and the organ voluntary was pealing under the vast arches and down the shadowy aisles striped with their dusty bars of sunshine, Elaine walked slowly and gracefully towards the side door that led into the Deanery garden. One gloved hand held her rustling silk skirts raised above the contamination of dust, the other held the beautiful ivory-backed prayer-book with its silver cross that her husband had given her to carry on her wedding day. It was a warmth to her chilled heart that every eye was on her, though not one of them was an eye worth having. Her way brought her past Miss Montague's bath-chair and the old lady looked up at her with a smile, wholeheartedly delighting in her beauty, even though a slightly mischievous sparkle in her eye recognized the histrionic perfection of Elaine's exit. Elaine inclined her head graciously but coldly. She could not stand Miss Montague. Upon the rare occasions when Adam went to call on the old lady every fibre in her body knew it.

CHAPTER 9   *The Mouse*

I

EVENSONG on Sundays was at three o'clock and was sometimes followed by one of the Deanery tea parties to the élite
of the Close and Worship Street. These parties on the whole
gave pleasure for the sandwiches and cakes melted in the
mouth, Elaine no matter how bored was always a good hostess,
and the Dean's painstaking courtesy was less alarming at his
wife's parties than at other people's because being less shy in
his own house he was also less hard of hearing. Yet at the same
time there was for the guests a sense of relief when it was over
and they could emerge safely from the Deanery portal without,
they hoped, having appeared too ignorant and dowdy in the
presence of the Dean's vast learning and his wife's elegance.
Out in the Close there was a tendency for them all to chatter,
even when they were not the chattering type. Like children let
out of school the making of a joyful noise was a psychological
need. A few of them felt a strong desire to go and see Miss
Montague; indeed Miss Montague always knew when there had
been a Deanery party because of the number of droppers-in
from which she suffered. "I was passing the door, my dear. I
thought I'd just look in." She was pleased to see them, but
always very tired on Sunday evenings because going to the

Cathedral in her bath-chair was rather an exhausting business.

For Adam Ayscough and his wife, after their guests had gone and Garland had replenished the fire and closed the drawing-room door noiselessly upon their loneliness, there was no sense of relief. They were perhaps at their happiest together when they were entertaining, for in this they worked as a team. Left to face the long Sunday evening together a sense of hopeless-ness, almost of panic, took hold of them. If Adam could have immersed himself in *The Spectator* Elaine could have taken her French novel and buried herself in that, but it was his habit to sit beside her on the sofa, to take her hand and stroke it mad-deningly while he made heartrending efforts to talk to her, to amuse her, to reach her at last. She longed to cry out, "You fool, there's nothing to reach," but that would have been to hurt him. She was almost thankful tonight to find the first light hammer strokes of one of her headaches beating on her fore-head. "Adam," she said, "I am so sorry but I have one of my heads. I think I'll go to bed before dinner."

He got up from the sofa in a condition of distress out of all proportion to the seriousness of her indisposition. That was another irritating thing about Adam; he got into such a ridi-culous state if she ailed. "My dear, I am so sorry." He took her in his arms, tender and clumsy, and with one heavy hand pushed the hair back from her forehead, shattering her coiffure so that she would be ashamed to face her maid when she went upstairs. "My dear, I wish you need not suffer so. I would give my right hand that you need not be always ill," he said sadly.

She knew that he spoke the truth and she tried not to grit her teeth. "I shall be quite well in the morning," she said. "Will you ring and tell Garland that I shall not want dinner? I will go now, Adam."

He took his arms from her reluctantly and let her go, and rang the bell for Garland. That worthy, entering, found the Dean standing with his back to the fire, his huge form drooping disconsolately. "Mrs. Ayscough is unwell, Garland. She has gone to her room and will not take dinner."

"I am sorry to hear it, sir," said Garland and proceeded to deal with the familiar situation with suavity and skill. He had been with the Dean for many years and was one of the very few who had come close enough to him to love him. He was unaware of his love but he would not have left the Dean for untold gold. "What would you fancy for dinner, sir?" he asked, knowing very well that when his wife was indisposed and he himself had just preached a sermon the Dean fancied nothing. "Grilled sole, sir? A glass of white wine? A lightly baked custard settles well, sir."

"Thank you, Garland," said the Dean.

"It's a nice evening, sir," suggested Garland. A breath of fresh air always did good. And he knew what would happen if the Dean did not go out. He would sit the whole evening with *The Spectator* held unread before his eyes, for appearance sake if a servant should come in, and worry about his wife until he could go to bed. He was a writer of scholarly books, and writing was his lifeline in times of distress, but on Sundays, bound by the Commandments, he could not write his book. Nor could he read the kind of book that helped him with his book, because that too was work, and other books did not hold his attention when Elaine was not well. There was of course the great duty and privilege of prayer, and to prayer he most humbly believed himself to be especially called of God, but on Sunday evenings after a long day of services he found it difficult to pray. He was tired, he supposed. Garland knew all this. "A very pleasant evening indeed, sir."

The curtains were still undrawn and the Dean looked at the evening. The trees in the Close were black and motionless against a clear sky. The moon was rising and presently there would be a blaze of stars. "I think I will take a little stroll," he said.

"Very good, sir," said Garland, and following the Dean out into the hall he helped him into the cloak that he liked to wear on his lonely walks. It was an old friend and shabby now. He could not wear it when Elaine was with him. Garland noticed

that he was a very bad colour. He was always sallow but now
his face had a leaden hue that Garland did not like at all. He
had been noticing it for some while and so had Miss Montague. "Dinner can wait your convenience, sir," he said.
"Grilled sole. Baked custard. They can be prepared when you
come in." He handed the Dean his top hat and stick, opened
the front door and saw him out. Then he came back to the
drawing-room to draw the curtains and tidy the cushions. The
Dean when he came in would go to the study. The drawing-
room fire which Garland had built up with such care would
now be wasted, and so would the dinner which cook had prepared for two. But that was the way of it with the gentry. Their
servants had to learn to accept wasted effort with equanimity.

The Dean walked slowly down the lime avenue. It was cool
and quiet. Though the moon had not yet appeared from behind the Rollo tower there was a silveriness about the branches
of the trees, magic in the air, a sensation as though bells that
could not be heard were still ringing somewhere. There was no
wind tonight and the city was silent. Over the fen the dome of
the sky was quiet, vexed with no cloudwrack, dark and vast.
Just over the edge of the horizon the dark sea breathed gently
and caressed the shore.

The Dean sat down for a moment on the seat in the lime
walk where Isaac had sat, his head bent, too tired to be much
aware of the beauty of the night but vaguely quieted, vaguely
ashamed of his own shame. What did it matter if he was incapable of preaching a decent sermon? Why be ashamed of
failure? Failure was unimportant. The fact was that mounting
the pulpit steps, standing there before all those bored men and
women who like the hungry sheep in Lycidas looked up and
were not fed, had become to him a sort of symbol of the failure
of his life. As priest and husband he had failed. They said he
had been a good schoolmaster but he believed them to be
wrong. His apparent success there had been due he believed
solely to a formidable presence. He had always been able to
impose discipline because people were afraid of him. There was

of course that other thing, that power that had been given him
of taking hold of an evil situation, wrestling with it, shaking it as
a terrier shakes a rat until the evil fell out of it and fastened on
himself. Then he carried the evil on his own shoulders to the
place of prayer, carried it up a long hill in darkness, but will-
ingly. Each time he felt himself alone, yet each time when the
weight became too much for him it was shared, then lifted, as
though he had never been alone. Yet if there had been no hope
of help he would still have been just as willing. But in that
mystery nothing was his own except the willingness, and willingness in no way mitigated failure. Nothing mitigated failure
except the knowledge that it did not matter. But how could he
bring himself to think it did not matter that he had failed
Elaine? It was impossible.

He got up abruptly and walked on through the Porta and
across Worship Street. At the top of Angel Lane he stopped.
The city lay at his feet, its tumbled roofs washed with moonlight, its dark walls patched with squares of orange fireglow.
The men and women in the houses would have been astonished
to know that the Dean knew the city like the palm of his hand.
In earlier years, when he had it in his grip and most men hated
him, he would go out into the streets night after night after
dark, when he could not be recognized, and walk up and down
there. After a month or two he knew every corner and alley as
well as Miss Montague knew them. The evil was more dreadful
in one street than another, and to these places he would return
again and again, exposing himself to them. He would stand in
dark doorways and pray there for the men and women within
the shuttered houses. If he lacked the common touch, if he was
not the priest he had longed to be, this at least he could do.
Sometimes, trudging wearily home up the hill, he would remember Michael towering above him in the dark sky, and
would be aware of some sort of communication, as though
Michael asked him, "Watchman, what of the night?"

Sometimes, when he got home on moonlight nights, he would
let himself into the Cathedral through his private door that he

might bring the needs of the city before God before he slept. For he loved the Cathedral as few men had ever loved it, more deeply even than William de la Torre who had built it or Prior Hugh who had died within it or Dean Peter Rollard who had been persecuted for it, or Tom Hochicorn the bedesman of the south door who thought he owned it. What it was like at night, with the moonlight piercing through the clerestory windows to illumine the great rood and gleams of silver touching now here and now there as the clouds passed, and the rest vast darkness, only he knew. But he could not have told what he knew.

2

Tonight, looking down at the city, he found himself thinking of one citizen only, Isaac Peabody. He had not seen him again for when Isaac had next come to wind the Deanery clocks he had been once more at matins. He wanted to ask him if in future he could wind the clocks a little later in the morning, so that they could have a few moments' weekly conversation together on the subject of horology, and he wanted to ask if he had in his shop a clock suitable for Elaine's Christmas present, some lovely thing such as Miss Montague's Lyre clock. He was always thinking of something new to give Elaine, some exquisite new thing to adorn her beauty. She always thanked him charmingly for the new jewel or the new fan but he did not often see again the treasure he had chosen for her and then he was sorry, for he knew his taste had blundered. But surely she would like a new clock. The cupid clock in the drawing-room, a relic of the disaster of her French marriage, she must surely dislike. He thought it was a dreadful thing. He wondered what Peabody thought of it.

He remembered suddenly that Isaac lived in Angel Lane at number twelve. He knew because he had asked Garland. He thought he would just stroll down the lane and see which of the old houses was number twelve. He would not go in, for it would be much easier for them both if he went to the shop, but he would just see where his friend lived. He would walk past,

go down the steps to the market place and then home up
Worship Street.

He found the house easily for the street lamp opposite
illumined the number. The front door was slightly ajar and
warm light spilled itself down the two worn steps and shone
diagonally across the pavement and the cobbles. It was the
only open door in the street. The Dean as a boy had had a re-
current dream about a little old house in a crooked street. Two
steps had led to its door, set in a small arch like this one, and
always it had been a night with stars in the sky and this light
spilling out over the pavement and across the cobbled street. To
the boy who had dreamed the dream, a small boy without a
mother and as an only child much addicted to dreams, it had
always seemed that something he wanted very much was inside
the house but he had been too shy to push the door and go in.
So he had knocked and waited. But no one had ever answered
his knock. Always he had said to himself, next time that dream
comes I will push the door. Yet when next time came he was
still afraid, and had knocked and waited, and then woken up.
Then he had been sent to boarding school and dreams had given
place to nightmares.

The Dean knocked timidly and waited, aware of laughter
somewhere in the house, but no one came, and then with that
boldness of panic that can precipitate even a shy person into the
wildest of actions, he pushed the door and went in. If he had
not done it quickly he would, once more, have woken up. Inside the little passage he suddenly, appallingly, came to himself, but it was too late. He had lost his footing on something
which slid from beneath him, and crashed into the umbrella
stand and sent it flying. He had also practically lost his own
balance. His top hat fell from his head and his walking stick
to the floor to join the stick and the vast umbrella of the
Reverend Robert Peabody.

The half-open kitchen door, through which the light had
been shining, flew wide, and Isaac, Polly and Job came hurrying into the passage. The Dean was too shaken to speak. He

did not know what had happened to him out there in the street
and he did not know how he came to be where he was now. He
had seemed to fall out of time. It was as though he had left his
body for a moment or two and coming back to it again had
found it not where he had thought it was. Isaac, unable to believe that he was seeing what he saw, bewildered and dumb-
founded, could not speak either. Job had melted back into the
kitchen. Polly alone remained in command of the unusual
circumstances.

She had never seen the Dean, only heard him in a rage that
one time at the workhouse, and so he was to her simply an old
codger who had slipped on the wool mat outside the parlour
door. In the light that shone from the kitchen she thought he
looked poor, ill and old and immediately, figuratively speaking,
took him to her bosom. "You've come to see Mr. Peabody,
sir?" she said. "You're welcome. You've not hurt yourself?
You slipped on the mat. Mr. Peabody, he's always doing the
same. Miss Peabody, she will make 'em. Let me take your
cloak, sir."

While she spoke she had been swiftly picking up the scattered
umbrella and sticks and restoring the passage to rights. Now
she gently took the Dean's cloak from him, hung it with his top
hat upon a peg and ushered him into the kitchen.

When she had him there, divested of the shabby cloak, she
saw that his clothes were of fine black broadcloth such as gentlemen wear. He wore white bands beneath his chin, over his
waistcoat, and his hands were very clean. She thought he
looked like a Beak and for a moment of dreadful terror she
wondered if Job, who had disappeared, had done anything.
With a blanched face she looked up at the Dean and saw her
own terror reflected in his eyes.

"It is the Dean, it is Doctor Ayscough," said Isaac, who was
recovering himself. "Another chair, Polly."

The relief was so intense that colour flooded into Polly's face
and still looking at the Dean she smiled, her eyes shining. Only
the Dean, not a Beak. Then she picked up a duster from the

dresser and carefully dusted a chair for him. "Please to sit down, sir," she said, and she was still smiling at him. She knew she should not be smiling at the gentry, but she had taken him to her heart in the passage; she remembered the splendid anger and could not help herself. The Dean thought he had never in his life received a sweeter, warmer welcome than from this child. He was trembling with anxiety lest he do something, say something, to frighten her or Peabody and break this dream that seemed to him a most fugitive thing, like a soap bubble. He was inside it now but the least clumsiness on his part and he would be outside.

"I hope I do not come at an inconvenient hour, Mr. Peabody," he said. "Would you, may I, will you permit me to share your meal with you?"

He was so obviously scared that Isaac could not help realizing that he was in the extraordinary position of having to set the greatly feared Dean at his ease. Courage came to him and a queer emotion which he did not until afterwards recognize as that compassion which Doctor Ayscough had once before aroused in him, and he managed to say that it was an honour, to explain that Emma was out and that in her absence they were having late tea in the kitchen instead of the parlour.

"I prefer the kitchen," said the Dean, accepting a large cup of strong sweet tea from Polly. "Mr. Peabody, was there not a boy here? I thought I heard young voices chiming together when I came in."

"It was Job," said Isaac. "Polly, where's Job?"

"He might be in the scullery with the cat," said Polly. "Job, are you there?"

There was a movement and the Dean, looking up, saw Job standing in the doorway with a large black cat dangling from his arms. He liked boys and some of them in his schoolmastering days had actually come to know it. Instantly he liked Job, though he did not identify him with the chimney sweep of years ago. He liked the square thin face with the high cheek bones, the defiant sensitive mouth and wary, dark eyes, one of which

had been blackened by a blow. The boy's clothes were ragged
and smelt strongly of fish; which was possibly why the cat was
purring so contentedly. But his black brows were drawn together and he was obviously not intending to advance farther
than the scullery door.

"That's your chair, Job," said the Dean, nodding towards
the chair on the other side of Isaac. "If you do not come back
and finish that piece of cake I shall not be able to forgive myself that I called upon Mr. Peabody at this unprecedented
hour."

The Dean had never yet been disobeyed by a boy, and did
not expect to be. Job came across the room and slid into his
chair, but he could not lift his eyes from his plate. He had
recognized the old man instantly and was terribly upset. That
great figure of his dreams had through the years become so exclusively his own that it had been a profound shock to find him
here in this house, to find he was the Dean of the city, a man to
whom Job Mooring could in the world of reality mean nothing
whatever. It was obvious that he meant nothing to the Dean
because he did not remember him. The man of his dreams
would have remembered him. Yet there could not be two men.
One of them must be false, and the man sitting on the other side
of the table was real enough. It was the great figure of his
dreams who was false, and if he was false so was Job's world. A
depth of anguish opened inside him, and fear. Bereaved of his
chief strength and consolation he seemed to have lost himself.
It was his first experience of the frightening sense of lost
identity.

The Dean was aware, suddenly, of danger, and almost in the
same moment he perceived a robin beside his cup and saucer.
It was as though someone nudged him and pointed it out. With
a sudden exclamation he perched his eyeglasses on the summit
of his nose and picked it up. It was shaped out of a rough bit of
wood, its breast and wings coloured perhaps with the juice of
wild berries. It was an earthy thing, not the robin of a Christmas card but like one of the birds that a craftsman of William

de la Torre's day had carved under the miserere seats in the choir, a wild and living creature that had been not so much carved from wood as liberated from it. The Dean turned it round and round in his big ugly hands, silent in delight, for he loved birds. He remained absorbed in it until Polly put a chaffinch by his plate. Then he put the robin down and picked up the chaffinch with reverence. Then he peered short-sightedly round the table. There was a mouse beside the jam pot and a snail by the bowl of dripping. There was a willow wren of shy and slender elegance but no lark. The Dean turned to Isaac. "There's no lark. Ah, but you put the lark on top of Miss Montague's Lyre clock. Mr. Peabody, I am dumb in the presence of your genius."

The Dean was astonished at Isaac's delight. His seamed old face was flushed, his eyes sparkled and the rubicund point of his button nose was a point of fire. The delight seemed excessive for a few words of appreciation. "Not me, sir," said Isaac. "Job."

The Dean was not sure that he heard aright and he leaned forward with his hand behind his ear, as forgetful of the nuisance the deaf can be as he had already been forgetful, when he helped himself to a large piece of bread and butter, that he could never fancy food on a sermon Sunday. "Eh?" he asked.

"Job made them," said Isaac, raising his voice. "That boy there. Job Mooring." The Dean turned his gaze on the boy, his hand still absentmindedly behind his ear, his sad eyes kindling. "Job Mooring," he repeated. "Job Mooring."

The reiteration had an extraordinary strength about it, like the grip of his hand on Job's shoulder long ago. It gave back the lost identity and Job lifted his head and looked straight across the table at the Dean. It was years before he was to realize that a sense of identity is the gift of love, and only love can give it, but for the rest of his life he was to remember this moment and be able to recall at will the tones of the harsh deep voice, the kindling in the eyes. It was the moment when life began for him, real life, the life of spirit and of genius which his world had foreshadowed. Years later, when silence was called for him and he rose to make his first speech as Master of the Clockmakers' Company, he was suddenly back again in the city in the fen country, hearing his name spoken by the old Dean. He sat tongue-tied, his face white but as vividly alive as white flame.

"The boy must be your pupil, Peabody," said the Dean after a moment or two. "Your apprentice?"

"No, sir," said Isaac. "I never set eyes on Job till today, except just that one time when I saw him looking in through my shop window at the cuckoo clock. During divine service this morning I found that mouse by the coal scuttle. Then Job, he came in this afternoon, knowing my sister was out, and Job and Polly they showed me what he'd made for her. No, sir, I've no apprentice, though many's the time I've thought I'd find one handy. Could you fancy some dripping, sir? It's good beef dripping."

The Dean helped himself and said, "Are you apprenticed, Job?"

Job nodded speechlessly and Polly spoke up for him. "To Albert Lee the fishmonger, in Swithins Lane by the North Gate. Him what has that stall in the market, sir."

"I know Swithins Lane," said the Dean thoughtfully. "And I've noticed the shop. Do you like gutting fish, Job?"

"No, sir," whispered Job.

"Have you ever been in the Cathedral?"

"No, sir."

"One day perhaps you will let me show you the carvings there. Have you ever seen a watch like this?"

He unfastened his watch from its chain and handed it across to Job. "Mr. Peabody, will you show him how to open it? I would like him to see the watchcock."

Isaac's bald head and Job's dark one were bent together over the watch. Job held it, his brown fingers trembling a little, while Isaac explained the mechanism, pointing out the great beauties of this loveliest of all watches, mentioning with pride that he had been an apprentice not far from the workshop where this watch had been made. Job's face grew wholly absorbed in wonder, like the face of a child seeing its first candle. Isaac's had a great tenderness and as he talked he watched Job as though he knew every thought, and was aware of every tremor, in the mind and body of a boy who sees a perfect piece of mechanism for the first time in his life. To hold a marvellous new thing is to a boy as though he held the world, and to touch or take it from him can drive him to frenzy. Isaac was oblivious of everything except the boy and the watch. The boy was oblivious of everything except the watch. The Dean turned to Polly but she was absorbed in the boy. Sooty was in front of the fire, one leg erected like a lamp post, intent upon washing his hind quarters.

The Dean sat back in his chair and was content to be forgotten. He felt suddenly exhausted, yet thankful. So far it seemed he had not blundered, and he had confidence that he would not, for it seemed to him that the thing was not in his hands, and had not been from the moment he had entered Angel Lane. Although his Cathedral was dedicated not only to Michael but to all the angels he had never thought very much about them. Legends, miracles, guardian angels, holy wells, relics and demons had been somewhat lumped together in his scholarly mind as irrelevancies to the great truths of his faith. But now he had a strange sensation that those walls of which he had been aware, thinking of them as the soap bubble walls of a dream, were not so fragile as he had thought. The odd thought came to him that four people and a cat were held within the containing wall of eight great wings. Not even the cat would leave this room until the wings chose. He reminded himself that he was unusually tired tonight.

Polly was the first to remember the presence of the distinguished visitor, but not for his own sake. Her eyes were full of a pleading so fierce that it startled him. He smiled at her, and she recognized the extraordinary contortion of his facial muscles as the assurance of understanding it was meant to be, and smiled back. Then Isaac remembered where he was and Job sighed deeply, closed the watch and gave it back to the Dean. His lips moved but no sound came.

"Would you like to be a clockmaker, Job?" asked the Dean.

"Yes, sir," said Job hoarsely, and then suddenly he pushed his chair back and dived for the scullery. They heard him dragging at the back door and Isaac called out, "Stop, Job!" and Polly ran after him. But it was too late. He had banged the back door behind him and they heard him running down the street. Isaac and Polly were in distress but the Dean remained unperturbed. Job would not have got through the retaining wall had not a wing been deliberately raised to let him through.

"You see, sir," said Polly, "Dobson's apprenticed Job to fish. He's got two more years, sir, and Albert knocks him about something cruel."

"If he was apprenticed to me," said Isaac eagerly, "I could make that boy such a clockmaker as we haven't had since Tompion's day."

"If you by yourself try and take Job from the fish you'll be had up before the Beak and put in quod," said Polly. "Likely you'll be hanged."

"I do not entirely understand the legalities of apprenticeship," said the Dean, "but I feel sure that Mr. Peabody's wishes could be met without quite such disastrous consequences to himself as you envisage for him. I feel sure that were it made worth his while Mr. Lee would be willing to relinquish Job. I will consult Mr. Havelock, our Cathedral solicitor. I will do so tomorrow. Will you be content to leave the matter in our hands, Mr. Peabody?"

"I shouldn't like to put you to any trouble, sir," said Isaac unhappily. "Nor to any expense. It wouldn't be right, sir."

"There's Job to be considered, Mr. Peabody," said the Dean. Isaac took his pipe from his pocket and twisted it about in his fingers, a habit of his when he was worried. His great domed forehead was wrinkled and his little beard wagged distressfully.

L

"I like boys," the Dean went on, "and since I retired from schoolmastering it has been little in my power to serve them."

Isaac yielded. "Thank you, sir," he said, "and I give you my word that I'll do my best for the boy."

"May I smoke a pipe with you before I go, Mr. Peabody?" asked the Dean. "I see that you smoke yourself."

"Turn your chairs to the fire," said Polly in a maternal tone, "while I clear."

The two men obeyed her. Their feet stretched to the comfortable warmth, their pipes alight, the cat between them, they arranged that Isaac should wind the Deanery clocks a little later every Saturday morning, to allow for a short instruction in horology, and that one day in the near future the Dean should visit the shop to choose a Christmas gift for Mrs. Ayscough. Then they talked clocks. Beside the kitchen mantelpiece hung a large wooden clock with a slow and solemn tick. Its big round dial was of wood, painted black, with gilt numerals, and below it was a plain wooden trunk to hold the pendulum.

"Compared to that ruffled courtier the Michael Neuwers, or to that dryad the Lyre clock, it's like an old woodsman, a peasant," said the Dean. "But I like its honest ugly face. What is its age, Mr. Peabody?"

"Getting on for a hundred years," said Isaac. "It's a Parliament clock. When William Pitt put a tax on clocks and watches, so that only the rich could afford 'em, the tavern keepers put these clocks in the taverns so that poor men could tell the time. There was vileness for you, sir! Taxing clocks and watches! A wicked man, that Pitt."

"Also a great man," said the Dean.

Isaac growled savagely. "Great! A man that brings clock and watchmakers nearly to ruin? The watches that were broken up! Men couldn't afford to carry 'em. Enough to break your heart. Watchcocks torn out and made into necklaces! Dreadful! But he's an honest old clock, my Parliament. Keeps good time."

While they talked Polly's quick light footsteps went backwards and forwards between kitchen and scullery. Then came the tinkle of washing up and little snatches of song, accompanied by the deep rumbling of one of Sooty's organ fugues. Michael struck, echoed by the Parliament clock and the Time and Death clock, but neither man paid any attention. Two oddities as they were, accustomed like the white blackbird to the loneliness of eccentricity yet never quite reconciled to it, they found in each other's oddness a most comforting compatibility.

Isaac was so at ease that he forgot that his companion was the Dean, but the Dean did not quite forget that Isaac was the clockmaker, a poor man as his world counted poverty, and his heart glowed. Presently Polly came in and sat down near them, just behind Isaac, and because it was Sunday, when she was not allowed to do any sewing, for once she sat with her hands in her lap. The Dean, as he talked to Isaac, was very much aware of her in her spotless white Sunday apron and a big mob cap that nearly obliterated her small, bright-eyed face. She sat very still as though to be able to do so was a pleasure that she held in her folded hands upon her lap, and though she held herself upright she was yet entirely relaxed. She was happy, he realized, for she had transferred the problem of Job's future from her own shoulders to his, and she had entire trust in him. This for the Dean was a familiar situation, but the burden in this case was not a heavy one and he could share her quietness. He might have been there for another half-hour had not Emma entered upon them. They had not heard her come. They only knew she was there because a shadow fell upon them, sad and strange.

Emma knew the Dean quite well by sight, for he had sometimes taken the chair at meetings which she attended and she had a great respect for him. Could she have entertained Doctor Ayscough in the parlour it would have been the proudest day of her life. But it was Isaac who was entertaining him, in the kitchen in his shirtsleeves and smoking a pipe; and that little hussy Polly was with them, daring to sit down in the presence of her betters. And upon the dresser was a collection of cheap little wooden toys. These things Emma saw as though in a clear picture, as it is said the drowning see their past life passing before them, and then she was submerged in a dark wave of jealousy and shame, and the picture began to disintegrate. Sooty leapt for the mantelpiece, Polly for the scullery. Isaac scrambled to his feet trying to hide his pipe, his hands trembling as he looked desperately about him for his coat. The Dean rose, his tall black figure seeming to Emma to fill the whole room, knocked out his pipe and bowed to her. Isaac stammered something and he held out his hand and Emma, drowning, caught at it.

The Dean knew she was drowning and held her hand in a firm grip until she had a little recovered herself. As he greeted her he was aware of much; of Isaac's fear of his sister and her contempt for him, of the despair in this woman's mind and her loveless rectitude. "Your brother is going to provide me with a clock for my wife's Christmas gift," he said. "It will be a great privilege to possess an Isaac Peabody clock. We are proud of your brother in the city. We are very proud that so fine an artist lives amongst us. May I bid you good-night, Miss Peabody, and my thanks for the happy hour I have spent in your home. Much obliged." He was in the passage now and she heard him talking to Isaac. "Will you convey to the little Polly my grateful thanks for the excellent tea? Havelock shall attend to that matter of the boy. Good-night. Much obliged."

Isaac and Polly returned to the kitchen in characteristic fashion, Isaac with the slow seep of a guilty conscience, for his coat was nowhere to hand, Polly with the alacrity of a quiet one, for she considered she had a perfect right to sit down in her own kitchen on a Sunday evening. If the gentry chose to invade it that was not her fault. Both had returned for the sole purpose of defending the other. Knowing this Emma stood between them slowly removing her cloak and drawing off her black kid gloves. Isaac had entertained the great Dean to tea in the kitchen in his shirtsleeves. He had praised Isaac, and sent an almost affectionate message to Polly. Shame and jealousy tore at her, and hatred that seemed almost a physical thing rose like a surge of hot blood from her breast to her throat and would have strangled her had she not given it an outlet. With a savage and skilful gesture she swept the little wooden toys off the dresser into the black silk apron she wore and flung them on the fire.

CHAPTER 10 *Bella*

I

Iₙ the reaction of next morning the Dean was not so sure about
those angelic wings and could only trust that he had not
done great harm. He was well aware that his visit had seriously
disturbed Miss Peabody, and that in escaping from her himself
he had left Isaac and Polly behind him to bear the brunt of
whatever it was he had unwittingly stirred up. He should have
remained and talked with her a little. The fact was that she
had much alarmed him and he had fled. Fear he was accustomed to, for he was not inside himself the fearless man that his
height and courage had led men to suppose, but by the grace of
God he had not until yesterday run away from what alarmed
him. Miss Peabody had taken him by surprise, entering suddenly upon a moment of relaxation when his armour, so to speak,
was on the floor. Yet he was deeply ashamed for relaxation,
while life lasted and evil endured, was not permissible except
in prayer in the presence of God. The poor woman was not
evil, she was he believed highly virtuous, but she was not good
and the absence of love left a most dangerous vacuum. "Much
ashamed, much ashamed," he murmured, and knew that
when opportunity offered he must go and see her, though he did
not want to. He said to himself that Miss Montague in urging

him to take a little joy had forgotten the alarming contingency of life. The gentle stream of his friendship with Peabody was showing every sign of developing into a roaring cataract.

And now he must see Havelock about the boy. "Where does Mr. Havelock live, Garland?" he asked as Garland helped him into his cloak to go to matins.

"Mr. Abraham Havelock lives at number twenty Worship Street, sir," said Garland. "His son Mr. Giles at number seventeen. But their office is in the market place, sir."

"I want to see Mr. Abraham Havelock after matins," said the Dean. "Will he be at home or at the office?"

"On a Monday morning, at home, sir," said Garland, who knew every detail of the private lives of the inhabitants of the Close and Worship Street by a process of suction, his mind lifting the knowledge out of the sacred ground of the ecclesiastical precincts as the sun draws vapour from the earth. "Being elderly Mr. Abraham leaves Monday morning to Mr. Giles. Monday morning at an office can be difficult, sir."

"No doubt, no doubt," said the Dean. "Thank you, Garland. Much obliged."

"I'll send a message, sir," said Garland.

"Message?" asked the Dean.

"Asking Mr. Abraham Havelock to wait upon you, sir."

"I thank you, no," said the Dean. "I will wait upon Mr. Havelock."

And he went away to matins leaving Garland much perturbed, for it was contrary to all his ideas of propriety that the Dean should wait upon anybody except the Bishop and Miss Montague. Nor, skilfully trained by Garland, had he done so before. Garland was not happy as he washed up the breakfast silver in his pantry. The Dean was most unaccountable just now. And Garland rather disliked these queer warm spells in late autumn. Indian summers, he believed people called them. For the first time in his life he dropped a silver spoon upon the floor and stooping to pick it up bumped his head on the draining board. He could have wept.

Matins over the Dean forged his way down Worship Street, peering shortsightedly from side to side in an effort to locate number twenty, oblivious of those who touched their hats to him, talking to himself. "Much ashamed, much ashamed," he said, for he had just realized that for many years past he had been guilty of a most contemptible arrogance. Why should he expect doctors, solicitors, bank managers and the humbler clergy (though not dentists owing to obvious technical difficulties) always to wait upon him as though he were a crowned head? He was not. He was a humble servant of the Master who had girded himself with a towel and knelt on the floor to wash the feet of twelve poor men. Abbot William de la Torre, and all the abbots and priors after him down to Prior Hugh, had done the same every Maundy Thursday, but he did not, nor did he think the twelve old men at the almshouses would appreciate the gesture if he should try to do so. Times changed and there was no greater tyranny that that of social custom, but he was to blame that he had let it fasten about him with quite such octopus strength. He would try now, God helping him, to loosen the coils a little.

He was at number twenty. It was at the humbler end of the beautiful winding Georgian street, the end nearest the market place. Those who had at one time resided in the Close lived at the Cathedral end, the slightly less privileged at the town end, poised as it were on the delicate tight-rope between trade and gentility. But the houses at the town end of Worship Street were just as beautiful as the others, if a little smaller. They lacked the porches and fluted pillars of the larger houses but they had fanlights over their front doors, white doorsteps snowily scrubbed, beautifully spaced windows kept scrupulously clean and shining and an air of contented solid comfort that was very reassuring. They did not look like houses in which anything could go very wrong. To pass them was to think of shining beeswaxed floors, pots of jelly on a scrubbed shelf and a walled garden behind the house where nectarines grew on the south wall. None of the houses in Worship Street was quite the same. Some had two windows on each side of the front door, others only one. Virginia creeper grew on some, wistaria on others. Number twenty was covered with a vine whose leaves were now deep crimson and pale gold. They made a brilliant setting for the green front door and the brightly polished brass knocker.

The Dean knocked and stood waiting, and he was conscious of a sudden lightness of heart that a little overcame his nervousness, for in spite of its Georgian dignity there was something about this trim gay exterior that reminded him of a doll's house. He had of course never possessed a doll's house, but in his childhood there had been a little girl who had one, a child with a blue bow in her hair, and out of the mist of the ages he remembered that it had been a green door, or was it a blue door? He was trying to remember when suddenly, noiselessly, this one opened, letting out the warm scent of geraniums and the piercing cacophony of a canary rejoicing in the beauty of the day. The rosy-cheeked maid who opened the door wore a pink print dress and a mob cap and apron and was so terrified when she saw the Dean that her wits deserted her.

"Is Mr. Abraham Havelock at home?" asked the Dean sepulchrally.

"Yes, sir. No, sir. Yes, sir. Will you please to come in?"

"Mr. Abraham Havelock is disengaged?"

"No, sir. Yes. I mean Squire Richards is with him, in from the fen. But he can go away and come later. I'll tell Mr. Havelock, sir."

"Do no such thing, I beg," said the Dean. "I would not wish to discommode the squire, who has come from far. I will wait. I am quite at leisure, quite at leisure." He looked a little helplessly at the scared little maid. "Could I sit here in the hall?"

But at this preposterous suggestion she came to her senses. "O no, sir! Mr. Havelock would not think that right. Will you please to sit in the dining-room? There's a fire there."

"Much obliged, much obliged," said the Dean, and was

ushered into a room at the right of the front door, and into the
presence of the canary.

When he came to himself a little, for even for his deaf ears the
noise was terrible, he found he still had his top hat on his head
and was grasping his stick, for he and the little maid had both
been too nervous to separate him from them in the hall. Much
distressed he laid them beside his chair on the floor. The room
was bright and warm and geranium-scented, and would have
been quiet but for the canary. Just by him on the mantelpiece
there was a clock that was probably ticking but he could not be
sure because of the canary. He got up to look at it. It was a
very elegant pedestal clock surmounted by two little brass owls.
He was thankful for their silence. He sat down again. The room
was very warm and the canary very loud. His head ached and
presently he closed his eyes.

Something touched him. He opened his eyes and saw what
he thought was a starfish lying on his knee. Intensely surprised he looked closer and saw it was a small hand. Almost
afraid to look lest the apparition vanish he put his eyeglasses on
his nose and dared to lift his gaze a little higher. A small girl
was planted sturdily before him. She wore a starched muslin
frock with short puffed sleeves and a frill round the neck. A
blue sash encircled that part of her anatomy where in later years
a waist would possibly develop, and her yellow curls were kept
out of her eyes with a snood of blue ribbon. She was plump,
with bracelets of fat round her wrists and a double chin. He
could not guess her age but as her chest was about on a level
with his knee he thought it to be tender. But she appeared to
have plenty of self-confidence and *savoir faire* and was addressing him with great fluency, though he could not hear what she
said because of the canary. She was not afraid of him.

Awe and trembling took the Dean. He had always adored
small children, especially little girls, but no one had ever known
it. Elaine thought he disliked them as much as she did, and
even Miss Montague had never guessed that he had this hidden
idolatry. For idolatry it was. Children to him were beings of

another world. The sight of one stabbed him to the heart, but he never dared to come too close to the heavenly delicacy and innocence that might be frightened and corrupted by his ugliness and sin. Children, he had always thought, were little angels, and had not Bella laid her hand upon his knee he might have continued in this misconception until the end of his days.

She was now gesturing towards the canary with one fat hand and shaking his knee with the other, and he realized that some stupidity on his part was causing her annoyance. She wished him to take action of some sort and her commands had fallen upon ears both deaf and deafened. He cleared his throat, painfully anxious to assure her of his desire to serve her, but she suddenly turned her back on him and darted away, making for the first time her woman's discovery that it is generally quicker to do a thing yourself than to ask a man to do it. Grabbing the velvet cloth from a small table as she passed it she leaped into the big chair beside the canary's cage and swarmed up its padded back, revealing as she did so that she wore the most enchanting lace-trimmed undergarments. Poised on top of the chair back, in an attitude of such extreme danger that the Dean's heart nearly stopped, she flung the velvet cloth over the canary's cage. Instantly there was silence, and seldom had silence seemed to the Dean more heavenly. But it was shortlived. Bella, throwing a glance of triumph over her shoulder at the incompetent male, overbalanced, rolled down the chair and off it on to the floor, where she lay and roared in a welter of frills and blue ribbons.

The Dean came hurrying over to her in much anguish of spirit but just as he reached her she stopped roaring and sat up, for she was not, she found, so badly hurt as she had thought she was. Virtue was not Bella's strong point but she had grit. Nevertheless she had bumped her head and she put her hand to her curls and hiccoughed.

"My dear child," said the Dean, assisting her gently and reverently to her feet, "have you a nurse whom I can summon?

I think that I should ring the bell." He looked round him anxiously. "Is there a bell?"

But Bella was suddenly herself again. Pushing him vigorously towards his chair she commanded loudly, "Sit on your knee." Having got him in the correct position she climbed there and said, "Kiss it." The Dean, his hand behind his ear, was at a loss. "Where I'm bumped," she said and placed the first finger of her right hand against a fat yellow curl behind her right ear. He kissed the curl, moved by the most extraordinary emotion, and the canary let out a tentative trill beneath the velvet cloth. "Stop that noise, Birdie!" called Bella shrilly.

"Is it kind to cover him up?" asked the Dean anxiously.

"Her," said Bella. "She lays eggs."

The Dean felt shaken and tried another topic of conversation. "There are two more birdies on the clock. They are owls, I believe."

Bella glanced contemptuously at the clock. "They don't move," she said. "The bird in the clock in the shop window moves. He flies out of a little door and wants to come to Bella." Suddenly she was seized with an attack of heartrending grief. Laying her head against the Dean's waistcoat she wept, not noisily now, for the grief was real, but with a couple of low sobs and a tear trickling down her left cheek. "No one will give it to Bella," she mourned. "Nurse won't. Grandpa won't. No one won't."

"Is it a cuckoo clock?" asked the Dean. He found to his joy that he could hear everything Bella said quite easily, so clear was her voice. Other people thought the stiletto clarity of Bella's voice hardly an asset, but to the Dean it was sweet as the autumnal song of the robins that he could just hear faintly now whenever he passed a garden wall.

"He says, cuckoo," said Bella. "He says cuckoo, cuckoo, Bella! Cuckoo come to Bella. But they won't let him come to Bella." And she wiped away the tear with the back of her hand. It was not followed by another, but the silence that followed was a deep well full of sorrow.

"Is this clock in Mr. Peabody's shop?" asked the Dean.

But Bella had not heard of Mr. Peabody. "A little shop," she said. "With two little steps to the door. There is a little man inside the shop. He is a fairy man."

"Ah!" said the Dean. "That is Peabody." And then, with that wild impulsiveness which was so foreign to his nature but which seemed to be more and more taking hold of him just now, he said, "Bella, my dear, would you like me to give you that clock?"

"Yes," said Bella cheerfully. "Now. We'll go now."

But the door opened and Mr. Abraham Havelock entered in something of a state. "Mr. Dean! I am distressed indeed! But it was not until the departure of Squire Richards that I was informed that you were here. Not for the world would I have kept you waiting. May I offer you my most humble apologies. May I—Bella!"

There was a certain likeness between Mr. Havelock and his grand-daughter, though his once yellow head was now bald and his magnificent whiskers and moustache snow-white. He was stout and rosy and his eyes, at first sight disarmingly round and blue, were very acute and unblinking. His mouth, though soft and slightly pursed, could show that purposefulness which in the old is called resolve and in the young obstinacy. He was full of resolve now and so was Bella.

"What are you doing here, Bella?" he asked in a voice of silk. "Go to the nursery at once."

Bella adhered. The Dean was conscious of a sense of increased pressure upon his knees, as though the silent and motionless child were putting on weight as she sat there. She looked at her grandfather and her grandfather looked at her. Then he rang the bell.

"Minnie, take Miss Bella to the nursery," he said to the little maid.

Bella adhered.

"I'd fetch nurse but she's been took bad," said Minnie, looking at Bella apprehensively.

The Dean had been momentarily silent through uncertainty

as to where his duty lay. As a schoolmaster he felt that discipline should be upheld, yet Bella undoubtedly had a claim upon his loyalty. His impulsive offer of that cuckoo clock had not perhaps been altogether wise. Like his unpremeditated call on Mr. Peabody he was aware that it was about to have consequences out of all proportion to his initial action. But he could not turn back now. Even if he had wished to do so Bella would not have permitted it.

"Mr. Havelock, there is a small legal matter which I would like to discuss with you, if you will be so good as to spare me a few minutes of your valuable time. At the conclusion of our business will you permit me to take Bella for a little walk? Only as far as Mr. Peabody's clock shop. I should count it a very great pleasure and I will detain her for a short while only." Then aware of utter stupefaction in Mr. Havelock he asked anxiously, "Will it perhaps be too great an exertion for one of her tender years? Should I send for my wife's carriage?"

Mr. Havelock pulled himself together. "Mr. Dean, the exertion of which Bella is capable would surprise you. I hesitated only because of—forgive me—the startling nature of your suggestion. That you should be seen walking through the streets of your Cathedral city hand in hand with Bella—well, sir, it will startle the city."

The Dean, aware in Mr. Havelock of a resistance to which he was not accustomed, felt a little nettled. And also a little reckless. What did it matter what the city thought? In for a penny in for a pound. "Would such a course of action be contrary to your wishes, Mr. Havelock?" he asked. "I should not wish to cross them but the fact is that Bella and I have anticipated this outing with considerable pleasure."

Mr. Havelock capitulated with grace. He could do no less, with that authoritative note in the Dean's voice and Bella adhering.

"You do Bella a great honour, sir. I thank you in her name and my own." He turned to the little maid. "Minnie, take Miss Bella upstairs and put her things on. When I ring the bell you may bring her in. Bella, go with Minnie."

Bella slid demurely to the ground, made a dangerous wobbly curtsey, for owing to her bulk curtseying was not easy for her, and left the room with Minnie in a sweet biddable manner.

"Mr. Havelock," said the Dean, much moved, "I feel unworthy. How unworthy we are, we old sinners, of the company of little children. They are as angels."

Mr. Havelock's spectacles slid a little on his nose and he looked at the Dean over the top of them, but father of five and grandfather of eight though he was he forebore to comment. "I trust Bella will do nothing to forfeit your good opinion, Mr. Dean," he said. "But I think I should tell you that she has until now lacked discipline. She was born in India and has been much in the care of native servants. My wife and I now have charge of her but she has been with us only a month as yet and is still I fear something of an autocrat."

"Her parents are alive?" asked the Dean anxiously.

"Very much so, sir. They brought her home to us, the climate being unsuited to white children, and have now returned to India."

"She misses them?" asked the Dean, still with anxiety. "She weeps for them?"

"Bella has shown great adaptability," said her grandfather evenly. "And now, sir, in what way may I have the honour to serve you? But I am grieved that you should have put yourself to the trouble of coming to see me. I should have waited upon you. I am at your command, sir, at any time."

"Why should you be?" asked the Dean unexpectedly. "I have come to see you, Mr. Havelock, about Job Mooring the fishmonger's apprentice."

Mr. Havelock's spectacles slid further down his nose. He replaced them. The moment he had come into the room he had thought the Dean looked unwell, and the oddness of the great man's behaviour had caused him to wonder anxiously if there could be any slight mental disturbance, consequent perhaps upon a disordered liver? Now he was sure of it and was much perturbed. Yet the Dean, when the legalities of apprenticeship had been fully explained to him, showed his usual grasp of affairs. He knew exactly what he wished done in order that Albert Lee should be fully compensated, and Mr. Peabody spared all expense in the taking of an apprentice, and showed no further signs of mental aberration until he said, "Would it be advisable for me to wait upon Mr. Albert Lee myself, Mr. Havelock?"

"Certainly not, sir!" ejaculated Mr. Havelock. "No, sir. I shall do myself the honour of acting for you personally in this matter. Your name should not be mentioned in connection with fish. You are the Dean of the city."

"Have you ever wished you were a shepherd, Mr. Havelock?" asked the Dean. "Or a ploughman, driving your bright share through our rich fen earth with the gulls about you?"

"No, Mr. Dean," said Mr. Havelock. "I have always felt that indoor occupations are better suited to the vagaries of our climate."

"We are what God wills," said the Dean. "But I should like to have been a shepherd."

"Shall I ring the bell for Bella?" asked Mr. Havelock.

"Thank you, Mr. Havelock," said the Dean. "Much obliged."

Bella entered. She had been attired in a blue pelisse trimmed with swansdown, with a blue bonnet to match. She had mittens on and a little white muff hung round her neck by a cord. Eyeing the Dean she gestured with one mittened hand towards the birdcage. "Birdie may sing now," she said. The Dean obediently removed the velvet cloth and a torrent of song poured out into the room. Mr. Havelock appeared to be in the grip of strong emotion but what he said to Bella and the Dean by way of reprobation and apology could not be heard above Birdie's rejoicing. He led the way out into the hall with some precipitation but here Minnie was waiting to help the Dean into his cloak and he could not express himself freely. He opened the front door to bow the Dean out but it was Bella who walked out first past his bow, her hands in her muff and her head in the air.

Out on the pavement she waited for the Dean and with great kindness took his hand.

With the door shut Mr. Havelock took out his handkerchief and wiped his forehead. "I tell you what it is, sir," said Minnie, "the Dean being so dark complexioned Miss Bella takes him for one of them darkies she was always ordering about."

2

Bella and the Dean walked down Worship Street. Bella chatted without cessation but he did not know what she said now because she was so low down. It was as though a robin was singing somewhere on a level with his knee. He could distinguish the music but not the meaning of it, apart from its general meaning of joyful satisfaction with the splendour of the world. Looking down he could not see Bella's face but only her bonnet. A few tendrils of yellow hair clung about the edge of the bonnet, and her muff, not in use at present, swung from side to side to the rhythm of her trotting footsteps. She trotted like a very determined pony, four steps to the Dean's one, but it was she who set the pace and the Dean, growing a little breathless, marvelled that anyone so young could simultaneously trot and converse so fast without any diminution of energy whatever. Worship Street led into the market place at a sharp incline and this they took almost at a run. The sight of them crossing the market place was an astonishment to all beholders, but they were oblivious of this. In Cockspur Street the incline was again very steep and the Dean's rheumatic knees slowed him up a little. Bella, impatient, broke away and flew off, skimming down the pavement like a swallow. He was in terror lest flight in one so plump should end in disaster but she landed safely at the window of the clock shop. Here she leaned motionless, her nose pressed against the glass. The Dean followed as quickly as he could, past the small crooked houses with their flights of worn steps leading up to low front doors recessed within porches, past small windows bright with geraniums, and bow-fronted shop windows. Cockspur Street was a gay little street, the happiest

M

in the city. The people who lived here were neither rich nor poor. They were for the most part contented people, good craftsmen who liked their work, and the little shops and homes had been handed down from father to son and were all their world.

With his eyeglasses on his nose the Dean leaned beside Bella to look at the cuckoo clock. He realized now why it was that they had had to hurry, for the cuckoo clock said six minutes to twelve. Another seven minutes and they would have been too late. He echoed Bella's deep sigh of relief.

It was a good cuckoo clock of carved and painted wood. Oak leaves and oak apples curved about the enchanting little double doors which were represented as though opening into the trunk of a tree. As an example of Isaac's art it was not one of his best clocks but then he had made it for such as Bella and as a joyous arcadian toy it was perfect of its kind. Five minutes to twelve. Bella had misted the glass with her passionate breathing and the Dean had to take out his white silk handkerchief and wipe it clear again. Four minutes to twelve by the cuckoo clock, kept slow by Isaac, and Michael began to strike. The golden notes rolled down Cockspur Street like flaming suns and after them came the silver star-chiming of little St. Nicholas and St. Matthew's at the South Gate, almost submerging the deep-toned and moony sadness of St. Peter's in the market place. Two minutes to twelve by the cuckoo clock. The glass was misted again and Bella wiped it with her muff. Now all the clocks in the window except the cuckoo were striking together, and it sounded as though someone was playing the harpsichord. One minute to twelve by the cuckoo clock. Bella stretched up her mittened hand and held the Dean's and both hands were trembling as they counted out the sixty seconds. Then the double doors in the oak tree burst open and the cuckoo, yelling joyously, exploded forth. Its voice was as shrill as that of Birdie the canary and for a moment the Dean was profoundly dismayed. Birdie and the cuckoo together in one house? Poor Havelock. What had he done? Into what further indiscretion

would this autumnal madness of his precipitate him? Poor
Havelock.

The row suddenly ceased and the cuckoo withdrew as suddenly as he had come out, the little doors closing behind him.
Bella withdrew her nose from the glass and pulled the Dean up
the steps into the shop. Isaac favoured one of those bells which
ring when the customer stands on the doormat. Bella was en-
raptured and impervious to all suggestions that she should come
off the mat. Isaac, entering from his workroom with all possible
speed, joined his entreaties to those of the Dean with no avail.
Suddenly the slumbering schoolmaster awoke in Adam Ayscough. "Bella!" he thundered. "Come off that mat immediately!" Bella, her muff lifted coquettishly to her chin, dimpled,
smiled, and came off the mat. But with no air of capitulation.
She had come off it because she had wanted to come off it.
Climbing on to the customers' chair, showing a good deal of
petticoat as she did so, she smiled adorably at the two men and
said, "Cuckoo!"

"Mr. Peabody, might we trouble you to show us the cuckoo
clock?" asked the Dean. "Much obliged. Do you like it,
Bella?"

Bella, with the clock beside her on the counter, did not bother
to answer the rhetorical question. With a small forefinger she
traced the pattern of oak leaves and oak apples, and caressed
the closed door. Her lips were slightly parted, her face raised
towards the clock like that of a cherub looking into heaven. Her
expression, so wicked a few minutes ago, was now rapt and
holy. Both men looked at her in awe. Imp though she was she
could still at moments trail her clouds of glory. It was not until
she took her finger from the clock, sighed, and began to swish
her legs backwards and forwards among her petticoats in imitation of the clock's pendulum, that the Dean could bring himself to break the charmed silence and explain the situation to
Mr. Peabody.

"Very good, sir," said Mr. Peabody. "I will deliver the
clock to Worship Street this evening."

"Will that inconvenience you, Mr. Peabody?" asked the Dean anxiously.

"No, sir, no trouble at all. I will leave it on my way home tonight."

"I want it now," said Bella.

"Not now," said the Dean. "Mr. Peabody is not at liberty until the evening."

"*You* carry it," said Bella, sliding off the customers' chair. "Now."

For a moment the Dean was as much taken aback by the suggestion as was Isaac. He was not in the habit of carrying things. He scarcely knew how one set about it. Then the curious recklessness that was reversing the habits of a distinguished lifetime took hold of him again. "Mr. Peabody," he said, "will you be so good as to wrap it up?"

"Sir, you cannot carry it," said Isaac in deep distress. "Even were it suitable for you to be seen carrying a large brown paper parcel through the streets of the city the weight would be far too great for your strength. Indeed, sir, the thing is impossible. Bella must wait."

"No," said Bella. Her face was crimson and her blue eyes were full of fiery points of light. Although neither man had as yet experienced Bella in one of her rages they both felt the deepest apprehension, as though they stood on the rim of a volcano's crater, with fire and rumblings down below. The Dean was aware that the schoolmaster's voice would be of no avail now. It had only been of use before because Bella's will and his own had happened to coincide. He suddenly felt very tired. Authority had always come easily to him, and sometimes in years past he had felt a slight contempt for masters who could not keep order. It was good for him, he realized, to know that even the strongest sometimes meet their match.

"If it is too heavy for me it is too heavy for you, Mr. Peabody," he said, looking down at Isaac from his great height. "How do you convey these heavy clocks from place to place?"

Isaac lowered his voice to tell a secret. "I have a little cart," he said. "A push cart. I made it."

"Could I push it?" asked the Dean.

"No, no, no!" said Isaac. "It is only a wooden box on wheels. I myself use it if possible only after dark."

"If ever a man needed an apprentice you do," said the Dean. Then he too dropped his voice. "I've seen Havelock. You'll have Job in a matter of days I hope."

Something in the quality of Bella's silence suddenly made both men look at her again. Her face was now a most alarming puce colour, her body looked strangely swollen and her mouth was slowly opening. "I'll close the shop," said Isaac suddenly. "I'll bring it now, Bella. Just a moment while I fetch my little cart."

He hurried back into his workshop and the Dean sat down rather suddenly on the customers' chair, for really he was extraordinarily exhausted. Bella laid her hand upon his knee. He looked at her and found she was another child. Her exquisite pink and white complexion was restored to her. Her blue eyes were infinitely gentle, her long eyelashes wet with tears that had been arrested on the brink. She stretched up her arms to him and then suddenly she scrambled up, her bonnet falling off, and wound them tightly round his neck, her warm cheek pressed against his. "Bella loves you," she whispered, and she spoke the truth. She was not an impartially loving child, later in life she would be considered a hard woman, but at a quarter-past-twelve on this particular autumn morning in the city Bella Havelock suddenly and completely loved Adam Ayscough. He had not known that children loved like this, so suddenly. He had never known this stranglehold about the neck, the velvet softness against his cheek, the scent of a child's hair, and within him something wept wildly for joy. When Bella whispered, "Get down now," he set her down very carefully, not knowing if he had held her for an hour or a minute, for time had stopped.

Isaac reappeared with his box on wheels, as queer a little box as he was a man, but beautifully made, for he could not make anything that was not a fine bit of handiwork. He was wearing his caped greatcoat, and his hat was under his arm. "I had thought to show you my clocks, sir," he said wistfully.

"Another time," said the Dean gently. "I will call in one evening just at closing time. That would be best I think. We shall be undisturbed then. But I am aware of your clocks, Mr. Peabody; beautiful things, alive all round me. Their tick is their pulse and breath."

There was a note in his voice that Isaac recognized. The man was happy, as Isaac himself had been happy that night in the workshop not long ago, and Bella was happy. Isaac's own good time had ended abruptly on Sunday night, its light put out by Emma's destruction of Job's treasures, and he was now so wretched that even his memory of the way light and air had flooded into the house when he had opened the front door had no power to help him. The worst of his dark times was that while they were at their worst his good times seemed to him just a betrayal; as though he had loved a wife and found her a whore. But he knew that the Dean and Bella were happy and it eased his breathlessness. He was very much afraid that one of his attacks of asthma was coming on.

"You've a cold, Mr. Peabody?" asked the Dean.

"No, sir," said Isaac, coughing peevishly. "But I wanted to show you my clocks."

The Dean was sorry for his disappointment but the peevishness added to his joy, for a man is only peevish to his friends.

"Come now, come now," he rallied him. "Matters of great moment need leisure and quietness for their consideration. Yes, Bella, we are going. Look, Mr. Peabody is putting the clock into the little carriage."

Isaac and the Dean lifted the cart down the steps, Isaac locked the shop door and poised his battered old hat at the back of his head while the Dean placed his immaculate one well down over his forehead, its rim nearly resting on his eyebrows, which was the top hat position he favoured. They set out,

Isaac trundling his cart up the hill over the cobbles with Bella
and the Dean beside him. When they were nearly at the top of
the hill he was taken with a sudden fit of coughing. It was a
bad one and it winded him. They had to stop while he wheezed
and gasped his way back to a hurried painful breathing that
greatly distressed the Dean. "What was I thinking of to let you
push that heavy cart up the hill, Mr. Peabody? Much distressed. My physical strength is greatly superior to yours." And
he picked up the handles of the little cart.

"No, sir," wheezed Isaac. "In a moment we shall be in the
market place. Sir, I beg of you."

But it was too late, for the Dean, pushing the cuckoo clock,
had already launched out into the market place. He was, as he
had said, stronger than Isaac and he strode forward with a mad
gay recklessness, Bella running beside him hopping and skipping
and joyously tossing her muff from side to side. Isaac could only
follow after, at first aware of nothing except the incredulous
astonishment, the horror and shock of the city, which in the
raw state of his feelings seemed to a man, woman and child to
be lined up all round the market square and gazing dumb-
founded from every door and window. Then he was abruptly
conscious of something that suddenly lit up his darkness as
though a shutter had swung back, then closed again, leaving a
picture illumined small and bright against the darkness of his
mind. Tall silver towers lifted up against the cloudless blue sky
above, old houses with crooked roofs and gables gathered about
the market place that was filled to the brim with a dazzle of
golden sunshine. In the gold a running child with yellow hair,
glinting and gay, and an old man as gay as she was, forgetful of
himself. Chimes rang out far up in the blue sky. Half-past-
twelve. Other bells answered as though ringing in another
world.

The Dean, Isaac and Bella gained the farther shore and made
their way into Worship Street. The small bright picture faded
from Isaac's mind but he had it somewhere, just as he had the
picture of Graham's little bow-windowed shop in Fleet Street,

its gables etched black against the stars and its walls washed by moonlight. And others, equally imperishable, small and precious as little pictures painted within a great gold letter in an illuminated manuscript. Sometimes he would fancy that strung together they would have been a sort of speech telling him something. They were all safely kept, all part of the imperishable landscape of the country where he made his clocks.

At number twenty Minnie answered the Dean's ring upon the instant and Mr. Havelock was just behind her, anxiety writ large upon his face.

"Mr. Havelock, I am anxious about this clock," said the Dean. "It cuckoos. I trust that you and Mrs. Havelock may suffer no disturbance of your rest." He stood very humbly, and he felt humble, though not as distressed as he felt he ought to have been. It was difficult to feel distressed with Bella refusing to let go of his hand and with gaiety still in his heart. Yet poor Havelock. "Pray forgive me," he pleaded.

"My dear sir," ejaculated Mr. Havelock, "Mrs. Havelock and myself are seasoned parents and grandparents. There is the canary. There is Bella herself. One learns a certain trick of disassociation. Bella, thank the Dean for his great kindness."

"I *have* thanked him," said Bella.

"Then let Minnie take you to the nursery."

Bella adhered.

"Thank you, Mr. Peabody, put the clock on the hall table," said Mr. Havelock, changing the subject, a ruse which on rare occasions had been known to unstick Bella. "Minnie will take it to the nursery. Mr. Dean, will you do me the honour of partaking of a little luncheon?"

"Most kind, most kind," said the Dean. "My grateful thanks, but my wife is expecting me. Remember me to Mrs. Havelock. . . . Bella."

Bella adhered.

"Bella!" thundered her grandfather.

The Dean bent down to her. "Bella, we must say good-bye. But not for long I trust. Be a good girl, my dear."

Bella suddenly gave in, lifting her face to be kissed. "Bye," she said, and kissed Isaac too. She went from one to the other, running between them as a puppy will do between two that love him, then disappeared up the stairs in the wake of Minnie and the cuckoo clock. With renewed civilities the three old gentlemen bowed to each other and the door was at last closed. Politeness was important in the city in those days. There was time for it.

"Do you go home for luncheon, Mr. Peabody?" asked the Dean.

"No, sir, I have it in the shop. I take sandwiches." And Isaac trembled a little at the thought of having to go home to Emma for his midday meal as well as for supper.

"I'll walk a short way with you."

"You will be late home, sir."

"Luncheon is at one-thirty. Just a few paces. That's a nice clock at Havelock's, the one with the owls on the dining-room mantelpiece."

"Edward East sixteen hundred and forty-four," said Isaac dispiritedly and began to cough again.

"Asthma?" asked the Dean gently.

Isaac nodded and they stopped where an old tall cherry tree leaned over a garden wall. The last of its crimson leaves drifted upon them. Isaac stopped coughing and the Dean put his hand on his shoulder. "Did the child not lighten it at all?" he asked.

"For a moment," said Isaac.

"The child has joy," said the Dean. "You stored your joy for her within the cuckoo clock. As I see it there is no giving without giving away. But joy is a homing pigeon. Good day to you, Mr. Peabody."

His hand tightened for a moment on Isaac's shoulder and then he turned away.

I

"THERE's a young person at the back door says she wishes to
see you, sir," said Garland in strangled tones. "I told her
it was impossible, of course, sir. She asked me why. I said you
were engaged. She said she'd wait. I told her to go away. She
smiled at me. I don't know what to do, sir, I don't indeed."

Bella and the cuckoo clock had been on Monday. Today
was Saturday morning. The Dean, at work at his writing table,
looked up. Garland's face was pale and his hands trembled
slightly. He was obviously much shaken, worsted, the Dean
thought, in some encounter which had not only been contrary
to routine but foreign to his whole experience. The Dean put
his hand behind his ear. "Could you repeat that, Garland?"

Garland repeated it, ending miserably, "I don't like to
trouble you with such a thing, sir. I don't know how it is that I
am standing where I am or she where she is. I am ashamed, I
am indeed. But Cook tried too, sir."

"Don't distress yourself, Garland," said the Dean. "Is this
young person small and sandy-haired? Quick in her movements? A chin of remarkable determination?"

"That's her, sir," said Garland.

"Then pray ask her to step this way." Garland could not

186

believe that he had heard aright but he took a few weak steps towards the door. "One more thing, Garland." The Dean hesitated, picked his pen up and put it down again. "I am the Dean of this Cathedral city and I should be accessible to all who want me. I fear that has not always been so in the past. You understand, Garland? Much obliged."

In a remarkably short space of time Polly, scared but courageous, stood before him. Her face was white inside her bonnet, all the whiter in contrast with the brave crimson ribbons tied beneath her determined chin, and both hands clung rather desperately to the handle of her loaded shopping basket. The Dean was saddened that she, possessed of so much pluck, had found it so hard to come to him. A strong smell of fish emanated from the basket.

"I could not persuade her to leave it at the back door, sir," said Garland.

"She was quite right," said the Dean. "We have a kitchen cat I believe. Sit down, my dear. Garland shall set a chair for you. Thank you, Garland."

Garland withdrew and Polly sat gingerly on the edge of her chair, still clinging to the basket. "Set it down, my dear," said the Dean. "It will be quite safe there on the floor."

Polly put it down beside her. "It's not my things, sir," she explained. "It's Miss Peabody's. I market for her on a Saturday morning. I'd be blamed, sir, if anything were to be missing."

"You can't be too careful," the Dean agreed. "Are you on your way from the market now? Did anything occur there to distress you?"

"Yes, sir. Job wasn't at the fish stall. Job's gone."

"Gone?" echoed the Dean.

"Run away, sir. He's been gone two days." She was near breaking point but she controlled herself. No longer able to cling to the handle of the basket her hands were twisting her handkerchief into a knot. The Dean, trying to see her face inside the bonnet, thought that she had wept but was dry-eyed now. "My dear," he said, "I had hoped that by this time Job was happily established as Mr. Peabody's apprentice. I saw Mr. Havelock last Monday and he assured me he would see to the matter. Pray tell me just what has occurred."

He leaned forward again with his hand behind his ear. This aid to hearing that he had never liked to use was becoming almost habitual with him now, so important was it that in his present contacts he should hear what the children said. A feeling of guilt was growing in him. He had been unusually busy the last few days and Isaac, Polly and Job, Bella and the cuckoo clock, had perforce slipped to the back of his mind. But that would not do. One could not deliberately enter the lives of others and then go in and out just as one wished. Deliberate entry committed one to entire service. "Much ashamed," he said to himself.

"Job come in on Wednesday evening," said Polly, "just as far as the scullery because Miss Peabody she was in the parlour and he couldn't come no further. He'd brought me a lark made out of a bit of crab apple wood. Ever so pretty it was. I was just going to tell him how he was to leave the fish and be apprenticed to the clocks when he says to me, 'Where's the box you keep my birds in? I want that robin. It's not right and I've got to get it better. The Dean liked it and I'm going to give it to him.' "

"Yes?" asked the Dean, listening painfully.

"Well, sir, I pretended I'd lost it. So he told me to fetch the box, and I said I didn't know where I'd put it. Then he got angry, for he's got a temper, Job has, and somehow I let it out. I didn't mean to, knowing how he'd take on, but I was flustered like."

"What did you let out, my dear?"

"About Miss Peabody burning the birds."

"Burning the birds?" ejaculated the Dean.

Polly went as crimson as she had formerly been pale. "I forgot, sir. I forgot it was after you went."

"What happened after I went?"

"Miss Peabody, she put all Job's birds, and the snail and all, in the fire. I think, sir, she was angry that you called when she was out."

Polly stopped, shocked by the deepening of the lines in the Dean's face, the horror in his eyes. He couldn't have looked worse, she thought, had there been a death in the family. She thought Job's birds were very nice but to her they were just pretty toys. To the Dean it seemed they were something more. "And then?" he asked.

"Job, he took on something dreadful. He looked as though I'd stuck a knife in him. And so to comfort him I tried to tell him about being apprenticed to the clocks. But he didn't listen, sir. He pushed me away and went out. Banged the door in my face, he did. I've never known him rough like that. Quick tempered now and again, but not rough. He's gentle, Job is." She paused, a little breathless with her pain. "You see, sir, Job's not like other boys."

"No, Polly," said the Dean. "What his clocks are to Mr. Peabody Job's birds are to him. Genius creates from the heart and when the artifact is broken so is the heart. You must forgive his roughness. What did you do then?"

"There was nothing I could do, sir, but wait for market day, for Miss Peabody she won't let me out except for the Saturday marketing. I couldn't tell Mr. Peabody for he's having one of his bad times, and asthma like he has so often when he's low, and I tries to keep cheerful with him when he's low. But Job wasn't at the market, and the fish stall was all anyhow, the fish not gutted proper, no clean rushes and no posies for old Keziah to sell. Job had gone, they said. He'd run away."

"Did they give a reason?" asked the Dean.

"Albert Lee, he wouldn't speak to me. Been drinking. Proper black eye he had. But Keziah she told me quiet like that Albert had knocked Job about something cruel. That was Wednesday night. Thursday morning they found he'd gone. Had enough and who's to blame him. But why did he not come to me, sir? I never thought Job could be in trouble and not come to me." Her voice caught suddenly and the

sodden handkerchief ripped in her twisting fingers. The Dean
had to lean forward to try and hear what she said next. It was
something about the river, and Job not being like other boys.

"No!" he said harshly. "Not that. There is some good
reason why he could not come to you."

"You don't know Job, sir," said Polly. "Mr. Peabody he
gets low but Job he takes things that hard you wouldn't believe."

"Take heart, my dear. I will wait upon Mr. Havelock and
find out what he did in the matter. I fear he has blundered.
Then I will wait upon Mr. Albert Lee. We will find Job."

Polly was cheered. She even tried to smile, and she looked
timidly about the beautiful room as though it reassured her.
The Dean guessed, rightly, that she was thinking that a man
living in a big house like this, with these grand servants, must
be able to do anything. Her faith in him, terribly shaken, was
coming back.

"I tell you, Polly," he said, " 'that all shall be well and all
manner of thing shall be well'."

His harsh voice had a kind of joy in it. Dame Julian's words
had been unpremeditated. They had come into his mind in a
manner that brought as much conviction to himself as to Polly.

"Thank you, sir," she said, and rose and curtseyed. "Please
don't ring for Mr. Garland. I can find my way."

But the Dean had already rung the bell. "You will lose
yourself in this big house, my dear." He spoke looking down
at her. She had great dignity in her sorrow as well as much
courage. Who was she? He thought of Perdita. "Nothing she
does or seems but smacks of something greater than herself."
Garland entered and he took her hand in his and bowed to her.
She curtseyed again and left the room with Garland, who had
aged five years in the last twenty minutes. The Dean grieved
for Garland. For the last ten years the life of the Deanery
had moved as on oiled wheels, not moving one inch from the
lines laid down by Garland. Now, the Dean knew, there was
change in the air. To him it was as though the wind had set
south, but for Garland he feared it might be veering north for a

while. And for Elaine? He did not know but he prayed for a
west wind and the breaking of the wells.

2

The Dean made a hasty luncheon and after it he set out immediately for Worship Street. Under the Porta, beneath her
room, he remembered Mary Montague. "Take a little joy," she
had said. Had he sinned in trying to obey her? He believed
not. Joy being of God was a living thing, a fountain not a
cistern, one of those divine things that are possessed only as
they overflow and flow away, and not easily come by because
it must break into human life through the hard crust of sin
and contingency. Joy came now here, now there, was held and
escaped. But worth the travail of the winning both for himself
and the children. He would have liked to go in and see Miss
Montague, and tell her what had happened, but she rested
after luncheon and he dared not delay in his search for Job.
It did not matter. Such prayer as hers was, like joy, an overflowing fountain that flowed where it was needed.

Mr. Havelock's luncheon had not been as hasty as the Dean's
and he was still enjoying his post-prandial nap, his beautiful
white silk handkerchief spread over his bald head, his hands
serenely folded over the peaceful processes of his excellent
digestion, when his visitor was shown into his study.

"Good afternoon, Mr. Havelock," said the Dean hurriedly,
and then, becoming aware of his host's predicament, his attention was immediately caught by a shimmer of colour beyond
the windows. "Wonderful dahlias," he murmured, adjusting
his eyeglasses and turning a courteous back upon Mr. Havelock.
"You have a good gardener." They were chrysanthemums but
he did not see them very clearly, for time pressed. But he did
see a little wooden horse on wheels, abandoned on the lawn. It
was a dappled creature with scarlet reins, bright and gay on the
vivid green grass. Bella's horse. He felt a pang of keen pleasure
at the sight, as keen as though he had been a lover seeing his
lady's gloves lying on a chair. He saw the little picture as

vividly as though he had impeccable eyesight; or as though a
shutter had suddenly swung open in a dark room. He would
not forget it.

"Mr. Dean, I was just on the point of waiting upon you. In
another moment I should have left the house."

Mr. Havelock, smiling, suave and self-possessed, might never
have lunched at all. The Dean thought for a moment that the
spread handkerchief and folded hands must have been an
optical delusion of his poor sight, then remembered the legal
gift of swift adjustment. If Havelock had erred in the matter
of Job his adjustments would be agile. But he must not be
allowed to escape along by-paths for there was no time.

"What arrangements did you come to with Mr. Lee?" he
asked, his voice an abrupt bark. "The boy has run away." The
Dean could be alarming in an abrupt mood. "The Great
Beast is barking," had been a word of warning that in school
and college alike had caused men and boys to melt into the
landscape, but Mr. Havelock was unperturbed.

"Mr. Dean, I beg you will take this chair. Run away? I am
distressed to hear it. Is the reason known?"

"Not by me, Mr. Havelock. I am seeking information from
yourself." Mr. Havelock, in an armchair opposite the Dean,
put his finger tips together with a maddening deliberation.
"And without delay, I beg."

"I called on Lee on Wednesday evening," said Mr. Havelock,
with no delay but in tones so calm and unhurried that they
held a subtle rebuke. "The boy was out but both Lee and his
mother were at home. Disreputable parties, both of them. I
was thankful, Mr. Dean, to have spared you personal contact
with such a low sort of people. Swithins Lane is not a salubrious
part of the city."

"I know all about Swithins Lane," said the Dean. "What I
don't know is what sort of reply Mr. Lee gave to my proposal."

"Unfavourable, sir."

"You offered him the compensation we had in mind?"

"He refused it."

"I told you I was ready to increase the sum we had agreed upon as fair and just in order to save the boy."

"You did, sir, but I did not bargain with the fellow. The first offer was more than generous. To have increased it would have been for you a concession lacking in dignity. Nor do I believe that Lee would part with that boy for treble the sum." The Dean remembered what Polly had said about the market stall being in confusion. If Job's genius stood between his master and destitution here was another complication. "And you must remember, sir, that he has legality on his side."

The Dean suspected that Mr. Havelock's sympathies were entirely with Albert Lee, and suddenly he liked him for it. He was a lawyer. The law was perhaps to him what his birds were to Job. It was in a gentler tone that he asked, "And did you come away without more ado, Mr. Havelock?"

"I did, sir. I have those, including Bella, who are dependent on me."

"You mean the man was violent?"

"He is of gypsy origin and a heavy drinker. My interview with him was quite an experience."

"I am sorry, Mr. Havelock, to have subjected you to it. I am glad to see you physically unharmed, and I am obliged to you for your exertions on my behalf." The Dean rose, Mr. Havelock following suit. "And you can throw no light on the disappearance of the boy?"

"No, sir. Do you wish me to act further in this matter? I am at all times at your disposal."

"No, Mr. Havelock, do no more. As you say, legally we are in the wrong. But I wish that you had informed me sooner as to the failure of your visit."

"I was just about to do myself the honour of waiting upon you, sir," said Mr. Havelock suavely, but the Dean saw a gleam of astonishment in his eyes, quickly veiled. All this to-do over an orphanage brat, a fishmonger's apprentice. Adam Ayscough struggled with his anger. Yet what right had he to be angry? Absorbed in other work he had permitted Job to go

N

to the back of his mind. Probably it had been the same with
Havelock. "Much obliged," he said humbly, and going into
the hall began to feel rather blindly for his hat. "Bella is upstairs?" he asked with the wistful shyness of a young and
abashed lover, as Mr. Havelock gave him his hat and cloak and
stick.

"I fear she is out for her afternoon walk with her nurse."

"Yes, yes, of course. Good-day, Mr. Havelock. Much
obliged."

3

Adam Ayscough was in great distress as he made his way
down through the narrow twisting streets of the city towards the
North Gate slums. He was momentarily forgetful that all was to
be well and blamed himself entirely for Albert Lee's fury and
Job's disappearance. He should not have allowed Havelock to
act for him in the matter. The breaking of an apprenticeship
contract by the use of bribery had been against Havelock's
legal conscience, and one should never use a man where his
conscience in not persuaded. Bribery. The word he had
used himself had been compensation, which sounded better but
meant much the same. In this affair it appeared to him now
that Albert Lee had an impregnable moral position and he
himself a very poor one. If Job's skill was necessary to Albert
Lee in the prosecution of his business then he had been en-
deavouring to deprive him of the means of livelihood by means
of bribery. Most reprehensible! Yet he intended to continue to
do so for he believed a boy's salvation to be at stake. Job must be
rescued from the sin of this man whatever sin stuck to himself
during the process. Only the saints could rescue a soul from
evil without falling into the mud themselves. But on the
other side of this he must do what he could for Albert Lee.

He forged his way along the street as though against a high
wind, talking to himself, seeing no one, his hat a little crooked
and his stick whirling round and round in his hand. The
rumour that the Dean was going queer in the head had whis-

pered round the city after he had been seen wheeling a cuckoo clock across the market place in company with Isaac Peabody and Bella Havelock, and now it blew up in his wake like the rustle of autumn leaves, stirred by the wind of his peculiar passing. By nightfall it had curiously softened the city's feelings towards him. Perhaps the great men of the Close were not as immune from worry as had been generally supposed. Perhaps even the great Dean had his troubles. And if he had them, he who was so curiously the city, were they not the city's also?

The flight of steep steps that led down to Swithins Lane was well known to the Dean both in darkness and daylight, but in the strange pallid half-light that was creeping over the city on this autumn afternoon the dirty twisting steps, and the dark doorways on either side, looked more than usually sordid and evil. It was a queer sort of light, yellow and murky. All day the clouds had been gathering and it had been obvious that the spell of calm and lovely weather was over. Was there going to be a storm? The Dean trusted that Elaine and Bella were safely within doors and was glad that the market was now over. A deluge upon those bright gay stalls was not to be desired. The market ended at two-thirty in the winter in order that the beasts might be driven home before dark. Albert Lee, the Dean hoped, would now be at his shop again.

He reached Swithins Lane and opposite him across the street was St. Nicholas at the North Gate. St. Nicholas was a daughter church of St. Matthew's at the South Gate, so small as to be hardly more than a chapel and so old that it looked more like a rock than a building. It had been called after Saint Nicholas, the mariners' saint, because the North Gate beside it had opened directly on the river steps where the great barges had in days gone by unloaded their gear. South Gate, East Gate and West Gate were only names now, their sites marked by the two foundations of Dobson's and by the old pub that stood where once the South Gate had been, but the great arch of the North Gate still spanned the river steps, with the church on one side and on the other a portion of the old city wall that now formed one side of the tannery.

The Dean stood for a moment under the arch at the top of the steps. They were old and broken now and not at all salubrious, for the inhabitants of Swithins Lane could not be cured of a centuries' old habit of standing at the top of them and chucking garbage down to the water, but they still had a graceful curve. Just beyond the steps the river flowed with a strong calm power that was immensely impressive but not reassuring today, with the wide flood lit to a sulphurous yellow by the stormy light. In wet seasons the river could rage up the steps into Swithins Lane, flooding the houses and causing much illness and suffering among the people. There was little about suffering that the Swithins Lane people did not know, and thinking of them the Dean was back again in the heartbreak of his long fight to deliver them. Inbred, dug in, as violently attached to where they were as limpets to a rock, they had not wanted to be delivered, and selfish men had exploited their ignorance and fed their wealth upon it. It broke his heart that that bitter battle, of all his many battles in the city, should have been the only one he had ever lost.

Standing under the archway with the smell of the garbage and the tannery in his nostrils, the evil slums behind him and that menacing water lapping at the steps below, he suddenly straightened his sagging shoulders. He would reopen that fight. His plan had been a good one. The famous architect, his friend, who had helped him in the work on the Cathedral, had worked upon it with him and together they had designed well built, simple and good-looking houses that built upon high ground beyond the West Gate would have been no blot upon the city's beauty. The North Gate and the old church would have remained intact, and public gardens beside the river would have taken the place of the verminous cottages. He had planned those gardens himself and they were dear to him; he often dreamed of them. It would have cost a great deal but there was wealth in the city, not least his own, which would

have been at its disposal. He'd fight again. Swithins Lane
should no longer harbour Albert Lees to bludgeon young boys
to flight and death.

Death? No! But he had no time to stand here planning
fights to come with this boy still in danger. It was Job now.
Job. He did not know what he was going to say to Albert Lee,
he felt tired and stupid, but experience had taught him that
the mere fact of charging into the arena could most wonderfully
clear the mind.

He forged his way through the tortuous tunnel of Swithins
Lane. It was like an evil man's mind, he sometimes thought,
full of twists and turns, darkness and confusion. Even in sunlight, with the wind blowing in the opposite direction from the
tannery, it never seemed wholesome, for the tottering ruins of
old houses that leaned across it shut in the smell and darkness.
The hollows between the cobbles held filmed stagnant water,
and rotting cabbage leaves and shreds of paper clogged the
gutter. "We want a good rain," thought the Dean. "If there
is a storm coming we need it." The lane seemed deserted, for
the children were not yet back from school or the men from
work, and so dim that already the pallid flicker of candlelight
shone in a few of the grimy windows. When he reached the
fish shop he found the gas flares already lighted.

The Lees were home from the market and busy in the shop,
for on Saturday nights they did a brisk trade in fried fish. The
cod and whiting that had gone off in the market were fried in a
loathly kind of oil flavoured with onions and sold cheap for
Swithins Lane suppers. A nauseous preparatory stench took
the Dean by the throat as he walked into the circle of gaslight,
took off his top hat to Keziah and asked if he might be allowed
to speak a few words to Mr. Albert Lee. Keziah stopped what
she was doing and stared, her slack old mouth dropping open.
Albert emerged from the back of the shop and came warily
closer, shoulders hunched like an advancing prize-fighter, one
eye closed up within its purple bruises, the other fixed on the
Dean with a gimlet stare of mixed misery and insolence. They

knew him well by sight for he had been continually up and
down Swithins Lane during the years when he had been fighting for its demolition, and it had been Albert who had flung
the egg which upon one occasion had splashed his immaculate
top hat with rottenness. It was the remembrance of that egg
that was making Albert's approach so wary.

The Dean, as he stood in the flaring yellow gaslight with the
darkness of the coming storm behind him, was a formidable
figure. Even with his top hat in his hand he seemed to touch
the ceiling; his long black cloak added to his breadth of
shoulder and was thrown about him like a thunder-cloud.
Yet when he spoke his voice, even though harsh and grating,
brought a sudden sense of quietness to the tumultuous wretchedness that was Albert's habitual state of mind when, as now, he
happened to be completely sober.

"I owe you an apology, Mr. Lee. I fear I have been the
cause of your losing a valuable apprentice."

Albert looked stupidly at the large clean hand held out to
him, then wiped his own on his greasy trouser leg and took it.
The strong grip further steadied him. "And you, too, Mrs.
Lee," said the Dean, and bowed to her. "I fear you will miss
Job." Keziah was too awed to speak. Her lips worked nervously and her dirty hands kept folding and unfolding themselves in her dirtier apron. She was a terrible old creature to
look at, with her mumbling mouth and rheumy eyes and the
pitiful strands of her greasy hair falling over her face from
beneath a battered black bonnet, more repulsive even than the
drink-sodden brutal Albert. Yet the Dean was repulsed by
neither of them. They had that childlikeness that makes so
many criminals less repulsive than the sophisticated worldly
sinners. They were ruined creatures, both of them, but there
had once been something to ruin. The woman's face retained
its beauty of bone, and the man still had a queer panther grace
and strength. Gypsies, the Dean thought, whom greed for
money had brought from the wilds to the town, and separated
from their kind they had suffered the fate of so many exiles.

Loneliness made or ruined a man. It frightened him so that he must either sing and build in the face of the dark, like a bird or a beaver, or hide from it like a beast in his den. There were perhaps always only the two ways to go, God or the jungle. And all men were exiles. It was a common bond between them, the bond between himself and this man and woman.

"It was I who asked Mr. Havelock if he could arrange a transference for Job," said the Dean. "I did it because of the boy's great skill as a craftsman. I had been shown some excellent little birds that he had whittled out of wood and they showed, I thought, that he had it in him to become a better clockmaker than a fishmonger. But I fear I showed insufficient consideration for yourself, Mr. Lee, and for that I offer you my apologies." Albert growled something under his breath. In spite of that quietness he was not to be won over by a few courteous phrases. "I confess I had another reason. You knocked that boy about too much, Mr. Lee."

Albert looked up sharply, instantly on the insolent defensive, and met the Dean's glance. With his closed-up eye struggling to open and aid the other he stood and looked at the Dean, right into his unhappy eyes and beaky bony face. It was queer how he had to go on looking at the ugly old codger. And what he said was not in the least what he had meant to say.

"That bloody lawyer, ee proper got me back up, the way ee talked. I took it out of the boy."

"Not for the first time," said the Dean.

"You're right, sir. Scraggy, wey-faced, stubborn little beast that ee was, you see, sir."

"Yes, I know," said the Dean in what sounded almost like a tone of sympathy and understanding. "Weak enough to be at your mercy yet kept his mouth shut when you skinned him. They egg a man on, that sort. What you need, Mr. Lee, is a boy who'll yell and kick your shins. Give as good as he gets." He eyed Albert's black eye speculatively. "Or did he, at the end?"

"Yes, sir," said Albert in almost confidential tones. "Couldn't

'ave believed it. I stops to get me breath, an' sudden ee ups
and gives it me straight in the eye. Then ee was up the stairs
to the attic, where ee sleeps, before I could stop 'im. When me
ma went to rouse 'im in the mornin' ee'd gorn. Out the attic
winda. Sheer drop it is. She thought she'd see 'im there with
all 'is bones broke. But ee weren't there, sir. Queer, it was."

"He won't come back," said the Dean.

"No, sir," said Albert slowly. "There's the river out the
back. Ee couldn't swim."

"He is, I trust, alive," said the Dean. "But he will not come
back. You went too far. I believe I could find you a boy of the
type you need, Mr. Lee. He would not have Job's artistic skill,
which I know you have found invaluable, but he would drive
you to drink less often. I think, weighing one thing with another, your business would not suffer in the exchange." He
took a small packet from his pocket and laid it on the filthy
chopping block beside him. "Mr. Lee, Mr. Havelock offered
you compensation if you would forgo your legal claim upon the
boy. Slightly more than the amount he offered you is there.
Will you accept it with my apology for the inconvenience I have
caused you, giving me your word that if Job is found you will
not force him to return to you? I ask for no assurance except
your word."

Albert looked at the hand held out to him, once more placed
his own within it and mumbled an agreement. He had not
understood more than half of what the Dean had said to him
but that grip seemed now to hold not only his hand but his
being. It was as though he had been turned round to face in a
different direction.

"I will find you that new apprentice," said the Dean. "You
can rely on me. Much obliged. Good afternoon, Mrs. Lee.
Much obliged."

He bowed, replaced his hat and walked out of the shop.
Albert Lee, after a moment of stupefaction, let flow a flood of
language so lurid that even old Keziah had never heard it sur-
passed. He'd been foozled, had the bloody wool pulled over his

eyes and he as sober as a judge. His opinion of the Dean, and of all the grinders of the faces of the poor the world over, echoed up and down Swithins Lane and in no time at all a crowd was at the shop. He did a brisk trade that night, his fury and his language sauce to the fried fish. Yet all the time that grip held him. Shutting up shop that night he was suddenly silent, and when he had given Keziah one on the ear and kicked the cat he went to his bed with extraordinary meekness and lay awake till dawn.

4

The Dean walked back down Swithins Lane towards the North Gate. He was utterly exhausted, drained of strength and virtue. Yet the hidden tussle with the soul of the man had not been as hard as he had expected, for he was not entirely evil yet. Nor was the old crone. Cruel, yes, but who was not? Down at the bottom of the most crystal cup there seemed always to be left a few dregs of the poison. He could remember how, flogging boys, there had once or twice spurted up in him a desire to lay it on a bit harder, get a whimper out of a stubborn culprit, and then he had instantly dropped the cane in horror and revulsion and when the boy had gone he had repented and prayed. He himself was a cracked and polluted vessel. What could one do? Nothing. Only repent and pray and love and await God's mercy.

He reached the North Gate and walked down the dirty steps to the path at the edge of the river, then turned to walk along it behind the Swithins Lane houses, for he wanted to see the attic window from which Job had escaped. The backs of these houses always made him feel as though he were in a nightmare. The broken windows, stuffed here and there with rags or boarded up to keep out the bitter wind that swept across the fen, looked out on filthy backyards and poor little patches of ground running down to the river path, filled with nettles, cabbage stalks, broken glass and crockery. The path was strewn with rubbish and the river water that lapped against it was always oily and foul. It was here that the Dean had planned his beloved garden, with grass and flowering shrubs, and seats beside a clean and wholesome river. He could see it in his mind's eye now, as he picked his way among the cabbage stalks and bits of broken crockery, and his mouth set almost savagely in determination.

When fish bones and decaying fish heads made a slime under his feet he knew that he had reached the back of the shop and stopped and looked up. He saw the attic window, a crazy little dormer window that appeared about to fall out of the roof. The central wooden bar had been wrenched away and the two casements hung drunkenly outwards. There would have been room for a slim boy to squeeze through and drop into the bed of nettles below. It was a considerable drop and the Dean wondered that he had not injured himself. Perhaps he had. If so, where was he? The Dean turned to look at the scum on the river, which here looked almost solid with decay, and the sight reassured him. Job was not the boy to plunge down into that filth. Adam Ayscough was experienced in the vagaries of humanity. He knew well that the desperate can sometimes entirely forget those who love them and yet be influenced in what they do by old habits of fastidiousness. Habit in times of misery can be stronger than love. "Many waters cannot quench love" was said of divine, not human, love, which the Dean knew was not always tough enough to survive the indifference of misery. That was one of the chief reasons why he so struggled to do away with misery. He had been aware of fastidiousness in Job and of aspiration like a flame. Indeed there had been something flamelike in the boy's whole appearance, in his flickering nervous movements, in his genius that seemed to come and go like some spiritual presence, like some other boy looking out of his eyes. He could see Job plunging into fire but not into scummy water.

He lifted his eyes from the filth and looked across the river to the stretch of the fen beyond, and up to the great sky, and the sight was so amazing that he stood where he was. The storm clouds were massed overhead, blue-black and motionless. They had crept up stealthily from the east but they had not yet covered the sky. To the west there was a break over the horizon and through this the light of a wild sunset streamed across the fen, lighting the pools and waterways to gold against the darkness of the shadowed land. Where the Dean stood the air was breathless but out in the fen puffs of hot wind seemed darting this way and that, uneasy as evil spirits, frightening the rushes and ruffling the water, a surface of restless fear moving upon the leaden stillness of the crouching earth. There were no birds to be seen or heard. Usually one of the joys of the river and the fen were the birds, the swans and herons, the ducks, dabchicks and moorhens, wagtails and sedgewarblers. There was always a rustling and a thin sharp piping, a quacking and fluting, and sometimes the tremendous beat of the swans' wings as they passed overhead. But the birds had disappeared. They had all hidden in the rushes. The loneliness and silence of land and water without them was strange, like a ship with sails reefed and passengers below hatches. To the north there was still a band of gold between earth and sky, and against this the village on the hill that Job had seen rose starkly from a thicket of silver willows, its tall church spire black as ebony against the narrow band of light. It was one of the loneliest of the fen villages, it was Willowthorn, and it had about it a courage that riveted the Dean's attention.

To the mutter of thunder he followed the path to its ending at a dilapidated iron bridge. Once there had been a grand old bridge here, crowned by a chapel dedicated to Our Lady, and a paved way from the North Gate had crossed it and continued into the fen. This was the way that Prior Hugh's monks had followed on the night of storm when they had left the city. Of this bridge there was nothing left now but the stone piers that held up the rusty ironwork of the new bridge. As the North Gate came down in the world, and a bridge to the east of the city came into more general use, the old north bridge had gradually fallen into disrepair. The Dean's plan for his garden had included the taking away of the iron bridge and its replacement with a stone one, simple and strong, with a parapet of the right height for the accommodation of fishermen. For the people loved to fish here. Draping themselves over the iron railing of the present bridge was one of the few innocent pleasures of the men and small boys of Swithins Lane.

But there was no one here today and the Dean was alone as he stood on the crown of the bridge and looked down at the rough drove that followed the track of the old road. Between wind-twisted hedges of crab apple and hawthorn it led waveringly from the bridge to the village that still stood out so courageously against the narrowing band of golden sky. Nowadays more modern roads linked the villages and the monks' way was overgrown and deserted. But not today, for the Dean could see a lonely figure coming towards him, now seen where the way opened out, now hidden as the hedges drew closer. He came as unsteadily as the way, wavering from side to side as though drunk or exhausted. In the whole terrible landscape he seemed the only living creature, as though he were the last man left to face alone the doom of all things. As the first flash of lightning lit up the stretch of the fen, so that it seemed for a blinding instant as though every reed and every twig were simultaneously visible, proclaiming aloud the preciousness of its identity before the darkness overwhelmed it, the Dean started forward from the bridge. That wavering figure was not Job, he knew, but it had the loneliness of Job and he could not leave it to face the doom alone.

I

THE wind and rain came together as the Dean stumbled forward over the tussocks of rough grass, driving into his face and nearly blinding him. The windings of the drove hid the other man, he could see nothing but the sheeting rain and the stripped hawthorn boughs tossing in the wind. It was like struggling in a trough of waves, and took him back in thought to the days before the dykes had been built, when in a great storm the sea would come raging in over the fen to join the overflowing waters of river and stream. Men had struggled then somewhat as he was struggling now, battling their way through rising water with children on their backs or lambs under their arms, trying to reach rising ground and safety before the waters covered the earth. But he had no more than rain and mud to contend with and was hampered only by his ridiculous top hat and flapping cloak. He felt a quirk of amusement at the thought of the absurdity of his appearance. A poor sort of parody of those courageous shepherds of old days! And with his poor eyesight he was likely to pass the lost sheep in the drove and never even see it. He battled on and presently ceased to feel amused, for he was feeling extremely ill. The thudding of his heart made it difficult for him to get his breath. He stopped, supporting himself on his stick. Fool that he was to go in for such capers at his age!

"Are you mad?" asked a hoarse high-pitched voice, and he was aware of a bony hand pressed against his chest, gripping the clasp of his cloak. Peering through the deluge he saw a tall dripping skeleton or scarecrow reared up before him, supporting itself by its grip on his chest. He seemed to see dark rags flapping about the bones of the thing, dark pits for eyes and mouth. But the hoarse voice was human. " 'O, let me not be mad, not mad, sweet heaven! Keep me in temper: I would not be mad!' "

The Dean was in no state to support the crazy creature. They were in danger of both falling headlong. There was a slight slackening of the rain and he saw to his right an old hawthorn tree whose branches, bent all one way by the prevailing wind from the sea, gave some hope of slight shelter if they sat on the bank beneath it. He steered them both towards it and they fell, rather than sat, upon the bank. The hand that had gripped the Dean's cloak fell away and was clasped by the other in an attitude of prayer. Holding them before him, his head lifted in a queer sort of proud ecstasy, he prayed in a voice that was suddenly strong and resonant.

> " 'Poor naked wretches, wheresoe'er you are,
> That bide the pelting of this pitiless storm,
> How shall your houseless heads and unfed sides,
> Your loop'd and window'd raggedness, defend you
> From seasons such as these? O, I have ta'en
> Too little care of this!' "

His voice broke and he said uncertainly, "I don't remember. How does it go on? How did he finish his prayer? Do you know?"

The Dean finished it for him.

> " 'Take physic, pomp;
> Expose thyself to feel what wretches feel,
> That thou mayst shake the superflux to them
> And show the heavens more just.' "

"Yes, yes, yes," said the man, and lifted one hand, dripping with water, in a childish gesture to his face, as though he

thought to wipe away the raindrops that were trickling down
his grooved cheeks and plastering his few wisps of white hair like
seaweed to his bald pate. The Dean felt for his handkerchief,
not too wet since it had been in his coat pocket beneath the
shelter of his cloak, and handed it pitifully to the lunatic. Yet
he doubted if he was mad. He doubted if lunatics could quote
Shakespeare with such accuracy. An eccentric, rather, an
eccentric who had suffered greatly.

"I think the storm is passing," he said gently. "These
autumn storms are violent but soon over."

A sudden gleam of sunshine glinted like a sword through the
rain, then vanished again. But it was lighter and the wind had
dropped.

"I have been to see Letitia," said the man. "I always go to
see Letitia on a Saturday."

The Dean found his eyeglasses and putting them on turned
to have a good look at his companion. He was an old man, tall
and thin and almost as bent as the ancient hawthorn that
sheltered them. His eyes were blue and bewildered, his mouth
hung a little open and raindrops dripped from the point of his
thin nose. He wiped them off with the Dean's handkerchief
but the hawthorn was not an adequate protection from the
downpour and to his distress they gathered again. The Dean
was better off. His top hat, tipped a little forward as usual,
made a gutter for the rain. Where the bend came in front it
shot off to the ground as though through one of the waterspouts
on the Cathedral roof, leaving his face dry.

"Your daughter?" asked the Dean.

"My wife."

"Does she live in Willowthorn?"

"Not now. She's dead. I go to see her on a Saturday. I sit on
her grave and we talk."

The Dean looked again at his companion. He saw now that
his greenish rags of clothes might once have been decent
clerical black, and the sodden wisps of white under his chin
a parson's bands. From the first there had seemed to him

something vaguely familiar about the figure. Who was he? Suddenly he remembered Augustus Penny, the vicar of St. Peter's in the market place. He had only seen the old man once or twice for he seldom attended clerical gatherings, and had never accepted any of his invitations to the Deanery, but the Dean remembered that in years gone by, before he himself had come to the city, Augustus Penny had been Vicar of Willowthorn. He also remembered being told that Penny was a recluse, and odd, and that he had felt a desire to call upon him, but he had not done so because he feared to intrude on his privacy. For this he now blamed himself. The reasons for seclusion were many. One should find out why a man is alone before one lets him alone, for he may not want to be alone. This he had not done.

"Mr. Penny," said the Dean, "I believe it has stopped raining. We are both old men. Shall we help each other home?"

Mr. Penny showed no surprise at being recognized; age, bewilderment and suffering had brought him long past the point of ever being surprised at anything. He was never quite sure these days whether he was living in memory, dreams, this world or the other. The frontiers were not clearly distinguishable now. There had been a time when he could lose himself in memories of the past and then with a deliberate exercise of the will leave them and come back to the present. He had known then when he was dreaming and when he was awake, and whether the glow of comfort that warmed and reassured him was that of heaven or the kitchen range. It was difficult to be sure now except when he was doing his work. Reading the liturgy, ministering the sacraments, teaching the children, preaching, doing what he could for those who suffered, that life-long routine still held and was still his lifeline. It had always been for him the utterance of his love of God, the expression in works of his adoration and delight. He would hold on to it while he lived. He would praise his God while he had his being. Suddenly he struggled to his feet, feeling the tug of the lifeline. He was needed at home. Someone needed him.

"I am needed at home," he said.

"Our way lies together," said the Dean. "Could you help me up? I do not seem to be able to get a proper purchase in this mud. You are nimbler than I am. Much obliged. Much obliged."

Augustus Penny was surprisingly strong and had swung the Dean to his feet in a trice. "Ah, see there!" he cried in his high-pitched voice. "The waters have abated. The dove has found rest for the sole of her foot. She has not returned."

The storm had passed and the whole fen lay bathed in spent sunlight. Every stream and stretch of water among the rushes, that had been whipped and tormented by the storm, lay quiet now, reflecting the piled masses of white and silver clouds that floated like swans on the far deep pools of the sky. Every twig was strung with sparkling crystal drops, and every drop had a rainbow caught in its heart. The Dean could not see these rainbows, he could only see the dazzle of light, but Augustus Penny could see them and he laughed and clapped his hands like a child. And then looking back up the drove he saw something else. "Look there! Look there!" he cried, pointing a lean forefinger at what he saw. "That's where she is. That's it! That's it!"

The Dean looked too and this time he saw something of what Mr. Penny saw, for his long-distance sight was better than his near sight. From this point onwards the drove ran fairly straight, a green way narrowing to vanishing point in what looked like a floating silver cloud, so ethereal in the evening light was the grove of willow trees that grew about the lower slopes of Willowthorn. Above this shimmering cloud rose a small dreamlike city, as delicate as though carved out of aquamarine or opal, roof rising above roof to cluster about the church that rose to the sky like a lifted sword, with a bright point of light twinkling at the summit of the spire. It looked far away, not close at hand as it had appeared before the storm. It had looked then attainable by living man, but not now. They would not get there now. Not until they were as utterly changed as the city. He took the bemused Mr. Penny gently by

o

the arm and turned him round to face the other way, towards
the mortal city where they must finish it out.

"You are needed at home," he reminded Mr. Penny.

"I don't remember," murmured Mr. Penny. "Who is it?
Did I tell you anyone wanted me at home? Generally I'm not
much needed, you know. Not now. Are you?"

"No," said the Dean, and the thought of Elaine was a hard
pain at his heart. "No, not much needed. But we have to
finish it out."

2

There was still a bank of dark cloud low down in the west and
the sun soon dropped behind it. By the time they reached the
bridge it was dusk, but the Dean could make out the soft white
blur of the floating swans and the arrowed gleam of darting
moorhens. The birds had come back. He heard a cock crow
and a dog bark. The terror was over and a cool breath came
from the face of the river. It was so dusky, and there were so
few people about, that no one recognized the two old men as
wet and exhausted they struggled up the steep streets of the
city towards the market place. As they went there was another
shower of rain but they were already so wet that it could not
make them much wetter. Five o'clock struck as they reached
the market place and the Dean was astonished to find it still so
early. He seemed to have lived through a lifetime since he had
left home after luncheon. And he had accomplished nothing.

"There won't be a fire at home, you know," said Mr. Penny
gloomily. "Not till I light it. No fire."

The Dean had intended to leave Mr. Penny at his door but
now he changed his mind. He would go in. There must surely
be someone to be found who would light a fire for Mr. Penny
and dry his clothes. He could not go back to his own luxurious
home and leave him comfortless.

St. Peter's vicarage was behind the church and was reached
by a narrow lane that led off the market place between the
church and the Swan and Duck. "This is my church," said Mr.

Penny proudly, pausing at the entrance to the lane and looking up at the weight of darkness beside him and above him. St. Peter's was not a large church but with its low square tower and storm-grey buttressed walls it had an air of sturdiness and strength, and in this duskiness looked less like a church than a great rock upon the seashore. The deserted market place, with the wet cobbles reflecting the last of the afterglow as ripples do on calm water, and the street lamps like the riding lights of ships at anchor, seemed to the Dean to be the sea lapping gently against the worn stone.

"Shall we go in?" whispered Mr. Penny. "I hide the key in the porch."

The Dean could see the porch, a pitch black cave in the storm-grey rock. The beautiful gold-flecked water washed into it and out again, but silently. He felt he could not presume to go inside. He saw a broken marble floor through which there welled up a clear cool spring that mirrored a few stars, for there was a rent in the roof. The water was living so that the stars trembled. There was a freshness in the air. One could not go in.

"Another day," said Mr. Penny, disappointed. "We'll go home now." They went on down the lane into a garden overgrown with trees and saw through the tangled boughs a gaunt house where all the windows but one were darkened. In that one there was the wink and glow of firelight. "It *is* lighted," said Mr. Penny. "There's someone there. How very odd."

"We will understand when we go in," said the Dean. He still thought he had better go in. It might be that Mr. Penny had lighted the fire himself before he went out, and had forgotten what he had done. In that case there was no one to see that he changed his wet clothes.

Mr. Penny stumbled up the cracked steps to the battered old front door, from which the paint had long since peeled away, and pushed it open. Then with an uncertain stumbling courtesy, the remnant of something that had once been sure and proud, he took off an imaginary hat and holding it against his breast with his left hand gestured with his right towards his home. "Please to come in, sir. You are very welcome. Just a glass of wine and a biscuit. I am honoured, sir. A glass of wine and a biscuit."

His voice trailed off uncertainly and the Dean saw that he must go in first. The hall was a vast chill darkness, crossed by a thin beam of light from a door that was not quite closed. It illumined a curtain of cobwebs, swaying in the draught, but nothing else. The sickly-sweet smell of mildew, unaired rooms, dust and mice, made the Dean's head swim and for a moment he was utterly bewildered. "Most extraordinary!" he said to himself.

For some while now he had found it hard to remember that this was the city, and that not a mile from him Garland was washing up the tea things and Elaine was sitting by the fire with her embroidery. The silence of birds by the bridge, the drenching storm and the old mad king clutching at his chest, the celestial city at the end of the long green way, the riding lights of the ships and the hidden place where the living water welled up through the broken floor, and now this house of windy darkness. Who could have believed that they were there beneath the crust of things? Life had taken on a strange richness since Mr. Peabody had sidled like a terrified crab into his study, had lifted the thin gold shell of his watch and shown him the hidden watchcock. Until now life for him had meant the aridity of earthly duty and the dews of God. Now he was aware of something else, a world that was neither earth nor heaven, a heartbreaking, fabulous, lovely world where the conies take refuge in the rainbowed hills and in the deep valleys of the unicorns the songs are sung that men hear in dreams, the world that the poets know and the men who make music. Job's world. Isaac's world. The autumn song of the robin could let you in, or a shower of rain or a hobby-horse lying on a green lawn.

The strange dark hall was flooded with light, and in the oblong splendour of the opened door stood a beautiful boy.

His dark hair was tumbled on his forehead and his broad fine-boned face was fiercely flushed across the cheek-bones. His eyes, dark and brilliant, swept the hall with that effortless certainty of the young who see so well that they are in no doubt about what they see. His head was flung back, his hands raised to each side of the door, and the garment of soft olive green that he wore belted about him flowed to the ground. His figure was defiant, glorious, and for a moment or two the Dean placed it with the riding lights and the broken marble floor, something he would not have seen a month ago. "Sir! Sir!" cried the boy, but still it took him a few minutes to identify this young god with Job attired in a woman's faded velvet dressing gown, and a few moments more to realize that the change was the change from normal health to the defiant courage that will not submit to fever and pain. Job had guts. He took two long strides across the hall and put his arms round him that he might take his taut hands from the sides of the door. Job sagged for a moment, tried for his footing and failed to find it. The Dean picked him up, feeling his body burning hot under the dressing gown and as surprisingly light as the body of a dead bird can feel, held upon the palm in the days of snow and frost-bound earth. In his mood of exaltation he did not find it hard to carry him to the old sofa with broken springs that stood at right angles to the fire.

"Of course, now!" said Mr. Penny, standing behind them and rubbing his hands happily together. "How could I have forgotten who it was? David? Joshua? Job! Job Mooring. He comes to my church. Attends at St. Peter's. No one young comes except Job and the king's daughter. Did you light the fire, Job?"

"Yes, sir."

"Good boy. Good boy. And you've put the teapot on the hob. Good boy. Letitia's dressing gown. I've always kept it. Now we'll have tea."

"Mr. Penny, you are very wet," said the Dean. "I beg that first of all you will go upstairs and put on some dry clothes."

He spoke with authority and Mr. Penny ambled off murmuring to himself, "Tea and toast. I like tea and toast. Tea and toast." The Dean could hear him stumbling up a long flight of dark stairs and he pictured them as going on for ever. What a vast height darkness had, and what depth. The fire, and the one guttering candle on the mantelpiece, did not illumine the further reaches of Mr. Penny's vast cobwebbed study. Beyond the torn carpet, the piles of books on the floor, and the tall chair where he had put his hat and cloak, the walls vanished in a shapeless infinity of darkness. He thought the clouds must have come over the first stars.

"You're wet too, sir," said Job shyly.

"No matter," said the Dean, "I shall change when I get home. Did you escape from that window, Job?"

"Yes, sir. I sprained my ankle."

The Dean looked at the clumsy bandages that protruded from beneath Letitia's dressing gown. They were obviously the combined work of Job and Mr. Penny, not of Doctor Jenkins. Dark ridges were gouged out under Job's eyes and there were beads of sweat on his forehead. He must have broken the ankle. "Could you tell me what happened?" he asked gently. "I know that Albert Lee beat you and that you tried to run away. I know no more than that."

Job sat up straight on the sofa. "I could be making the toast, sir. Mr. Penny likes toast."

The Dean saw his hand tighten on the edge of the sofa as he moved. Yes, the boy had courage. He liked courage in a boy. He was proud of Job. Adjusting his eyeglasses and looking about him he perceived a platter of grimy-looking bread in the hearth before the fire, with a toasting fork. A pat of butter and milk in a cracked jug stood on the mantelpiece beside the guttering candle. "Stay where you are, Job," he croaked commandingly. "I used to make toast at your age. I can't have forgotten the trick of it."

A three-legged stool was near him. He lowered himself down to it with the utmost care, for he doubted if any article of

furniture in this house could be used with any assurance of
safety, spread a piece of bread on the toasting fork and held
it hopefully towards the fire. The steam from his wet garments
rose about himself and Job like smoke from a bonfire. He was
divided between sorrow that Mr. Penny should be living out
his old age in this cobwebbed darkness, and he had not known
it, amusement at his own situation, and a return of that strange
joy that once or twice lately had suddenly arisen within him
as he had seen the spring rising through the cracked marble of
the floor. It was strange because until now foreign to his
experience. He took it when it came with a humble startled
gratitude.

"I had meant to go to Willowthorn, sir," said Job. "You can
see Willowthorn from the drove where I used to get the flowers
and berries for Keziah's posies. I like Willowthorn. I thought
I might get work there. But first I thought I must tell Polly
where I was going, so she shouldn't worrit. But I couldn't go
then, it was late and dark and she'd have been in bed. So I
hid in the rushes by the river till the morning. My ankle hurt
but I held it in the river and that eased it. The water was cool."

"It's dirty there," said the Dean, his eyes on Job.

A strong shudder passed through the boy's body. "Yes, sir.
It's horrible there. Slimy. And then there was Polly—"

He broke off in confusion and the Dean found himself intensely and absurdly happy. So Job's love for Polly had not
been quenched. It had about it something of the divine toughness. Polly would be a happy woman.

"Go on, Job," he said jubilantly.

"I started for the city as soon as it was light, sir, for Polly
gets up early. But my ankle made me slow, it was swelled up
so much, and when I got to the market place and was passing
St. Peter's I thought I'd rest it a bit, and I sat in the porch.
There's a seat there under the notice board."

"Mr. Penny found you there?"

"Yes, sir. He gets up early and goes to the church for his
office. I couldn't tell you what an office is, sir, only that it's

something Mr. Penny does in the church before breakfast. He saw that I'd hurt myself. He said to come to his house and he'd give me a bandage for my ankle. But when we'd got the bandage on I didn't seem to be able to stand on the foot, so he said to stay a while. Tomorrow I hope I'll be better and get away. I don't want to burden Mr. Penny but he says he likes the company."

"You didn't think of writing to tell Polly you were safe?"

"I did write, sir, and Mr. Penny he said he'd send it by the milkman." He paused and asked sharply. "Didn't he, sir?"

"I'm afraid not," said the Dean.

"No, sir? But he's a very kind gentleman."

"Kindness, thank God, we can keep until the end. Memory, not always. It is no matter. Is this toast as it should be, Job?"

Job looked at the charred bread. "You turn it round to the other side now, sir. Does Polly know I ran away?"

"Yes. She is much concerned on your account. On my way home I will do myself the honour of calling at Angel Lane and assuring them of your safety. And, Job, this afternoon I called on Mr. Albert Lee and came to a satisfactory arrangement with him. You will not go back there. You are released from your indentures and will go to Mr. Peabody and learn to be a clockmaker."

Job was silent for so long that the Dean allowed the charred bread to burst into flames while he adjusted his eyeglasses and looked at him anxiously. But Job, sitting upright on the sofa, was merely happy. The Dean thought he had never seen such happiness in a human face. It seemed to light the whole room. Even the shapeless dark appeared to go down before it, as utterly annihilated as is a man's shadow when he swings round to face the sun. It occurred to the Dean that he had never before been a witness of one of those moments of entire reversal that come only once or twice in a human life. For Job, in the space of one moment, death had become life. It was like seeing the son of the widow of Nain sit suddenly bolt upright on his bier. The Dean turned to shake the burnt bread off into the fire, then spearing another piece on the toasting fork he tried again.

"I fear I lack concentration," he said to Job. "These domestic tasks are not as simple as they appear to those who do not habitually perform them."

Job suddenly found his voice. "Thank you, sir. This is the second time you've taken me out of hell."

"That sounds over-dramatic, Job. What do you mean? The second time?"

"You wouldn't remember the first time, sir. I was a sweep's climbing boy and my master and I came to sweep a chimney at the Deanery. I wouldn't go up it, for I'd got that I couldn't sweep another chimney. You sent me to Dobson's."

Job's eyes were fixed on the Dean's face in an agony of pleading as dramatic as his speech. He wanted the Dean to remember more than he had ever wanted anything in this life; yet he had just said that old men did not always remember. For a moment the Dean looked puzzled, then slowly his face lit up. To see the hard lines soften, and tenderness and delight beaming in the eyes that looked at him over the top of the Dean's spectacles, was a greater joy to Job than the fact of his own deliverance.

"Dear me!" ejaculated the Dean. "Most extraordinary! I have never forgotten that little urchin. In your early years at Dobson's, Job, I enquired now and again as to your welfare. You, and boys like you, have been continually in my prayers. You must forgive me that I did not recognize you when we met at Mr. Peabody's. You must remember that I am short-sighted and that you have altered considerably. I am obliged to you, Job, for making yourself known to me. Much obliged."

The strange, tall, dusky room, lit by the light of the flames, was like a cavern in a mountain. It might have been in Job's world. It was in his world. He and the old man were close together in his world, and his world was real. The great figure of his dreams was once more exclusively his own.

The Dean broke a silence in which he too had been aware

that he belonged to this boy, and the boy to him. This sense of belonging was one of the profounder satisfactions of love. "Job," he said, "I am perplexed upon one point. Where are you to lodge whilst working for Mr. Peabody?"

"Could I lodge here, sir?" asked Job. "With Mr. Penny? He needs company. I could look after him, night and morning. Make his bed, cook him a kipper. I'd like that, sir."

While the second piece of toast blackened the Dean considered the suggestion. At first sight he thought it bad. This house was no place for a boy. But then this boy was not as other boys. He could see Job finding books that he liked among the masses scattered on the floor. He could see him digging in the old garden whose wild trees pressed against the windows, and finding peace deep as a well in quiet empty rooms, the shadow of leaves, moonlight moving on a wall. If some good woman could be found who would be willing to sweep up the cobwebs in this house, and upon occasions cook something more substantial than a kipper, these two might do very well together.

"We will think of it, Job," he said. "And thank you that you wished to give me that robin. Polly told me of your intention and I am much obliged to you for your kindness." He paused, searching for words. "I should like to offer you my sympathy in the loss of all those little birds so lovingly created. The snail, too, and the mouse. It is a loss whose magnitude I am myself perhaps not able to estimate, for my clumsy fingers have never known the artist's skill. I did once, I recollect, make wool roses but they were not recognizable. But I do write books and were the manuscript of one to be burnt before publication I should, I know, feel it at my heart."

His words seemed to have gone over Job's head for when he looked at the boy he saw nothing in his eyes but a blazing hatred that deeply shocked him. Job, it seemed, could be as virulent a hater as he was a tough lover. "Don't hate, Job!" he said sharply, but he was so shocked that he could say nothing more. It was a relief when Mr. Penny came in.

Mr. Penny, attired in strange but dry garments, an old pair of cricketing trousers and the frock coat he wore for funerals, was almost in merry mood. While the Dean toasted with more concentration and less eccentricity than before he made the tea, hot and strong and sweet, and poured it into cracked cups. Long ago he had liked being hospitable and guests around his fireside had been one of his joys. Suddenly it was so again. From the deeps of his old memory funny stories that he used to tell began floating mysteriously up to the surface, stories that he had not told for forty years. He told them again, chuckling over them, his thin hands wrapped lovingly about his hot tea-cup. The Dean capped them with others. Job, whose pain was not unbearable if he kept still, kept still and ate buttered toast. For the rest of his life buttered toast would seem to him the nectar of the gods.

The pealing of bells all over the city brought the Dean to his feet. Seven o'clock. He must go, for he had much to do, but for the first time in his life he took leave of a social occasion with regret. "Good-night, Job," he said. "I shall be sending Doctor Jenkins to look at your ankle. Keep still until he comes. I will inform Mr. Peabody and Polly of your safety. Be at peace now and let the tide carry you into calm water. That is all you have to do for the moment. God bless you. Thank you, Mr. Penny, for an excellent tea. Yes, that is my cloak. Much obliged. I am glad, sir, that we met each other in the drove this afternoon. To have had some speech with you has been a privilege."

By this time they were in the hall and Mr. Penny had just opened the front door. Outside was darkness, the cool breath of night, the faint rustling of overgrown trees in the wild dark garden. "A privilege," repeated the Dean. He meant what he said. Mr. Penny under the bludgeonings of disaster had not lost his sense of direction or of allegiance. He never would. Love still owned him, steered him, drew him to itself. No matter how eccentric he became he would never go off course.

"Thank you, sir," he said now with sudden dignity. "May I

know your name, my friend? I should like to know your name."

He had met Adam Ayscough before, but he did not remember. The Dean did not want him to remember and he replied, "My name is Adam."

"Adam," said Mr. Penny. "A good name. Adam and Job. Both good names. Good-day to you, sir. I am needed at home."

He suddenly abandoned the Dean, forgetful of him, and shuffled back across the hall to Job. Adam Ayscough shut the front door behind him and felt his way down the broken steps with the help of his stick. The firelight shining from the study window illumined his way through the dripping garden to the lane, and out in the market place the riding lights were ready with their welcome.

He climbed up the steps to Angel Lane and knocked at the door of number twelve. It was opened by Isaac and in the lighted oblong of the kitchen door stood Polly, holding a soup tureen to her chest, her figure taut with anxiety. A crack of light shone along the line of the parlour door, slightly ajar, where instinct told the Dean that Emma was listening.

"Good evening, Mr. Peabody. Job is safe with Mr. Penny, the Rector of St. Peter's. He had a fall and hurt his ankle. There is I think no cause for anxiety but I am on my way to ask Doctor Jenkins to look at it. I have seen Mr. Lee and Job's connection with him is now ended."

Polly had disappeared from the lighted doorway and the steaming tureen was reposing on the kitchen table. The Dean thought he heard the back door opening and closing and was aware of someone slipping silent and ghost-like behind him, and then running like the wind down the street. He was also aware that the line of light down the parlour door was a little wider than before. What would Emma do to Isaac when she discovered that Polly had fled without leave to attend to the comfort of Job and Mr. Penny? He raised his voice. "Will you be so good, Mr. Peabody, as to present my compliments to your sister? Would it be convenient, do you think, if I were to

wait upon her after evensong on Monday, about the hour of
five? I would come in now but I was caught in the rain and I
am too wet to enter a lady's parlour. I owe Miss Peabody an
apology and I would count it an honour and privilege if I might
be allowed to make her acquaintance."

Isaac, nodding like a mandarin, murmured incoherently.
When he had opened the door his shoulders had been sagging
and he had been coughing. A dejected grey woollen muffler
with one end wrapped round his neck and the other trailing on
the floor had seemed the very symbol of his misery. Now,
seeing the conspiratorial gleam in the Dean's eyes, his own lit
up. He straightened himself and saw that there were stars
above the roofs across the way. One great planet burned with
a rosy glow. Each street lamp, reflected in the wet cobbles,
had its own glory. The smell of onion soup that flowed out
from the little house into the street had a remarkable pungency.
Isaac was fond of onions. Job was safe and Emma was mollified,
for the parlour door had closed softly. The rosy planet so
dazzled his eyes that he did not for the moment realize that the
Dean had left him. When he did realize it he did not mind,
for his love was creeping like a girdle round the whole city and
nothing he loved was absent from him. Job was safe. No one
he loved was in danger. Nor was he. He had been cold and
shivering for days but now he was warm. Gathering up the
trailing end of muffler as though it were a dowager's train he
turned back into the house, shut the door and called out
cheerily, "I'll bring in the soup, Emma."

3

The Dean walked along Worship Street, knocked at Doctor
Jenkins's door and left a message with the astonished parlour
maid. Then he turned homeward, flogging his weary mind to
the remembrance of his next duties. He could now leave Job
and Mr. Penny in the competent hands of Doctor Jenkins
and Polly, but he must find a permanent housekeeper for St.
Peter's vicarage. He would ask Elaine. He would ask her

tonight. He must see Havelock. He must find an apprentice
for Albert Lee. The things he must do went round and round
in his head. It seemed a long way from Worship Street to the
Deanery and when Garland opened the door to him he
stumbled clumsily on the mat.

"You're wet, sir!" said Garland angrily, taking off his cloak.
"You're wet through, sir!"

"No matter," said the Dean. "If I change quickly I shall not,
I trust, be late for dinner. Mrs. Ayscough has not been anxious?"

"Mrs. Ayscough has had her dressmaker with her, sir," said
Garland, and shut his mouth like a trap.

"Ah!" said the Dean with a sigh of relief. "She has been
occupied."

He was going upstairs, Garland with him. Presently he was
in his dressing-room, changing his wet things, and Garland
was presenting him with a small but fiery drink on a tray. He
waved it aside but Garland appeared to have taken root in the
carpet and his silent fury was so intimidating that the Dean
drank it. Subsequently he felt warmer, but more muddled.
Garland moved soft-footed about the room, and presently the
Dean found himself impeccably dressed for dinner. Then he
was in the drawing-room with Elaine, not very sure whether
Garland had inserted him through the door, as a nurse inserts
the small boy she has brought down from the nursery for his
hour with his mother, or whether he had not. The gong
boomed and he and Elaine went in to dinner.

Hot food made him feel more like himself and after dinner,
when they were by the drawing-room fire, she with her embroidery, he asked her, "My dear, what happened to that
housemaid we had? The one you sent away."

"Which one, Adam?" asked Elaine. "The fen girls are so
heavy and stupid, so unteachable, that I have sent away a good
many."

"Her name was Ruth and she had been badly burnt in her
youth. Her face was much scarred."

"You mean Ruth Newman." Elaine shuddered. "What a

revolting creature she was! I only kept her two months. But she left two years ago, Adam. What makes you remember her? Her ugliness, I suppose."

"I did not think her ugly," said the Dean. He was looking thoughtfully at the fire. He remembered Ruth very well, a woman of middle age, a country woman, moving with a slow and quiet strength. The drawn purple scars had been a disfigurement, certainly, but not an ugliness, for what one had chiefly noticed about her face had been the broad lined forehead and the extraordinary softness of the dark eyes, widely spaced beneath fine brows. He had reason to remember her, for it was during the two months when she had been with them that he had been seized with an unusually bad bout of lumbago, at a time when Garland had been laid up with a feverish attack. He had stumbled and fallen upon the stairs one evening, and had found himself unable to get up again. He had not known what to do, for if he had called out for help Elaine might have heard him and been alarmed. The shock might have brought on one of her headaches. But Ruth, crossing the landing above, had seen him and came to his assistance, and subsequently looked after him, applying remedies which she assured him had been of great service to her own grandfather. The remedies had seemed strange to him; the application to the afflicted part of salt warmed in the oven, and subsequent anointing with hog's grease. But though strange they had been remarkably effectual and he had never forgotten her sensible matter-of-fact kindness and the peculiar tenderness of her broad strong hands. He had been deeply sorry when Elaine had sent her away. And she, he remembered, had been sorry too. He had given her a gift upon parting and she had been hard put to it to keep herself from weeping. "No, not ugly," he said, adding with a smile, "but perhaps a fellow feeling made me over partial to her looks. Where is she now, my dear?"

"Adam, how should I know?" said Elaine airily, her voice bell-like in sweetness. "She left two years ago."

The Dean held out his hands, still chilled, to the blaze of the fire. He did not look at Elaine and a heavy grief pressed upon him, for she was lying. He wished he did not always know when she was lying but to know these things was one of the penalties of love. He did not need to look at her to see her in her sofa corner in that wonderful sea-green gown, the lamplight on her hair, her needle flashing in and out of her embroidery in its small round tambour frame. There was a suggestion of a smile on her mouth and her long lashes cast faint lovely shadows on her cheek. When she deceived him, managed him, there was always that airy music in her voice, the small smile, the shadow of the lashes on her cheek because she had hooded the amusement in her eyes. Until now he had always let it alone, never pressed her, lest she perjure herself further, but now he had to go on.

"Has she never written to you, my dear?"

"Why should she? There was no intimacy between us."

"Where did she subsequently find employment? You were applied to for a reference, were you not?"

"Adam, how can I remember where all the servants go when they leave us?"

"Try to remember, my dear. It is of importance. I am anxious to find a housekeeper for Mr. Augustus Penny, the Vicar of St. Peter's. I believe Ruth Newman to be the very woman he requires."

Elaine dropped the tambour frame in her lap in sudden exasperation. "Adam, since when has it been one of the duties of a Dean to find servants for the parochial clergy?"

"Elaine, all my life I have prayed much, and as I could I have endeavoured to love much and to grapple with the evil about me, but in the equation of love and prayer with the service of small things I have failed. In the mercy of God it is not, I trust, too late."

He spoke with such sadness that a sudden shiver of inexplicable apprehension went down her spine. The skill of her evasiveness no longer amused her and before she could stop herself she had answered plainly, "She went to work on a farm in one of the villages. Willow something."

"Willowthorn?"

"Yes."

"Is she there now?"

"No. They could not afford to keep her after the failure of last year's harvest."

"She wrote to you asking to return to us?"

"She suggested she should come back as scullery maid. Keeping to the kitchen regions her disfigurement, she said, would not give offence. She had, quite naturally, failed to find another place on leaving the farm."

"What reply did you make to her?"

"I am not sure that I did reply. I considered her suggestion presumptuous."

"You sent her no assistance in her trouble?"

"Possibly. I don't remember."

She picked up her work and dropped it again. Never before had Adam spoken to her like this. His ugly voice had lost none of the tenderness that was always there for her, but the questions were coming fast as arrows. She began to understand how the arrows, without tenderness, had always mown down their victims. It no longer puzzled her that he should have been considered such a great headmaster.

"How long ago did she write to you?"

"Three weeks. A fortnight perhaps."

"You still have the letter?"

"Adam, you know I do not usually keep letters. You know how I dislike mess and clutter."

"Look in your escritoire. I do not think you would have closed your heart to that poor woman. I believe you will find her letter there. You would have remembered it in a day or two and sent her help."

It was he who was lying now, to himself as well as to her. He tried hard to believe his own lie but he still could not manage to warm his hands as he held them to the fire. Elaine rustled to

P

her escritoire and sat there turning over her papers, unhurried and lovely. The abominable cupid clock ticked on and on in a lengthening silence. Adam was praying childishly, with a grief and intensity out of all proportion to the smallness of the incident, "Let her find the letter, O God of mercy." Elaine was wondering how long it would be politic to keep up this farce. Another five minutes by the cupids, she decided, and reached her long white fingers to the back of a pigeon-hole. She was not looking for the letter at all, for she was certain she had destroyed it, but for some patterns of rose-coloured velvet for an evening gown. She had received them three weeks ago but had mislaid them, which had annoyed her intensely for she wanted the gown for the Bishop's new year dinner party. She removed a little bottle of perfume from the pigeon-hole, and a ball of crimson embroidery silk, and then her husband, watching her face intently, saw it light up with sudden pleasure. His heart beat so fast and hard that it nearly choked him. She withdrew her fingers, holding some shreds of bright stuff and a bit of crumpled paper, and turned her head aside as she smoothed out the paper. Then she turned round to her husband with her rare smile like light upon her face, and held it out to him. "Here it is, Adam."

He jumped up and came to her and she rose to meet him. He put his arms round her and held her close to him, dizzy with relief. He had misjudged her, and though he would never forgive himself his remorse was like the dew of heaven because it exonerated her. "Forgive me, my dear," he whispered.

"What for, Adam?" Her voice was cool and amused as she withdrew herself gently from his arms. He was crushing the lace fichu on her gown to a limp rag.

"I spoke sharply, I believe." How could he tell her what he had believed? And how could he have believed it? She would have written to the poor woman in a few days. That fountain of joy was playing within him again.

"Well, never mind," said Elaine. "There's your letter. Do you wish me to deal with it?"

"No, my dear. I've given you trouble enough already. I'll deal with it myself."

She gave him the letter and went back to her embroidery. He sat down again, the cheap bit of paper held on his knee. The letter was written in a laborious copperplate hand, beautifully clear and without blots or erasions. Ruth must have copied it out many times to get it so perfect. A few phrases caught his eyes. "Forgive me, madam. I am ashamed to trouble you . . . I was happy at the Deanery . . . The last few months at the farm I did not get my wages. The mistress died, poor soul, and at the end I had to use my savings for the things she needed. I was glad to do what I could . . . I would not trouble you, madam, were it not that I am desperate." He put the letter in his pocket. It would be discourteous to Elaine to read it now, and the longing came upon him to talk to her, to try once more to come a little closer to her, only he did not know what to talk about.

"What have you been doing today, my dear?" he asked lamely, but when he looked up he found that she was already putting away her embroidery. She so often seemed to be doing that when he felt that he would like to try and talk to her.

"It's late, Adam. You were late for dinner you know. I am tired. I'll go to bed, I think."

"I tired you, making you look for that letter," he said contritely. He got up and kissed her and went with her into the hall to light her candle for her, and stood watching her with adoration as she went slowly up the stairs, her hair haloed in light. Then he went into his study and wrote a long letter to Ruth about Job and Mr. Penny. He made some bank notes up into a packet for her and rang for Garland, for they must be delivered by hand to her tomorrow. She must not remain another night and day in desperation. That she was still at Willowthorn, and still available for Mr. Penny, he did not doubt. "All shall be well and all manner of thing shall be well."

"Garland," he said, when Garland had received his instructions, "where do we get our fish?"

"Sir?" asked the astonished Garland.

"I asked you, Garland, where do we get our fish?"

"At Catchpole's, sir, in the market place."

"We must not leave Mr. Catchpole but I shall be obliged, Garland, if in the immediate future the Deanery order could be divided between Mr. Catchpole and Mr. Lee of Swithins Lane."

Shock and displeasure kept Garland silent for a moment, then he said, "Not very reliable, sir, Lee's isn't. The cat's fish could be purchased there if that should be your wish."

"Mine also, if you please," said the Dean sternly. "I wish to give Mr. Lee a trial. No more. But I think you will find that he will serve us with excellent fish. I shall be obliged if you will inform Cook of my decision and ask her to make the necessary arrangements. Thank you, Garland. Good-night."

CHAPTER 13   *The Umbrella*

I

IT was the proudest day of Emma's life. She, who of late
years had hardly been accounted of genteel birth in the
city, was expecting the Dean to tea in the manner of Miss
Montague and other ladies of the Close. It was true he had
said nothing about tea, and five o'clock was late for it, but he
would not be able to resist Polly's seed cake and her own
speciality of lace-thin bread and butter, cut with a knife dipped
in hot water and rolled up into delicate fingers. She had put
out the best Derby china, that had not been used since her
father had died, and the best linen table cloth with its deep
crochet border. She had also unearthed from the attic, and
polished till they shone, the George I silver teapot and some
very old teaspoons, thin as moonlight. The house was very
quiet in these awed moments of expectancy, soundless except
for the ticking of the clock and the low hum of Sooty's appreciation of the first good parlour fire they had had in years.

All over the city the clocks struck five. He would soon be
here now. She turned to look at herself in the spotted old
mirror above the mantelpiece. She was looking her best, with
her mother's shawl softening her angularity and a tall tortoiseshell comb set high in her hair. There was a little colour in her

usually sallow cheeks and it was not impossible today to realize that in her youth she had been a handsome girl. She was very much aware of it herself for like so many spinsters she had remained oddly oblivious of the effects of time. The years had been long and she had not moved with them, supple to their ring and change, but had withstood them in the cold frustration of her virginity. She would have been shocked if anyone had told her that she was not adult, yet in her dreams she ran and ran in the dark, doubling back upon her tracks to find her father. She had never, like Polly, dreamed of the quick bright water running out into the mystery and of herself upon it in her dancing boat.

There was a heavy step upon the pavement and the window was momentarily darkened by the passing of a tall black figure. Then came a knock on the door and the eager feet of Polly in the passage. Emma stood waiting in stately dignity. She was not shy, for this was her right, but a little anxious as to how Polly would acquit herself. She had coached her in the correct procedure but the girl had been in a troublesome mood over the week-end, constantly bursting into song and what could only be described as dance, so quick were her footsteps as they moved about the house. But she had promised not to sing while the Dean was in the house, to move quietly and slowly, to let no words pass her lips except the necessary, "The Dean, ma'am," when she showed him in, and not to push the parlour door with her knee when she brought in the teapot and hot water jug. But listening intently Emma fancied she heard whispering in the passage, a sound silken and light as the stirring of new leaves on a poplar tree. Then the door opened, Polly flattening herself against it. "There's no need to feel for the mat, sir," she said. "I've took it away. The Dean has caught a cold, ma'am. Which tea did you say, best or kitchen?" Emma ignored her as the Dean bent courteously over her hand. "Best or kitchen?" persisted Polly. "Kitchen's the stronger and him with a cold."

"Might I be allowed to put in a plea for the stronger brew?"

asked the Dean. "I did not intend, ma'am, to put you to the trouble of giving me tea but I am much obliged."

He was very hoarse but he had not, he assured Emma, caught a cold, or he would not have waited upon her. He had got wet on Saturday and the reading of the lessons at the Cathedral services yesterday had a little acerbated the vocal cords. And now the weather had turned very chilly. "This good fire, ma'am," he croaked, his hands stretched to its blaze, "hot tea and a rest will do wonders for me."

"You have been busy today?" asked Emma.

"A couple of committee meetings, a visit to the workhouse and my lawyer. Just routine business. No more. What a charming parlour this is, ma'am. Is that your worthy father? There's a likeness, ma'am. I see a strong likeness. I am sorry that I did not know him."

They stood together before the portrait of the Reverend Robert Peabody while Emma expatiated on his merits. Behind their backs Polly came in with the tea and went out again. When the parlour door had shut behind her the Dean felt like a child whose mother has left it alone in a strange and frightening place. Firelight and Polly had lent a momentary charm to the parlour but now, looking up at the portrait, he was aware of having passed under the shadow of a dark hand. Emma, he realized, lived under it always. Her parlour was her past, and Issac's, and if Isaac in tearing himself out of its grip had torn himself too he was better off with his asthma and his nerves and his eccentricity than Emma. Better to struggle through life with a broken wing than to have no wings at all.

When he was seated opposite Emma at the tea table he said, "Will you forgive me, ma'am, that I left so hastily when I called the other evening? I gave myself no opportunity for the privilege of a little conversation with you. I fear I must have appeared discourteous."

"I beg you will not mention it, Mr. Dean," said Emma graciously from behind the George I teapot. "You are a busy man, I know." She had forgotten now that at the time she had been jealous and resentful. To have the great Dean apologizing to her, seated here at her table, eating her bread and butter and drinking her tea, even though it was the kitchen tea, was giving her a satisfaction greater than anything she had known in years. She cut generous slices of the seed cake and the Dean's heart sank. He had had a cup of tea with Elaine already, he had an unworthy detestation of seed cake, and his throat was in that condition when every swallow is a matter of painful difficulty. Such a vast and stupefying fatigue weighed upon him that he could scarcely remember what he was here for, and what it was that he had thought he had to say. The child. Something about the child. What child?

"A piece of cake, Mr. Dean?" suggested Emma coyly. "I know gentlemen like cake."

"Thank you, ma'am," said the Dean. "Much obliged."

Struggling in the deepest depression to masticate seed cake he ruminated in alarm on Emma's sudden coyness. An unloving woman, he had thought at their first meeting, torn with dark passions, and though he had felt profound pity yet he had instinctively disliked her and had cravenly fled. Well, he was back here again because he had fled, and would have to return all over again were he to retreat before her coyness. Why was she coy? As he talked laboriously of the weather, of her revered father, of the affairs of the city, he watched her and saw that she was not so much coy as strangely happy. Her eyes rested upon the seed cake as though it had lighted candles upon it, and her fingers, touching the tea things, had a sort of joyous deftness that made him think of a child untying birthday presents . . . When was Bella's birthday? he irrelevantly wondered . . . She did not use this lovely china and these thin silver spoons very often, he realized. She had no friends for whom to make a party. Possibly her shadowed childhood had never known parties, and the child in her watched still for her birthright, shaking the barren tree, puzzled because no treasure fell in her lap. Suddenly his dislike of her cracked and fell apart, and the warmth of profound relief flooded through him. He disliked so seldom, was so increasingly prone to love much, that to dislike even a little was a great distress to him. Poor child! This woman was no monster, merely another of the children. "The child!" he said with sudden jubilation, unaware that he had spoken aloud.

"The child?" asked Emma, puzzled, for a moment before they had been speaking of Alderman Turnbull, who had just been elected mayor, a man well past middle age.

"The boy, ma'am," said the man, suddenly remembering what it was that he had thought he would say to her. "I want to ask your help for him. I badly need your assistance in a project dear to my heart."

Emma was astonished, touched, curious, enormously flattered. "What boy, Mr. Dean? I shall gladly do all in my power."

"Job Mooring, ma'am, whom I have persuaded your good brother to take as his apprentice. I believe him capable of becoming an excellent craftsman. Indeed I believe that with our encouragement and affection, yours, ma'am, and Mr. Peabody's and my own, he will become a great man. His story is a tragic one. Let me tell it to you."

He told her all he could about Job and she listened rigidly, her eyes on her plate. When he had finished she asked in a cold remote voice, "Do you consider those little toys he makes show promise?"

"Ma'am, I consider them to show genius," he said gently.

There was a silence and he waited anxiously. She did not know that he had heard that she had burnt the little birds. If she would now of her own will tell him about it he could not think of anything that would make him happier. But the silence lengthened and she said nothing. His heart sank. He waited for another minute, then changed the subject with as much cheerfulness as he could muster.

"Do you number Miss Montague among your circle of acquaintances, ma'am?" he asked.

"I have not that pleasure," said Emma, but still she did not raise her eyes from her plate. She had a feeling that if she did the Dean would see in them that she had burnt the birds. And he must never know. "With our encouragement," he had said, linking her with himself, and now he was taking it for granted that she and Miss Montague moved in the same social circle. He knew she was a lady. He was a man who could recognize gentility when he saw it. He was a perfect gentleman.

"I wish, ma'am, that you could know her," said the Dean. "But she is an invalid now. I believe that she would take it very kindly were you to call upon her. I fear that life can be lonely in the latter years."

The idea of loneliness in connection with Mary Montague was laughable and the Dean had an uncomfortable feeling that the strict veracity he so much prized was not the hall-mark of this conversation. He scarcely knew what he was saying. In his heavy fatigue he felt like a top heavy bumble bee, his blunderings past his control. He could only put his trust in those invisible tides that do sometimes lift and carry a man when his own sense of direction is entirely lost.

"I will do so most gladly," said Emma. "As you say, life can be lonely for the old."

They talked platitudes for a while and then the Dean rose to go. "I can rely on you, ma'am?" he asked anxiously as he said good-bye. "You will in your woman's kindness do what you can for that boy? And you will not forget Miss Montague?"

Emma was at a loss to understand his anxiety but was immensely flattered by his reliance upon her. It meant, she was sure, that he had taken a fancy to her. "You can rely on me, Mr. Dean," she said earnestly.

At the parlour door, just as he was leaving her, he suddenly said, "There is another matter, ma'am, in which you can help me. When you were a little girl was there anything you particularly longed for? There is a child to whom I should like to give a birthday gift. She has, I think, the usual toys. I know she has a hobby horse. I am at a loss to know what to give her. You, ma'am, will be able to advise me."

Emma cast her mind back over the years. She thought a little and then she said shyly, for she was speaking of a deep symbolical longing that she had never disclosed to a living soul, "I remember that I longed for a little red umbrella."

"Thank you, ma'am," said the Dean. "I am much obliged to you."

He went out into the little passage, where Polly gave him his cloak and hat and stick. He said a few words to her and went out into the street, into the cold mist that was swirling up from the river. From the doorstep she watched, for she did not like to see him go. After a few moments the mist seemed to come down like a wall, and he was on the other side. She came back into the house to clear away the tea, oddly troubled. The parlour door was open and looking in she saw Emma standing by the fire. Her back was to the door but it appeared to Polly she was weeping.

"My!" thought Polly, and went noiselessly back to the kitchen without clearing away. Making up the fire she began to sing under her breath, for oddly enough the sight of Emma weeping had done away with her sense of trouble. Instinct told her Emma's tears would do a power of good.

2

There was an umbrella shop in the market place. The Dean opened the watch that was now so valued a possession and saw that he had time to go there before calling on Miss Montague. He went down Angel Lane, turned towards the steps and went slowly down them. Half-way down he felt suddenly quite extraordinarily ill. During the last year or so he had become accustomed to sudden attacks of giddiness and malaise, unpleasant while they lasted but soon over, and to constant fatigue. But this was something different. There was a sudden constriction of the throat, a drum-like thundering of the heart, like the sounding of an alarm, a queer sense as though his whole body were in mortal terror. Not himself but his body. He himself felt curiously detached, even elated, though the swirling mist seemed choking him and he found he had sat down suddenly on the steps. He had a brief vision of himself sitting on the steps in his top hat, as vivid as though he looked at himself from outside himself, and its comicality twisted his grim face into a quirk of amusement. Then it passed in a roaring blackness. Then that too passed and the grey mist came slowly back and he was still sitting on the steps in his top hat. "I've been here for hours," he thought, felt for his handkerchief and wiped the sweat from his face. Then with great difficulty he took out his watch, opened it with fumbling fingers and looked at the flower-encircled dial. Only eight minutes had passed since he had last looked at it in Angel Lane.

"Most extraordinary!" he ejaculated, and feeling disinclined for movement sat on where he was. He felt curiously peaceful and exceedingly happy, indeed happiness was mounting in his spirit in much the same way as a short time ago panic had been mounting in his body. Though happiness was a poor word for that which was rising within him. "Light," he thought. "Light." That was a poor word too but there was no other. His consciousness moved out from himself and he became aware of the city. It was extraordinary how deeply he had come to love it during the ten years that he had lived here. Behind him, he knew, the Cathedral rose into the sky, the mist wrapped about its towers. Below him there was a faint rosy glow in the greyness, and he guessed that the shops in the market place had lit their lamps. The rumble of wheels on cobble stones, the sound of children's voices, came up to him very faintly. He prayed for God's blessing on the city and then he remembered Bella's red umbrella. "I must get it at once," he thought. "Anything that has to be done must be done quickly."

With the help of his stick, and with one hand on the wall, he found he could get up. He descended the steps with caution, but down in the market place he felt almost himself again. Joshua Appleby's bookshop was lighted up and he could distinguish the books inside, their coloured ranks glowing in the soft lamplight. There is no more satisfactory sight than a lighted bookshop in the dusk, and his heart glowed. He passed St. Peter's church and looked up the lane to the trees of Mr. Penny's garden. Behind their tangle he fancied he saw a light gleaming. Job was probably making toast. His ankle, Polly had whispered to him in the passage, was mending nicely now that Doctor Jenkins had attended to it. The messenger he had sent to Willowthorn had brought back a grateful little note from Ruth Newman. If she was not yet installed she would be in a day or two.

He crossed the market place to the little old umbrella shop, tucked in between Catchpole the fishmonger and Mrs. Martin's bakery. He had never been inside it but he had always liked the look of its small bulging bow window, and the little umbrella, made of tin and painted in stripes of red and blue, that swung like an inn sign over the shop door.

The proprietor of the shop was Miss Bertha Throstle. When the Dean came in she had just clambered up on a chair to light the oil lamp that hung over her counter. Too intent upon her task to look round she murmured, "Just a minute, dear," and went on with what she was doing. Everything she did now needed a bit of concentration for though hale and hearty for her age she was eighty. She was thin and small but also round because of the number of petticoats she wore as protection against the draughts of the shop. Her scarlet tippet was crossed over her chest and a large black bonnet almost extinguished her tiny crumpled face. Her eyes were black and beady and she needed no glasses. Her shop was scarcely bigger than a large cupboard and crammed with umbrellas of every size and shape, from large green carriage umbrellas to dainty parasols with silk fringes. The counter was to scale, reaching no higher than Miss Throstle's waist.

"There now, dear," she said, her task completed, and turned round on her chair to survey the newcomer. When she saw who it was she was astonished but not at all flustered.

Miss Throstle had never been flustered, and never would be. "Well!" she said in her tiny piping voice. "Who'd have thought it? Good afternoon, sir. I took you for Matty Wilcox come for her pa's umbrella."

"Allow me, ma'am," said the Dean, holding out his hand to help her down.

She took it and climbed off the chair with surprising nimbleness. "Turning chilly," she said, when she had bustled round behind her counter. "What can I do for you, sir?"

"I want an umbrella for a little girl," said the Dean. "A scarlet umbrella."

"What age would she be, sir?" asked Miss Throstle, her head on one side like a bird listening for the worm, her bright dark eyes on the Dean. He felt she was summing him up pretty shrewdly. He on his side knew her to be sound as a nut and kind to the kernel of her. He knew this instinctive kindness of the good countrywoman. Ruth Newman had it. They were kind as the bird sings or the fish swims for they seemed not to have shared in the complications of the primeval fall. This kindness was a lesser thing than the love of a Mary Montague, because not willed or fought for, but it had the freshness of all natural beauty and was as balm to him here among the umbrellas.

"I think perhaps four years old," said the Dean. "Or five. I am not knowledgeable about the ages of small children. She has blue eyes and yellow curls."

"The pretty dear!" said Miss Throstle. "I should suggest an en-tout-cas, a parasol and umbrella combined. You know what a child is with a new toy, sir, they can't be parted from it, and wet or fine she'll be able to take an en-tout-cas out walking. I've a scarlet one here, very tasty. And a green and a rose pink."

She laid all three on the counter, and then opened them for the Dean's inspection. They were so small that they were like flowers. The scarlet one had a handle shaped like a poppy head and a silken fringe. The pink had a shepherdess's crook for handle and was tied with a large pink bow. The third was a bright emerald green and its handle was a yellow and green parrot. In the soft lamplight, against the background of the chill grey day, they were infinitely gay. How could one choose? Under each one of them Bella would look equally enchanting. "I'll take all three," said the Dean. He spoke with the abandoned desperation of the true lover and it was as a lover, a creature not quite in possession of his proper senses, that Miss Throstle dealt with him.

"Now, sir, the little puss scarcely needs three," she said. "You must not spoil the child, sir. She's had the cuckoo clock."

The Dean was startled by this, unaware to what extent his latest idiosyncrasies were the talk of his Cathedral city, but his chief concern was with a slight suggestion of kindly asperity in Miss Throstle's voice.

"I do not think Bella is an acquisitive child, ma'am," he pleaded. "A high spirited child, with an artist's eye for what pleases her taste, but not acquisitive."

"A dear little girl," said Miss Throstle soothingly. "But if I may advise you I should say just the one, sir. Children grow quickly. A year from now she'll be needing a larger one."

"Then I'll take the crimson en-tout-cas, if you please, ma'am," said the Dean. But Miss Throstle did not seem anxious for him to buy the crimson. Instead she held the green one up under the lamp, so that the light shone through its silken shimmer like the sun through beech leaves. "You think she would prefer the green?" he asked humbly.

"It's the green she's after, sir," said Miss Throstle. "Whenever her nurse brings her this way she's flat against my window as a winkle to a rock, pointing at the parrot, and that persistent, sir, that Nurse has a lot of trouble. 'Best take her along the other side of the market,' I says to Nurse, and Nurse she says she does that, but as soon as her back's turned for a moment Miss Bella she's across in a twinkling of an eye, right under the horses' feet. It's a pretty green, sir, and as you see it has a little yellow tassel."

"Thank you, I'll take it," said the Dean. "How much do I owe you, ma'am?"

The en-tout-cas was paid for and Miss Throstle wrapped it up in soft green tissue paper, and then in sober brown paper to make it a more suitable object for the Dean to carry across the market place. Then it was time to say good-bye but each was reluctant to do so. Miss Throstle was amazed that the Dean should be so feared in the city. She was not afraid of him. Looking up at him she felt much as she did when looking up at the Cathedral. Here was a rock! He made her feel as though she had firm ground under her feet. Hale and hearty though she was being eighty did at times make her feel a little insecure. The Dean was thinking how many little tucked-away shops there were in the city that he had never entered, kept by men and women whom to his eternal loss he would now never know. His tall hat in his left hand he held out his right to Miss Throstle across the counter. "I am much obliged to you for your assistance. Much obliged. God bless you, ma'am."

He bowed to her, replaced his hat and went out into the gathering dusk with the little umbrella tucked under his arm. Fifteen minutes later, still carrying it, he was in Miss Montague's drawing-room. He had not been there since that day when they had talked of the nature of love. The lamp was lighted and the curtains drawn against the chill mist, the lovely room warm and sweet-scented with chrysanthemums and burning apple logs. The two friends greeted each other with delight and satisfaction, for to both it seemed a long time since they had been together.

"I have something to show you, ma'am," said the Dean, when the correct courtesies had been exchanged and he was seated in the comfortable arm-chair opposite Miss Montague, the little parcel on his knee.

"Where did you catch that cold?" she asked.

"It is not a cold, ma'am, merely a slight hoarseness due to the inclement weather."

"It has been remarkably inclement," agreed Miss Montague. She did not look at him again. For the moment she could not, so violent was her sense of panic. He did not look any more ill than he had looked for the past year or so, but there was something new in his face this afternoon. To her fancy a shadow lay upon it, yet not from any inward melancholy. It was like the shadow of a wing and behind it she believed he was hiding an awed if profound joy. While she tried to quiet the panic, at her age and with her faith a thing both selfish and ridiculous, she watched his large clumsy hands fumbling at the brown paper and string. Their slowness would have reduced Elaine almost to screaming point. To Miss Montague they restored quietness. She was slow too now that she was old. With time a thing so soon to be finished with it was right to let the last strands pass very slowly through the fingers. One had liked time.

"There, ma'am!" said the Dean.

"What an exquisite little umbrella," said Miss Montague.

"It is not an umbrella, ma'am. It is an en-tout-cas."

"For Bella?"

"Now how did you know about Bella?"

"Sarah knows everything, and sometimes out of her vast store she shares a few crumbs of knowledge with me. I am so delighted about Bella. I did not know you loved children. Is it not odd that I should not have known?"

"It was not a thing that I had mentioned to you, ma'am."

She smiled. There was so much that he had not mentioned to her and yet that she knew. Aloud she said, "Are you glad that I persuaded you to take a little joy?"

"Yes, ma'am, but the complications, and indeed the anxieties, have been and are very great."

"Naturally," said Miss Montague. "If you turn for your joy to the intractable and explosive stuff of human nature it's in for a penny in for a pound. The contemplation of sunsets and vegetable matter has its serene pleasure, and involves no personal exertion, but that I think was not what you wanted in old age?"

"No, it was not. And I am not complaining. But I should

Q

like to tell you of these children. They all seem children. Some
people, ma'am, never seem to reach maturity."

"Few grow up in this world," agreed Miss Montague. "We
should all like each other better if we could realize that. But
tell me another day. You have no voice tonight."

"I must tell you now, ma'am," barked the Dean urgently.
"These children need your prayers."

Miss Montague saw that he wanted to tell her and yielded.
She sat without movement or comment while he told her of Job
and Polly, of Emma and Bella, Keziah and Albert Lee, Mr.
Penny, Ruth Newman and Miss Throstle. Her listening quietness was deeply receptive and Adam Ayscough felt as always
that what he told her was not only safe but likely to undergo a
sea-change. When he had finished she said, "I shall be glad
to know Emma Peabody. I am glad she is coming to see me.
I have always wanted to know her."

"Then why did you not invite her, ma'am?"

She looked at him in surprise. "I never thought of it. I am
one of the antiquities of the city, and as such there are those
who make a ridiculous fuss of me, but that does not give me the
right to ask a busy woman to visit me just because I have a
fancy for her company. Who am I that I should presume to do
such a thing?"

He smiled. It was as he had always thought and she had not
the slightest idea of what she was and what she did. That was
as it should be for to have begun to know her value would have
been to begin to lose it. "Miss Peabody will come, I am sure of
it," he said. "I wish I could be as sure that Job will stop hating
her."

"He will," said Miss Montague. "Do not forget to show him
the Cathedral. I wish I could see Bella."

"I will bring her to see you tomorrow, ma'am."

"You will do no such thing. You will stay indoors tomorrow
and see Tom Jenkins."

"Not yet, ma'am!" said the Dean in alarm. "I have too
much to do. There's Albert Lee. That great hulking boy they're

sending him from the workhouse will suit, I think, but he
needs to get about more. He's a gypsy. He should, I think,
have a little cart, with a smart pony, and drive to the villages
two or three times a week with his fish. With more variety in
his life he'd drink less. I must see to it. And Swithins Lane,
ma'am, it *must* come down." If he had not been so hoarse he
would have shouted, and he brought his fist violently down
upon the arm of his chair. It was no way to behave in a lady's
drawing-room. "Ma'am!" he ejaculated in horror. "I must
ask your pardon. I believe I spoke too loud. I had not intended, ma'am, I mean I was not aware—"

"You were hardly aware of what you were saying," Miss
Montague finished for him, "and should see Doctor Jenkins, as
I said before."

"It is impossible, ma'am."

"I will not argue," said Miss Montague. "I have not the
right."

Something in the tone of her voice startled the Dean. He got
up and stood before the fire looking down at her. "Surely our
long acquaintance gives you the right to say what you wish?"

"Not a very long acquaintance. Only a few years," said Miss
Montague. "Though time, I suppose, has nothing to do with
it."

"Nothing whatever," said the Dean, and his voice took on
sudden strength and depth. There was a silence in which
he could not say what he wanted to say. To let it lengthen
would have been painful, and also unnecessary since she had
understood him. She chose to accept the fact that he was
standing as his farewell and held out her hand. He bent over
it, murmured the customary courtesies and went away.

CHAPTER 14

Advent

I

IT was after closing hours and Isaac and Job were in the workshop. It was a wild night in late November, with a north-
wester pouring icily across the fen. At times the gusts almost
reached gale force, and sleet crashed against the small dark
square of window. It was an eerie night, with the sort of tumult
abroad that pulls the thoughts outward to itself, and most men
and women in the city were very aware of the rushes lying flat
in the wind, the ruffled water, bare branches twisting and turning and smoke torn from chimney tops like ripped lace. The
clouds raced low and about the towers of the Cathedral the roar
and clamour of the wind was like waves breaking in a cave.
When the clock struck the boom of the great bell, usually so
tremendous, was caught and cast away by the wind and the
city scarcely heard it. This was the kind of night that usually
terrified Isaac, filling him with a sense of doom and setting all
his nerves jangling, for he hated noise, but tonight he was not
afraid of the storm and Job was enjoying it because by contrast
it increased his joy. He was out of it. He was in harbour.

The workshop, lamp-lit tonight, seemed to him a world to
itself, a self-sufficient star swinging in the roaring blackness as
unconcernedly as the planet that could be seen shining in the

dark window pane between one hailstorm and another. Job was aware of both stars, his awareness in itself a glowing thing, and thought to himself that that was how it was with him now; light held him and beckoned him and burned within him. What would happen if the three lights fused? What if the fire inside him could dart out into the glow that held him, and the two together could flame down the wind to the splendour of that planet? He laughed, suddenly, and Isaac looked up and smiled. He was used now to these sudden peals of laughter from Job. The first one had surprised him, for he had thought of Job as a quiet sort of chap. He knew better now. Job's depression had had its roots in fish and frustration and had vanished with them. Quiet he would always be, so concentrated was his whole being on work that he adored, but his present quietness was as different from the other as life from death. His laughter, like most laughter, was occasioned by awareness of contrast, by the sudden striking of one thing upon another like flint upon tinder. It was the spurt of the happy flame.

"Feeling good, Job?" he asked.

"I feel like God," said Job.

For a moment Isaac the unbeliever was slightly scandalized. Then he realized that Job, with exquisite precision, was indeed engaged in embedding stars in the firmament. Seated at Isaac's work-bench, with the candle behind its globe of water giving added light, he was at work upon the celestial clock. Isaac could not have believed that he would ever have allowed another to touch his masterpiece, and indeed for a few weeks after he and Job had started working together he had tried not to see Job's longing glances, to be unaware that the boy was eaten up with hunger to get his hands on the exquisite thing. He had worked steadily at the simple tasks that Isaac had considered within his capacity and Isaac had worked at the clock, his back turned on the boy except at such times as Job needed his help and instruction. But Job had learnt so rapidly that Isaac had been almost terrified. It was like having a young hawk with him in the workshop, for the boy swooped upon

knowledge like a wild thing on its prey, and devoured it like
flame running through dry grass. Isaac had been a little taken
aback at first. This was not at all the conventional apprentice,
running meekly upon errands and grateful for any crumbs of
knowledge that his master might vouchsafe to impart to him.
Job did not mind the errands, and he was not ungrateful, but he
had suddenly discovered his own power. He was a finer craftsman even than Isaac, and he knew it, and so, presently, did
Isaac.

There was a greatness in Isaac. One evening at supper, between one bit of sausage and another, he was able to acknowledge that it was so. "He must increase, but I must decrease," he said to himself. He did not know where the quota-
tion came from, or that in taking it to himself he had taken a
fence at which many baulked or fell. He finished the sausage
without having the slightest idea that he was not the same man
that he had been when he embarked upon it. The next morning
he smiled at Job and asked him if he would like to help him with
his clock. Job went crimson to the roots of his hair and unable
to speak bent to pick up a tool he had dropped under the work-
bench. When he reappeared he was no more able to speak than
he had been before but his face was shining like the morning
sun. From that moment the two increasingly loved each other.

They worked now in that companionable silence, broken by
an occasional word or two, which between two who are as
attached to the work they do together as they are to each other
is one of the most satisfactory things in life. Love of the work
strengthened the love of each other. Love of each other enriched the work. "This is good," thought Job. "There will
never be anything better than this. Me and the old codger together. It's good." Aloud he said, glancing at the working
drawing at his elbow, "Sir, why did you put the sun behind the
fish? Wouldn't it have been better balancing the moon?"

"It wouldn't stay there," said Isaac.

This ridiculous answer was one that Job understood. Polly
had once wanted him to make her a dabchick with its head

under its wing. But it wouldn't put its head under its wing. It wanted to preen a feather in the centre of its back. Though Polly had not minded she had laughed at him and had not been able to understand that though he talked about carving the bird from wood that was only a manner of speech. What he really did was to set free the living bird imprisoned in the wood. That dabchick had been unusually lively, and Miss Peabody had burnt it. His face hardened. She was being nice to him now, letting him come into the kitchen, even allowing him to have supper there with Polly once a week, asking him how he did, making him sit with her and Polly in church, and he tried to be polite for Polly's and Isaac's sake, but still he hated her. The hatred surged up in him now, and his tool slipped. He laid it down. A moment before there had been such quietness in him but now it had gone. He could not go on working until he had it again.

Isaac, working at a second bench at his fret of the two swans, felt the sudden disturbance of peace and looked over his shoulder. "Tired, boy?"

"No, sir," Job swallowed, trying to push the hatred down out of sight, below the quiet reeds and water. He asked, "Does the sun behind the fish mean anything, sir?"

"I don't know," said Isaac. "I shall in time."

Again Job understood him. Once he had whittled out of a bit of cherry wood a bird he had never seen. A fortnight later he had seen his first gold-crested wren in the Willowthorn drove. He wondered if poets ever wrote of experiences with which they had not yet caught up. Time as one understood it seemed oddly non-existent when one made things. "The Dean would know," he said.

"We'll ask him," said Isaac, and his voice was warm with delight. Job's hatred disappeared without any further effort on his part and he picked up his tool again and went on working. Beneath their contentment in work and in each other they had tonight a deeper satisfaction, for this morning Garland had let it be known that the Dean was up though not down. He would,

Garland trusted, be down shortly and out for Christmas. The news had spread through the city by midday and the city breathed again.

The Dean had had laryngitis followed by an attack of pneumonia, which though mild Doctor Jenkins had pronounced to be touch and go owing to the Dean's age. When the specialist had arrived from London a curious dismay had fallen upon the city; curious because of the Dean's unpopularity. Day by day they had prayed for him in the Cathedral, and from the Canon in residence to the smallest choir-boy they had attended to what the precentor was saying when he intoned the prayer for all sorts and conditions of men, and impeccable musician though he was neither he nor anyone else had noticed that emotion invariably sent him a semitone flat when he reached "those who are anyways afflicted, or distressed, in mind, body or estate". Michael had struck the hours as usual, but the youngest choir-boy, looking up at him as the choristers in their black gowns and mortar boards scuttled two by two up the steps for matins and evensong, had not thought he looked himself. Through the days of anxiety the invariable greeting of people meeting each other in shops and streets had been, "Vile weather. Have you heard how the Dean is today?" They had all agreed that the weather, which since the day of that extraordinary thunderstorm had been consistently abominable, made it somehow worse. The city had seemed like a ship riding out a dangerous storm, and when they had looked up at the captain's bridge it was empty. That tall grim stooping figure had been no longer there. The Bishop, who had been away, came home, though there was nothing he could do except prowl about and be disagreeable to everybody. Several people who had been away came home, they had not quite known why. On the night when Garland had let it be known that the crisis was at hand no one had slept very much, least of all Garland, and when it was past the Bishop had ejaculated, "Reprieved, thank God!" as though, his butler had reported, he himself had expected to mount a scaffold at noon. Still, for a few days, anxiety had continued, for there was this thing referred to by Doctor Jenkins as "the Dean's age". The harmless phrase had an ominous ring about it, as though it were not what it seemed.

But today, in spite of the weather, hearts had been light in the city, and all the afternoon little bursts of gaiety had kept blowing up here and there like the fires of spring. Faces had smiled under dripping umbrellas and in the shops people had lingered and gossiped and laughed. The muffin man had done a brisk trade for everyone suddenly had a fancy for muffins for supper. The Dean was up and would be down shortly. At the Christmas Eve carol service in the Cathedral, the glory and climax of the city's year, he would be in his stall as usual and he would read the lesson as usual. Not to hear his ugly voice grating out, "In the beginning was the Word," would have been, well, there was no need now to think what it would have been.

"When he's down," said Job to Isaac, "could I go with you to wind the clocks?"

Isaac looked at him, for he found this a hard request to grant. There had been no time as yet for the Dean and himself to combine clock-winding with instruction on horology, as they had planned to do, though he had sent the Dean some books to break up the fallow ground of his ignorance. They would, he thought, begin as soon as the Dean was down, and he did not want Job there. "He must increase and I must decrease." He swallowed his disappointment and said, "Yes, Job. You should learn to wind the clocks. If I was to be taken poorly at any time I'd like to think you knew them all. You've come on fine, Job. I'd trust you even with Miss Montague's Michael Neuwers and the Jeremiah Hartley in the Dean's study. More than that, Job, I could not say."

It was the proudest moment in Job's life. He was aware that there was a sudden quietness beyond their small warm world of clockmaking, not a lull in the storm but the ending of it. He could see a whole cluster of stars in the window pane and in the silence Michael began to strike seven, his notes no longer torn away but round and full and golden. The man and boy smiled

at each other, laid down their tools and listened. All the clocks
of the city were striking now and hard upon their heels came the
chiming of the clocks in the shop.

"Next week," said Job, "the celestial clock will be finished."

2

The following morning the world was blue and rain-washed,
rather as though the azure of the sky had fallen into the rain
and faintly tinctured all that the rain had touched. The trees,
stripped by the storms of the last vestige of their leaves, were
shadowed with blue and the houses were limned with it as
though a paint brush loaded with blue had underlined each sill
and lintel and moulding, and splashed pools of bluebell-colour
under the eaves. Even the Cathedral towers seemed drenched
with the sky and the vast fen was like an inland sea. The pale
gold of sunlight, the orange-tawny and brown and lavender that
stained the blue about the boles of the trees, the rosy glow of
roofs and chimney pots, were subordinate colours, for it was not
their hour.

"We shall have a green Christmas," said Doctor Jenkins, at
the window of the Dean's room, and was not surprised when
Adam Ayscough answered, "Why do we talk about the green
earth? In this painted manuscript of a world the colour varies
with each turn of the page and green, to my mind, does not
predominate. I should like a white Christmas this year. I
remember them in my childhood but none since. Is that the
universal experience? It never rained in the summer when I
was a child either. Memory is not wholly reliable."

Doctor Jenkins turned from the window and there was an
almost imperceptible tautening of his whole frame. The Dean,
with a slight smile, pushed aside the papers that littered his
counterpane, for they were now coming to business. It always
amused him to watch Tom Jenkins turning from man to
doctor. A little chat about the weather was the correct thing
when he entered the room, and he was hesitant, even a little in
awe of his distinguished patient. Then it seemed that something

clicked and he moved smoothly into action, concentrated and wholly happy. Something of the same sort of process was familiar to the Dean when he settled down to the writing of a book. A wave of self-loathing, of self-distrust, would go over him at first. Who was he that he should dare to take a pen into his hand? And how puerile was the result when he had done it. He would struggle wearily through a page or two and then forget himself, coming to the surface an hour later knowing that his book was his artifact, and whatever the result he could no more not make it than fail to breathe.

"Breathe deeply, please," said Doctor Jenkins curtly.

The Dean did meekly all that he was told and straightened his nightcap. He was not yet up all day. During the morning hours he sat upright in his curtained fourposter like an ogre in his cavern, gazing out balefully upon all comers and goers, for his convalescence had now reached the point when he was having a little difficulty with a slight irritability of temper. For reading or writing in bed he was obliged to put on his eyeglasses, which in conjunction with a nightcap would have made a comic figure of a lesser man. But the Dean retained his immense dignity quite unimpaired.

"What's all this, Mr. Dean?" demanded Doctor Jenkins with a touch of anger, indicating the papers on the counterpane.

"Architectural plans, correspondence and estimates relating to the new houses beyond the West Gate," said the Dean. "Plans and sketches of the garden beside the river at the North Gate. You will remember that this important work was momentarily abandoned a few years ago owing to the opposition encountered in the city. As soon as possible the whole question must be reopened. You know as well as I do that this work is essential for the well-being of the city."

Doctor Jenkins was standing at the foot of the bed. The Dean poised his eyeglasses on the summit of his nose and they glared at each other. "You are right," said Tom Jenkins. "Those slums are foul. But you will do no work upon those plans at present."

"In this one instance, Doctor Jenkins, you must allow me the exercise of my own judgement," said the Dean. "Time is short."

"And if you labour too soon at those plans," retorted Doctor Jenkins, "it will be shorter."

He caught himself up. Before the Dean attempted to plunge back into active life it would have to be said, but not yet. But he had checked himself too late; or else had fallen into a trap deliberately laid for him by his patient.

"Ah!" said the Dean with relief. "I shall be glad to have your opinion on this point. That somewhat pompous individual who visited us from London was a heart specialist, I believe. How long have I got? Three months? Four months? I have much work on hand of one sort or another and should like specific information."

"I cannot tell you, Mr. Dean."

"Are you hedging, Jenkins?"

"No. You are seriously ill. How long you will live will depend on how faithfully you carry out my instructions."

"Which are?"

"The diet I have already given you. Plenty of rest. The avoidance of all undue exertion. No hills, no country walks such as I understand you attempted on the day of that thunderstorm. Mental and emotional strain should also be avoided. If you fight such another battle for the demolition of the North Gate slums as you fought before it will kill you."

"Would you consider it advisable that I should tender my resignation as Dean of this Cathedral?" asked the Dean mildly.

A curious panic rose in Doctor Jenkins. He fought it down and replied slowly, "Speaking as your doctor I should say, yes, most certainly you should. Speaking as a man I would like to say that it is hard to imagine the city without you."

He had dropped his voice and the Dean was not quite sure he had heard aright. Could he have heard that? "Thank you, Doctor Jenkins," he said. "I am much obliged to you for your advice."

"And you will take it, I trust. It is advice not lightly given."

"Much obliged. There is just one further point. You will remember that at the commencement of this illness I had your promise that you would make light of it to Mrs. Ayscough. I hope you will continue to do so. You know her delicacy. She must be spared all anxiety."

"Of course."

"Thank you. I trust Mrs. Jenkins is well?"

"I am glad to say she is in tolerable health. I will call again tomorrow, Mr. Dean." He looked meaningly at the papers on the counterpane. "And I shall hope to find you reading Boswell."

"At what time will you call tomorrow?" asked the Dean.

"At about the same time."

"I am much obliged to you for the information," said the Dean suavely. "Much obliged. Good-day."

When he was alone he remained for some while as quietly relaxed as even Doctor Jenkins could have wished. He was so still within the shadows of his fourposter that he might have been carved out of wood. His first reaction was the same joy that he had felt when he had been taken ill upon the steps. Was it a sin in him that he should feel so thankful? He hoped not. Old people were surely allowed to be glad if they could get to the end in a manner that would not impose too great a burden upon others. Only God knew how he had dreaded being a burden to Elaine. If he could get the building scheme well started and see Albert Lee going round the villages with his spanking pony and cart, if he could see all the children happy and Isaac possessed of a faith in God as strong as his own, and if he could just get his book finished he would feel his work was done. There would be no more for him to do. Then he checked himself, for such a manner of thought was a presumptuous bargaining with God. Who was he that he should think himself necessary to any piece of work, to any living soul, even for a short while? Surely by this time he knew his own worthlessness. Looking back upon his life he could see no good thing that he had done, and apart from Mary Montague and, for the moment, little Bella, he could think of no one whose love he had won, not even the love of his own wife.

Elaine. Elaine. He said her name over and over to himself. He was incapable of self-pity but the thankfulness that he had felt began slowly to pass into grief. For he must leave Elaine. He grieved not for her sake, for his loss would be for her pure gain, but for his own. Never again to rest his mortal eyes upon her beauty or hear her voice. Not to see her stitching at her embroidery beside the fire, walking among the roses in her garden, not again touch her hair or her cheek. She had been both the grief and the glory of his life and gladly in the life beyond death would he have still endured the grief if he could have kept the glory. "God is my glory," he whispered to himself. But here again there was sorrow. He was going empty-handed to his God. He had no sheaves to bring with him. Nothing. He had failed his God as miserably as he had failed Elaine. That was the bitterness of death. He was motionless for perhaps an hour in his bed and towards the end he wept.

He was aware of a shadowy figure standing beside him. It was Garland. "I did not ring," he snapped, for Garland had startled him.

"It's been a long time, sir," said Garland. "It is your custom to ring as soon as Doctor Jenkins leaves you."

"I dozed, no doubt," said the Dean. "My apologies, Garland. I must get up at once. I must not keep Mrs. Ayscough waiting."

She came daily to sit with him when he was installed in his arm-chair by the window. She was careful to come just twenty minutes before luncheon, for the ringing of the gong provided her with a natural and easy means of escape. She hated illness. Above all she hated it in Adam because it intensified her physical shrinking from him. And in this illness of his, the first serious one he had had in their married life, she had been astonished by a strange wild bitter sorrow. Why must he always spare her, indulge her, deceive her? He had been near death, she knew, yet the knowledge of it had been kept from her. Throughout his illness he had struggled in her presence to hide every symptom that might distress her, and even now that he was better he told her nothing of what he had suffered, was perhaps still suffering. He had often tried to talk to her of things beyond her comprehension but she could not remember that in all their married life he had ever confided any trouble to her; not even to the extent of telling her that he had a headache. Not yet ready to hate herself she almost hated him. Long ago he should have done some sort of violence to her, taken hold of her and shaken her into some semblance of a wife. Now it was too late.

Or was it not yet too late? Sitting beside him at the sunny window with her embroidery in her lap she wondered, if she wooed him now, would he at last confide in her? He had never refused her anything. She dropped her work and put her hand on his, lying on the arm of his chair.

"How do you feel today, Adam?"

"Very well, my dear, thank you."

"Did Doctor Jenkins give you a good report?"

"Excellent," said the Dean heartily. He expected, her wifely duty done, that she would withdraw her hand, but instead she held his a little more closely.

"The illness has left no weakness behind it? If there's anything of that sort I want you to tell me."

"There is no cause for anxiety, my dear. I am doing excellently."

The answer came with the ease of long habit and though he returned the pressure of her hand he seemed not aware that she was pleading with him. But she was aware, perhaps through the physical touch, perhaps because this new sorrow had made her more sensitive, that death had laid a hand on the body of her husband. She caught her breath sharply, as though its hand was laid also on her own breast.

"Please, Adam," she pleaded, "please."

"What is it, my dear?" He looked at her, smiling indulgently. "What can I do for you?"

She realized he was expecting her to ask for new sofa cushions, or fresh upholstery for the drawing-room chairs. The pressure on her breast felt like a band of iron. The gong rang and Adam raised her hand and kissed it. "Your luncheon, my dear. Tell me another time what it is that you require."

She left the room proudly. She would not ask again.

3

A few days later, Garland, passing through the hall, heard a peculiar knocking on the front door. Callers were not in the habit of knocking, for an imposing bellpull was displayed in a prominent place. The knocking was rather low down on the door, insistent and imperious. Garland was reminded of the knocking of a woodpecker but was nevertheless astonished, when he opened the door, to find himself confronting a green and yellow parrot on the wing. It got him on the knee and it needed all his years of training to suppress a yelp. But he had the presence of mind to grip the parrot, lest it attack again, and found himself engaged in a tug-of-war. He was gripping the parrot end of a minute green umbrella, and clinging to the ferrule end was a small girl in a large bonnet. Bending down to try and see the face within the bonnet Garland relaxed his grip upon the parrot. It was immediately pulled from his grasp and the child marched past him into the hall.

"I wish to see the man," she said.

Her head was tipped back now as she looked up into Garland's face and he recognized the round pink countenance and yellow curls of Bella Havelock.

"You've run away from your nurse, Miss Bella," he said reprovingly.

"I have come to see the man," said Bella.

"If you mean the Dean, Miss Bella, he has been ill and is not yet sufficiently recovered to see visitors."

"He's down," said Bella.

Garland regretted that he had let this fact be known throughout the city only yesterday. What was he to do now? He hesitated and was lost. Bella's pelisse and bonnet today were cherry red trimmed with beaver, a mid-winter outfit which she found oppressive in the warm Deanery. She took off the bonnet and handed it to Garland. Then she kicked off her goloshes and tugged at the buttons of her pelisse. "Undo it," she commanded.

"Another day would be better, Miss Bella," said Garland feebly, but as he spoke he found himself mechanically undoing buttons. "Another day," he repeated, bending to retrieve a minute golosh from under an oak chest. But when he had straightened himself he saw Bella speeding off down the corridor in her white muslin frock, the umbrella brandished in one hand. He gave chase but it was too late. Though she had never been in the Deanery before her woman's intuition led her straight to the study door. Dropping the umbrella she stood on tiptoe and grasped the round brass handle with both hands, turned it and pushed the door open. Then she grabbed the umbrella again and marched in. Garland found the door pushed vigorously shut in his face but nevertheless he opened it again and followed her.

"Sir," he panted, "I beg pardon. I tried to stop the young lady, sir, I did indeed but—"

He paused, shocked and horrified by what he saw, for Bella was sitting upon the Dean's knee with the umbrella up. From beneath its silken beech-green shade she looked out triumphantly at Garland, her blue eyes sparkling and her yellow head a froth of dancing curls. Or so it seemed to Garland. Though it was a grey bleak day he thought confusedly of kingcups growing in a water meadow and white washing on a green hedge, some forgotten scene from his own childhood. The Dean, a west-country man, was remembering the first primroses in a Somersetshire wood. The Dean smiled at him and hardly knowing what he was doing he returned the smile, standing stupidly by the door. He was very tired. The past weeks had told on him considerably.

"There is no need for you to distress yourself, Garland," said

R

the Dean. "I shall be much obliged if you will ask Cook if there is a sugar biscuit in the house. A glass of milk, perhaps. She will know what would be suitable. I am much honoured by this visit but I think someone should take a message to Worship Street lest there should be anxiety on Miss Bella's account. But make it clear, Garland, that I am honoured."

"Very good, sir," said Garland, and closed the door behind him. Bella put the umbrella down and showed the Dean her new shoes, which were tied with cherry coloured ribbon. Then sitting very upright on his knee she gazed round the big book-lined room, the biggest room she had ever been in. She was a little awed and the Dean marvelled at the courage of the small creature in coming to see him. "Did you run from your nurse?" he asked her. "Were you not frightened, my dear, to come alone?"

Bella shook her head. "I runned all the way from the Porta," she said. "And I knocked on the door with my umberella." She felt in her little hanging pocket and brought out a small heart-shaped comfit. "For you," she said, holding it up. The Dean thanked her courteously and ate it. It tasted of peppermint, which of all things he disliked, but he could not disappoint her for he knew it was a great treasure and that she was not parting with it lightly.

"Thank you, my dear, for your letter," he said, and putting finger and thumb into his waistcoat pocket he brought out a scrap of pink notepaper on which she had inscribed, with anguished labour, a few words of thanks for the umbrella. The words had obviously been dictated by a higher power, whose hand had perhaps guided Bella's, but the blots and rows of kisses at the foot of the page were Bella's own. "You see I have it safely. I was much honoured to receive it."

"I writed you another letter," said Bella, "on blue paper. Grandma didn't tell me what to say. I writed it myself. But it fell on the fire."

The Dean felt a pang of keen disappointment. "What did you say, Bella?" he asked.

"I told you about my cuckoo clock," said Bella after some thought. "It caught a mouse at three o'clock. Cuckoo did. I told you Nurse had new garters. Red ones. I put kisses. That was all."

It was enough, thought the Dean. Even the report of such a letter was enough to ensure his bliss. Yet his heart ached that a work of so much labour and difficulty should have perished in the flames. And a labour surely of love. Could it be possible that the child's affection had not been only the thing of a moment that he had thought it? That children could love with extraordinary suddenness he had discovered in Isaac's shop. Could they also love enduringly? It seemed to him that Bella's love had already endured, for to a child the short period of time that had elapsed since they had last been together must have seemed an aeon. He could remember from his own childhood how vast a period of time had been covered by a summer's day. The sense of worthlessness, of failure, was eased a little as he held her on his knee. He wished humbly that she would kiss him again but he did not expect it. She was not, he fancied, very free with her kisses.

"Will you come with me one day to see an old lady called Miss Montague?" he asked her.

"Has she a cat?" asked Bella.

"I believe so," he said. "I believe Miss Montague is never without a cat. Yes, I distinctly remember a cat."

"Kittens?" asked Bella.

"I do not recollect kittens when I last waited upon Miss Montague," said the Dean anxiously, for he feared a kittenless Miss Montague would not appeal to Bella. "But I trust so."

"White kittens," said Bella. "I've a new petticoat."

She lifted the hem of her dress and both heads were bent in admiration of its glory when Garland entered with a round silver tray scarcely bigger than a water lily leaf. Cook had known what would be suitable. On a small plate, with rosebuds on it, lay an equally small queen cake iced in pink. In a rosebud cup with a gold handle was some warm sugary milk.

Having assured himself with a quick glance that the Dean was none the worse for Bella Garland placed this on the writing table, piled cushions on a chair and lifted her to their summit. His movements as he turned to go were not as precise as usual. The Dean was aware of a slight hesitancy.

"Wait, Garland," he said. "Then you can take the tray away."

Garland waited. He was a bachelor, having been jilted in youth by a barmaid who had eloped with a sergeant-major in the marines. Devotion to the Dean had largely filled the gap, but watching a young thing eat a sugar cake is one of the major pleasures of life. Bella wriggled herself forward on the cushions and lifted her chin imperiously. For a moment both men were at a loss, then with the inspiration of genius Garland took out his clean handkerchief and tucked it into her frock. "She's accustomed to a bib, sir," he explained sotto voce to the Dean.

Bella ate like a mouse, her small sharp teeth demolishing the sugar cake very daintily but with an almost inexorable concentration. It disappeared without pause. Then Garland stirred the milk for her with a little apostle teaspoon and that went in and down almost it seemed in one intake. For a moment or two the rosebud cup remained in an upside-down position over Bella's nose, then she replaced it in the saucer and rescued the last remnants of sugar from the bottom with the little spoon. When there was no more she sighed deeply and permitted Garland to wipe her mouth. Lifted down she ran instantly back to the Dean and laid her hand on his knee.

"Does your watch tick like Grandpa's?" she demanded.

The Dean had been wondering if he might show her his watch. It was almost as though in her affection for him she had read his thoughts. He took it out and held it to her ear beneath her curls. Then he opened the pair cases that she might see the wreath of flowers about the face. Neither of them heard Garland leave the room or noticed when ten minutes later he came in again.

"There's a little man inside!" Bella was exclaiming. "It's the little fairy man from the shop!"

"No, Bella," said the Dean, peering through his eyeglasses. "I think not. This man carries away the sin of the world . . . What is it, Garland?"

"Miss Bella's nurse, sir. She offers her apologies. She turned her back only for a moment, she assures me, to speak to Miss Montague's Sarah who was cleaning the letter box. Miss Bella, sir, is very quick upon her feet."

"My compliments to Nurse," said the Dean. "And I beg she will not distress herself. Miss Bella's visit has been a source of great happiness to me. Could it be repeated at any time I should count it an honour. Must she go now?"

"I think so, sir. Nurse is waiting in the hall with Miss Bella's bonnet and pelisse."

"Bella, my dear, we must say good-bye," said the Dean sadly.

"No," said Bella, and climbed back upon his knee. He felt that sense of increasing weight, of adherence, that he had experienced before, and looked anxiously at Garland.

"Now, Miss Bella," said Garland.

Bella ignored him, stretched out her hand and grabbed the Dean's gold pencil from his writing table.

"Perhaps we should call Nurse?" suggested the Dean.

"I doubt if it would do much good, sir," said Garland gloomily. "Come along now, Miss Bella."

Bella dropped the pencil and grabbed the inkpot.

"Put that down, Bella!" said the Dean with sudden sternness. "And now, my dear, listen to me. Do not spoil this happy time that we have had together by disobedience. If you are a good girl and go now I hope and trust you will be permitted to visit me again. But if you are naughty I fear the pleasure may be denied me. It will be a sorrow to me, Bella, if I do not see you again."

Bella withdrew the inky fingers of her left hand from the inkpot and with a queenly gesture held them out to Garland to be

wiped upon his spotless handkerchief. Her right hand she laid
against the Dean's cheek. But she was no longer adhering, and
her body felt light now upon his knee. He remembered having
heard or read that small children sometimes had the strange
power of levitation. They could take off at the top of a staircase and float down; some echo, surely, of powers possessed in
the innocent morning of the world when spirit and not body was
the master. For a flashing moment he knew very intimately the
bright spirit of this child. Then she slipped off his knee and ran
straight out of the room without looking back. She had not
given him the kiss he had hoped for but the touch of her hand
had seemed to wish him God-speed more surely and lovingly
than a kiss could do. On Christmas Eve, when he always
visited Miss Montague, he would take her with him.

4

The following Saturday an expected knock at the back door,
at the expected hour, was a pleasure to Garland. Mr. Peabody,
to wind the clocks, and not a moment late. During the Dean's
illness Isaac had wound the clocks as usual, in the correct order,
not deviating an iota from the accepted procedure, and Garland
had followed him round with a chamois leather in one hand and
a silver milk jug in the other, feverishly polishing as they whispered anxiously together, and finding in Isaac and routine his
one comfort in days of darkness and dismay. The days were
not so dark now, but Garland was not yet easy in his mind and
had a corresponding queasiness in his stomach whenever he
looked at the Dean, and it was still a comfort to him to hear
Isaac's knock. He hurried to the door and opened it, and could
have cried with disappointment because it was not Isaac.

"Good morning, sir," said the slim dark-eyed boy who stood
correct and composed at the door. "I am Mr. Peabody's
apprentice, come to wind the clocks. Mr. Peabody is indisposed."

"Peabody now," said Garland crossly. "What's the matter
with Peabody?" He felt annoyed with Isaac. He had quite

enough anxiety with the Dean without Isaac also taking it into his head to fall sick.

"He has one of his great colds," said Job.

"A cold is no reason for a man not doing his duty," said Garland. "The colds I've had, and kept on my feet!"

"Mr. Peabody dare not run the risk of giving a cold to the Dean," said Job.

"I should not have permitted him to see the Dean," snapped Garland.

"You might have caught it yourself, sir," said Job, "and given it to the Dean." He smiled delightfully at Garland. "I'm quite able to wind the clocks. I've been trained by Mr. Peabody."

He was in the passage without Garland quite knowing how he'd got there, composed and smiling. The impudence, thought Garland. He was just such another as that young hussy who had penetrated into the study with a basket of stinking fishheads. Yet when he looked at the boy again he was standing humbly enough, holding Mr. Peabody's bag. Yet there was an authority about him, the assurance of a man who is master of his craft and means to practise it. Garland led the way down the passage. On the other side of the green baize door Job looked quickly round the hall, his eyes resting joyously for a moment upon the face of the Richard Vick. "I believe I know my way, sir," he said. "I have been here once before. I need not trouble you to come with me."

"The hall, the drawing-room, the dining-room, but not the study," said Garland firmly. "Not the study. That must wait for Mr. Peabody. The Dean is down."

Job smiled, turned quickly to the drawing-room, opened the door, went in and shut it behind him, leaving Garland much annoyed. The boy should have begun in the hall. He'd got the order wrong. The hall came first. Too sure of himself. They all were, these days. No respect for their elders. And yet Garland felt he could not exactly accuse the young gentleman of disrespect. Gentleman? What was he saying? The boy was Isaac Peabody's apprentice and no gentleman, though he might give himself the airs of one. Yet the airs, or rather the air, had seemed natural to him. Garland gave it up and went back to the other side of the green baize door. Yet a few minutes later he was back in the hall again, keeping his eye. Job came out of the drawing-room, smiled and moved towards the dining-room. Garland looked up at the Richard Vick. "Ten minutes," he said to Job. "Mr. Peabody takes fifteen, seeing that all is as it should be."

"I'm a little quicker than Mr. Peabody, sir," said Job courteously and shut the dining-room door behind him.

This time Garland thought it his duty to walk as far as his pantry, but he was back in the hall again as Job opened the Richard Vick clock face. "That is a very valuable clock, young man," he said.

"Yes, sir," said Job. "It is a very beautiful one too. Mr. Peabody thinks the world of this clock." He wound the clock, looked at the pendulum, gently dusted the clock face and polished the winged cherubs with Isaac's old silk handkerchief, all with a careful dexterity that Garland could not help admiring.

"Have you been long with Mr. Peabody?" he asked. "Odd I've not heard him speak of having an apprentice."

"Not long, sir," said Job, "but Mr. Peabody likes to teach and I've learnt quickly." He closed the clock face and turned round to face Garland. "Sir, may I go in and wind the Jeremiah Hartley? I think the Dean would like me to do so. I will not disturb him."

"I have already told you," said Garland severely, "that the study clock must wait for Mr. Peabody." He eyed Job with growing anger. "Had I returned a few minutes later, young man, I believe I would have found you knocking at the study door."

Job looked him straight in the eye. "No, sir, I would not have done that. I would not have disobeyed you. But if he is well enough I would like to see the Dean. He has been very good to me."

There was a short angry silence in which Garland suddenly

remembered something the Dean had said after the visit of the young hussy with the fishheads. He had finished by saying, "You understand, Garland? Much obliged." He swallowed his anger. "I will enquire," he said, and advanced majestically upon the study door. He returned in a moment saying coldy, "The Dean would be much obliged if you would wind the Jeremiah Hartley. Come away, young man, as soon as you have done so."

"Thank you, sir," said Job. He walked to the study door, knocked and entered.

The Dean was writing at his littered table. "Good morning, Job," he said.

"Good morning, sir," said Job, and came up to the table. "I hope you are better, sir?"

"I am quite recovered. How are you, Job? How is your ankle?"

"It has mended, sir. I am very happy working for Mr. Peabody and I like living with Mr. Penny and Ruth."

"You like Ruth?"

"Yes, sir." He paused. "I would like to thank you, sir."

The strong beat of profound happiness was in Job's quietly spoken words. It seemed to the Dean's fancy that clear golden wine was filling the room and his own being too. For a moment he thought that neither of them could stand it. The room was an old man's room, its walls rigid with antiquity, he himself tired to death, patched like an old kettle. They had lost the power of resilience and would crack at the seams. Then the gold slowly ebbed, drawn back into the depths of Job's singing spirit, leaving only a ripple of light on the ceiling, as though reflected from a dancing sunbeam, and a gentle warmth about the Dean's heart. Fancy, all fancy, he told himself, like the fancy that the scent of spring had come into the room with Bella and the green parrot.

"Shall I wind the clock, sir?"

"Much obliged," said the Dean, thankful to sit back in his chair and adjust himself quietly to this new Job.

How did the young effect these sudden changes? Did they, in one of those deep dreamless sleeps of youth, lying cheek on hand graceful and enchanted as though Oberon had touched them, know a metamorphosis such as Bottom knew? Or was it just what they ate? Undoubtedly Ruth fed Job well. In just a few weeks he had grown and filled out astonishingly. There was colour in his face and the hollows in his cheeks and the dark lines under the eyes had vanished. His hair, cut shorter, grew now with a strong wiry twist, full of vitality. He held his shoulders straight and his head well up, as though he respected himself and his work. He had changed from boy to young man. His hands on the clock were deft and sure and whilst he was attending to it he took no notice of the Dean. He had forgotten him. The Dean too was respectfully silent. One did not disturb an artist at his work or a saint at his prayers.

Job finished his work and shut the bag. Then he turned back to the Dean, his eyes sparkling with excitement. "Sir! I'm reading Mr. Penny's books."

"I thought you would," said the Dean. "What do you read?"

"Just what I pick up off the floor, sir. Plato. Shakespeare. Charles Lamb. Wordsworth. It's all grand stuff, even when I don't understand it. But Mr. Penny helps me. Polly never learnt to read properly at Dobson's, like I did, so Miss Peabody lets me go up one evening a week after supper and we sit in front of the fire and I teach her."

He had come back to the Dean's table and the words poured out as he told him of his affairs. Adam Ayscough had thought him changed from boy to man, but now he was back in some childhood he had never had, telling a grown-up he loved and trusted the glorious tale of his accomplishments without the slightest doubt that the other would be as thrilled as he was. The Dean could not remember that such a thing had happened to him before. He listened with one hand behind his ear, fearful lest he should miss a word of it.

Job suddenly caught himself up, aware of some slight sound

outside the door, as of a prowling presence there. He flushed scarlet. "Please forgive me, sir. I should have gone away when I had wound the clock. That's what Mr. Garland told me to do."

"Had you done so, Job, you would have deprived me of a very great happiness. I am more obliged to you than you can well know. Before you go tell me of Mr. Peabody. I understand he is indisposed? Is it his asthma?"

"No, sir, only a cold. He's well over his asthma."

"Had he had asthma previously?"

"Yes, sir. It was only to be expected, Polly said."

"The weather has been very inclement."

"It wasn't the weather, sir, it was you."

"Me?" asked the Dean, his hand behind his ear again.

"Being ill, sir. Mr. Peabody always has asthma when he is miserable."

The Dean did not like to ask Job to repeat himself, but he believed he had heard aright. Bella. Job. Isaac. It appeared that they all felt affection for him. He struggled for speech and when it came at last its banality shocked him.

"My compliments to Mr. Peabody. You will tell him, if you please, that during my illness I have been continuing my study of horology. To the books he lent me I have added others from the library." He moved the sheets of manuscript and architectural plans that were piled on his table and showed Job the books that lay under them, calf-bound histories of clocks and clockmakers. "Tell Mr. Peabody I am his humble pupil and I shall hope soon to visit you both at the shop to choose the clock for my wife. My compliments to Miss Peabody, Mr. Penny, Polly and Ruth. I hold you all in my heart. There is Garland at the door. Good-bye, Job. Much obliged."

CHAPTER 15

I

CHRISTMAS was less than a fortnight away and already its light
shone upon the days. Through all the city there was a quiet
hum of preparation. Serious housewives had made their
Christmas pudding and mincemeat weeks ago but the giddy
ones, those who did not perform their duties until crisis was right
upon them, were doing it now and delicious smells of brandy
and spice mingled with the smell of ironing, gingerbread and
beeswax that floated out into the streets from open windows
and doors left ajar. For the weather had turned warm and
springlike, violet-scented in the early morning and fragrant
with wood smoke at night, and musical with the chatter of
astonished birds who could not understand it. People said to
each other that it was like the Christmas when Dean Rollard
had ridden home from prison. It was proper Dean's weather.
Doctor Jenkins alone regretted the warmth, so passionately had
he wanted the Dean to have his white Christmas. The shops
were gay and stayed open for an extra half-hour every evening,
the lamps shining upon books and toys, sweets and apples and
nuts and festoons of coloured paper. In the market place they
were selling Christmas trees and piles of oranges like golden
moons. The children and dogs were in a permanent state of

over-excitement and every house, and indeed almost every room, had a secret.

The Cathedral towered over it all, benignly great in this quiet weather, the sound of the bells falling gently from the height of the Rollo tower. At evening, when dusk fell, men looked up and saw light shining from the windows of the choir and heard music, for the choristers were practising for the carol service. Michael seemed dreaming. So many Christmases had gone since he had stood here looking out to the edge of the world, looking down at the city, looking up to heaven. So many Christmas Eves he had stood waiting through hours of snow and storm, of wind and rain or of rapt stillness bright with moon and stars, waiting for the mid-course of the night when he should lift his fist and strike out on the great bell the hour of man's redemption. Then when the boom of the last echo had died away over the plain to the sea he would veil his face with his wings, for love was running down the steps of the sky, running fast from cloud to cloud, from star to star, leaping and laughing. He dared not look upon the face of love but he would hear the laughter in that moment of profound quietness between the last echo of midnight and the pealing out of the Christmas bells.

"Last Christmas," said Job, "I did not know what Christmas was." When he had first come to Mr. Peabody he had not wanted to look back for he had felt like someone just awake after a nightmare, and afraid to think about it lest it catch him again, but now the evil had receded so far that he liked to set it as a backcloth to the procession of his shining days. "I did not know what it was," he repeated. "Shall I put the shutters up?"

"Another five minutes," said Isaac. "I don't like to close too soon before Christmas."

"Thirty minutes late now," said Job, but he laughed and leaned his arms on the counter, content to wait. He was tired, and so was Isaac, for it had been a busy day with people in and out buying Christmas presents, but they had enjoyed it to the full and their tiredness was of the pleasant sort that invests the thought of supper and bed with haloed glory.

Isaac did not call himself a jeweller but he did in his odd moments make pinchbeck brooches, heart-shaped lockets and earrings whorled or delicately pointed like shells or stars. He also made eternity rings set with imitation jewels whose first letters spelt words like regard, dearest, and adored, adjectives nicely graded to express the degree of feeling which ravaged the breast of the enamoured male at the moment of purchase, and these as well as his clocks had a great sale before Christmas. Job had proved as expert as Isaac at making these trifles but one of the rings that he had made was not for sale. It was in a leather heart-shaped box in his pocket, burning a hole there until such time that he could give it to Polly for her Christmas present. As well as jewellery he had created flights of little birds, angels and stars, and silver reindeers with golden antlers to hang upon the Christmas trees that were sold in the market.

There had been moments during the past week when it had scarcely been possible to move in the shop for excited children, papas, mammas, uncles, aunts and nannies, but now most of the pretty trifles had been sold and the ticking of the clocks, that for days had been drowned by the babel of voices and laughter, had come back into the silence as the singing of birds comes back when the wind dies at dusk. It was dark now beyond the bow windows of the shop, the sky clear after a passing shower and spangled with stars above the crooked roofs of Cockspur Street. The windows of the houses were small squares of orange and gold, reflected in the shining cobbles. The lamplighter had passed down the street and the muffin man had passed up it, but now there was no one about, not even a cat. Yet they waited in the lamplight, leaning on the counter, and listened to the voices of their clocks as other men listen to a harpsichord or the slap of small waves against the hull of a boat. It was to them the music of their hearts, that pulsed in time to the heart-beat of the celestial clock.

It was there in the window, finished five days ago, the best clock that Isaac had ever made. He had thought that he would not be able to put it in the window, so much did it seem to be a part of himself, yet suddenly he had put it there, in the centre, the other clocks grouped about it like lesser stars about the moon. He had put it there because it was Christmas. To him it was only a fairy tale that love had leaped from heaven on fire for the manger and the cross, but tales are potent things and this one was in his blood, and so he had had to give his best to the city. The celestial clock, his masterpiece, must shine in the window for the city to see. And the city had seen and liked it. For five days rows of faces had been pressed against the window, rejoicing in his Christmas clock that chimed as sweetly as the singing stars.

But he would not sell it. It would kill him to part with that clock. When anyone asked the price he named one so exorbitant that the questioner backed laughing from the shop. His clock had become something of a joke in the city. Everyone knew he did not mean to sell it, yet they would ask the price for fun, and every time they asked it soared higher.

It was Job who heard the heavy footsteps first, and he thought again that he knew now what Christmas was. It was expectancy. This time last year he had expected little except the dreary continuance of misery but now the horizon of his expectations was lost in glory.

"You can put up the shutters now, Job," said Isaac.

"Just a minute, sir," said Job, "there's someone coming."

In another moment or two the black silhouette of the Dean's cloaked and top hatted figure had blocked out the crooked houses opposite, the sky and the stars. Isaac, with an exclamation of delight, was just starting forward when Job checked him. "He's seen the clock!" he whispered.

The Dean with his poor sight had not seen the two weary workmen inside the shop but he had indeed seen the clock. He took off his eyeglasses, polished them and put them on again. He stood perfectly still gazing at the clock, and his face was as still as his body. Both might have been carved out of dark and ancient wood. At first Isaac was disappointed, used as he was to the eager faces pressed against the window and the exclamations of delight. He was afraid the Dean did not like his clock. His expressionless stillness could only mean disapproval. Or else homage. It could not be homage. He watched intently and saw a smile creep about the Dean's lips. He had seen that smile outside his shop window many times this last week but always on a young face, not an old one. The young men of the city, the ones with not much money, had looked like that when they had seen exactly the right heart-shaped pinchbeck locket to give their girl for Christmas, and then they had slouched in, blushing crimson, and counted out half their week's poor wages on his counter. But it shocked him to see that same smile on an old face. Such an intensity of feeling could be borne through the time of courting and first love but he did not know how a man could support it through a lifetime.

Then suddenly fear gripped him as he realized the meaning of the smile. The celestial clock was the one the Dean wanted to give to his wife and he would be content with nothing else. Isaac knew these lovers and their obstinacy. They wanted the one thing and the one thing only and there was no fobbing them off with something else. He would have to tell the Dean the clock was not for sale. What a fool he had been to put it in the window. What a fool! And now he would have to disappoint the one man of all others whom he most loved and admired; the only man, if it came to that, for though his love embraced the whole city he felt a deep personal love only for the Dean, Miss Montague, Polly and Job. He must do it quickly. He must tell the Dean as quickly as he could that the clock was not for sale. Get it over.

Adam Ayscough had moved from the window and Job had leaped to open the door. Then the three of them were together in the shop exchanging the greetings of the season and only Isaac's rang hollow. "You are well again, Mr. Peabody?" asked the Dean, peering at him a little anxiously.

"Yes, sir," said Isaac.

"You must be much fatigued," said the Dean. "Overburdened with customers. And I am yet another, and a late one. I was with Mr. Turnbull, our mayor, talking with him of a project that I have at heart, and I could not get away as early as I had intended. Much distressed." He paused and then said as shyly as a schoolboy, "That clock for my wife, Mr. Peabody. There is one in the window, a very lovely clock. I do not think I have ever seen one I liked better."

Isaac wetted his lips. "Which one, sir?" he asked.

"It is a clock of the heavens," said the Dean.

Isaac looked up at him. Now he must say it. No good beating about the bush. He must say it at once. The Dean's eyes, usually rather dim, seemed boyishly bright in the lamplight. Isaac rehearsed in his mind what he had to say. "The celestial clock is not for sale, sir." He rehearsed it several times and then swallowed and said, "Job, bring the celestial clock through to the workshop. Then put up the shutters and close the shop that we may be undisturbed." He opened the workshop door and stood back. "Will you come this way, sir?"

In the workshop he turned up one of the lamps and cleared a wide space on his work-bench. "Put it here, Job," he said. "You see, sir, there is more space here. You can stand back and get the effect as it will be when it stands on Mrs. Ayscough's mantelpiece. I shall be proud indeed, sir, if you choose this one for her but would you like Job to bring any others through for you to see?"

The Dean had taken off his hat and was standing before the clock. "I need not trouble Job," he said quietly. "There is only one clock in the world that I want to give my wife."

"I am glad, sir," said Isaac. "When you have put up the shutters, Job, you may come back. I must tell you, sir, that I had Job's help in making this clock. He was of great assistance to me."

"That increases the clock's value," said the Dean.

Job went out to the street and put up the shutters in a state of great bewilderment. What ever had made Isaac part with the

s

clock? It was to the Dean of course. Yet he had thought that Isaac would have cut the heart out of his body sooner than part with the clock. The shutters in place he came back to the workshop and stood in the shadows behind the two old men, who were talking in low voices of the glory of the clock. It *was* a glorious clock. It seemed to Job that until this moment he had not himself realized what a masterpiece had been achieved. It stood illumined by the lamplight, shining out against the shadows behind it as sometimes the setting sun is illumined against the dusk. The golden fret that hid the bell was the loveliest Isaac had ever made. The two swans were just rising from the reeds, one with wings fully spread, the other with his pinions half unfolded. Job could understand from experience, and the Dean through intuition, what an achievement it had been to form those great wings and curved necks into a pattern that was a fitting one for a clock fret and yet alive, but only Isaac knew how he had laboured and sweated over it. This had been a costing clock. Yet the figures of the signs of the zodiac were as fresh and lively as though they had stepped with ease to the clock face. The ram, the bull, the heavenly twins, the crab, the lion, the scales, the scorpion, the archer, the sea goat and the man with the watering pot were bright as their own stars, gay as the little figures in an illuminated manuscript. But the virgin and the fish had something more than life and gaiety.

"She stands in her blue robe at her own hour of vespers, full of the peace of that hour," said the Dean. "Expectancy too. A great expectancy. Only six hours to midnight."

Isaac was startled. He had intended no Christian symbolism when he had painted his virgin in a blue robe. He had chosen blue merely to balance the blue of the watering pot at nine o'clock and the blue fillet that bound the archer's head at three o'clock. But the pretty Christmas story was a part of him and had obtruded itself.

"Six hours to midnight," repeated the Dean. "There you have combined the two symbols very excellently, Mr. Peabody.

The fish, the ancient Christian symbol of Christ our Lord, and the Sun of Righteousness, the Light of the World."

With a pang of something remarkably like jealousy Mr. Peabody realized that the Dean's homage, that he had seen through the window, had not been entirely for his clock, if for his clock at all. And what had he been thinking of to put only one fish at twelve o'clock? Pisces, the sign of the zodiac, had two fish. He could only suppose that out of the deeps of his memory that one fish had come swimming up into the light, to remind him now suddenly of his father. For it was his father who had told him how the martyrs had painted that fish on the walls of the catacombs, and traced it in the dust that one Christian might recognize another.

"My homage is a double one," said the Dean, and Isaac's spirits rose again until he remembered the virgin, when they sank, but lifted once more when the Dean added, "You are a master craftsman, Mr. Peabody. I hope the price you are asking for that clock is sufficient for its great merit."

"No price, sir," said Isaac in a low voice.

"What did you say, Mr. Peabody?" asked the Dean, and put his hand behind his ear.

Isaac raised his voice. "I cannot let you pay me for that clock, sir. I shall be happy if Mrs. Ayscough will accept it."

He was looking very dejected. How could he explain to the Dean that he was only able to part with the clock if he could give it? It was himself. A man does not give himself to his friend for payment. The Dean, his hand still behind his ear, was looking at him in puzzled distress. But he could not explain. He had not got the words. Job, he noticed, was escaping quietly out of the room and he saw him go with panic. Now he was alone with the Dean and could not escape. It was not of the man himself that he was afraid but of that which reached out for him through his friend. The Dean's huge shadow leapt up over the ceiling in the same sort of way that the Cathedral loomed up in the night sky. He began to cough.

"Mr. Peabody," said the Dean gently, "do you not wish to

part with this clock? If that is the case I beg that you will tell me. I can assure you that whatever your motives may be I shall understand them."

"I want to give you the clock," mumbled Isaac. "That's what I want."

"Much distressed," murmured the Dean, and indeed he was groping in a fog of distress. One thing however was clear to him, and that was that Isaac was speaking the truth and he must, for the moment at any rate, humbly accept the clock. After Christmas, he trusted, God's guidance would show him some happy way of persuading Isaac to accept payment, or if that was not possible then some way of service to his friend that should reveal without patronage or pride the depth of his gratitude.

"I want it too," he said quietly. "For my beloved wife. With all my heart I thank you, Mr. Peabody. I cannot just now express my feelings as I would. I shall hope to do so at some future time when I have a little more collected myself. My friend, may I stay for a few moments and talk with you?"

"It is getting late, sir," said Isaac. "Dark too. You should be at home."

"To be here with you is a pleasure," said the Dean, "and to walk home in the dark will be no burden. The city at night is a continual joy to me. Do you fear the dark?"

"Not of the city at night," said Isaac.

"Of death?" asked the Dean. "If so you are not alone in your fear, for the dark auditorium with its unseen crowd of witnesses is a frightening thing, pressing in upon our poor little garish stage, frightening because we know nothing of it. Yet when our play is ended and the house lights go up we shall see many kindly faces. It is a house, remember, a friendly place. There is a prayer by the great Dean John Donne that I often repeat to myself. 'Bring us, O Lord God, at our last awakening, into the house and gate of heaven, to enter into that gate and dwell in that house where there shall be no darkness or dazzling, but one equal light; no noise nor silence, but one equal music;

no fears nor hopes, but one equal possession: no ends nor be-
ginnings, but one equal eternity; in the habitations of Thy
glory and dominion, world without end!"

To Isaac this seemed just another finely spun web of words.
Men made so many to hang between themselves and their fear.
They glittered in the eyes but the dark was still behind them.
He was perched tensely on his work stool and the Dean was
sitting in the old battered chair. He had dreamed of having the
Dean here like this, sitting with him in the soft lamplight of the
workshop, and now that it had happened he only wanted to
escape. He was very much afraid one of his bad times was
coming. That would happen, just at Christmas. They always
came just when he was planning to enjoy himself. He coughed,
pressing his thin hands together between his knees, dreadfully
sorry for himself. The Dean went on talking, saying the first
thing that came into his head. " 'The house and gate of
heaven.' I always say that to myself when I go into the Cathedral, especially when I go in through the west door. Men think
of heaven under so many symbols. The garden of paradise, the
green pastures and so on. I think simply of the Cathedral, for
within it I have so often found my God. Before my illness I told
Job I would show him the carvings in the Cathedral. I would
like to redeem my promise this Christmas. Will you come too,
Mr. Peabody."

He turned to smile at Isaac and was astonished to see terror
in the little man's bright blue eyes. "No, sir, no! I have never
been in the Cathedral."

"Never been in the Cathedral?" The Dean could scarcely
believe his deaf ears.

"No, sir," said Isaac hoarsely.

"Did not your father take you there as a child?"

"He tried to take me but I would not go. He beat me but
still I would not go."

"Why not, Mr. Peabody?"

"It is too big. Too dark. If it fell on you it would crush you
to powder." And Isaac began to cough again.

"Dreadful as your father's God," said the Dean. Isaac stopped coughing and looked at him in amazement. "Do not misunderstand me, Mr. Peabody. I know your father was an excellent man whose memory is revered in the city. But we always tend to make God in our own image and your father was perhaps a man of stern rectitude. Is that so?"

"I hated him," whispered Isaac. "When I was a child I hoped he'd die. That's murder." It was out. He had never said that to anyone before. Nor had he ever told anyone about his father thrashing him because he would not go inside the Cathedral. He suddenly began to cry in the manner of the child that he was and then stopped crying as abruptly as he had begun. He twisted his red knobly hands together in his misery. Now the Dean would get up and go away and leave him and never speak to him again.

"And no doubt as a boy you hated God as much as you hated your father," said the Dean calmly. "But all your hatred, Mr. Peabody, God took into his own body that it might die with him. You now are free of it."

"I don't believe in God," said Isaac obstinately.

"I wish I could believe you," said the Dean. "I should be thankful to believe you had parted company with the God of your boyhood. But I fear he is with you still in a darkness that shadows your mind at times. Disbelieve in him, Mr. Peabody. Believe instead in love. It is my faith that love shaped the universe as you shape your clocks, delighting in creation. I believe that just as you wish to give me your clock in love, refusing payment, so God loves me and gave himself for me. That is my faith. I cannot presume to force it upon you, I can only ask you in friendship to consider it. I believe I have your affection, Mr. Peabody. You are aware I think how deeply you have mine."

Isaac surreptitiously dried his eyes and began to feel a little better. The last sentence was the only one he had really got hold of, the only one that had done him any good.

"I have been so interested in reading of Plato's water clock, that he introduced into Greece," said the Dean. "I had no idea

Plato was a horologist. And Holbein too. I wish I could see one of his sundials. And the Dean of Ely, Richard Parker, carried a horologium in the top of his walking stick. All good men. Soon, Mr. Peabody, I shall have no opinion of any man who is not a horologist."

"Sir, I could make you a walking stick with a horologium," said Isaac eagerly.

The Dean laughed. "A celestial clock is enough for now, Mr. Peabody. More than enough. No man ever received a more princely gift or was more deeply grateful or more profoundly touched by its reception. Can you explain to me, Mr. Peabody, the mechanism of a falling ball timekeeper? I have not a mechanical mind and in my recent study of horology have found myself much handicapped by the lack of it."

Isaac's face lit up. The phrase was literally true in his case for his cheeks and the tip of his nose shone rosily and his blue eyes were suddenly as flooded with light as sapphires held to the sun. In the country of his mind the advancing shadows were halted and rolled back upon themselves like the fen mists when the wind suddenly freshened from the sea. He glowed and the Dean felt a pang of sadness. What would this man have been, what would he have done, had he not been so wrenched from the true by the sufferings of his boyhood? Yet perhaps without them he would not have been Bella's fairy man. Such twistings sometimes forced out poison but at other times honey. It depended what was at the heart of a man.

"Come into the shop, sir," said Isaac eagerly. "I will show you all my clocks. Their mechanism will be easier to understand with the living thing before your eyes. Come this way, sir."

For nearly an hour Isaac instructed the Dean in horology and Adam Ayscough was no longer amazed at the rapidity with which Job had learnt his craft. The schoolmaster in him delighted in Isaac's lucid explanations, and he delighted too in this experience of being shut in with all these ticking clocks. The sheltered lamplit shop was like the inside of a hive full of amiable bees who had no wish to sting, only to display for his delight the beauty of their gold-dusted filigree wings and gold-brown bodies. They spoke to him with their honeyed tongues of this mystery of time that they had a little tamed for man with their hands and voices and the beat of their constant hearts, and yet could never make less mysterious or dreadful for all their friendliness. How strange it was, thought the Dean, as one after another he took the busy little bodies into his hands, that soon he would know more about the mystery than they did themselves.

Michael struck his bell above the buzzing of the lesser bees and he remembered the sacred hour of dinner. Elaine must not be kept waiting however great his pleasure here in the hive. "I must go," he said. "I am obliged to you, Mr. Peabody, for a most enjoyable hour. I do not recollect having spent a happier." Isaac brought him his hat and cloak and he put them on. "I wish, Mr. Peabody, that I could give you something of the same pleasure that you have given me. I wish I could show you my Cathedral as you have shown me your clocks. Will you not give me that privilege?" Isaac, looking up at him, looked hastily away again, for the Dean's longing to take him to the Cathedral was plain to see and he did not wish to see it. He mumbled something, shaking his head, then opened the shop door for the Dean to go out.

"I'll send up the celestial clock to the Deanery before Christmas, sir," he said.

The Dean was outside on the pavement in the moonlight, his hat in his hand. "My deep gratitude, Mr. Peabody," he said sadly. "My deep gratitude. God bless you."

He bowed, put on his hat, and turned away. Isaac went back into the shop, shut the door and began to put the clocks and watches back in their places. Then he went to the door again, opened it and looked out. The Dean was walking so slowly and heavily that he had not got far up the street. He walked much more slowly now than he had been used to do. An impulse came to Isaac to run after him and say that he would go with him to the Cathedral, and he did crawl crabwise down the worn steps. Then he scuttled back into the shop again. No, he would not go to the Cathedral. If he did it would get him.

On the day before Christmas Eve, at breakfast, Isaac suddenly found himself telling Emma about the celestial clock. It came into his head because tomorrow he was going to take it to the Deanery. This was the last day that the glorious thing would be with them in the shop. Tomorrow it would pass into the keeping of the Dean and on Christmas Day it would be Mrs. Ayscough's. Isaac's adam's apple felt too big for his throat whenever he thought of tomorrow. Yet he did not regret his gift. Deep inside himself he felt a profound satisfaction because of it, a new sort of stability. He felt more of a man because he had been able to do it. It was this new steadiness that had made him suddenly speak to Emma of his affairs in the sort of way a man speaks to his wife, taking it for granted that she will be interested. He was astonished at himself, and even more astonished at her, for she answered pleasantly. Isaac was a self-absorbed man yet even he had noticed that she had seemed happier lately. She had been consistently kind to Job and she had bought herself a new bonnet to wear when she drank tea with Miss Montague. This she had done twice already, meeting the precentor's wife by special invitation upon the second occasion.

"It must be a lovely clock, Isaac," she said. "Will you take another cup of tea, my dear?"

She never called him dear. He was so astonished that he dropped his fork on the tablecloth and she did not reprove him. He believed there had been a slight wistfulness in her voice. Surely she could not wish to see the clock? He could not ask her to come to the shop for she hated it and never came there. She had never forgiven him for disgracing them by going into trade.

"Emma," he said shyly, "would you like me to bring the clock back with me this evening so that you can see it? It will be quite safe here tonight and tomorrow I will take it to the Deanery."

"Has the Dean paid for it yet?" asked Emma. "If he has it would not be right to have it in the house tonight."

"Not yet," said Isaac, for he had not told her, and would never tell anyone, that he had given the clock to the Dean.

"Then I would like to see it," said Emma. "Thank you, Isaac."

After breakfast she further astonished him by coming out into the passage to help him on with his coat. As she lifted her arm he saw that there was a split in the seam of her bodice and a ridiculous notion came to him that the hard black sheath of her dress was a chrysalis and something would presently burst out of it. The thought was so alarming that he bade her a hasty good-bye and bolted out of the door and down Angel Lane with all possible speed. What sort of creature was likely to burst out of that cracking chrysalis? Would it be good or bad?

A slight uneasiness remained with Isaac through the day and when the time came to shut the shop and go home he felt reluctant to take the clock with him. Job had already gone home to Mr. Penny and Ruth and he was alone in the workshop as he stood before it and wondered what to do. He could not bear to think of the lovely thing standing in the shadows of the parlour, of his sister's long yellow fingers touching it, and his father's dark glance resting upon it as he gazed out from his portrait in sour disapproval of all things that he saw. Yet he had told Emma that he would bring it. What would the Dean say? It was his clock now. Undoubtedly his great courtesy would not wish to disappoint Emma. Isaac lifted the clock and wrapped it gently first in the old silk handkerchief and then in a length of wine-coloured velvet that he sometimes used in the shop window. Then he put on his hat and cloak and with the clock held like a child in the crook of his arm he went out into the street. He noticed as he came out that it was turning cold.

He carried the celestial clock very carefully through the streets of the city, his head a little bent to catch the faint ticking from within the folds of velvet and silk. Now and then he murmured a few quiet words, speaking of the beauty of the night, of the lighted windows and the shadows of the children behind the blinds, of open doors spilling light across the pavements. The clock was a citizen of this city even as he was but they would not again walk its streets together. He would see it in future only for a few minutes on Saturdays, when he wound it and dusted its starry face with the old silk handkerchief.

When he reached number twelve he took it into the parlour, unwrapped it and put it on the round plush-covered table beside the family Bible. All through supper it shone there in the lamplight and Emma was pleased that he had brought it and said it was very pretty. Polly, coming in and out with the dishes, was wide-eyed with delight. Isaac's own uneasiness vanished as he ate tripe and onions and baked apples and gazed at the clock. There was not a thing wrong with it. Every bit of mechanism in it was hiddenly perfect, as lovely in its particular function as the swans' wings and the slender arrow-headed hour and minute hands, moving imperceptibly from one exquisite star symbol to another around the azure heaven. There had been a tiny scratch on the clock face where Job had confessed that he let his tool slip, but they had been able to smooth it away. But it had been an extraordinary thing that so good a craftsman as Job had let his tool slip and Isaac had not been able to understand it.

After supper he and Emma sat for a little while in front of the fire, Emma reading the evening chapter, and they were more at ease together than they had ever been. And then Isaac suddenly got to his feet.

"I never locked the shop!"

Emma clicked her tongue in disapprobation. "Isaac! Whatever made you so careless?"

"I had the clock in my arms. I was thinking of that alone. I must go back at once."

"Put your muffler on," said Emma. "Good-night, dear. I expect I shall have gone to bed when you come back. I have a slight headache."

Isaac said he was sorry and hurried across the room. At the

door he looked back once at the clock and the silver fish shone out against the golden sun behind it as though a lighthouse had flashed a message to him. All the city clocks were striking as he put on his cloak and muffler in the hall, and as he opened the front door the celestial clock also began to strike. He stood outside on the steps, and listened to it. He had never made a bell with a sweeter tongue. It seemed calling after him all the way down Angel Lane.

Emma had just gone to her room and Polly was darning in front of the kitchen fire with Sooty at her feet when a knock came at the back door. She was surprised, for it was not Job's night. Yet it was Job outside, bright-eyed and laughing.

"Whatever are you doing there, Job Mooring? The mistress only lets you come on Wednesdays and that you very well know."

"Let me in, Polly," pleaded Job. "I want to see you."

"No more than five minutes then," said Polly severely. "The mistress is upstairs with a headache, and Mr. Peabody down at the shop, and I'm not one for more deceitful goings on than are necessary and that you very well know too. Wipe your feet on the mat and speak soft. I'll not have the mistress disturbed, let alone she'd skin us alive if she found you here after dark and it not Wednesday. Wipe your feet on the mat, I said."

She spoke all the more severely because of the mad beating of her heart and the exquisite joy that was sweeping over her, like a wave over the ribbed sand in the sunlight, pouring over the rocks and filling the pools. Her sharp words came breathlessly and she did not look at Job as she pulled him in and shut the scullery door behind him, for if she had looked at him she would have been on tiptoe in a moment, her mouth pressed to his and her hands clinging to his shoulders because her knees had turned to water and would no longer support her. For this growing up of Job was doing extraordinary things to Polly. As his shoulders broadened and his height increased, lifting him away above her head who once had been a scared child at her shoulder, so her breasts rounded out and colour came into her cheeks and all her hard tasks seemed light as air. At night she felt lonely in her bed and yet in bliss because in her dreams she ran and ran along the sparkling sand, or down green alley ways under flowering trees, and though she never caught up with Job she knew that he was just on ahead of her and that one night he would swing round and come speeding back to meet her, and then the whole green world, the whole curve of heaven, would belong to the two of them made one.

She pushed him into the fireside chair, then bustled about getting him a drink of warm milk, an apple and two little tarts on a plate. With Ruth such a good cook there was now no need for her to save her own food for him, yet still she did it some-times because of the joy it gave her. And there seemed no limit to what he could eat these days. His stomach, stretching and relaxing itself after the years of semi-starvation, appeared to be bottomless. With Sooty draped like a muffler round his neck he absorbed the tarts as rapidly as though they were oysters and then crunched his strong white teeth into the apple. Polly watched him with profound satisfaction, her hands folded in her lap, her eyes as they followed his every movement mak-ing up for the time lost when she had not dared to raise them to look at him. For while he enjoyed his food there was no danger that she would suddenly find herself with her mouth on his. Just now he wanted it for other purposes. His plate empty and the mug of milk drained he sighed, happily replete, and after his sigh came the distant music of a bell ringing the half-hour in the next room.

"That's the celestial clock!" he ejaculated.

"Mr. Peabody brought it home for the mistress to see," said Polly. "It's ever so pretty."

"Pretty?" snorted Job. "It's the most beautiful clock that was ever made. You can't have seen it properly just to call it 'pretty'." He lifted Sooty from his shoulders and picked up the lamp. "Come on, Polly. We'll go and look at it together."

"Hush now," she whispered as she opened the parlour door.

"The mistress. What would she say if she found you in the parlour and it not Wednesday?"

"I wouldn't care what she said," Job whispered back fiercely. In the parlour he placed the lamp on the high bookshelf so that its light fell full on the clock. "There!" he said.

They stood together looking at the clock while in a whisper he told her about the signs of the zodiac, and the sun and the silver fish. The clock ticked sweetly and cheerily but the house, and the city beyond the house, were so still that they felt themselves alone in the world with the sun and moon and stars like Adam and Eve. Polly slipped her hand into Job's and leaned a little closer, so that she felt the glowing warmth of his young body. Her hand tightened in his. "Why did you come tonight?" she whispered.

"To bring you something," he said. "I meant to keep it till Christmas but I can't."

"Another bird?" asked Polly.

"No, not a bird," he said, and putting his free hand in his pocket he brought out the small heart-shaped case. He took his other hand gently from hers and opened the box. Inside was a small bright ring. He took it out and laid it on his palm. "I made it for you," he whispered. Polly gasped, for words were beyond her. They leaned with their heads close together, bent over the ring. "The stones spell a word. Can you read it? Diamond. Emerald. Amethyst. Ruby. Emerald again. Sapphire. Topaz. They're not real jewels, of course. I couldn't afford that. But one day I'll make you a ring with real jewels. Can you read it?" She shook her head for she was not yet such a fine scholar as he was. "Yes you can, Polly. Hold out your left hand and I'll put it on. DEAREST. You know that word, my dearest Polly."

Suddenly she cried out, a cry of young ecstasy, cut short as his mouth came down on hers and his arms went round her. The celestial clock ticked merrily on, sparkling in the lamplight, but the boy and girl did not hear it for time had stopped for them. "This is Job," thought Polly, and though she did not know it she was crying and there was a salt taste on their lips. "It's Polly," he thought. They had known each other so long yet now each was made new for the other. The whole world was made new. Polly put up her hand to touch Job's curly hair as his left arm strained more closely round her tiny waist. Neither of them heard the heavy footsteps floundering down the stairs or the opening of the parlour door, but the shrill voice frightened them by its sheer hideousness, as though all lovely things had suddenly turned to ugliness.

Emma was shouting vile things as she stood with her candlestick in her shaking hand, her black shawl clutched about her shoulders, her face so old and distorted that for a moment Polly did not recognize her. When she did she was more terrified than ever, and clung shivering to Job. It was more fearful to see Emma, with whom she had lived for so long compassionately and companionably, turned as suddenly to this evil than it would have been to see Appollyon come up through the parlour floor. Then the candlestick in Emma's hand lurched suddenly, spilling grease on the carpet, and instinctive duty sent Polly darting forward. "The candle, ma'am! Mind the candle!" Emma dropped the candle and boxed Polly's ears, and she struck so hard that Polly cried out in pain as a short while ago she had cried out in joy.

It was the contrast between the two cries that sent Job mad. A moment before he had been frozen with fear and horror, the next moment he had seized Emma's wrists and flung her away from Polly. His strong fingers bit like steel into her flesh and his eyes blazed their hatred down into hers. For a moment she thought he was going to fling her into the fire as once she had flung his birds, and she screamed. Wrenching away one hand she clutched at the plush cloth on the table behind her. Trying to save her from falling he stumbled too and they went down together, Emma still clutching the cloth. The celestial clock crashed into the grate and was smashed on its marble slab.

"Have you hurt yourself, Emma?" asked Isaac, and bending down he helped her up and put her weeping and shivering into

her chair. Job and Polly gazed at him stupefied, for they had
not heard him come in. He was quiet, and more composed than
any of them, but his face was ashen and his eyes were like hard
blue stones. Only Job was aware of his terrible anger, but Polly
thought he looked dreadful and timidly stretched out a hand towards him. He pushed it away and turned to his sister. "Be
quiet, Emma! You have done enough harm for one night. Go
to bed." Slumped in her chair, her face blotched with tears, she
was to Job the most repulsive sight he had ever seen, and he
looked away in miserable embarrassment. But Isaac gazed at
her fixedly, as though, Polly thought in terror, he was seeing her
clearly for the first time and hating what he saw. "What a
carry-on just because a clock's been smashed," she thought with
a sudden return of commonsense, and loving Isaac and Job as
deeply as ever her sympathy nevertheless swung so suddenly
over to Emma that she went to her and put her arms round her.

"Don't take on so, ma'am," she said. "It's only a clock
smashed. It can likely be mended. Come, ma'am, I'll take you
to bed." She lifted her up and took her to the door where with
her arms round Emma she looked back to Job, her eyes soft
and bright. "There now, lad, don't you take on neither," she
said. "Mr. Peabody, he'll understand when you tell him what
happened." Her eyes went to Isaac but he had his back to her.
He was bending over the grate, picking up the pieces of the
clock. She said to him pleadingly, "Mr. Peabody, it was because she never had a man," but his back remained as im-
placable in hatred as his face had been. There was nothing she
could do except take Emma away.

Job fetched a box from the kitchen and kneeling beside Isaac
he tried to help him pick up the bits of the clock. It was odd
how silent the room seemed without its ticking. The Time and
Death clock still ticked, but its heart beat was slow and leaden
and that of the celestial clock had been so merry. Job was so
cold with misery that his fingers only fumbled at the bits as he
tried to pick them up, and then dropped them again as though
they were slippery as the guts and heart of a dismembered

body. "It's only a clock," Polly had said. But she did not understand about making things. And it was not only the clock. There was a blackness in his mind, a sickening sort of stench in the room that had nothing to do with any physical odour, and yet made him feel as sick as he had used to do when Albert Lee flogged him. And he was afraid, as though some appalling presence were here in the room with him and Isaac. The fear too was familiar, though lately he had imagined he had forgotten the choking blackness of the chimneys and the fire beneath his feet. Only imagined, because no man forgets hell. But this hell he was in now was worse than the others for they had not emanated from himself and this one did. From himself and Isaac and Emma. Only Polly tonight had not hated.

"I came to see Polly," he said hoarsely to Isaac. "We came in here to look at the clock and I gave her the ring. She cried out, she was so pleased, and we kissed each other. Miss Peabody must have heard and she came in. She said things. They were not true, for I've never touched Polly till tonight. I can kiss her, can't I, without foul things being said? I'm going to marry her. She boxed Polly's ears and I pulled her away so roughly that she clutched at the tablecloth and we fell and the clock went over. I've hated her ever since she burnt my birds. It's my hating her that smashed the clock. I wouldn't have smashed the clock if she hadn't burnt my birds. It's her fault."

Isaac seemed not to hear a word. He said coldly, "You need not drop the only part of the clock that can still be given to the Dean. Pick it up again."

A shining thing had just dropped from Job's fingers and lay in the ashes. It was the fret of the two swans. The clock face was smashed into a hundred pieces, and the delicate mechanism of the works was jarred and twisted, but the fret of the two swans was uninjured. Job picked it up and dusted it on his sleeve.

"Tomorrow morning," said Isaac harshly, "you can take that to the Dean and tell him what you did. You need not come to work tomorrow. I shan't want you." And with the box holding the ruins of the clock under his arm he walked out of

T

the room and out of the house, his footsteps echoing down the street.

Job sat crouched over the fire. There had been a moment not long ago when he had seemed to wake suddenly from darkness to light. It had been the day that the Dean had come to St. Peter's vicarage. But now the darkness was again as thick as death. Isaac would not forgive him for what had happened and his love and Polly's was soiled. That wicked old woman had flung it like a flower into the mud and now it would never be the same again. They would pick it up and make the best of it but it would never be the same again. He was so soaked in misery that he did not hear Polly come lightly into the room. He did not know she was there until she sat down beside him and slipped her arm round his neck. "I'm going to make a pot of tea," she said cheerfully. "Where's the cat?"

"Lord, Polly, how should I know?" Job asked irritably. "Surely there's enough trouble without you fussing about the cat."

She laughed and leaned her cheek against his. "Mend the fire while I make the tea," she said. "I'll take a cup up to the mistress, poor soul, and then we'll have ours here. Where's Mr. Peabody?" She looked at the Time and Death clock. "Not closing time yet, and likely he'll drink more than is good for him. I'll sit up for him and when he comes back I'll get him to bed with a nice hot brick to his feet. He'll be himself in the morning if he don't get asthma."

She went out and Job heard her singing softly to herself as she got the tea, and talking to Sooty, who had thought discretion the better part of valour and remained aloof from disturbances in the kitchen. Her equanimity in disaster, her immunity from the strains and miseries of the artistic temperament, the way evil ran off her like water off a duck's back, was to exasperate him all their life together and yet be his delight and salvation also. Even now he found himself smiling as he heard the clink of china, and mending the fire as though it was important. All the material sources of comfort mattered extremely to Polly and one could not love her without in some sense loving them too, since all comfort seemed a part of her.

He heard her take the tea to Emma and then she was back again with two steaming cups on a tray. " 'Ot", she said, and the word seemed the promise of all bliss. With their hands round the hot cups they sat together on the hearth rug and sipped the scalding liquid. Then Polly stretched out her left hand and the stones in her ring winked in the firelight. "Pretty, ain't it?" she said. "While I'm working I'll wear it on a bit of ribbon round my neck. It'll never be off me, Job, never until I die. Don't you think no more about the things Miss Peabody said. She got 'em off her mind and now she's having a good cry and she'll be herself in the morning."

Job doubted it, but he no longer doubted the texture of their love. It was no camellia flower to be bruised by a rough touch but tough as a heather stalk. They sat in silence when the tea was finished, leaning against each other. Then Polly said, "You'd best be going, Job. You don't want to be here when Mr. Peabody comes in. Now don't fret, lad. Sleep well and have a good breakfast in the morning and go and tell the Dean. He'll tell you it don't matter, just the breaking of a clock."

"Good-night, Polly," he whispered. "Good-night, dearest Polly."

She went with him to the door and stood there as he walked down Angel Lane. He looked back several times, the last time at the top of the steps that would take him out of her sight, and she was still there, outlined against the light and waving to him. Presently she would go upstairs again to look after that horrible old woman, and then she would take care of a tipsy Isaac, and when at last she gained her hard little bed in the attic she would still be as cheerful as a cricket.

CHAPTER 16 *The Cathedral*

I

THE cold increased during the night and by morning the wind was from the sea and the sky was grey and lowering. The Dean had difficulty with his breathing as he stood through the psalms at matins, for the Cathedral was intensely cold. It would be warmer for the carol service tonight when the lamps and candles had been lit and nearly the whole city was here, each body giving out its quota of warmth for the good of all. How unselfishly useful a warm body could be in the winter, as useful as a glowing spirit like that of the little Polly. He rubbed his cold hands together but he could no more comfort them than he could comfort himself. He was not like Polly. His sad spirit had warmed no one. That he had spent so much of his life in sadness seemed to him now the chief of his sins. If he had had the drive of joy he might not have failed the city.

Once again he had been beaten over the North Gate slums. For the whole of the last week he had been bitterly fighting the matter out again with the mayor and corporation and the landlords, but he had made no headway against their greed or the hatred of his old enemy Josiah Turnbull. How hardly shall a rich man enter into the kingdom of heaven. He was a rich man too and he shared their guilt, for if he had been able

292

to put a little more of his own private fortune at the disposal of the city things might have gone better. He had not done so because he must leave Elaine enough, and more than enough, for the life she would enjoy in London after his death had set her free. Even at the expense of the city Elaine had to come first.

His thoughts were wandering appallingly this morning. Usually it was not difficult for him to bring them back to the matter in hand but just lately his mind had felt like a battered bird that cannot find the window. He had not yet been able to concentrate sufficiently to finish his sermon for Christmas morning. "Much ashamed!" he said aloud, his ejaculation falling sadly into the pool of silence that had come as the aged canon in residence, at the lectern for the reading of the first lesson, searched for his spectacles. No one was startled, for these ejaculations were a common occurrence at matins and evensong.

The old canon found his spectacles and the Dean closed his eyes to concentrate better, but he could only mutter to himself of what he had to do today. He must finish his sermon. He must see Havelock at his office. He must see Albert Lee. He had promised Miss Montague that he would take Bella to see her. And then there were other duties belonging to Christmas Eve, all small things, yet they loomed up like nightmare apparitions and his mind beat about among them in growing panic until it blundered into the clock and suddenly found rest. The clock! He saw it against the darkness of his closed eyelids and knew without any doubt that Elaine would like it. This Christmas, at last, he would please her with his gift. He began to feel a little warmer and a little happier. Throughout the rest of matins he clung to the thought of the clock as to a life line.

He came out through the south door, held open for him by Tom Hochicorn, and shivered as the cold air met him. His cloak had slipped a little and he groped for it uncertainly. Tom Hochicorn helped him. "Cold today, sir," said Tom shyly. The Dean looked down at the old bedesman in his caped dark blue gown and crimson skull cap. He too was shivering. His eyes were watering and his long white beard stirred in the draught. He bowed low, expecting the Dean to pass on quickly with his usual brief greeting. But the Dean did not pass on. Instead he adjusted his eyeglasses and smiled at Tom. Then he looked troubled. "You are cold here, Hochicorn," he croaked. "You should sit inside in cold weather. It's too cold for you outside. Why did I not think of it before? Much distressed. You must go inside, Hochicorn."

"No, sir," said old Tom decidedly. "I must be outside to open and close the door, and to see that no one unsuitable, thieves and such, goes for to push theirselves into the Cathedral. That's my duty, sir."

"How many years have you been sitting on this hard bench?" asked the Dean.

"Six years come next Michaelmas, sir."

"It's a long time."

"It doesn't seem so to me, sir."

"You are fond of the Cathedral?"

" 'Tis my pride, sir," said Tom.

"Yes," said the Dean, "I understand. God is my glory. But I wish you would go inside, Hochicorn."

"No, sir," said Tom, a little vexed. "I must see who comes. Here's a young fellow coming now, sir. Up to no good by the look of him."

The Dean peered down the narrow cloister and saw a slim boy mounting the steps. When he was nearly at the top he stopped and the Dean recognized him. "It's Mr. Peabody's apprentice, Hochicorn," he said. "He will not harm the Cathedral." He walked down the cloister and stood at the top of the steps peering down into Job's face. "What has happened, Job?" he asked sharply. "Did you go to the Deanery to find me?"

Job swallowed. "No, sir. I was afraid Mr. Garland would not let me in. Sir, I have broken the celestial clock."

"You have what?" asked the Dean.

"The celestial clock is broken, sir, and it was my fault."

"Come back with me into the Cathedral," said the Dean. They turned back and Tom opened the door for them with another low bow. "Thank you, Hochicorn. Much obliged. If you won't go inside you must have a brazier outside. A small one. Those inside are too large. A small brazier. I'll see to it. We'll go this way, Job."

He took Job into the chantry of the Duchess Blanche and they sat down where Miss Montague had sat so long ago. The vast Cathedral soared about them and high up in the shadows there was a great rood. Job could not see it properly because it was too dark. The organist was practising for the festival. He was playing the Shepherd's Music from Bach's Christmas Oratorio. Its gentle heartbreaking loveliness contrasted strangely with the dreadfulness of the Cathedral and yet it seemed a part of it. Job began to tremble.

"You are cold?" asked the Dean.

"No, sir, but I have not been in the Cathedral before."

"No. I remember. I shall be obliged to you, Job, if you will tell me about the clock."

Job told him about it slowly and accurately, out loud to the vast darkness where they were all listening in their ranks. The sordid little story sounded very vile to his ears as he told it. When he had finished there was silence. The Dean seemed abstracted. Looking miserably up at him Job saw only his hand supporting his bent head. "That wasn't the first time I hurt the clock, sir," he said. "When I was gilding the stars I was thinking how much I hated Miss Peabody and my tool slipped and I scratched the firmament."

The Dean was still silent. Was he too angry to speak? The organist ceased playing and the echoes of his music died away and away down the dark aisles of the forest, out to the bleak fen and the cold sea.

"It does not matter, Job," said the Dean at last. "I mean it does not matter that the clock is broken. What matters is that the clock was made."

"There's a bit left, sir," said Job. "I've brought it for you."

He felt in his pocket and brought out something wrapped in his handkerchief. He took out the fret of the two swans and gave it to the Dean. He thought he could not have been more miserable but when he saw it gleaming in Adam Ayscough's ugly strong hands he felt an added pang of twisting anguish.

"I am obliged to you," said the Dean. "The fret is in itself a thing of great beauty." He put it in his pocket and went on, "I beg that neither you nor Mr. Peabody will distress yourselves. It is Christmas and your hearts should be light."

"Mr. Peabody is very angry with me, sir," said Job. "He told me not to come to the shop today."

"You should disregard that prohibition," said the Dean. "You should go to the shop and offer your apology and assistance. He will need you on Christmas Eve."

"Yes, sir, especially if he was at the Swan and Duck last night. He's very low the day after."

"Ah yes," said the Dean. "I have no experience myself of the condition but I have observed it to be very distressing once the initial exhilaration is past. I do not think, Job, that you will find him angry today. Mr. Peabody is by nature a gentle man."

"Yes," said Job in a low voice. "That is why the clock should not have been broken. He was at our mercy in his clock."

The Dean perceived that Job was about as wretched as a boy could be and he said, "Now we are here together shall we look at those carvings I told you of? The light is growing, I think."

"You are not busy, sir?"

"No, Job. I am quite at liberty and there is nothing I should like better than to show you my Cathedral. I dare to call it mine, and I believe Tom Hochicorn does too. Our presumption appears great but the glory delights to be possessed as well as to possess."

He got up and moved out from the chantry to the nave and Job followed him, at first as passively and dumbly as a whipped dog, then with awed self-forgetfulness, and finally with surging excitement. As he walked with the Dean he was almost dancing with the compulsion he had to put upon himself not to outstrip the old man beside him. Who could have told it was like this inside the mountain? Who could have known such glory existed? Why had nobody told him? What a fool he had been not to come inside before! What a fool! If Isaac had felt he had a hawk with him in the workshop the Dean thought first of an eagle, so fierce and strong was the joy beside him, and then of a terrible young archangel, incapable of fatigue, the touch of whose hand against his shivering mortal flesh was a touch of fire. The boy had forgotten there had ever been a clock. All his sorrows were under his flaming feet and his joy set a nimbus about his head. Yet he retained his awe, listening to what the Dean said, glad to the depth of him that it was with this man and no other that he was for the first time in this place.

He would see them all in years to come, Canterbury, York, Ely, Chartres, Notre-Dame, San Marco and the golden churches of Palermo, but none of them would exalt and wring him quite as this one did today. The light grew and there were shafts of silver through the gloom. He remembered how he had dreamed of walking in a forest, where from the great-girthed boles of the trees the branches leapt to the sky, and of looking up at the dark stone cliffs of the mountain and wondering what such walls could hold, and of being below the sea where the tides washed in and out of the green gloom of caverns. Marvellous colours glowed in the windows far above him, the deep jewel colours of very old glass. There were lords and ladies here, angels and haloed saints, bishops and knights lying on their tombs, figures such as he had seen in some of Mr. Penny's old books, and fabulous creatures such as lions and unicorns, dolphins and griffins. Sometimes there was music, sounding like wind in the trees or water falling from the heights of the mountain, and sometimes silence and the far sound of a bell. There was dust here, for when he unconsciously put out his hand to feel the shape of a dolphin his long fingers came away coated with the friendly stuff. And under the miserere seats there were homely men and boys and creatures such as he knew, woodcutters and millers and ploughmen and young thieves stealing apples, foxes and owls, and small birds such as he made himself. From these he could not tear himself away. To him they were the best of of all. They made him laugh and yet they brought him nearer to weeping than anything else because the men who had made them had been dead for centuries and he could not know these men. The whole world was in this place, the earth, the sky and the sea, angels, men and creatures. He looked up often at the great rood, but that he did not understand, except that it seemed to him that nothing else could have been here without that.

"It is all here," he said.

"It is all here in microcosm," said the Dean. "The whole work of God."

He lowered a miserere seat and sat down, for he was trembling with exhaustion and the saints in the window above him seemed to be emptying buckets of cold water over his head. He hoped he might be forgiven for keeping the tireless Job in ignorance of the existence of the Lady Chapel, the crypt and the chapter house.

The boy was kneeling beside him, his head bent, intent upon a man and two yoked oxen ploughing a field. The furrows of the black fen earth shone as though newly turned and at the ploughman's right a bird was singing in a thorn bush under a high midday sun, as though to cheer the labouring man and toiling beasts. The scene was full of the sense of hard driving effort. Every muscle of man and beasts seemed at full stretch. With his finger tips he lightly touched the bird, and the ploughman's bent back. "I think it is the best of all," he murmured.

"I think I am most attached to the one I am sitting on," said the Dean. "The shepherd with his sheep. But then I have always wished that I could have been a shepherd. You no longer fear the Cathedral?"

"Not now I know these are here, sir," said Job. "I don't see how anyone could come here for the first time and not be afraid, but then this bird is here and it's no bigger than my thumb." He paused, placing his hands one on each side of the carving. "This is just the one man but the Cathedral is filled with them all."

The Dean was a little startled. "You mean filled with the men who made it?"

"Yes, sir."

The Dean sought about in his battered mind for the words he wanted, and then fell back in relief upon the words of another man. "If you remember, Job, I showed you a bishop with mitre and crosier carved on the capital of a pillar in the south transept and told you he was Saint Augustine, a man born in North Africa in 354, long before a stone of this Cathedral was laid in place. He said this, 'And who is that God but our God, the God who made heaven and earth, who filled them because it is by filling them with himself that he has made them.' Man is made in the image of God and as you said just now what he makes he fills with himself, either with his hate or with his love."

Job did not answer. He sprang lightly to his feet and moved up and down before the long line of exquisite small carvings, as though he could not bring himself to leave them. The Dean got up unsteadily and raised his seat so that Job might look again at the shepherd bringing his sheep home to their fold. He carried a crook and had a dog at his heels and a lamb over his shoulder, and above his head the sickle moon hung in the sky. The scene was as full of peace as the other of stress. The Dean glanced from one to the other and suddenly realized something that he had not noticed before. The toiling ploughman and the peaceful shepherd were the same man. He had the same stooped shoulders, the same tall hat and heavy serf's boots. He was Everyman. He pointed this out to Job.

"Yes, I saw that," said Job. "The same craftsman must have carved both and you can see, sir, that he loved the man."

They walked towards the south door in silence but the Dean was well aware of the strong confident vow that Job had made. They thought, these young creatures, that they could bind their passions with their vows and did not know the appalling strength of human passion. Yet it was good that they made them, for under the midday sun the vows were bit and bridle upon the wild horses, and as the day drew on to evening the creatures quieted.

"I shall endeavour to wait upon Mr. Peabody during the course of the day," said the Dean, "but meanwhile I beg that you will keep him from grieving over the loss of the clock. And before going to the shop will you take a message from me to Miss Peabody? Will you present my compliments and say what pleasure it would give me if she would come to the carol service tonight. And Mr. Peabody, too, and yourself and Polly. I must explain that the Christmas services this year have for me a special significance. I am deeply thankful to Almighty God that I have been spared to attend them, and it will give me deep pleasure to have my friends about me to share in my thanksgiving."

"Miss Peabody may not let me into the house, sir," said Job doubtfully. "And if she does she's not very likely to listen to what I say."

The Dean thought for a moment and then he sat down on a bench and taking a notebook and his gold pencil from his pocket wrote a few words on a page, tore it out and folded it, addressing the note to Miss Peabody. "I have written down what I said to you, Job. And I beg that before giving her this you will apologize for the hastiness of your behaviour last night."

"Yes, sir, I will," said Job, flushing scarlet. "And thank you for showing me the Cathedral."

"I have shown you only a fraction of its glory. You will come here many times by yourself I trust. It is your own, and all its citizens alive or dead. You have an inheritance to be proud of but when you are named one of the great men of the city remember that the poorest boy possesses all that you possess and yourself into the bargain. You have borne patiently with my prosing. Much obliged."

The Dean seemed to Job not so much to move away as so to unite with the shadows of the Cathedral that he could no longer be recognized as a separate entity. Job walked out through the south door smiling at Tom Hochicorn as he passed, his head up, his whole air confident and happy. Yet Tom Hochicorn was not conscious of arrogance as he passed by, indeed he received an impression so much to the contrary that it caused him to change his opinion of the boy he had thought up to no good. Here was another of them, akin to the Dean and himself. You could always tell when the Cathedral had got them by the way they left it, not proud of themselves, but proud of what had got them.

2

The Dean went back to the chantry of the Duchess Blanche and knelt down. The breaking of a pretty clock was such a small disaster, scarcely noticeable among the vast tragedies that wrenched the world, yet this small happening, he did not doubt, had wrenched the world of Isaac Peabody and his sister. All that was vile in Emma had contributed to the breaking of Isaac's clock, and Isaac would find it as hard to forgive her as Job had done. He did not know what would come of it all and there was nothing he could do, he who had come into their humble lives seeking his own comfort at the cost of theirs. And now he had no Christmas present for Elaine. He had found the perfect gift for her and it was broken. He would not now see on her face that look of delight that he had pictured so often but never seen.

With horror he realized that he was pitying himself. For that prayer was the only cure but when he tried to pray he could find nothing in the thick darkness which enclosed him except all the things he had to do. He had better get up and do them. There was one more now, that brazier for old Hochicorn. For six years the old man had sat there shivering through the winter and he had never given it a thought. "I have ta'en too little care of this." Where did one buy a small brazier? In the town somewhere. He must go to the town. He stumbled to his knees, walked past Hochicorn, the object of his concern, without noticing him, and set out for the town. Under the Porta he collided with the Archdeacon, and so blindly that when they had recovered themselves the Archdeacon made so bold as to ask him where he was going.

"To buy a small brazier," said the Dean.

"A brazier?" ejaculated the Archdeacon.

"For Hochicorn. It is too cold for him outside the south door and he won't go inside. He must have a brazier but I do not know where to acquire one."

"Just at this moment, neither do I, Mr. Dean," said the Archdeacon. "After Christmas perhaps."

"It is today it is so cold," said the Dean sadly. "Much obliged to you, Archdeacon, much obliged. I remember that I have to see Havelock. He will perhaps know where I can acquire a brazier," and raising his hat he turned away up Worship Street. The Archdeacon looked after him anxiously, for he did not think he looked very steady on his feet. The mind too seemed a little disturbed. What did Hochicorn want with a brazier? The poor did not feel the cold.

In Mr. Havelock's office the Dean sat down gratefully by the fire and said he wanted to add a codicil to his will. Mr. Havelock felt as uneasy as the Archdeacon, for the Dean had added a number of codicils to his will during the last week and each had seemed to him slightly crazier than the last; excepting only the little legacy for Bella when she came of age; that he considered both gratifying and sensible. But the others he feared all indicated a mind disturbed. There had been, for instance, the annuity for Garland, and the gift of the Dean's gold pencil. The man had had good wages, sufficient to have something laid by, and what would a butler want with a gold pencil? And then that large sum of money left to Josiah Turnbull the mayor, his avowed enemy, to be used for the good of the city in whatever way the mayor thought fit. What an extraordinary thing to do. An annuity for Mr. Penny's housekeeper seemed as pointless as the sum left in his charge for the purchase of a pony and cart for that scoundrel Lee. What next?

"Just one more, Havelock," said the Dean, as though reading

Mr. Havelock's agitated mind. "I leave to my friend Isaac Peabody my watch and my faith in God." Mr. Havelock's head went round. He picked up his pen and laid it down again. "I beg that you will write out the cocidil exactly as I have dictated it," said the Dean with some asperity. "Thank you, Havelock. Much obliged."

The codicil was added to the will and witnessed by Mr. Havelock's son and the clerk. Then the Dean rose to leave. He had a little difficulty in getting to his feet and Mr. Havelock assisted him with a slight irritability, caused by the queer sense of desolation that came over him whenever he had to bring his mind to bear upon the Dean's will. "You should not come to the office in this way, Mr. Dean," he said curtly. "You must send for me to the Deanery when you wish to see me."

"Poor men must come to your office," said the Dean, "and I in the dereliction of my days am the poorest of the poor. Do you know, Havelock, where I can buy a small brazier?"

Now Mr. Havelock was quite sure about the mental disturbance and he spoke gently and persuasively as to a child. "It is time for your luncheon, Mr. Dean. I beg that you will go straight home to luncheon." As he opened the office door and ushered the Dean out into the market place he laid his hand for a moment on his arm. "God bless you, sir," he said.

To be blessed by Havelock of all people so astonished the Dean that he felt stronger, and the walk down through the city to Swithins Lane did not seem so impossibly far as it had seemed to him when he had thought of it during matins. The dark clouds had parted now and a cold silver sunlight illumined the city, catching in its net all the colour and gaiety of the Christmas shops and shoppers. The Dean had not walked through the city since his illness and he looked at it as a man looks at the spring after a long hard winter. He had forgotten how beautiful it was, he had forgotten how poignantly he loved it, and he wanted to stretch out a hand to hold it lest its beauty pass away from him before he had had time fully to feast his eyes and heart upon it. But he could not do that, and the streets and the happy crowds seemed to flow past him like a quick bright river, these Christmas streets and people, and the streets and people that he remembered on spring and autumn days in past years, and summer nights of moon and stars. He did not distinguish very clearly between the past and the present, between this century or another. Some of the men and women who passed by, smiling at him, seemed to him to be not of this age. But he was not surprised to see them and he returned each shy greeting with a smile and a courteous lifting of his tall hat. People spoke for many days afterwards of the way the Dean had walked down through the city that morning, not forging along in his usual fiercely abstracted state but looking at them with great kindness, smiling and lifting his hat even though many who greeted him were strangers to him. But when he reached Swithins Lane the Dean smiled at no one, so dreadful did it seem to him after the gay and happy streets that had flowed past him up above in the city. The silver sunlight did not seem to penetrate to Swithins Lane and there were no decorated Christmas trees in the dark and dirty windows. And he had failed to cleanse this place. The men and women and children who rotted and died here must continue to rot and die because he had failed. The crash of the celestial clock falling to pieces was in his ears as he entered the fish shop and lifted his hat to Keziah.

The old crone was in a flutter of pleasure at seeing him and Lee wrung his hand so strongly that he could have cried out with the pain of it. The great lout of a boy whom he had procured from the workhouse was grinning in the background and it was obvious to the Dean that he was in a state of well-being, and that one blow of his huge red fist would have felled a tipsy Albert instantly to the ground, and probably had already done so. The warmth of the greeting he received took the Dean entirely by surprise. He had prayed much for this man and woman but his humility never expected, or even much desired, to have the answer to prayer presented to him like the head of John the Baptist on a plate. Yet in this place there was undoubtedly a change. The atmosphere was less dark and evil. Giving thanks to God alone he said to Albert, "I have come to thank you, Mr. Lee, for your faithful service to the Deanery. During my recent illness I fancied only a light diet and was much obliged to you for the delicious fish with which I was served." A pang of guilt went through him, for he seldom noticed what he ate and did not suppose that Garland had allowed the Swithins Lane fish to penetrate to his sick room, but the pleasure of Albert and Keziah seemed almost to justify a probable lie, and Keziah muttered something about business being better now it was known they supplied the Deanery.

"I wish you and your son could have a shop in a better locality, ma'am," said the Dean. "And I would like to see Mr. Lee driving out to the villages with a pony and trap. Were you born in the fen, Mr. Lee?"

Albert looked at him with stupefaction. How did the old codger know about him wanting a pony and trap? He said, "I was born in the fen, sir. Out beyond Willowthorn." Old Keziah began to mumble something about the smart painted van she'd had out in the drove and Albert chimed in with reminiscences of varied types of horse flesh, and the dog Pharaoh. He'd fancy a dog again, to run behind the trap. Even with his hand behind his ear the Dean was not very sure what they said but was most happy that they should be saying it. "Much obliged," he murmured gratefully when it was time to say good-bye. "A happy Christmas to you." He went to the back of the shop and shook hands with the lout of a boy, and pressed a five shilling piece into his huge red palm. At the door, replacing his hat after bowing to Keziah, he suddenly remembered something else and said anxiously, "Do you know, Mr. Lee, where I can procure a small brazier?"

Lee and Keziah shook their heads doubtfully but the lout of a boy remarked hoarsely from behind them, "There's one out the back." Lee slapped his thigh, remembering that he'd come by it two years ago when old Cobb, the roast chestnut man, had been took to the workhouse. He'd put it in the shed and forgot

U

it. He and the boy went out to the shed and the sound of crashing ironmongery told of its exhumation from beneath a heap of scrap iron and empty tins. Back in the shop it was dusted down and bent back into shape and emerged as a very nice little brazier indeed.

"What would you be wanting to do with it, sir?" asked Albert.

The Dean explained about Hochicorn, and also remarked anxiously that he did not know to whom he should apply for charcoal. "I am not a practical man, I fear," he said sadly. "I should have informed myself as to these matters earlier in life."

"Leave it to me, sir," said Albert. "I knew old 'Ochicorn when I was a boy. I used to go round sellin' clothes pegs with me poor grannie and 'e'd always buy a few. I'll take it up to 'im and git it goin'. I can come by a bit of charcoal."

"I am much obliged to you," said the Dean with profound relief, and took his purse from his pocket. But Albert shook his head. "No, sir," he said. "There's nothin' I wouldn't do for you. An' I didn't pay nothin' for that brazier. I come by it."

"I thank you, Mr. Lee," said the Dean. "I am grateful for your kindness. You know your way to the south door?"

"No, sir. I ain't ever been to the Cathedral."

The Dean explained the route with sadness. How many of the men and women of the city had never been inside the Cathedral? To some of them it was no more than a great stone mountain in their midst. He said good-bye once more and went away wondering how it had happened that in this nineteenth century the poor of the city were not at home in their Cathedral. In past centuries it had not been so. Had he and his kind in some way barred it to them? The shepherds had allowed themselves to become wealthy and the sheep were frightened of the rich man's house. Nor did they follow a shepherd who did not share with them their own rough weather and hard going.

He went grieving up through the empty streets of the city, deserted now because the sun had gone in and the weather looked threatening, and did not notice that they were empty.

But he knew he had to go to Cockspur Street and presently he found himself inside the little shop, sitting on the customers' chair and facing Isaac across the counter. Job had gone home and there was no one else in the shop. They looked at each other in mute distress and neither knew what to say.

"It may be for good," said the Dean at last. "It has taught Job something. It may prove to be the casting out of evil for your poor sister. I pray so. You must take great care of your sister, Mr. Peabody. Go back now to the point when you took the clock home to give her pleasure, forgive what came after and build up the work of love from there. Think that she is a woman who has had a severe illness. If you do not help her to recovery no one will."

"Will you choose another clock for Mrs. Ayscough?" asked Isaac dully, as though he had not heard a word.

"No," said the Dean, "I will give her the fret of the two swans." He had not known until he spoke that this was what he was going to do but now it seemed to him right that he should do so. "It is more beautiful by itself than when it surmounted the clock."

There was a flash of anger in Isaac's blue eyes at the idiocy of this remark, and the Dean was glad to see it for it brought back life to his miserable sullen old face. "By itself it is nothing but a bit of bent metal, sir," he said.

"It is much more than that, Mr. Peabody. The fret of the two swans, creatures who it is said sing for joy at their death, says to me that my affection for you, and yours for me, will always endure." The Dean put his clasped hands on the counter and to avoid looking at his eyes, for he was not going to be compelled into forgiving Emma against his will, Isaac looked at the hands and remembered suddenly that he had seen them clasped in that way on that Sunday morning that seemed now several centuries ago. They had lain then on the velvet cushion of the Dean's stall and had been clasped in prayer for the city. Isaac rubbed his nose irritably. There was no escape from that which pursued him in this terrible man.

"Mr. Peabody, I beg that you will listen to me and endeavour to believe what I say. The love that created and gave the clock is of more value because the clock is broken. It has entered into eternity, as does the soul when the body fails and dies. If I die before you, Mr. Peabody, I shall find the love that made and gave the clock awaiting me. Perhaps I might not have done so had it not been broken. It will give me welcome." Isaac was still sullenly silent and after a moment or two the Dean unclasped his hands and got up. "I must go, Mr. Peabody, for I am already late for luncheon and I do not wish to alarm my wife. Will you be at the carol service this evening? It would give me infinite pleasure to see you there with your sister and Job and Polly."

Isaac helped him into his cloak, handed him his stick and did not answer. He was not going to live with Emma any more. Why should he live with a woman he hated? Once Christmas was over he would leave Angel Lane and live at the shop.

"Good afternoon, sir," he said politely, opening the shop door. "I trust that you and Mrs. Ayscough will spend a happy Christmas."

"Good afternoon, Mr. Peabody," said the Dean gently. "Much obliged."

Isaac went back to sit behind the counter and his cruelty frightened him. But he was not going to forgive Emma. He sat there hugging his hatred to him.

The sky had darkened still more while the Dean talked to Mr. Peabody and when he reached the market place a shower of cold sleety rain beat full in his face. Passing St. Peter's church he stopped a moment, feeling breathless and ill.

"Come inside, sir, come inside," piped a high quavering old voice. "Come in here and shelter."

The Dean stepped inside the porch and sat down beside old Mr. Penny, who peered up at him inquisitively and enquired, "Who are you?"

"Adam," said the Dean.

"Adam," said Mr. Penny. "Do I know you?"

"We were together once, sir, in another storm. We were Lear and his fool taking shelter together as we are now. I am Lear's fool."

"Lear's fool wasn't called Adam," said Mr. Penny decidedly. "Not that I know of. Would you like an apple?"

He had a large basket at his feet filled with apples and oranges and little parcels wrapped in coloured paper. "For the children of my parish," he said importantly. "Ruth wrapped them up. I shall take them round when the rain stops. I've had my luncheon. Have you had yours?"

"Not yet," said the Dean.

"Then have an apple," said Mr. Penny, and diving into his basket he took out the largest and rosiest.

"Much obliged," said the Dean, and ate it gratefully, for he found he was hungry.

Mr. Penny watched him for a little while with a seraphic smile and then suddenly his soft old face crinkled with childish distress. "I can't write my sermon for tomorrow," he said. "I can't think what to say."

"Nor can I," said the Dean.

"Have you to preach tomorrow?"

"I have," said the Dean.

"Where are you going to preach?"

"At the church of St. Michael and All Angels."

"Where's that?"

"At the top of the hill."

"I don't know where that is," said Mr. Penny. "Ruth will know." Then suddenly a bright idea struck him. "I'll bring my congregation to hear you preach and then I shan't have to preach myself. Would that be a sin?"

"I am not sure," said the Dean slowly. "Ruth will know."

Mr. Penny took a handkerchief out of his pocket and tied a knot in it. "That's to ask her," he said. "People call me forgetful but I'm not forgetful if I've tied a knot. The sun's out again. I must go to the children." He got up and laid his hand kindly on the Dean's shoulder. "Stay there and rest, my friend.

What did you say your name was? Adam. Remember, Adam, if there's anything I can do for you at any time, if you're short of money, or hungry, or anything of that sort, you've only to come to the vicarage and I'll do all in my poor power. God bless you."

Mr. Penny grasped the handle of his basket and went out into the sunlight. The Dean watched him trotting across the street to the market place and disappearing into Mrs. Martin's bakery like an ancient rabbit into its burrow. Mrs. Martin must have her grandchildren with her for there was a Christmas tree in the window. Mr. Penny was changed since the Dean had seen him last. He was not so thin and his eyes were happy. His mode of progression was no longer that sad aimless waver but a fairly brisk trot. "Ruth and good food," thought the Dean, and he thanked God.

In spite of all the things he had to do he went on sitting in the porch, for fatigue encased him like lead. He felt too tired to go inside the church and as he sat with his eyes shut, thinking of it, he saw the tombs decorated with holly and the ancient windows with their colours staining the paving stones. And welling up through the broken floor was that spring of water. It refreshed him where he sat in the porch, as though the cracked old paving stones were the crust of his own mortality. After a while he pulled himself to his feet, remembering with joy that the next thing he had to do was to take Bella to call on Miss Montague. But first he must reassure them at home. He got himself back to the Deanery and Garland opened the door.

"I lunched out, Garland," he said, for he did not want to put the household to the trouble of getting him luncheon now, at two-thirty.

"You did not mention that you were doing so, sir," said Garland irritably, for the last hour had not been a happy one for him.

"I apologize, Garland," said the Dean humbly. "I trust Mrs. Ayscough has not been anxious?"

"Yes, sir," said Garland without mercy. "Mrs. Ayscough has suffered considerable anxiety."

"Much distressed," murmured the Dean and hurried to the drawing-room, past the tall Christmas tree which stood in the hall tastefully decorated by Garland.

"Wherever have you been, Adam?" asked Elaine. She was kneeling on the floor surrounded by parcels and piles of tissue paper and coloured ribbons, packing up the servants' presents for Garland to hang on the tree. All their married life Adam had insisted on having a tree and presents for the servants. After tea on Christmas Day they stood ranged in their ranks according to seniority, Cook at one end and the tweeny at the other, and Garland took the gifts from the tree and Adam presented them with heavy anxious courtesy. He found this a great ordeal, she knew, but it was nothing to what she had to do, buying and packing the gifts. Each Christmas she was freshly exhausted. She rose wearily to her feet, pushing her hair back from her face. "Where have you been? Why didn't you tell me you were lunching out?"

"My dear, it was unexpected. I lunched with the vicar of St. Peter's. Forgive me that I did not inform you."

Her beauty, with her face a little flushed and her hair ruffled, took him freshly by surprise, though it was always surprising him. This shock of surprise was in all real beauty, he thought. If one was not surprised it was only a counterfeit. He took her in his arms and asked her to forgive him and for once she did not hold herself rigid but leaned against him in the relaxation of re-lief. She had been genuinely anxious. "Oh, Adam, I am so tired," she murmured.

"Why, my dear?"

"All these parcels for the servants! It's too much for me. And I can't even ask my maid to help me since you don't want them to know what presents they are having. I must get them done before tea for I'll be far too tired after the carol service."

"I'll help you," said the Dean. "I'll help you at once. I must speak to Garland for a moment in my study and then I will be with you. Did you, my dear, get the doll for little Bella?"

"It's here somewhere," said Elaine, and stooping she picked up a large cardboard box from the floor. "Though I think you make a great mistake, showering that child with presents. It will only lead to jealousy in other quarters."

The Dean thought sadly that it was only too likely. He thought of Isaac and the broken clock and his heart was heavy. What harm unpurified and undisciplined human love could do. He believed it must pass through death before it could entirely bless. Then he lifted the lid of the box and forgot his sorrow in pleasure.

In the world of toys he lacked experience but he believed this to be the most wonderful doll ever created. It was rosy-cheeked and blue-eyed with a dimpled chin and hair of a yellow as startling as Bella's own. It was clothed in pink satin and its rosy bonnet was lined with lace. Very shyly he lifted the stiff satin skirt with his forefinger and perceived that its under-garments also were trimmed with lace. He lowered the skirt reverently and saw that it had pink leather shoes and a small gilt reticule hanging from its tiny waist.

"Thank you, Elaine," he murmured. "Thank you, my dear, with all my heart. You must have gone to great trouble in choosing this beautiful doll."

"Oh, no," said Elaine airily. "I ordered it from Town with the servants' things. But it is a pretty doll. I believe it says mama if you stand it upright."

The Dean stood it gingerly upright and it said mama. He was immensely cheered. "I'll be back with you in a moment, my dear," he said, and took it with him to the study in its box.

It was very difficult to write and tell Miss Montague that after all he feared he would not be able to take Bella to see her this afternoon, for this would be the first time for some years that he had not visited her on Christmas Eve. He had to write the same news to Mrs. Havelock but he trusted that Bella's sanguine spirit would not be cast down if, as he suggested to Mrs. Havelock, the doll were presented to her concurrently with the reception of the news. He sealed the two notes and rang for Garland. "These must go at once," he said. "The doll for Miss Bella too. Do you like it, Garland?"

"A very fine doll indeed, sir," said Garland. "Miss Bella cannot fail to be gratified."

He put the box under his arm and moved rather slowly towards the door. He wished he could take it round himself. Wouldn't take him more than a few minutes. She might be about and he'd see her face when she took the lid off. The Dean watched him with a smile. "I would be obliged, Garland, if you would yourself be my messenger this afternoon. Have you the leisure?"

"Certainly, sir," said Garland briskly.

"Much obliged," said the Dean. "It will be of no consequence if tea is a little late."

He went back to the drawing-room to help Elaine. His clumsy hands were not very efficient at folding paper and tying ribbon, and the sweat poured off him with the labour and concentration involved, but he managed fairly creditably and Elaine was set free to sit at her escritoire and write out the little labels that were to be attached. After tea he made her put her feet up on the sofa and he read aloud to her to rest her until it was time for the six o'clock carol service. To the pealing of the bells they walked across the garden to the Cathedral together and as they walked she took one gloved hand from her muff and slipped it into his.

I

EVERY year, at half-past-five on Christmas Eve, Michael lifted his great fist and struck the double quarter, and the Cathedral bells rang out. They pealed for half-an-hour and all over the city, and in all the villages to which the wind carried the sound of the bells, they knew that Christmas had begun. People in the fen wrapped cloaks about them and went out of doors and stood looking towards the city. This year it was bitterly cold but the wind had swept the clouds away and the Cathedral on its hill towered up among the stars, light shining from its windows. Below it the twinkling city lights were like clustering fireflies about its feet. The tremendous bell music that was rocking the tower and pealing through the city was out here as lovely and far away as though it rang out from the stars themselves, and it caught at men's hearts. "Now 'tis Christmas," they said to each other, as their forbears had said for centuries past, looking towards the city on the hill and the great fane that was as much a part of their blood and bones as the fen itself. " 'Tis Christmas," they said, and went back happy to their homes.

In the city, as soon as the bells started, everyone began to get ready. Then from nearly every house family parties came out and made their way up the steep streets towards the Cathedral. Quite small children were allowed to stay up for the carol service, and they chattered like sparrows as they stumped along buttoned into their thick coats, the boys gaitered and mufflered, the girls with muffs and fur bonnets. It was the custom in the city to put lighted candles in the windows on Christmas Eve and their light, and the light of the street lamps, made of the streets ladders of light leaning against the hill. The grown-ups found them Jacob's ladders tonight, easy to climb, for the bells and the children tugged them up.

Nearly everyone entered by the west door, for they loved the thrill of crossing the green under the moon and stars, and mounting the steps and gazing up at the west front, and then going in through the Porch of the Angels beneath Michael and the pealing bells. Some of them only came to the Cathedral on this one day in the year, but as they entered the nave they felt the impact of its beauty no less keenly than those who came often. It was always like a blow between the eyes, but especially at night, and especially on Christmas Eve when they were full of awe and expectation. There were lights in the nave but they could do no more than splash pools of gold here and there, they could not illumine the shadows above or the dim unlighted chantries and half-seen tombs. The great pillars soared into darkness and the aisles narrowed to twilight. Candles twinkled in the choir and the high altar with its flowers was ablaze with them, but all the myriad flames were no more than seed pearls embroidered on a dark cloak. The great rood was veiled in shadow. All things alike went out into mystery. The crowd of tiny human creatures flowed up the nave and on to the benches. The sound of their feet, of their whispering voices and rustling garments, was lost in the vastness. The music of the organ flowed over them and they were still.

But a few came in through the south door and Tom Hochicorn gave them greeting as he stood bowing by his brazier. Albert Lee had worked quickly, had come by some charcoal and had it lighted and installed by the time the bells began to

ring. He had sat on the bench chatting to old Tom for a while
and then, as people began to arrive, he took fright and was all
for escaping back to Swithins Lane, but old Tom grabbed him
and held on with surprising strength. "Go inside, Bert," he
commanded.

"What, me?" gasped Albert Lee. "In there? Not bloody
likely!"

"Why not, Bert?"

"Full of toffs," said Albert Lee. "'Ere, Tom, you leggo. I
don't want to 'urt you."

"You won't see no toffs," said old Tom. "Not to notice.
Just a lot of spotted ladybirds a-setting on the floor. That's
all they look like in there. You go in, Bert. Not afraid, are
you?"

"Afraid?" scoffed Albert Lee. "I ain't been afraid of nothink
not since I was born."

"Go in, then," said Tom. He opened the door and motioned
to Albert. "Look there. See that pillar? The one by the stove.
There's a chair behind it. No one won't see you if you set behind that pillar. If you look round it when you hear the Dean
speaking you'll see him."

He had hold of Albert by his coat collar. Albert didn't want
to make a scene or own himself afraid. He found himself inside
with the door softly closed behind him. Sweating profusely he
crept to the chair behind the pillar and sat down on its extreme
edge. Cor, what a place! It was like old Tom had said. No one
didn't notice you in here. You were too small. Cor, this was a
terrible place! It was like night up there. But the door was
near, and so was the homely-looking stove. For a while his eyes
clung to the door, and then as the warmth of the stove flowed
out to him his terror began to subside. It was nice and warm in
his corner. No one couldn't see him. He'd sit for a while. The
bells were pretty but he didn't like that great humming rumbling music that was sending tremors through his legs. Then
it stopped, and the bells too, and there was silence, and then
miles away he heard boys singing.

They came nearer and nearer, singing like the birds out in the fen in spring. One by one men's voices began to join in, and then the multitude of men and women whom he could scarcely see began to sing too. The sound grew, soaring up to the great darkness overhead. It pulled him to his feet. He didn't know the words and he didn't know the music but he had sung with the Romany people in his boyhood, sitting round the camp fire in the drove, and he'd been quick to pick up a tune. He was now. He dared not use his coarsened voice but the music sang in his blood like sap rising in a tree. When the hymn ended there was a strange rustling sound, like leaves stirring all over a vast forest. It startled him at first until he realized that it was all the toffs kneeling down. He knelt too, his tattered cap in his hands, and the slight stir of his movement was drawn into the music of all the other movements. For the forest rustling was also music and that too moved in his blood. There was silence again and far away he heard the Dean's voice raised in the bidding prayer. He could not distinguish a word but the familiar voice banished the last of his fear. When the prayer ended he said Amen as loudly as any and was no longer conscious of loneliness. From then until the end he was hardly conscious even of himself.

There were not many who were. It was that which made this particular Christmas Eve carol service memorable above all others in the city's memory. The form of it was the same as always. The familiar hymns and carols followed each other in the familiar order, the choir sang "Wonderful, Counsellor, the Mighty God, the everlasting Father, the Prince of Peace," as gloriously as ever but not more so, for they always put the last ounce into it, the difference was that instead of the congregation enjoying themselves enjoying the carol service they were enjoying the carol service. They were not tonight on the normal plane of human experience. When they had climbed the Jacob's ladders of the lighted streets from the city to the Cathedral they had climbed up just one rung higher than they usually did.

There was another difference. The form of this service was
the same as always but the emphasis was different. Generally
the peak of it all was the anthem but tonight it was the Christmas gospel, read as always by the Dean.

Adam Ayscough walked with a firm step to the lectern, put on
his eyeglasses and found the place. As he and Elaine had left
the Deanery to go to the Cathedral he had been in great fear,
for he had not known if he would be able to get through the
service. Then as they crossed the garden she had slipped her
hand into his and he had known he would do it. "All shall be
well and all manner of thing shall be well." He cleared his
throat. "The first verse of the first chapter of the gospel according to St. John," he said. His sight, he found, was worse than
usual and the page was misty. But it was no matter for he knew
the chapter by heart. He raised his head and looked out over
the congregation. "In the beginning was the Word, and the
Word was with God."

His voice was like a raucous trumpet, it had such power behind it. The people listened without movement, but though
they had all come filled with thankfulness because he would be
here tonight they were not thinking of him as they had thought
of him on other Christmas Eves, thinking how ugly he was, how
awkward, but yet how in place there in the lectern, looming up
above them in his strange rugged strength, they were thinking
only of what he was saying. "The Word was made flesh and
dwelt among us." Was it really true? Could it be true? If it
was true, then the rood up there was the king-pin that kept all
things in perpetual safety and they need never fear again. To
many that night Adam Ayscough's speaking of the Christmas
gospel was a bridge between doubt and faith, perhaps because
it came to them with such a splendid directness. He stood for a
moment looking out over the people, then left the lectern and
went back to his stall. His sight had been too dim to see them
when he looked at them and he had no knowledge that he had
been of service to them.

Nor, when at the conclusion of the service the Bishop and

clergy, the choir and the whole congregation, flocked down to the west end of the nave for the traditional singing of "Now thank we all our God," did he know that his presence with them all was one of the chief causes of their thanksgiving. But when the Bishop had blessed them, and the clergy and choir had turned to go to their vestries, he did what no Dean had ever done before and moving to the west door stood there to greet the people as they went out. To break with tradition in this manner was unlike him, for he revered tradition, yet he found himself moving to the west door.

He had no idea that quite so many people as this came to the Cathedral on Christmas Eve. Surely nearly the whole city was here. Most of them only dared to smile at him shyly as they passed by, but some bolder spirits spoke to him, saying they were glad he was better and returning his good wishes when he wished them a happy Christmas. To his astonished delight almost all those who in the last few months had become so especially dear to him, like his own small flock of sheep, were among those who gave him a special greeting.

Bella was there, in her cherry-red outfit, clasping her doll. "She would come," her grandmother whispered to him, "though it's long past her bedtime, and she would bring her doll. I knew it was not right but I could not prevent it." Mrs. Havelock was looking extremely tired and the Dean took her hand to reassure her. Bella, who had been looking as smugly solid as a stationary robin, suddenly became airborne and darted off into the night. Mrs. Havelock, abruptly dropping the Dean's hand, fled in pursuit.

Mr. Penny was there, not identifying the Dean in his robes with Lear's fool, and bowing very shyly as he passed, and Ruth with her wise calm smile and little Miss Throstle of the umbrella shop. Albert Lee was there, borne along by the crowd as an integral part of it and quite comfortable in his non-entity, and yet bold as well as comfortable for he was one of those who paused to wish the Dean a happy Christmas. Polly and Job were there, as he had known they would be, but they smiled

at him as though from a vast distance, and he was glad of it.
They were in their own world. Polly wore her bonnet with the
cherry-coloured ribbons and her left hand lay on Job's right
arm in the traditional manner of those who are walking out.
She had left her glove off on purpose that the world might see
her ring.

With them was Miss Peabody, looking not so much ill as
convalescent. She was one of those for whom despair, to which
she had lived so near for so long, had receded during the reading of the Christmas gospel. Yet she would have slipped past the
Dean unnoticed had he not stopped her and taken her hand.
"A happy Christmas, Miss Peabody," he said cheerfully, as
though there had been no clock. "I am obliged to you for
coming tonight. Much obliged. God bless you."

But the one he had most wished to see, Isaac, was not there.
As he walked home he was deeply unhappy. Isaac and Elaine,
he feared, he had loved only to their hurt, and he prayed God
to forgive him.

Back in the Deanery again there were many matters to attend
to and it was not until late in the evening that he went to his
study to finish writing his Christmas sermon. He turned back
to the beginning of it, to refresh his mind as to what he had already written, and as he read he was in despair. It was a
terrible sermon for its Christmas purpose of joy and love. It
was academic, abstruse, verbose. Why was it that he could
write a book but could not write a sermon? He told himself
that a sermon was a thing of personal contact, and in personal
contacts he had always failed most miserably. Already, as he
turned the pages of this most wretched sermon, he could feel
the wave of boredom and dislike that always seemed to beat up
in his face when he tried to preach, and he shrank miserably
within himself. Nevertheless the sermon had to be written and
it had to be preached and he picked up his pen, dipped it in
the ink and began to write.

But presently he found to his dismay that he could not see
what he wrote. He turned back to the earlier pages and found

they were as blurred as the page of the gospels had been when he stood in the lectern. He realized that he was too tired to prepare this sermon, too tired even to sit here any longer at his desk. Fear took hold of him. This dimming of his sight had not mattered this evening, for he had known what he had to say, but in the pulpit it would be fatal, for he had never been able to preach in any other way than by reading aloud from the written page. The gospel he had known by heart. "By heart." It seemed to his bewilderment and fatigue as though a voice had spoken. A great simplicity had come into his life these last months, a grace that had been given to him with the friendship of humble people. Could he tomorrow preach from his heart and not his intellect? Could he look upon his heart with his inward eyes and speak what he found written upon it? A man's heart was the tablet of God, who wrote upon it what he willed. He took up the manuscript of his sermon and tore it across, flinging the fragments into the waste paper basket.

Then he lit the candle that stood upon a side table, put out the lamp and went out into the darkened hall. When there was much work to be done he often went to bed very late and by his command no servant waited up for him. He climbed the stairs slowly with his candle, and as he climbed the clamour of the bells broke out once more. It was midnight, the hour of Christ's birth. At the top of the stairs there was a window. He put his candle down on the sill and stood for a moment in prayer. Then he opened the old casement a few inches and the sound of the bells swept in to him on a breath of cold air. He closed the window again and saw that a snowflake lay on his hand.

2

He slept deeply that night, a thing he had not done for months past, then woke at his usual early hour, dressed and made his meditation. Then he left the house for the first service of Christmas Day. As he closed the garden door behind him he stood in amazement, for he had stepped not into the expected

x

darkness but into light. It was neither of the sun nor moon but of the snow. The sky was a cold clear green behind the dark mass of the Cathedral, the wind had dropped and the stillness was absolute. The snow was not deep but it covered the garden with light. He moved forward a few steps and looked about him. The roof of the Cathedral, every parapet and ledge, the roofs of the houses and the boughs of the trees all bore their glory of snow. He walked slowly through the garden in awe and joy, thinking of the myriad snowflakes under his feet, each one a cluster of beautiful shapes of stars and flowers and leaves, all too small to be seen by any eye except that of their Creator, yet each giving light. That was why he always wanted a white Christmas. Almighty God had been so small, as small as the crystal of a snowflake in comparison with the universe that he had made. "Such light!" murmured the Dean as he opened the door into the Cathedral. "Such light!"

In the Cathedral it was still dark, for he was very early, as he liked to be, and only the lights in the sanctuary were as yet lit, but he could have found his way about the Cathedral blindfold. He went into the chantry of the Duchess Blanche and knelt down and as he began his prayer he found that light was in his mind and spirit. The darkness of yesterday had been taken from him.

3

After breakfast Elaine stood in the drawing-room, one hand on the mantelpiece, looking down into the fire, steeling herself for the moment between breakfast and matins when she and Adam always gave each other their Christmas presents. She never knew what to give him, for he had no hobbies apart from this recent rather ridiculous one of horology, and he was indifferent to what he ate. This year she had a book of travel for him which she had chosen at Joshua Appleby's bookshop. If he did not like the reading matter it was at least a book, and she believed that he liked books not only for their contents but for their shape and feel, for she had seen him touch and turn their pages as though each one were a unique thing of beauty, like the petals of a flower. She had only noticed this just lately, during his illness. There were many things about him that she had not noticed until just lately. But even more difficult than her gift to him was his to her. Once again she would have to simulate pleasure at sight of some trinket that she would never be able to wear. Her beauty being her *raison d'être* it was impossible for her to desecrate it by some jewel that was not in keeping with its perfection. Adam's taste in clothes and jewels was atrocious.

He came in and she gave him his book and saw that she had truly pleased him. "The Isles of Greece, Elaine," he said as he turned the pages. "You have remembered how I went there as a young man. My dear, I love you for it." She had not remembered but she smiled very sweetly at him and accepted his tribute. When sensitive apprehensions were attributed to her she was always able to appropriate them quickly. It was a part of her charm.

Adam laid the book aside and now it was her turn. Her heart sank. But he produced no jeweller's velvet case from his pocket, instead he said to her, "My dear, I have no real gift for you this year. I must tell you why." Then he told her about the celestial clock, describing its beauty, telling her that by some mischance it had fallen and been broken. "There is only the fret left," he said. "I am so sorry that it is all I have to give you."

He put it into her hands and she carried it to the window and gave an exclamation of pleasure, so delighted was she to find it was nothing she might be expected to wear. The Dean was startled. She stood in the wonderful snowlight, which could not dim her beauty but only enhance it, and on her face was the look of pleasure he had longed to see, called there by the fragment of a broken clock. Truly there was no understanding women. He did not try to understand. She was pleased and he was content to love her beauty and her pleasure.

"I am so sorry the clock was broken, Adam," she said, "but I like this fret. I shall use it as a paper weight." She looked at him with a smile. "It will help me not to lose my letters as I did Ruth's. The bells have started. I must put on my things."

"I'll wait here for you, my dear," said the Dean. "We will go together."

Waiting for her he had a moment of panic about his sermon but he put it from him. What a peculiar thing the mind was. Yesterday had been full of darkness and distress, both pressing sorely upon him, but today he was happy and at peace, and though physical malaise never left him now it seemed pleasantly relaxed, like a hand that has relinquished its grip though not its hold.

Elaine came back wrapped in her furs and this time, instead of going through the garden, they went out into the Close, to look at the wonder of the lime avenue under snow. The sun shone now in a cloudless blue sky and the splendour of the white world awed even Elaine. All over the city the bells were ringing and the shining silence of the white snow seemed to answer them. They walked slowly towards the south door along a path swept clear of snow. On either side it was piled in miniature snow mountains, silver-crested and pooled with azure. "We used to have white Christmases like this when I was a boy," said the Dean with satisfaction.

"How do you feel today, Adam?" asked Elaine. She was already beginning to dread his sermon and there was genuine anxiety in her voice.

"I feel very well," he answered. "Do you remember our walking through the garden together yesterday evening? You gave me strength, my dear, when you put your hand in mine. It is so, through every touch of love, that God strengthens us."

They had reached the south door and Hochicorn was beaming and bowing beside his brazier. The Dean stopped to speak to him and Elaine went on into the Cathedral. Although she was looking superbly beautiful in her sables and holly-green velvet her progress to her seat lacked something of its usual dramatic perfection. It was graceful but unstudied and Mary Montague, in her usual place in her bath-chair, noticed it.

"Did she feel the Dean's illness at all?" she wondered. "Can the wells have broken? No, not yet, but the wind has changed."

The congregation in the Cathedral on Christmas morning at matins was not the large one of Christmas Eve, when the carol service was the only one in the city, it was the usual Sunday congregation, but larger than was customary because it was Christmas Day. It was a distinguished congregation, containing all the élite of the city. As the Dean walked in procession to his stall past the long rows of well-dressed, well-fed people, his nose was assailed by delicate perfumes, the scent of rich furs and shoe polish, and in spite of his happiness panic rose in him again, and this time he could not subdue it. How could he have imagined that he could preach a simple extempore sermon to people such as these? They would be outraged. He would bring shame upon the Bishop and his learned brethren of the chapter, upon the Cathedral and upon Elaine. He did not know how to preach extempore. Nervous and anxious as he always was when he had to speak in public he had never attempted such a thing. He was so dismayed that by the time he reached the choir his hands were clammy and trembling. Then, as he settled into the Dean's stall like a statue into its niche, reassurance came to him from the great joyous Cathedral. He was as much a humble part of it as the shepherd under the miserere seat, as the knights on their tombs and the saints and angels in the windows, as the very stones and beams of its structure. They all had their function to perform in its Christmas adoration and not the humblest or the least would be allowed to fall.

As the Te Deum soared to the roof, to the sky, and took wings to the four corners of the earth, he felt himself built into the fabric of the singing stones and the shouting exulting figures all about him. The stamping of the unicorns, the roaring of the lions and the noise the angels made with their trumpets and cymbals almost drowned the thunder of the organ. The knights sang on their tombs and the saints in their windows, and the homely men and boys and birds were singing under the miserere seats. Adam Ayscough was not surprised. He had had a similar experience long ago as a child, although until this moment he had forgotten it. The human brain was an organ of limitation. It restricted a grown man's consciousness of the exterior world to what was practically useful to him. It was like prison walls. Without them possibly he could not have concentrated sufficiently upon the task he had to do. But in childhood and old age the prison walls were of cloudy stuff and there were occasional rents in them.

The tremendous music sang on in him after the Te Deum had ended but it did not prevent him from doing efficiently all that he had to do. He made the right responses, he walked to the lectern to read the second lesson and returned to his stall again, and during the hymn before the sermon he knelt in his stall to pray as he always did. But today he did not pray for strength to mount the huge pulpit under the sounding board, for he hardly remembered it. He prayed for the city.

Yet when he was in the pulpit he instinctively steeled himself against that wave of boredom and resignation that always rose and broke over him when he stood above the distant congregation like Punch on his stage. It did not come. There was no distance. They were all as close to him as his own body. His sight was better today and he looked down at them for a moment; at Elaine in her pew, her head bent and her hands in her muff, at Mary Montague in her bath-chair, at Mr. Penny over to his right, quite close to him. The knot in Mr. Penny's handkerchief had done all that was asked of it and Mr. Penny sat in the midst of his flock, Miss Peabody on his right and Job and Polly on his left. He was looking up at the Dean in a state of rapture and bland attention. He had not had to preach himself this morning. It was years since he had had the pleasure of listening to another man's sermon and he was enjoying himself. The Dean forgot all about the well-dressed critical men and women who had so alarmed him while he walked past them. He suddenly remembered Letitia and it was to this old shepherd that he preached his last Christmas sermon.

He took his text from Dean Rollard's psalm, the sixty-eighth,

"God is the Lord by whom we escape death." He spoke of love, and a child could have understood him. He said that only in the manger and upon the cross is love seen in its maturity, for upon earth the mighty strength of love has been unveiled once only. On earth, among men, it is seldom more than a seed in the hearts of those who choose it. If it grows at all it is no more than a stunted and sometimes harmful thing, for its true growth and purging are beyond death. There it learns to pour itself out until it has no self left to pour. Then, in the hollow of God's hand into which it has emptied itself, it is his own to all eternity. If there were no life beyond death, argued the Dean, there could be no perfecting of love, and no God, since he is himself that life and love. It is by love alone that we escape death, and love alone is our surety for eternal life. If there were no springtime there would be no seeds. The small brown shell, the seed of an apple tree in bloom, is evidence for the sunshine and the singing of the birds.

He came down from the pulpit and walked back to his stall and fitted comfortably into his niche in the fabric. Presently, when the last hymn had been sung, he went up to the altar and blessed the people.

4

All over the city men and women and children poured out of the chapels and churches exclaiming at the beauty of the day. It all looked as pretty as a picture, they said. The frost kept the sparkling snow from slipping away from roofs and chimney pots, but it was not too cold to spoil the sunshine. There was no wind. On their way home, whenever a distant view opened out, they could pause and enjoy it without having to shiver. The stretch of the snow-covered fen almost took their breath away, it was so beautiful under the blue arc of the sky. It was like the sea when it turns to silver under the dazzle of the sun. When they turned and looked up at the Cathedral its snow-covered towers seemed to rise to an immeasurable height. Then a wonderful fragrance assailed their nostrils. In steam-filled

kitchens the windows had been opened now that the day was
warming up. The turkeys and baked potatoes and plum
puddings were also warming up and in another forty minutes
would have reached the peak of their perfection. Abruptly
Christmas Day swung over like a tossed coin. The silver and blue
of bells and hymns and angels went down with a bang and
was replaced by the red and gold of flaming plum puddings and
candled trees. Everyone hurried home as quickly as they could.

Christmas Day at the Deanery was one of the busiest of the
year. When the morning services were over there was the ritual
of the Christmas dinner, to which the Dean insisted that Elaine
invite all the lonely people connected with the Close, such as
bachelor minor canons and widows of defunct Cathedral dignitaries. This was usually something of an ordeal for all concerned but today not even the sight of the vast dead turkey
could depress the Dean, and old Mrs. Ramsey, whose terrifying
privilege it was to sit upon his right, found him almost a genial
host. When the guests had gone Elaine dissolved upon the sofa,
but the Dean went out to visit the old men at the almshouses
until it was time for evensong. Then there was a late tea, followed by the ceremony of the servants' Christmas tree. The
difficult occasion had never seemed so happy. The servants
almost forgot their shyness in their pleasure at seeing the Dean
looking so much better. Elaine had never been so successful in
disguising her boredom or the Dean in overcoming his trepida-
tion, and Garland was so happy that he unbent sufficiently to
utter a few mild jokes as he cut the presents from the tree. Yet
he did not hold with the Dean going round to the choir school
Christmas tree as soon as he had finished with the servants'. It
was his custom on Christmas Day, and boys were his delight,
but Garland considered that Cook was in the right of it when
she remarked that the boys should have made do with the Archdeacon this year. They'd scarcely have noticed the difference;
not with their stomachs full.

Elaine went to bed directly after supper, her husband carrying
her candle for her to her room.

"Are you very tired, my dear?" he asked her. "It has been a long day for you."

"Not so tired as usual," she said, pulling off her rings and dropping them on her dressing-table, and she added softly, looking away from him, "It has been a happy Christmas Day. I liked your sermon, Adam."

She had never said that before and his heart seemed to make a physical movement of joy. "It is true, Elaine," he said. "All I said so haltingly is true. I'm glad you liked it. Good-night, my dear. Sleep well."

She lifted her face and as he kissed her smooth cool cheek he felt suddenly that he could not leave her. He wanted to ask if he might sit in her arm-chair for a little while, in her warm scented room, and watch her brush her hair. It was years since he had seen her glorious hair down on her shoulders. But her eyes were drowning in sleep and he feared to weary her. He tiptoed from her room and closed the door softly behind him.

He went into his study, where Garland had lighted the lamp for him. He was deeply grateful that the labour of the last two days was now accomplished, and most thankful to find himself so well. He was abysmally tired, but he did not feel ill. He would work for a little longer before he went to bed.

He opened a deep drawer in his table and took out two piles of papers. One was the manuscript of his book and the other the architectural plans. The unfinished book cried out to him in its plight but he put it to one side. It was himself and so must be denied. For the hundredth time he unfolded all the plans and opened them before him. They were dog-eared now, and stained in several places, for they had been through so many hands and had been argued over so hotly for so long. And now it was all to do again. Tomorrow he would start the fight once more. He thought of it with dread, but that cancer could not be left in the body of the city. He remembered Dean Rollard singing the sixty-eighth psalm. "This is God's hill, in the which it pleaseth him to dwell." With what grief must God look upon the North Gate slums, and the rotting human bodies there. The Dean pulled a piece of paper towards him and wrote out the words in his fine handwriting, laying it upon the plan of the city. Then upon another piece of paper he began to calculate the cost of demolition and rebuilding all over again. If he could only get expenditure down a little he might meet less opposition. But he feared he had many enemies. In past years, stung nearly to madness by the sufferings of the poor, he had forced through reforms with too much anger and too much contempt for the oppressors. He was a gentler man now, but it was too late. Yet for an hour he went on working until the figures blurred and his gold pencil slipped from his hand.

"I must go to bed," he thought, and tried to get up from his chair. Then it came again, the rising panic in his blood, the constriction of his throat, as though a rope were being drawn tighter and tighter about it, a roaring in the ears and the agonizing struggle for breath. He did not feel the joy this time, for it was too bad, but a great voice cried out in the crashing blackness of his mind, "Blessed be God."

I

GARLAND did not let it be known for a few hours. "Let them have their breakfast first," he said to Doctor Jenkins. "And then an hour or two for the children to play with their new toys. Eleven o'clock is time enough."

And so it was not until between eleven and twelve on St. Stephen's Day that the city became aware of the tolling of the great bell. The day was overcast and windless with a few snow-flakes drifting down from the grey sky, and the tolling travelled far across the fen. In the city every man and woman stood aghast, stricken by a sense of appalling calamity, and for a few strange moments the memory of each ceased to be a personal thing. This had happened before. Then they came out into the streets, as they had done in centuries past, and stood in frightened groups looking up at the Cathedral, grim and vast today against the grey sky, and each boom of the great bell trembled slowly through their bodies. No one supposed for a moment that it was the Bishop or the Archdeacon. They knew who it was as they had known when Duke Rollo died, and William de la Torre and Peter Rollard. Only this man was greater than those others, great though they had been. What would become of them now? What would become of the city?

The Dean was dead. Those who had hated him were as stricken as those who had loved him. Of all the stunned men standing about in the market place the mayor was the first to move. He went back into his house, and into his plush mahogany dining-room, and slammed the door.

A few moments afterwards Isaac left the group in Cockspur Street with whom he had been standing and crept back into his shop. He locked the door and went into his workshop. No shops were open but he had decided to spend the day in his workshop so as not to have to speak to Emma. He had said he had work to do and Polly had packed up some food for him. Throughout their uncomfortable Christmas Day he had spoken to Emma only when he was obliged, he had hated her so much.

Now he had forgotten Emma. All the miseries that had obsessed his mind twenty minutes ago had vanished. His arms folded on his work-table and his head on his arms he could think only of one thing. The Dean was dead. Ever since the day when Emma and Job between them had smashed the clock he had been in the grip of one of his bad times, the worst he had ever had. And now the Dean was dead. It was too much. For perhaps an hour he lay drowning in sorrow and self-pity and then he began to cry. And presently he wanted to blow his nose. His handkerchief was in the tail pocket of his coat and he was sitting on it. He had to get up to find it and while he was blowing his nose his eyes fell upon his sandwiches. He ate them. He could not taste anything but it was something to do. After that he felt better and gradually began to remember all the times when the Dean had tried to talk to him, and obstinately wrapped up in himself and his own opinions he had scarcely bothered to listen. That great man had given of his time and strength to try and comfort an insignificant little worm of a clockmaker and he had not bothered to listen. He tried to remember the times, to remember what the Dean had said. That morning in Worship Street, something about giving away joy. Here in the shop, something about the friendly house of God. And on Christmas Eve, he had thought it had not mattered about the breaking of the clock. There had been something too about himself and Emma, but he could not remember what it was. He struggled to remember the words and could not. And the Dean had pleaded with him to go to the Cathedral but he had not gone; not even to the carol service, when he might have seen him once more and taken his hand. Self-reproach gnawed at him. It felt like a rat inside his head gnawing at his skull. It drove him to potter about the workshop trying to do a few jobs, but he couldn't fix his mind on them. And so the afternoon passed and the window of the workshop was filled with gold. It was the sunset and he must go home to Emma.

It seemed impossible to do so, hating her as he did, but until he had been able to arrange a separate home for himself his bed and his food were where she was and he had to go home. He locked the shop and crawled up Cockspur Street. It was empty. The market place was empty too and the whole city was silent. He was aware of the Cathedral towering up above him but he would not look at it for it was now not only a terror to him but a reproach. He toiled up the steps to Angel Lane and it was not until he was in sight of his home that he at last became aware of the sunset that had broken through the grey clouds. He had to notice it for the light was beating upon his eyes. He looked up. It was one of the great fen sunsets, flaming across the sky from horizon to horizon, burning up the earth beneath it to nothingness. But it could not subdue the Cathedral. Isaac was looking straight up at the three great towers and the flaming clouds were streaming out from them like banners. Yet there was no wind, and no movement in the sky except just above the Rollo tower where two small white clouds were in gentle flight. They soared and sank again, infinitely graceful and lovely, the golden light touching their wings and breasts. Then they soared once more and were lost in the light. They were two white swans.

Isaac had stood watching the sky for perhaps ten minutes, and he had forgotten where he was. Then he came gently back to awareness of Angel Lane. He said to himself that he had imagined it. No swans ever flew as high as that, and not in that manner. The two swans of the broken celestial clock had come into his head as he watched the sky and transformed themselves there into what men call a vision. That sky was enough to make a man imagine anything, it was in itself so unbelievable. He watched it all the way up the lane, so intent upon its glory that he did not realize that he was feeling much happier. As he opened the front door of number twelve he suddenly remembered what the Dean had said about himself and Emma. It came into his mind like the beginning of one of his good times. It came in like light.

Emma was in the passage and her presence took him so utterly by surprise that he did not shut the door, and the light pouring in from the empty street illumined her tear-stained face. Emma was by nature a less self-centred person than Isaac and during the afternoon she had suffered neither self-pity nor self-reproach but just natural sorrow, demonstrative and simple. "Isaac! Isaac!" she cried, and felt in her pocket for her handkerchief. "What a dreadful thing! Give me your coat, my dear." She wiped her eyes and helped Isaac off with his coat and hung it up. That split in her dress that he had noticed when they had last stood in the passage together was still there and for a moment he remembered how he had feared what might come out of Emma's chrysalis. Well, it had come out, and gone. Now he must go back to that day, before the clock was broken, and start again from there. "Emma," he said, "forgive me that I was so surly over Christmas. It does not matter about the clock."

Polly, red-eyed but mopped up, appeared in the kitchen door with a tea tray. "I've made the tea," she said. "It's 'ot."

2

In the glow of the sunset Doctor Jenkins and Josiah Turnbull the mayor rang the Deanery bell and were admitted by Garland. All the windows were closed and the blinds down and the golden light could penetrate into the house only through a crack here and there. The atmosphere was hot and heavy, restless with the intolerable comings and goings that succeed a death. Garland had been on his feet all day answering the door to lawyers, undertakers and clerics, receiving notes of condolence and answering enquiries for Mrs. Ayscough. He was calm and imperturbable and looked more like an elder statesman than ever. Cook had remarked through her tears to Elaine's maid that she had thought Mr. Garland would have felt it more than this, especially since it had been he who had found the Dean. Garland had in fact not yet begun to feel anything much except a pain at the back of his head and a distaste for food. He had too much to do, and in everything he did he had to think quickly what the Dean would have wished.

There had been no time for him to think whether the Dean would have wished him to admit the mayor, for Doctor Jenkins, the mayor just behind him, had stepped quickly in before he could place either of them in proper focus. The pain at the back of his head was making it a little difficult for him to be quite certain, at once, who was there. But he was quickly in command of himself again and in answer to the mayor's hoarse enquiries answered that he feared Mrs. Ayscough was entirely prostrated.

"She is taking the sedative I prescribed?" asked Doctor Jenkins curtly.

"Yes, sir," said Garland. "Do you wish to see Mrs. Ayscough again?"

"I do not," said Doctor Jenkins, a man whom sorrow always robbed of his good manners. "Has anyone touched the Dean's study table?"

"No, sir," said Garland.

"Then will you be so good as to take the mayor and myself to the study."

Garland swallowed and his face went red. He knew very well that the mayor for years had been the Dean's bitterest opponent, and the study was the room where the Dean had died. But he was also aware that Doctor Jenkins was looking very fixedly at him, and he trusted Doctor Jenkins. With stately tread he led the way to the study, and obeying the doctor's gesture pulled up a blind. His hands at his sides he stood looking out into the garden while the two men spoke in lowered voices behind him.

"Mr. Mayor," said Doctor Jenkins, "I am sure it will be your wish to inform the city yourself of the manner of the Dean's death. He suffered a heart attack last night while he was working at these plans. You were, I believe, working at them together. That is why I thought you would like to see this table before the papers are put away. I think he had been making calculations on this piece of paper."

"Could I see it, Doctor?" asked the mayor.

"Certainly," said Doctor Jenkins, and gave it to him.

The mayor held the paper in his large red hand and adjusted his spectacles. He was silent for a while, breathing heavily. He read right through the paper, missing nothing, for he was a sharp business man. He noted that the Dean had subtracted the sum for the garden from the total. The Dean had been passionately attached to the idea of the garden. He noted also how the neat handwriting had run suddenly away into a scrawling line when the Dean had dropped the pencil. His own hand shook a little as he held the paper.

"May I keep this, Doctor?" he asked.

"Certainly," said Doctor Jenkins. "He would wish you to do so. This one too. It was lying on the plan of the city. It is part of a verse from a psalm I believe. What about the plans?"

"Havelock had better have 'em for the time being," said the mayor. "But I'll need 'em later. The matter of a memorial to the Dean will soon be under consideration in the city."

Garland's nails bit into his palms as he clenched his hands. Though he did not look round he could see the mayor's fat hands folding those two bits of paper, the last things the Dean had touched, except the pencil. He would have given his soul to possess either of the three. It hurt him to breathe.

"Thank you, Garland," said Doctor Jenkins. "That is all, I think."

Garland led the way majestically from the room. He doubted if Doctor Jenkins had the slightest right, even legally, to do what he had done, but as he opened the front door and bowed them out it occurred to him that, in this matter, things were moving in the direction the Dean would have wished.

3

After the funeral everyone called on Miss Montague and she hardly knew how to bear it. Never had she so longed to be alone, but as soon as she took the cat on her lap and felt quietness taking hold of her the lid of the letter box was lifted again. Why did they all want to talk about it so much, and with such excessive sentiment? Hadn't they known? The multitude who had come to the funeral service, not only flocking up from every lane and street in the city but journeying to it from all over England, a crowd of men who at one time or another, as public schoolboys, schoolmasters, dons or undergraduates had had contact with the Dean, had apparently taken the city by surprise. Miss Montague supposed it was always the same. Men and women needed the shock of a death before they could humble themselves to realize that anyone with whom they had lived in daily contact was of far greater stature than they were themselves. And when they had realized it they swung over the other way and did their best to dissolve the strong memory of a great man in a mush of sentimentality. That was human nature. In these days of sorrow and the irritability of fatigue Miss Montague came very near to disliking human nature.

But a quiet evening came at last and she sat down by the fire. It was dark and Sarah had drawn the curtains. There was a west wind and rain, one of those quiet rains that do no more than whisper at the window pane, soothing or melancholy according to one's mood. She took the cat on her lap and was at peace, for she found the sound of the rain restful. She had, she found, passed beyond the first sharpness of sorrow to that

Y

state of thankfulness that should have been hers from the beginning. She was ashamed now of the way she had wept by
night and snapped at Sarah by day. The fact was that no one
had been nearer to her in understanding than he had been and
she missed him. Well, she would miss him till she died, and
must expect to do so. Her feelings were of no consequence.
Would she never understand that? Nothing ever had been, or
ever would be, of any consequence except that which had given
such power to this man's life and death. She settled back in her
chair and closed her eyes, one hand passing lightly over the
cat's soft back. The cat purred and the ash settled in the grate.
She was so tired that she was nearly asleep.

The bell clanged and she started up. Who was it? No one
she knew well, for intimate friends did not ring the bell. She
heard Sarah's voice, and the opening and shutting of the door,
and then Sarah's footsteps coming up the stairs, but the woman
who followed her trod so lightly that she did not hear her step.
Half asleep as she had been the absurd thought came to her,
"It is the Duchess Blanche."

Sarah opened the door and stood back. "Mrs. Ayscough,
ma'am," she said.

Miss Montague struggled up from her chair, scattering the
cat. She had never been more astonished in her life. "Elaine!"
she exclaimed, though she had never called Elaine by her
Christian name before. "My dear, I am very glad to see
you."

She sat down again, for her knees refused to support her.
Elaine, ignoring the arm-chair behind her, stood in front of the
fire, her hands held out to it. She seemed to have forgotten to
put on her gloves but otherwise she was exquisitely and correctly dressed in deep mourning. She raised her hands and
lifted her crêpe veil back over her bonnet. The gesture was so
graceful that Miss Montague was sure she was witnessing a
dramatic performance. Then Elaine turned round to her and
she realized with a shock that she was looking into the face of
grief. The lovely gestures were merely automatic.

"Do you think I am doing right about Adam's grave?" Elaine asked sharply.

"Sit down, dear," said Miss Montague. "What are you doing about Adam's grave?"

"It's in the south aisle of the nave," said Elaine with that same abruptness. "Close to the other dean with a book held between his hands."

"Peter Rollard," said Miss Montague. "He flung the book at Cromwell."

"And the chapter and the city want an elaborate tomb with a sculptured effigy lying on it."

"And you are against that?"

"I think it should be a plain stone slab, like the one Adam showed me once up by the altar where some other dean is buried."

"Abbot William de la Torre," said Miss Montague.

"I want that because Adam liked it. I remember now that he liked it. But he never said what he wanted himself."

"He was not the type of man to be interested in his own tomb. What would you like inscribed on the stone?"

"Just his name, and that he was dean, and the text of his Christmas sermon. It was, 'God is the Lord by whom we escape death.' I liked that sermon."

"What does Garland think?" asked Miss Montague.

"Garland is no help," said Elaine. "That's why I've come to you, because you knew Adam so well. Garland just says that the Dean would have wished what I wish."

"So he would," said Miss Montague. "And how lovely it is, my dear, that the insight of your love has chosen the thing that is perfect and right."

A moment later she said to herself that experience should have taught her to avoid that type of remark. At this stage it broke a woman down. What was she to do with this wildly sobbing creature kneeling beside her? "Take off your bonnet, my dear," she said. "It is impossible to cry comfortably in a tight bonnet." Elaine pulled at the velvet strings and flung the bonnet from her. Then she cried herself exhausted with her head in Miss Montague's lap. Now and then Mary Montague could distinguish words of bitter lamentation.

"Now that will do, Elaine," she said at last. "Self-reproach is always inevitable and perhaps for a short while right. To continue to indulge it is futile and wicked, especially in your case, for you were your husband's pride and delight, and always will be. Go to my room and wash your face, dear. It is the second on the landing. Then come back to me again."

When Elaine had come back, quiet and composed, and they had talked for a little, Miss Montague asked, "Will you live in London, Elaine?"

"I shall stay here. There is a little house in Worship Street that's empty now."

"Stay here?" ejaculated Miss Montague, for Elaine's dislike of the city was well known.

"Yes. What's that old word you see on tombstones? Relict. I am Adam's relict. I shall stay here."

"Well, my dear, that will be a pleasure for me," said Miss Montague, and meant what she said. She would come to love Elaine, she believed. By dying and leaving her Adam Ayscough appeared to have been the making of her. Or else through the years he had formed something in her that only the shock of his loss could have brought to fruition. "Will Garland stay with you?"

"Yes, Garland will come with me."

"Does he like the house?"

"He thinks it is too small."

The difficulty of adapting large furniture to small rooms occupied them until Elaine rose to go. Then they kissed each other quietly and she went away.

Miss Montague's next visitor was Garland himself. He came by appointment and brought Bella, who had refused to leave her umbrella in the hall. Garland held her firmly by the wrist while he made his prepared speech to Miss Montague.

"It had been the Dean's wish, madam, to call upon you with Miss Bella on Christmas Eve. I believe he made the appointment but owing to pressure of work it had to be postponed. I felt, madam, that the Dean would not wish Miss Bella to miss the opportunity of your acquaintance."

"Perhaps it is more the other way round, Garland," said Miss Montague. "The Dean was anxious, I believe, that I should not miss the happiness of Bella's friendship while she is still so young. Would you like to have a few words with Sarah? I will ring the bell when Bella is tired of me. And then, if you please, I would like a few words with you."

"Very good, madam," said Garland, and let go of Bella, who dived for the cat.

"Never mind, Garland," said Miss Montague. "I can manage her, and so can the cat. You will be scratched, Bella, if you hold my cat so tightly."

Garland, as he closed the door behind him, gathered that the cat had already taken action. Bella was not a child to squeal but he heard her slap the cat.

"Cats take care of themselves," Miss Montague explained to Bella. "Take off your pelisse and bonnet, my dear, and fetch me that little silver box from the table."

Bella fetched the box. It had small chocolate dragées in it, with white hundreds and thousands on top. Miss Montague had one and Bella had two, and then she was told to open a cupboard door and inside in a box was the baby doll Miss Montague had had when she was a little girl. It was very old, a wooden doll whose hair had come off, not to be compared with Bella's Marianne that the Dean had given her, but she was content to sit on a footstool and nurse it while Miss Montague nursed the affronted cat. Conversation flowed easily between them and the firelight gleamed on Bella's hair. In the right company, and once she had asserted herself, Bella could be surprisingly good and gentle. Presently she sang a lullaby to the wooden baby, and put it to sleep. Miss Montague watched entranced, storing up pictures in her mind. The back view of Bella, when she was bending over and showing all her lace-trimmed under-garments, was not to be forgotten, and nor was the white nape of her neck where the yellow curls lay like spun silk, or her strong little wrists with their bracelets of fat. There was vitality pressed down and running over in her sturdy beauty and a few of the years of her great age seemed to drop off Miss Montague. The future, with Bella and Elaine in it, was a less empty thing to face than it had been. When she at last rang the bell it was not because either she or Bella were tired of each other but because she thought Garland must be weary of waiting.

"Give me a kiss and go with Sarah, Bella," said Miss Montague, when Sarah and Garland appeared. "She will put your bonnet and pelisse on in the hall. Good-bye, my dear. I will ask your grandmother if you may come and see me again." Bella, sitting upon the footstool, adhered, and Garland shot out his cuffs ready for action. "Do you hear me, Bella?" asked Miss Montague gently.

Bella met her eyes, rose and kissed her. She knew when she had met her match. She accepted a third chocolate and left the room with dignity.

"She will be a joy to me, Garland," said Miss Montague. "Will you sit down and tell me if there is anything I can do for you?"

Garland pulled forward the most uncomfortable chair he could find and sat stiffly upon its edge. Only his eyes gave any indication that life was now without savour for him. It was not, however, while Elaine lived, or while any one of the Dean's possessions remained in his care to be dusted or polished, without purpose.

"Nothing, madam, thank you. The Dean left a book he was writing unfinished upon his study table. Mrs. Ayscough is anxious that it should be published though unfinished, and she has sent it to the Dean's publisher. My only fear is that that may not be in accordance with what the Dean would have wished."

"I am sure Mrs. Ayscough is right, Garland," said Miss Montague. "The Dean was a very careful and polished writer. As far as he had gone his book would have been as perfect as he could make it. An unfinished book can be like a young life cut

short, all the more persuasive because so poignant. Is there anything else that worries you, Garland?"

Garland's face flushed. "Not that worries me, madam, but
that makes me so angry I could do murder."

"Murder would not be in accordance with the Dean's wishes,
Garland."

"No, madam. It's this memorial to the Dean. Sir Archibald
Gervase the architect who, if you remember, madam, was of
assistance to the Dean in the work done in the Cathedral when
the Dean first came to the city, is here and was with the mayor
all yesterday, I'm told. All those new houses on the high ground
where its healthy. The North Gate slums to come down. The
garden by the river, that's to be called the Ayscough Memorial
Garden. It's all to cost a mint of money." Garland gripped his
hands together and the words poured from him. "For years,
madam, the Dean fought for these improvements for the city,
and what happened? A campaign of vilification against him
carried on by certain persons in this city whose names, madam,
I will not mention in your presence, as not fit to be spoken in
the presence of a good lady. Scum, madam, that's what they
are. Scum. And now these same persons pose as benefactors to
the city. It's they who will get the credit for what's done, not
the Dean. Had they done what they're doing in the Dean's lifetime he'd have had the joy of it. And now the Dean's dead.
They should have done what they're doing while he lived." He
stopped and the fury went out of him. His hands dropped
limply between his knees.

"They would never have done it while he lived," said Miss
Montague. "Men are so obstinate. They run on in the course
they have chosen until some shock jolts them out of it. Only
then do they change course. Garland, believe me when I tell
you that nothing stems and turns wickedness more certainly
than the death of a good man. I have seen it happen again and
again. Sometimes it seems to me that the only thing we really
know about death is that it is creative."

"That's true, madam," said Garland thoughtfully. "There's

the saying about a grain of wheat. I don't remember it rightly but you'll know what I mean." He got up stiffly. "I must be going, madam. Thank you."

"I am so glad you are staying with Mrs. Ayscough. That would please the Dean."

"Thank you, madam."

"Mrs. Ayscough tells me that you fear the new house in Worship Street will prove to be too small?"

"Yes, madam," said Garland, "and it is at the wrong end of Worship Street. It is not the kind of establishment that the Dean would have wished for Mrs. Ayscough. I trust her residence there will be merely temporary."

Miss Montague was thoughtful for a few moments and then she said, "Garland, you can help me come to a decision. I have been thinking of the matter ever since Mrs. Ayscough came to see me the other evening. It is about Fountains. I have not known to whom to leave it at my death for none of my nephews wants it. They do not want to live in the city. Shall I leave it to Mrs. Ayscough? If you remember, Garland, a duchess once lived here, the Duchess Blanche, the widow of Duke Jocelyn who was one of the builders of the Cathedral. I believe that Mrs. Ayscough would be happy in this house. Do you think it would be a suitable establishment for her?"

Garland looked round the room and she saw that he was mentally arranging the Deanery drawing-room furniture within it. He seemed to fit it in. "Yes, madam, I think this would be suitable. It is a house of dignity, not too large but large enough for Mrs. Ayscough's position, intimately connected with the Cathedral and within easy walking distance from it. And then, madam, this was a house of which the Dean was very fond. Yes, madam, I think it would do nicely." Suddenly he checked himself. "But I trust, madam, that you will be spared to us for many years yet."

Miss Montague laughed as she held out her hand to him. "I trust not, Garland. My body is now so aged that I feel I shall enjoy Mrs. Ayscough in this house far more than I enjoy myself in it. Good-bye, Garland. I beg that you will take comfort. Time passes, you know. You will be surprised how the days slip along. Human life, even the longest, is not very long."

Garland bowed over her hand and went downstairs to find Bella.

4

Isaac crept up the steps to the Cathedral like a fly slowly ascending a vast wall. The cold weather was over, and though it was still only February it was almost warm and the sun shone from a sky like blue silk. But the bright day was not making it any easier for Isaac for it only intensified by contrast the darkness of the Porch of the Angels. It looked like the threshold of a great pit. It was here that long ago he had stopped short and fought with his father rather than go in. But he had to come this way because if he had gone in through the south door he would have got involved in conversation with old Tom Hochicorn, who might have wanted to go in with him. He was not acquainted with the bedesman of the west door, who in any case sat inside and not outside and could be more easily avoided. For this was something he had to do alone. Yesterday Mr. Havelock had given him the Dean's watch, and with it a piece of paper on which Mrs. Ayscough had written, "I leave to my friend Isaac Peabody my watch and my faith in God." Now Job had Isaac's old watch, and the Dean's, attached to its fine gold chain, was ticking quietly within Isaac's waistcoat pocket. And so he had had to do what the Dean had so often wanted him to do, and come to the Cathedral. It was too late, for the Dean was dead, but all the same he had to do it even though the Dean would never know.

He plunged into the darkness of the porch, stumbled through it and fumbled at the great iron-bound door. It had a handle but in his fear he did not see it. He had never acquired the adult and saving grace of standing aside from himself and laughing at his own absurdities. Like a child, the experience of each moment absorbed him far too intensely for him to be able to look at it. He was in a panic now because the great door would not yield when he pushed it, and he beat on it with his fists. It was opened quietly from within by the bedesman, and he passed in.

The splendour seemed to fall upon him like a vast weight, but the door had closed behind him and he could not go back. He began to creep up the nave, seeing nothing, for after the first glance he had kept his eyes on the ground. He saw only the ancient paving stones, worn into hills and valleys by the tread of many feet. They were stained with colour because the midday sun was shining through the south windows. Veering sideways like a crab he nearly collided with a pillar, its girth greater than that of any tree he had ever seen. To steady himself he leaned his hand against it. The stone felt rough and somehow friendly under his hand and he noticed that just beyond the pillar there was a wooden bench. He let go of the pillar and went to it and sat down, his head on his chest and his hands between his knees. He noticed that the colour that lay upon the paving stones was lapping over his old cracked boots. Now and then a small cloud passed over the sun and it faded but a moment later it was back again. His breathing grew a little easier and his sight cleared.

Beyond the toes of his boots was another of the big old paving stones and then a flat black marble slab let into the floor. Words were cut upon it, "God is the Lord by whom we escape death", and above that the name of his friend, and the date, and that he had been Dean. The colour was lying on the dark slab just as it was lying on Isaac's boots. Just that, he thought, only that. He liked the simplicity but he could not understand why they had put those words. The Dean had not escaped death. His grave was under that stone.

He did not move on any further for he was tired, and still he did not look up, but he began to feel less frightened. The pillar and the bench and the humble grave patterned with colour began to take on a look of familiarity. Beyond the sunlit patch was the terror of the Cathedral but here there was a homeliness. And something more. He had been bitterly cold when he climbed up the steps to the porch but now he was glowing with warmth. He felt as though someone had wrapped him about with a comfortable old coat, yet the glow was within him too and about it he wrapped himself. He had experienced something of the sort so many times before in his good times, but not quite like this. Before he had not known what the warmth was but now he did know.

He took the beautiful watch out of his pocket and looked at it, holding it cradled in both hands. He looked at the monogram A.A. and on the other side of the pair cases the words from the sixty-eighth psalm, "Thy God hath sent forth strength for thee", encircling the mailed hand holding the sword. He remembered the watchcock inside, with the little man carrying the burden on his back, and the wreath of flowers within the hour ring. And this watch was his. Whatever had made the Dean take such a fancy to him, a cowardly, selfish, obstinate, ugly old fellow like him? He would never understand it. He took the piece of paper out of his pocket and looked at that too. Faith in God. God. A word he had always refused. But the Dean had said, put the word love in its place. He did just that, speaking to this warmth. "Bring us, O Love, at our last awakening, into the house and gate of heaven." The words had slipped as gently into his mind as the colour came and went over his boots. Just lately so many things that the Dean had said to him were coming back to his memory. He had scarcely attended to them at the time but they must have sunk down below the surface of his mind to its deeps, because now they were slowly being given back to him. Sentence by sentence he quietly remembered the whole prayer. Though it said "at our last awakening" he felt himself to be already in the house. It wasn't any different anywhere else to what it was here. If he moved on through the Cathedral all of it would be as homely as it was here because of this warmth, and when the house lights went up the great darkness would be full of friendly faces.

He put his watch and the piece of paper back in his pocket,
got up and went out into the centre of the nave. He walked
back a little way towards the west door, and then stopped.
There it was, the other Michael clock. It was just as it had been
described to him. Above the beautiful gilded clock face, with
winged angels in the spandrels, was a canopied platform. To
one side of it Michael in gold armour sat his white horse, his
lance in rest and his visor down. On the other side the dragon's
head, blue and green with a crimson forked tongue, rose
wickedly from a heap of scaly coils. The stillness of both figures
was ominous. They waited only for the striking of the bell to
have at each other. It was a wonderful bit of work. The tip of
Isaac's nose glowed rosily, so happy was he in the contemplation of this clock. And to think that he had lived in the city all
these years and had not seen it! To think he had lived here for
nearly a lifetime and never come inside the Cathedral. Fool
that he had been! Slowly he turned his back on the clock and
looked down the length of the Cathedral. For a moment he
ducked his head and gasped, as though a wave had crashed over
him, and then he went steadily on down the nave.

For an hour he wandered round the Cathedral. Once, far
away, he heard the clock strike twelve, and knew that Michael
was fighting the dragon. The splendour, the vastness and the
beauty no longer terrified him, though they made him feel like
an ant. For he was at home. He was not able to take in very
much today but he would come again and learn this glory by
heart, like a man turning over the leaves of some grand old
painted book. But the Dean would not be with him to turn the
leaves. He thought this, and suddenly the tears started to his
eyes. A few trickled down his cheeks and he fished in the tail
pocket of his old coat for his scarlet spotted handkerchief. He
blew his nose and was startled by the noise it made in the great
silence of the place. It was not fitting. Tears were not fitting.
He put his handkerchief away and looked about him.

He was in a small enclosed place like a chapel, where a lady
lay upon her tomb. Close to the tomb was a plain stone altar

and beside it a recess in the wall, like a cupboard, though the door was no longer there. Over it was a small beautifully carved arch. Though he did not know what it was it appealed instantly to the craftsman of small things that he was himself and he walked over to it. He had never heard of an aumbry but he thought to himself that some holy thing had once been housed here. It was a house, the Cathedral in miniature. He touched the tracery of the small arch with his fingers, delighting in it, and then without realizing what he was doing he put his right hand inside the recess, and found that the roof of the tiny place was carved as a replica of the great ribbed roof of the choir. With his heart pounding with excitement he slipped his fingers along the delicate curved flutings, like the convolutions of a sea-shell. They were hidden away here in the darkness where no one could see them. Here was this loveliness, and his craftsman's fingers could read the beauty as the eyes of a musician read a score of music, and it was hidden. But the treasure within had known of it. Love, that had made it, had known. None else.

"The watchcock, Mr. Peabody."

He stood where he was, without moving. He had heard the Dean's voice, though not with his ears. Yet he had never heard anything more clearly. There was a chair near him and presently he moved to it and sat down. Yes, that is how it is, he thought. He had known it when he had sat on the bench by the pillar. Love was vast and eternal as this great fane appeared to his sight, yet so small that he could possess it hiddenly, as once the cupboard in the wall had housed its treasure. He did possess it. When his good times lifted him to the place of safety he was always in love with something. The love of Adam Ayscough was not dead but at every step that he had taken within the Cathedral had accompanied him. Love, and nothing else, was eternal. "Love is the Lord by whom we escape death."

He sat and thought of his father and he no longer hated him. "Now I shall get to know him better," he said. "And I'll get to know Emma." He sat for a long time and thought to himself that he wished he knew how to pray, yet he knew, untaught, how by abandonment of himself to let the quietness take hold of him. Then he got up and wandered away, and found a door and went through it. Outside, sitting on a stone bench by a small glowing brazier, was old Tom Hochicorn.

"Good day, Isaac," said Tom. "Been in there long?"

Far up above their heads Michael struck his bell. Isaac took out the Dean's watch and verified the fact that Michael was correct in recording the hour as one o'clock. "About an hour, Tom," he said.

Tom Hochicorn's eyes twinkled with amusement. He said, "So it's got you, eh? I allus thought it would."

Isaac walked out into the sunshine and said to himself, "I shall make the celestial clock again. I shall make it for Mrs. Ayscough."